Praise for #1 *New York Times* Bestselling Author David Baldacci's
WISH YOU WELL

"UTTERLY CAPTIVATING . . . BALDACCI TRIUMPHS WITH HIS BEST NOVEL YET. . . . What the novel offers above all is bone-deep emotional truth. . . . Its myriad characters—each as real as readers' own kin—grapple not just with issues of life and death but with the sufferings and joys of daily existence in a setting detailed with finely attuned attention and a warm sense of wonder. This novel has a huge heart."

—*Publishers Weekly* (starred review)

"REALISTIC AND READABLE. . . . Baldacci's fans will enjoy this entertaining detour into his past."

—*Washington Post Book World*

"SUCCEEDS AS A DEPARTURE FOR BALDACCI . . . a tender . . . inspirational story. . . . Some wonderfully lyric prose."

—*Denver Post*

"BALDACCI PROVES HE CAN WRITE IN ANY GENRE WITH THIS WONDERFUL BOOK . . . a moving story . . . a must-read."

—*Southern Pines Pilot* (NC)

more . . .

"READERS WILL KEEP TURNING THE PAGES OF THIS DELIGHTFUL TALE."

—*Orlando Sentinel*

"AN EXCITING AND ENGROSSING STORY . . . a fine, rewarding book."

—*Mansfield News Journal* (OH)

"AFFECTING. . . . [The] richly textured setting of southwestern Virginia in the 1940s draws on the reminiscences of Baldacci's mother and grandmother. . . . Readers of historical fiction will welcome his debut in the genre."

—*Library Journal*

"KNOT-TIGHT, DRIVEN, AND, IN THE END, AN UPLIFTING GOSPEL that speaks to the strength of family bonds, WISH YOU WELL adds a new dimension to Baldacci the writer and to the code of Appalachia-inspired artistry. . . . The ending is pure Baldacci, uncertain until the last page."

—*Richmond Times-Dispatch*

Also by David Baldacci

Absolute Power

Total Control

The Winner

The Simple Truth

Saving Faith

Last Man Standing

DAVID BALDACCI

WISH YOU WELL

WARNER BOOKS

A Time Warner Company

WARNER BOOKS EDITION

Copyright © 2000 by Columbus Rose, Ltd.
All rights reserved. No part of this book may be reproduced in any form or by any electronic or mechanical means, including information storage and retrieval systems, without permission in writing from the publisher, except by a reviewer who may quote brief passages in a review.

Cover design by Jackie Merri Meyer
Cover photography by Swanstock/Christine Rodin
Photo illustration by Franco Accornero

Warner Books, Inc.
1271 Avenue of the Americas
New York, NY 10020

Visit our Web site at www.twbookmark.com.

For information on Time Warner Trade Publishing's online publishing program, visit www.ipublish.com.

 A Time Warner Company

Printed in the United States of America

Originally published in hardcover by Warner Books
First International Paperback Printing: June 2001
First United States Paperback Printing: September 2001

10 9 8 7 6 5 4 3 2 1

To my mother,
the inspiration for this novel

AUTHOR'S NOTE

The story in *Wish You Well* is fictional, but the setting, other than the place names, is not. I have been to those mountains, and also was fortunate to grow up with two women who called the high rock home for many years. My maternal grandmother, Cora Rose, lived with my family in Richmond for the last ten years of her life, but spent the prior six decades or so on the top of a mountain in southwestern Virginia. At her knee I learned about that land and the life there. My mother, the youngest of ten, lived on that mountain for the first seventeen years of her life, and while I was growing up she passed along to me many fascinating stories from her youth. Indeed, both the hardships and the adventures experienced by the characters in the novel would not be unfamiliar to her.

In addition to the stories I listened to as a child, I spent considerable time interviewing my mother in preparation for writing *Wish You Well*, and it was an enlightening time for me, on many levels. Once we reach adulthood, most of us assume we know all there is to know about our parents and other family members. However, if you take the time to ask questions and actually listen to the answers, you may find there is still much to learn about people so close to you. Thus this novel is, in part, an oral history of both where and how my mother grew up. Oral histories are a dying art, which is sad indeed, for they show appropriate respect for the lives and experiences of those who have come before. And, just as important, they document those remembrances, for once those lives are over, that personal knowledge is lost forever. Unfortunately, we live in a time now where everyone seems to be solely looking ahead, as though we deem nothing in the past worthy of our attention. The future is always fresh and exciting, and it has a pull on us that times past simply can never muster. Yet it may well be that our greatest wealth as human beings can be "discovered" by simply looking behind us.

Though I am known for my suspense novels, I have always been drawn to stories of the past in my native Virginia, and tales of people living in places that sharply limited their ambitions, yet provided them with a richness of knowledge and experience few have ever attained. Ironically, as a writer, I've spent the last twenty years or so hunting relentlessly for story material, and utterly failed to see a lumberyardful within my own family. However, while it came later than it probably should have, writing this novel was one of the most rewarding experiences of my life.

WISH YOU WELL

CHAPTER ONE

❧

THE AIR WAS MOIST, THE COMING RAIN TELEGRAPHED by plump, gray clouds, and the blue sky fast fading. The 1936 four-door Lincoln Zephyr sedan moved down the winding road at a decent, if unhurried, pace. The car's interior was filled with the inviting aromas of warm sourdough bread, baked chicken, and peach and cinnamon pie from the picnic basket that sat so temptingly between the two children in the backseat.

Louisa Mae Cardinal, twelve years old, tall and rangy, her hair the color of sun-dappled straw and her eyes blue, was known simply as Lou. She was a pretty girl who would almost certainly grow into a beautiful woman. But Lou would fight tea parties, pigtails, and frilly dresses to the death. And somehow win. It was just her nature.

The notebook was open on her lap, and Lou was filling the blank pages with writings of importance to her, as a fisherman does his net. And from the girl's pleased look, she was landing fat cod with every pitch and catch. As always, she was very intent on her writing. Lou came by that trait honestly, as her father had such fever to an even greater degree than his daughter.

On the other side of the picnic basket was Lou's brother, Oz. The name was a contraction of his given one, Oscar. He was seven, small for his age, though there was the promise of height in his long feet. He did not possess the lanky limbs and athletic grace of his sister. Oz also lacked the confidence that so plainly burned in Lou's eyes. And yet he held his worn stuffed bear with the unbreakable clench of a wrestler, and he had a way about him that naturally warmed other's souls. After meeting Oz Cardinal, one came away convinced that he was a little boy with a heart as big and giving as God could bestow on lowly, conflicted mortals.

Jack Cardinal was driving. He seemed unaware of the approaching storm, or even the car's other occupants. His slender fingers drummed on the steering wheel. The tips of his fingers were callused from years of punching the typewriter keys, and there was a permanent groove in the middle finger of his right hand where the pen pressed against it. Badges of honor, he often said.

As a writer, Jack assembled vivid landscapes densely populated with flawed characters who, with each turn of the page, seemed more real than one's family. Readers would often weep as a beloved character perished under the writer's nib, yet the distinct beauty of the language never overshadowed the blunt force of the story, for the themes imbedded in Jack Cardinal's tales were powerful indeed. But then an especially well-tooled line would come along and make one smile and perhaps even laugh aloud, because a bit of humor was often the most effective tool for painlessly driving home a serious point.

Jack Cardinal's talents as a writer had brought him much critical acclaim, and very little money. The Lincoln Zephyr did not belong to him, for luxuries such as automobiles, fancy or plain, seemed forever beyond his reach. The car had been borrowed for this special outing from a friend and admirer of Jack's work. Certainly the woman sitting next to him had not married Jack Cardinal for money.

Amanda Cardinal usually bore well the drift of her husband's nimble mind. Even now her expression signaled good-natured surrender to the workings of the man's imagination, which always allowed him escape from the bothersome details of life. But later, when the blanket was spread and the picnic food was apportioned, and the children wanted to play, she would nudge her husband from his literary alchemy. And yet today Amanda felt a deeper concern as they drove to the park. They needed this outing together, and not simply for the fresh air and special food. This surprisingly warm late winter's day was a godsend in many ways. She looked at the threatening sky.

Go away, storm, please go away now.

To ease her skittish nerves, Amanda turned and looked at Oz and smiled. It was hard not to feel good when looking at the little boy, though he was a child easily frightened as well. Amanda had often cradled her son when Oz had been seized by a nightmare. Fortunately, his fearful cries would be replaced by a smile when Oz would at last focus on her, and she would want to hold her son always, keep him safe always.

Oz's looks came directly from his mother, while Lou had a pleasing variation of Amanda's long forehead and her father's lean nose and compact angle of jaw. And yet if Lou were asked, she would say she took after her father only. This did not reflect disrespect for her mother, but signaled that, foremost, Lou would always see herself as Jack Cardinal's daughter.

Amanda turned back to her husband. "Another story?" she asked as her fingers skimmed Jack's forearm.

The man's mind slowly rocked free from his latest concocting and Jack looked at her, a grin riding on full lips that, aside from the memorable flicker of his gray eyes, were her husband's most attractive physical feature, Amanda thought.

"Take a breath, work on a story," said Jack.

"A prisoner of your own devices," replied Amanda softly, and she stopped rubbing his arm.

As her husband drifted back to work, Amanda watched as Lou labored with her own story. Mother saw the potential for much happiness and some inevitable pain in her daughter. She could not live Lou's life for her, and Amanda knew she would have to watch her little girl fall at times. Still, Amanda would never hold out her hand, for Lou being Lou would certainly refuse it. But if her daughter's fingers sought out her mother's, she would be there. It was a situation burdened with pitfalls, yet it seemed the one destined for mother and daughter.

"How's the story coming, Lou?"

Head down, hand moving with the flourishing thrust of youthful penmanship, Lou said, "Fine." Amanda could easily sense her daughter's underlying message: that writing was a task not to be discussed with nonwriters. Amanda took it as good-naturedly as she did most things having to do with her volatile daughter. But even a mother sometimes needed a comforting pillow on which to lay her head, so Amanda reached out and tousled her son's blondish hair. Sons were not nearly so complex, and as much as Lou wore her out, Oz rejuvenated his mother.

"How're you doing, Oz?" asked Amanda.

The little boy answered by letting out a crowing sound that banged off all sides of the car's interior, startling even the inattentive Jack.

"Miss English said I'm the best rooster she's ever heard," said Oz, and crowed again, flapping his arms. Amanda laughed and even Jack turned and smiled at his son.

Lou smirked at her brother, but then reached over and tenderly patted Oz on the hand. "And you are too, Oz. A lot better than me when I was your age," said Lou.

Amanda smiled at Lou's remark and then said, "Jack, you're coming to Oz's school play, aren't you?"

Lou said, "Mom, you know he's working on a story. He doesn't have time to watch Oz playing a rooster."

"I'll try, Amanda. I really will this time," Jack said. However, Amanda knew that the level of doubt in his tone heralded another disappointment for Oz. For her.

Amanda turned back and stared out the windshield. Her thoughts showed through so clearly on her features. *Life married to Jack Cardinal: I'll try.*

Oz's enthusiasm, however, was undiminished. "And next I'm going to be the Easter Bunny. You'll be there, won't you, Mom?"

Amanda looked at him, her smile wide and easing her eyes to pleasing angles.

"You know Mom wouldn't miss it," she said, giving his head another gentle rub.

But Mom did miss it. They all missed it.

CHAPTER TWO

AMANDA LOOKED OUT THE CAR WINDOW. HER prayers had been answered, and the storm had passed with little more than annoying patches of drizzle and an occasional gust of wind that failed to motivate the park trees to much more than a skimming of limbs. Everyone's lungs had been pressed hard from running the long, curvy strips of park grass end to end. And to his credit, Jack had played with as much abandon as any of them. Like a child, he had hurtled down the cobblestone paths with Lou or Oz on his back laughing riotously. Once he had even run right out of his loafers and then let the children chase him down and put them back on after a spirited struggle. Later, to the delight of all, he hung upside down while he performed on the swings. It was exactly what the Cardinal family needed.

At day's end the children had collapsed on their parents, and they all had napped right there, a huge ball of wild-angled limbs, deep breathing, and the contented sighs of tired, happy people at rest. A part of Amanda could have lain there the rest of her life, and felt as though she had accomplished all the world could ever reasonably demand of her.

Now, as they returned to the city, to a very small but cherished home that would not be theirs much longer, Amanda felt a growing uneasiness. She did not particularly care for confrontation, but Amanda also knew it was sometimes necessary when the cause was important. She checked the backseat. Oz was sleeping. Lou's face was turned to the window; she also appeared to be dozing. Since she rarely had her husband all to herself, Amanda decided now was the time.

She said softly to Jack, "We really need to talk about California."

Her husband squinted although there was no sun; in fact the darkness was almost complete around them. "The movie studio already has writing assignments lined up," he said.

She noted that he stated this without a trace of enthusiasm. Emboldened by this, Amanda pressed on. "You're an award-winning novelist. Your work is already being taught in schools. You've been called the most gifted storyteller of your generation."

He seemed wary of all this praise. "So?"

"So why go to California and let them tell you what to write?"

The light in his eyes dimmed. "I don't have a choice."

Amanda gripped his shoulder. "Jack, you *do* have a choice. And you can't think that writing for the movies will make everything perfect, because it won't!"

Her mother's raised voice caused Lou to slowly turn and stare at her parents.

"Thanks for the vote of confidence," said Jack. "I

really appreciate it, Amanda. Especially now. You know this isn't easy for me."

"That's not what I meant. If you'd only think about—"

Lou suddenly hunched forward, one arm grazing her father's shoulder even as her mother retreated. Lou's smile was big but obviously forced. "I think California will be great, Dad."

Jack grinned and gave Lou a tap on the hand. Amanda could sense Lou's soul leaping to this slight praise. She knew that Jack failed to realize the hold he commanded over his little girl; how everything she did was weighed against whether it would please him enough. And that scared Amanda.

"Jack, California is not the answer, it's just not. You have to understand that," said Amanda. "You won't be happy."

His expression was pained. "I'm tired of wonderful reviews and awards for my shelf, and then not even making enough money to support my family. *All* my family." He glanced at Lou, and there appeared on his features an emotion that Amanda interpreted as shame. She wanted to lean across and hold him, tell him that he was the most wonderful man she had ever known. But she had told him that before, and they were still going to California.

"I can go back to teaching. That'll give you the freedom to write. Long after we're all gone, people will still be reading Jack Cardinal."

"I'd like to go somewhere and be appreciated while I'm still alive."

"You *are* appreciated. Or don't we count?"

Jack looked surprised, a writer betrayed by his own words. "Amanda, I didn't mean that. I'm sorry."

Lou reached for her notebook. "Dad, I finished the story I was telling you about."

Jack's gaze held on Amanda. "Lou, your mother and I are talking."

Amanda had been thinking about this for weeks, ever since he had told her of plans for a new life writing screenplays amid the sunshine and palm trees of California, for considerable sums of money. She felt he would be tarnishing his skills by putting into words the visions of others, substituting stories from his soul with those that would earn the most dollars.

"Why don't we move to Virginia?" she said, and then Amanda held her breath.

Jack's fingers tightened around the steering wheel. Outside there were no other cars, no lights other than the Zephyr's. The sky was a long reef of suspect haze, no punctures of stars to guide them. They could have been driving over a flat, blue ocean, up and down exactly alike. One's mind could easily be tricked by such a conspiracy of heavens and earth.

"What's in Virginia?" His tone was very cautious.

Amanda clutched his arm in her growing frustration. "Your grandmother! The farm in the mountains. The setting for all those beautiful novels. You've written about it all your life and you've never been back. The children have never even met Louisa. My God, *I've* never met Louisa. Don't you think it's finally time?"

His mother's raised voice startled Oz awake. Lou's hand went out to him, covering his slight chest, transferring calm from her to him. It was an automatic thing now for Lou, for Amanda was not the only protector Oz had.

Jack stared ahead, clearly annoyed by this conversation. "If things work out like I'm planning, she'll come and live with us. We'll take care of her. Louisa can't stay up there at her age." He added grimly, "It's too hard a life."

Amanda shook her head. "Louisa will never leave the mountain. I only know her through the letters and what you've told me, but even I know that."

"Well, you can't always live in the past. And *we're* going to California. We will be happy there."

"Jack, you can't really believe that. You can't!"

Lou once more rocked forward. She was all elbows, neck, knees—slender limbs seemingly growing before her parents' eyes.

"Dad, don't you want to hear about my story?"

Amanda put a hand on Lou's arm even as she gazed at a frightened Oz and tried to give him a reassuring smile, though reassurance was the last thing she was feeling. Now was clearly not the time for this discussion. "Lou, wait a minute, honey. Jack, we can talk later. Not in front of the kids." She was suddenly very fearful of where this might actually go.

"What do you mean I can't really believe that?" Jack said.

"Jack, not now."

"You started this conversation, don't blame me for wanting to finish it."

"Jack, please—"

"Now, Amanda!"

She had never heard quite this tone, and instead of

making her more afraid, it made her even angrier. "You hardly spend any time with the kids as it is. Always traveling, giving lectures, attending events. Everybody already wants a piece of Jack Cardinal, even if they won't *pay* you for the privilege. Do you really think it'll be better in California? Lou and Oz will never see you."

Jack's eyes, cheekbones, and lips formed a wall of defiance. When it came, his voice was filled with a potent combination of his own distress and the intent to inflict the same upon her. "Are you telling me I ignore my children?"

Amanda understood this tactic, but somehow still succumbed to it. She spoke quietly. "Maybe not intentionally, but you get so wrapped up in your writing—"

Lou almost vaulted over the front seat. "He does not ignore us. You don't know what you're talking about. You're wrong! You're wrong!"

Jack's dense wall turned upon Lou. "You do not talk to your mother that way. Ever!"

Amanda glanced at Lou, but even as she tried to think of something conciliatory to say, her daughter proved swifter.

"Dad, this really is the best story I've ever written. I swear. Let me tell you how it starts."

However, Jack Cardinal, for probably the only time in his life, was not interested in a story. He turned and stared directly at his daughter. Under his withering look, her face went from hope to savage disappointment faster than Amanda could take a breath.

"Lou, I said not now!"

Jack slowly turned back. He and Amanda saw the same thing at the same time, and it pulled the blood from both their faces. The man was leaning into the trunk of his stalled car. They were so close to him that in the headlights Amanda saw the square bulge of the man's wallet in his back pocket. He wouldn't even have time to turn, to see his death coming at him at fifty miles an hour.

"Oh my God," Jack cried out. He cut the wheel hard to the left. The Zephyr responded with unexpected agility and actually missed the car, leaving the careless man to live another day. But now the Zephyr was off the road and onto sloped ground, and there were trees up ahead. Jack heaved the wheel to the right.

Amanda screamed, and reached out to her children as the car rocked uncontrollably. She could sense that even the bottom-heavy Zephyr would not maintain its balance.

Jack's eyes were silver dollars of panic, his breath no longer coming up. As the car raced across the slick road and onto the dirt shoulder on the other side, Amanda lunged into the backseat. Her arms closed around her children, bringing them together, her body between them and all that was hard and dangerous about the car. Jack swung the wheel back the other way, but the Zephyr's balance was gone, its brakes useless. The car missed a stand of what would have been unforgiving trees, but then did what Amanda had feared it would all along, it rolled.

As the top of the car slammed into the dirt, the driver's door was thrown open, and like a swimmer lost in a sudden rip, Jack Cardinal was gone from them. The Zephyr rolled again, and clipped a tree, which slowed its momentum. Shattered glass cascaded over Amanda and the children. The sound of tearing metal mixed with their screams was terrible; the smell of freed gasoline and billowy smoke searing. And through every roll, impact, and pitch again, Amanda pinned Lou and Oz safely against the seat with a strength that could not be completely her own. She absorbed every blow, keeping it from them.

The steel of the Zephyr fought a fearsome battle with the hard-packed dirt, but the earth finally triumphed and the car's top and right side buckled. One sharp-edged part caught Amanda on the back of her head, and then the blood came fast. As Amanda sank, the car, with one last spin, came to rest upside down, pointing back the way they had come.

Oz reached for his mother, incomprehension the only thing between the little boy and possibly fatal panic.

With a whipsaw motion of youthful agility, Lou pulled free of the destroyed guts of the car. The Zephyr's headlights were somehow still working, and she looked frantically for her father in the confusion of light and dark. She heard footsteps approaching and started saying a grateful prayer that her father had survived. Then her lips stopped moving. In the spread of the car's beams she saw the body sprawled in the dirt, the neck at an angle that could not support life. Then someone was pounding on the car with a hand, and the person they had almost killed was saying something. Lou chose not to hear the man whose negligent actions had just shattered her family. Lou turned and looked at her mother.

Amanda Cardinal too had seen her husband outlined there in the unforgiving light. For one impossibly long moment, mother and daughter shared a gaze that was completely one-sided in its communication. Betrayal, anger, hatred—Amanda read all of these terrible things on her daughter's features. And these emotions covered Amanda like a concrete slab over her crypt; they far exceeded the sum total of every nightmare she had ever suffered through. When Lou looked away, she left a ruined mother in her wake. As Amanda's eyes closed, all she could hear was Lou screaming for her father to come to her. For her father not to leave her. And then, for Amanda Cardinal, there was nothing more.

CHAPTER THREE

THERE WAS A CALM PIETY IN THE SONOROUS RING OF the church bell. Like steady rain, its sounds covered the area, where the trees were starting to bud and the grass was stretching awake after a winter's rest. The curls of fireplace smoke from the cluster of homes here met in the clear sky. And to the south were visible the lofty spires and formidable minarets of New York City. These stark monuments to millions of dollars and thousands of weary backs seemed trifling against the crown of blue sky.

The large fieldstone church imparted an anchor's mass, an object incapable of being moved no matter the magnitude of problem that assailed its doors. The pile of stone and steeple seemed able to dispense comfort if one merely drew near it. Inside the thick walls there was another sound besides the peal of holy bell.

Holy singing.

The fluid chords of "Amazing Grace" poured down the hallways and crowded against portraits of white-collared men who had spent much of their lives absorbing punishing confessions and doling out reams of Hail

Marys as spiritual salve. Then the wave of song split around statues of blessed Jesus dying or rising, and finally broke in a pool of sanctified water just inside the front entrance. Creating rainbows, the sunlight filtered through the brilliant hues of stained glass windows up and down these corridors of Christ and sinners. The children would always "ooh" and "ahh" over these colorful displays, before they trudged reluctantly into Mass, thinking, no doubt, that churches always made fine rainbows.

Through the double doors of oak the choir was singing to the very pinnacle of the church, the tiny organist pumping with surprising energy for one so aged and crumpled, and "Amazing Grace" trumpeted ever higher. The priest stood at the altar, long arms tenaciously reaching to heaven's wisdom and comfort, a prayer of hope rising from him, even as the man pushed back against the tidal wave of grief confronting him. And he needed much divine support, for it was never an easy thing explaining away tragedy by invoking God's will.

The coffin sat at the front of the altar. The polished mahogany was covered with sprays of delicate baby's breath, a solid clump of roses, and a few distinctive irises, and yet that sturdy block of mahogany was what held one's attention, like five fingers against one's throat. Jack and Amanda Cardinal had exchanged their wedding vows in this church. They had not been back since, and no one present today could have envisioned their return being for a funeral mass barely fourteen years later.

Lou and Oz sat in the front pew of the full church. Oz had his bear crushed to his chest, his gaze cast down, a collection of tears plunking on the smooth wood between skinny legs that did not reach the floor. A blue hymnal lay unopened beside him; song was really beyond the boy right now.

Lou had one arm around Oz's shoulders, but her eyes never left the casket. It did not matter that the lid was closed. And the shield of beautiful flowers did nothing to obscure for her the image of the body inside. Today she had chosen to wear a dress for one of the few times in her life; the hated uniforms she had to wear to meet the requirements of the Catholic school she and her brother attended did not count. Her father had always loved her in dresses, even sketching her once for a children's book he had planned but never got around to. She pulled at her white socks, which reached uncomfortably to her bony knees. A pair of new black shoes pinched her long, narrow feet, feet that were quite firmly on the floor.

Lou had not bothered to sing "Amazing Grace." She had listened to the priest say that death was merely the beginning, that in God's enigmatic way this was a time for rejoicing, not sorrow, and then she did not listen anymore. Lou did not even pray for the lost soul of her father. She knew Jack Cardinal was a good man, a wonderful writer and teller of tales. She knew he would be deeply missed. No choir, no man of the cloth, no god needed to tell her these things.

The singing stopped, and the priest once more took up his ramblings, while Lou picked up on the conversation of the two men behind her. Her father had been a shameless eavesdropper in his search for the authentic ring of conversation, and his daughter shared that curiosity. Now Lou had even more reason to do so.

"So, have you come up with any brilliant ideas?" the older man whispered to his younger companion.

"Ideas? We're the executors of an estate with nothing in it" was the agitated response from the younger man.

The older man shook his head and spoke in an even lower tone, which Lou struggled to hear.

"Nothing? Jack did leave two children and a wife."

The younger man glanced to the side and then said in a low hiss, "A wife? They might as well be orphans."

It was not clear whether Oz heard this, but he lifted his head and put a hand on the arm of the woman sitting next to him. Actually, Amanda was in a wheelchair. A wide-bodied nurse sat on the other side of her, arms folded across her flop of bosom; the nurse was clearly unmoved by the death of a stranger.

A thick bandage was wrapped around Amanda's head, her auburn hair cut short. Her eyes were closed. In fact, they had never once opened since the accident. The doctors had told Lou and Oz that their mother's physical side had been mostly repaired. The problem now apparently was only a matter of her soul's having fled.

Later, outside the church, the hearse carried Lou's father away and she did not even look. In her mind she had said her good-byes. In her heart she could never do so. She pulled Oz along through the trenches of somber suit coats and mourning dresses. Lou was so tired of sad faces, moist eyes catching her dry ones, telegraphing sympathy, mouths firing off broadsides of the literary world's collective, devastating loss. Well, none of *their* fathers lay dead in that box. This was *her* loss, hers and her brother's. And she was weary of people apologizing for a tragedy they could not begin to understand. "I'm so sorry," they would whisper. "So sad. A great man. A beautiful man. Struck down in his prime. So many stories left untold."

"Don't be sorry," Lou had started saying right back. "Didn't you hear the priest? This is a time to rejoice. Death is good. Come on and sing with me."

These people would stare, smile nervously, and then move on to "rejoice" with someone else of a more understanding nature.

Next, they were to go to the grave-site service where the priest would no doubt say more uplifting words, bless the children, sprinkle his sacred dirt; and then another six feet of ordinary fill would be poured in, closing this terribly odd spectacle. Death must have its ritual, because society says it must. Lou did not intend to rush to it, for she had a more pressing matter to attend to right now.

The same two men were in the grassy parking lot. Freed from ecclesiastical confines, they were debating in normal voices the future of what remained of the Cardinal family.

"Wish to God Jack hadn't named us as executors," said the older man as he pulled a pack of cigarettes from his shirt pocket. He lit up and then pressed the match flame out between his thumb and forefinger. "Figured I'd be long dead by the time Jack checked out."

The younger man looked down at his polished shoes and said, "We just can't leave them like this, living with strangers. The kids need someone."

The other man puffed his smoke and gazed off after the bubble-topped hearse. Up above, a flock of blackbirds seemed to form a loose squadron, an informal send-off for Jack Cardinal. The man flicked ash. "Children belong with their family. These two just don't happen to have any left."

"Excuse me."

When they turned, they saw Lou and Oz staring at them.

"Actually, we do have family," Lou said. "Our great-grandmother, Louisa Mae Cardinal. She lives in Virginia. It's where my father grew up."

The younger man looked hopeful, as though the burden of the world, or at least of two children, might still be shed from his narrow shoulders. The older man, though, looked suspicious.

"Your great-grandmother? She's still alive?" he asked.

"My parents were just talking about us moving to Virginia to be with her before the accident."

"Do you know if she'll take you?" the younger man eagerly wanted to know.

"She'll take us" was Lou's immediate reply, though in truth she had no idea at all if the woman would.

"All of us?" This question came from Oz.

Lou knew her little brother was thinking of their wheelchair-bound mother. She said in a very firm voice to the two men, "All of us."

CHAPTER FOUR

A S LOU STARED OUT THE WINDOW OF THE TRAIN, IT
occurred to her that she had never really cared
that much for New York City. It was true that during her childhood she had sampled many of its eclectic
offerings, filling her days with trips to museums, zoos, and
theaters. She had towered over the world on the observa-
tion deck of the Empire State Building, laughed and cried
at the antics of the city dwellers trapped in glee or doom,
observed scenes of emotional intimacy and witnessed pas-
sionate displays of public outcry. She had made some of
these treks with her father, who had so often told her that
the choice to be a writer was not the mere selection of an
occupation, but rather the choice of an all-consuming
lifestyle. And the business of a writer, he carefully pointed
out, was the business of life, in both its uplifting glory
and its complex frailty. And Lou had been privy to the results of such observations, as she had been enthralled by
the readings and musings of some of the most skillful writers of the day, many in the privacy of the Cardinals' modest two-bedroom walkup in Brooklyn.

And their mother had taken her and Oz to all the boroughs of the city, gradually immersing them in various economic and social levels of urban civilization, for Amanda Cardinal was a very well-educated woman intensely curious about such things. The children had received a well-rounded education that had made Lou both respect and remain ever curious about her fellow human beings.

Still, with all that, she had never really become that excited about the city. Where she was going now, that she was very eager about. Despite living in New York City for most of his adult life, where he was surrounded by a large supply of story material that other writers had culled with critical and financial success over the years, Jack Cardinal had chosen to base all his novels upon the place the train was carrying his family to: the mountains of Virginia that rose high in the toe of the state's topographical boot. Since her beloved father had deemed the place worthy of his life's work, Lou had little difficulty in deciding to go there now.

She moved aside so that Oz could look out the window too. If ever hope and fear could be compressed into one emotion and displayed on a single face, they were now on the little boy's. With any given breath, Oz Cardinal looked like he might either laugh till his ribs pushed through his chest, or else faint dead away from utter terror. Lately, though, there had only been tears.

"It looks smaller from here," he commented, inclining his head at the fast-receding city of artificial lights and concrete blocks stacked around welded threads of steel.

Lou nodded in agreement. "But wait until you see the Virginia mountains—now, they're big. And they stay like that, however you look at them."

"How do you know? You've never seen those mountains."

"Of course I have. In books."

"Do they look all that big on paper?"

If Lou hadn't known better, she would have thought Oz was being smart, but she knew her brother did not possess even a mildly wicked bone in his whole being.

"Trust me, Oz, they're big. And I've read about them in Dad's books too."

"You haven't read all of Dad's books. He said you weren't old enough."

"Well, I've read one of them. And he read parts of all the others to me."

"Did you talk to that woman?"

"Who? Louisa Mae? No, but the people who wrote to her said she really wanted us to come."

Oz pondered this. "That's a good thing, I guess."

"Yes, it is."

"Does she look like Dad?"

This stumped his sister. "I can't say I've ever seen a picture of her."

It was clear this answer troubled Oz. "Do you think she's maybe mean and scary-looking? If she is, can't we come back home?"

"Virginia is our home now, Oz." Lou smiled at him. "She won't be scary-looking. And she won't be mean. If she were, she never would have agreed to take us."

"But witches do that sometimes, Lou. Remember Hansel and Gretel? They trick you. Because they want to eat you. They all do that. I know; I read books too."

"So long as I'm there, no witch is going to be bothering you." She gripped his arm, showing off her strength, and he finally relaxed and looked over at the other occupants of their sleeper compartment.

This trip had been financed entirely by the friends of Jack and Amanda Cardinal, and collectively they had spared no expense in sending the children off in comfort to their new lives. This included a nurse to travel with them, and to stay with them in Virginia for a reasonable length of time, to care for Amanda.

Unfortunately, the hired nurse seemed to have taken it upon herself to act as the disciplinarian of wayward children as well as overseer of motherly health. Understandably, she and Lou had not particularly seen eye to eye. Lou and Oz watched as the tall, bony woman tended to her patient.

"Can we be with her for a bit?" Oz finally asked in a small voice. To him the nurse was part viper, part fairy-tale evil, and she scared him into the next century. It seemed to Oz that the woman's hand at any moment could become a knife, and he the blade's only target. The idea of their great-grandmother having witchlike qualities had not come entirely from the unfortunate tale of Hansel and Gretel. Oz held out no hope that the nurse would agree to his request, but, surprisingly, she did.

As she slid closed the door to the compartment, Oz looked at Lou. "I guess she's not so bad."

"Oz, she went to take a smoke."

"How do you know she smokes?"

"If the nicotine stains on her fingers hadn't clued me in, the fact that she reeks of tobacco would've been enough."

Oz sat next to his mother, who lay in the lower bunk

bed, arms across her middle, eyes closed, her breath shallow but at least there.

"It's us, Mom, me and Lou."

Lou looked exasperated. "Oz, she can't hear you."

"Yes, she can!" There was a bite to the boy's words that startled Lou, who was used to virtually all of his ways. She crossed her arms and looked away. When she glanced back, Oz had taken a small box from his suitcase and was opening it. The chain necklace he pulled out had a small quartz stone at the end.

"Oz, please," his sister implored, "will you stop?"

He ignored her and held the necklace over his mother.

Amanda could eat and drink, though for some reason unfathomable to her children she could not move her limbs or speak, and her eyes never opened. This was what bothered Oz greatly and also gave him the most hope. He figured some small thing must be out of sorts, like a pebble in a shoe, a clog in a pipe. All he had to do was clear this simple obstruction and his mother would join them again.

"Oz, you are so dumb. Don't do this."

He stopped and looked at her. "Your problem is you don't believe in anything, Lou."

"And your problem is you believe in *everything*."

Oz started to swing the necklace slowly back and forth over his mother. He closed his eyes and started saying words that could not be clearly understood, perhaps not even by him.

Lou stood and fidgeted, but finally could not take this foolishness any longer. "Anybody sees you doing that, they'll think you're loony. And you know what? You are!"

Oz stopped his incantations and looked at her crossly.

'Well, you ruined it. Complete silence is necessary for the ure to work."

"Cure? What cure? What are you talking about?"

"Do you want Mom to stay like this?"

"Well, if she does, it's her own fault," Lou snapped. 'If she hadn't been arguing with Dad, none of this would've aappened."

Oz was stunned by her words. Even Lou looked surorised that she could have said something like that. But rue to her nature, Lou wasn't about to take any of it back once it was said.

Neither one looked at Amanda right at that moment, out if they had, the pair would have seen something, only a tremble of the eyelids, that suggested Amanda had somehow heard her daughter, then fallen deeper into the abyss that had held her so very tightly already.

Although most of the passengers were unaware, the train gradually banked left as the line curved away from the city on its way south. As it did so, Amanda's arm slid off her stomach and dangled over the side of the bed.

Oz stood there stunned for a moment. One could sense that the boy believed he had just witnessed a miracle of biblical dimension, like a flung stone felling a giant. He screamed out, "Mom! Mom!" and almost dragged Lou to the floor in his excitement. "Lou, did you see that?"

But Lou could not speak. She had presumed their mother incapable of such activity ever again. Lou had started to utter the word "Mom" when the door to the compartment slid open, and the nurse filled the space like an avalanche of white rock, her face a craggy pile of displeasure. Wisps of cigarette smoke hovered above her head, as though she were about to spontaneously com bust. If Oz had not been so fixated on his mother, he might have jumped for the window at the sight of the woman.

"What's going on here?" She staggered forward as the train rocked some more, before settling into its narrow path through New Jersey.

Oz dropped the necklace and pointed at his mother, as if he were a bird dog in search of praise. "She moved Mom moved her arm. We both saw it, didn't we, Lou?"

Lou, however, could only stare from her mother to Oz and back again. It was as though someone had driven a pole down her throat; she could form no words.

The nurse examined Amanda and came away even more sour-faced, apparently finding the interruption of her cigarette break unforgivable. She put Amanda's arm back across her stomach and covered her with the sheet.

"The train went around a curve. That's all." As she bent low to tuck in the bedcovers, she saw the necklace on the floor, incriminating evidence of Oz's plot to hasten his mother's recovery.

"What's this?" she demanded, reaching down and picking up Exhibit One in her case against the little boy.

"I was just using it to help Mom. It's sort of"—Oz glanced nervously at his sister—"it's sort of magic."

"That is nonsense."

"I'd like it back, please."

"Your mother is in a catatonic state," the woman said in a cold, pedantic tone designed to strike absolute terror in all who were insecure and vulnerable, and she had an easy target in Oz. "There is little hope of her regaining consciousness. And it certainly won't happen because of a necklace, young man."

"Please give it back," Oz said, his hands clenched together, as though in prayer.

"I have already told you—" She was cut off by the tap on her shoulder. When she turned, Lou stood directly in front of her. The girl seemed to have grown many inches in the last several seconds. At least the thrust of her head, neck, and shoulders seemed emboldened. "Give it back to him!"

The nurse's face reddened at this abuse. "I do not take orders from a child."

Quick as a whip Lou grabbed the necklace, but the nurse was surprisingly strong and managed to pocket it, though Lou struggled hard.

"This is not helping your mother," the nurse snapped, puffing out the odor of Lucky Strikes with each breath. "Now, please sit down and keep quiet!"

Oz looked at his mother, the agony clear on his face at having lost his precious necklace over a curve in the track.

Lou and Oz settled next to the window and spent the next several rolling miles quietly watching the death of the sun. When Oz started to fidget, Lou asked him what was the matter.

"I don't feel good about leaving Dad by himself back there."

"Oz, he's not alone."

"But he *was* in that box all by himself. And it's getting dark now. He might be scared. It's not right, Lou."

"He's not in that box, he's with God. They're up there talking right now, looking down on us."

Oz looked up at the sky. His hand lifted to wave, but then he looked unsure.

"You can wave to him, Oz. He's up there."

"Cross your heart, stick a needle in your eye?"

"All of that. Go ahead and wave."

Oz did and then smiled a precious one.

"What?" his sister asked.

"I don't know, it just felt good. Think he waved back?"

"Of course. God too. You know how Dad is, telling stories and all. They're probably good friends by now." Lou waved too, and as her fingers drifted against the cool glass, she pretended for a moment that she was certain of all that she had just said. And it did feel good.

Since their father's death, winter had almost given over to spring. She missed him more each day, the vast emptiness inside her swelling with every breath Lou took. She wanted her dad to be fine and healthy. And with them. But it would never be. Her father really was gone. It was an impossibly agonizing feeling. She looked to the sky.

Hello, Dad. Please never forget me, for I won't ever forget you. She mouthed these words so Oz couldn't hear. When she finished, Lou thought she might start bawling herself, but she couldn't, not in front of Oz. If she cried, there was a strong possibility that her brother might also cry, and keep right on going for the rest of his life.

"What's it like to be dead, Lou?" Oz stared out into the night as he asked this.

After a few moments she said, "Well, I guess part of being dead is not feeling anything. But in another way you feel everything. All good. If you've led a decent life. If not, well, you know."

"The Devil?" Oz asked, the fear visible in his features even as he said the terrible word.

"You don't have to worry about that. Or Dad either."

Oz's gaze made its way, by steady measures, to Amanda. "Is Mom going to die?"

"We're all going to die one day." Lou would not sugar-coat that one, not even for Oz, but she did squeeze him tightly. "Let's just take it one step at a time. We've got a lot going on."

Lou stared out the window as she held tightly to her brother. Nothing was forever, and didn't she know that.

CHAPTER FIVE

IT WAS VERY EARLY MORNING, WHEN THE BIRDS HAD
barely awoken and thumped their wings to life, and
cold mists were rising from the warm ground, and the
sun was only a seam of fire in the eastern sky. They had
made one stop in Richmond, where the locomotive had been
changed, then the train had cleared the Shenandoah Valley,
the most splendidly fertile soil and temperate climate for
growing virtually anything. Now the angle of land was far
steeper.

Lou had slept little because she had shared the top bunk
with Oz, who was restless at night under the best circumstances. On a swaying train heading to a new, terrifying
world, her little brother had been a wildcat in his sleep. Her
limbs had been bruised from his unconscious flailing, despite holding him tight; her ears were hurting from his
tragic screams, in spite of her whispered words of comfort.
Lou had finally climbed down, touched the cold floor with
bare feet, stumbled to the window in the darkness, pulled
back the curtains, and been rewarded by seeing her first
Virginia mountain face-to-face.

Jack Cardinal had once told his daughter that it was believed that there were actually two sets of Appalachian mountains. The first had been formed by receding seas and the shrinkage of the earth millions of years before, and had risen to a great height that rivaled the present Rockies. Later these ridges had been eroded away to peneplain by the pounding of unsettled water. Then the world had shaken itself again, Lou's father had explained to her, and the rock had risen high once more, though not nearly so high as before, and formed the current Appalachians, which stood like menacing hands between parts of Virginia and West Virginia, and extended from Canada all the way down to Alabama.

The Appalachians had prevented early expansion westward, Jack had taught his ever-curious Lou, and kept the American colonies unified long enough to win their independence from an English monarch. Later, the mountain range's natural resources had fueled one of the greatest manufacturing eras the world had ever seen. Despite all that, her father had added with a resigned smile, man never gave the mountains much credit in shaping his affairs.

Lou knew that Jack Cardinal had loved the Virginia mountains, and had held high-angled rock in the deepest awe. He had often told her that there was something magical about this stretch of lofty earth, because he believed it held powers that could not be logically explained. She had often wondered how a mixture of dirt and stone, despite its elevation, could impress her father so. Now, for the first time, she had a sense of how it could, for Lou had never experienced anything quite like it.

The bumps of tree-shrouded dirt and slate piles Lou had initially seen really qualified only as small offspring; behind these "children" she could see the outlines of the tall parents, the mountains. They seemed unlimited by sky or earth. So large and broad were they that the mountains seemed unnatural, though they had been born directly from the planet's crust. And out there was a woman Lou had been named for but had never met. There was both comfort and alarm in that thought. For one panicked moment, Lou felt as though they had passed right into another solar system on this clickety-clack train. Then Oz was beside her, and though he was not one to inspire confidence in others, Lou did feel reassurance in his small presence.

"I think we're getting close," she said, rubbing his small shoulders, working out the tension of another round of nightmares. She and her mother had become experts in this. Oz, Amanda had told her, had the worst case of night terrors she had ever seen. But it was something neither to pity, nor to make light of, she had taught her daughter. All one could do was be there for the little boy and work out the mental and physical snarls as best one could.

That could have been Lou's own personal scripture: *Thou shalt have no greater duty than taking care of Thy brother Oz.* She meant to honor that commandment above all else.

The little boy focused on the landscape. "Where is it? Where we're going to be?"

She pointed out the window. "Somewhere out there."

"Will the train drive right up to the house?"

Lou smiled at his remark. "No. Someone will be waiting for us at the station."

The train passed into a tunnel slashed through the side of one of the hills, throwing them into even greater darkness. Moments later they shot clear of the tunnel and then how they climbed! Their degree of ascent made Lou and Oz peer out anxiously. Up ahead was a trestle. The train slowed and then eased carefully onto the bridge, like a foot at cold water's edge. Lou and Oz looked down, but could not see the ground below in the poor light. It was as though they were suspended in the sky, somehow carried aloft by an iron bird weighing many tons. Then suddenly the train was back on firm ground, and the climb was on again. As the train picked up speed, Oz took a deep breath interrupted by a yawn—perhaps, Lou thought, to stifle his anxiety.

"I'm going to like it here," Oz suddenly proclaimed as he balanced his bear against the window. "Look out there," he said to his stuffed animal, which had never had a name that Lou knew of. Then Oz's thumb nervously probed the insides of his mouth. He'd been diligently trying to stop sucking his thumb, yet with all that was happening he was finding it tough going.

"It'll be okay, right, Lou?" he mumbled.

She perched her little brother on her lap, tickling the back of his neck with her chin until Oz squirmed.

"We're going to be just fine." And Lou somehow forced herself to believe that it would be so.

CHAPTER SIX

THE TRAIN STATION AT RAINWATER RIDGE WAS NO more than a glorified pine-studded lean-to, with a single cracked and spiderwebbed window and an opening for a door but no door to fill the space. A narrow jump separated this wreck of nail and board from the railroad track. The channeled wind was fierce as it fought its way through the gaps in rock and tree, and the faces of the few folk hanging about, along with the runted trees, evidenced the blunt force of its chisel.

Lou and Oz watched as their mother was loaded into an ancient ambulance. As the nurse climbed into the vehicle, she scowled back at her charges, the confrontation of the day before obviously still rankling her.

When the doors of the vehicle closed, Lou pulled the quartz necklace from her coat pocket and handed it to Oz.

"I slipped into her room before she got up. It was still in her pocket."

Oz smiled, pocketed the precious item, and then reached on tiptoe to give his sister a kiss on the cheek.

The two stood next to their luggage, patiently awaiting Louisa Mae Cardinal.

Their skin was scrubbed raw, each hair on their heads assiduously brushed—Lou had taken extra time with Oz. They were dressed in their very best clothes, which managed barely to conceal their pounding hearts. They had been there for a minute when they sensed someone behind them.

The Negro man was young and, in keeping with the geography, ruggedly built. He was tall and wide of shoulder, deep-chested, with arms like slabs of ham, a waist not small but not soft either, and legs long but one oddly pushed out where calf met knee. His skin was the color of deep rust and pleasing to the eye. He was looking down at his feet, which necessarily drew Lou's gaze to them. His old work boots were so big a newborn could have slept in them with some room to spare, the girl observed. His overalls were as worn as the shoes, but they were clean, or as clean as the dirt and wind would allow anything to be up here. Lou held out her hand, but he did not take it.

Instead, with one impressive move, he picked up all their bags, then flicked his head toward the road. Lou interpreted this as "hello," "come on," and "I'll tell you my name maybe later," all wrapped into one efficient motion. He limped off, the bulging leg now revealed to be a bum one. Lou and Oz looked at each other and then trudged after him. Oz clutched his bear and Lou's hand. No doubt the boy would have tugged the train after them if he could have somehow managed it, so as to effect a quick escape if needed.

The long-bodied Hudson four-door sedan was the color

of a sweet pickle. The car was old but clean inside. Its tall, exposed radiator looked like a tombstone, and its two front fenders were missing, as was the rear window glass. Lou and Oz sat in the backseat while the man drove. He worked the long stick shift with an easy skill, nary a gear ever left grinding.

After the woeful state of the train station, Lou had not expected much in the way of civilization up here. However, after only twenty minutes on the road they entered a town of fair size, though in New York City such a meager collection of structures would hardly have filled one sorry block.

A sign announced that they were entering the township of Dickens, Virginia. The main street was two-laned and paved with asphalt. Well-kept structures of wood and brick lined both sides of it. One such building rose five stories, its vacancy sign proclaiming it to be a hotel at fair rates. Automobiles were plentiful here, mostly bulky Ford and Chrysler sedans, and hefty trucks of various makes adorned with mud. All were parked slantwise in front of the buildings.

There were general stores, restaurants, and an open-door warehouse with box towers of Domino sugar and Quick napkins, Post Toasties and Quaker Oats visible inside. There was an automobile dealership with shiny cars in the window, and next to that an Esso gas station sporting twin pumps with bubble tops and a uniformed man with a big smile filling up the tank of a dented La Salle sedan, with a dusty Nash two-door waiting behind it. A big Coca-Cola soda cap was hanging in front of one café, and an Eveready Battery sign was bolted to the wall of a hardware shop. Telephone and electrical poles of poplar ran down one side of the street, black cables snaking out from them to each of the structures. Another shop announced the sale of pianos and organs for cash at good prices. A movie theater was on one corner, a laundry on another. Gas street lamps ran down both sides of the road, like big, lit matchsticks.

The sidewalks were crowded with folks. They ranged from well-dressed women with stylish hairdos topped by modest hats, to bent, grimy men who, Lou thought, probably toiled here in the coal mines she had read about.

As they passed through, the last building of significance was also the grandest. It was red brick with an elegant two-story pediment portico, supported by paired Greek Ionic columns, and had a steeply pitched, hammered tin roof painted black, with a brick clock tower top-hatting it. The Virginia and American flags snapped out front in the fine breeze. The elegant red brick, however, sat on a foundation of ugly, scored concrete. This curious pairing struck Lou as akin to fine pants over filthy boots. The carved words above the columns simply read: "Court House." And then they left the finite sprawl of Dickens behind.

Lou sat back puzzled. Her father's stories had been filled with tales of the brutish mountains, and the primitive life there, where hunters squatted near campfires of hickory sticks and cooked their kill and drank their bitter coffee; where farmers rose before the sun and worked the land till they collapsed; where miners dug into the earth, filling their lungs with black that would eventually kill them; and where lumberjacks swept virgin forests clean with the measured strokes of ax and saw. Quick wits, a sound knowledge of the land, and a strong back were essential up here. Danger roamed the steep slopes and loamy valleys, and the magisterial high rock presided over both men and beasts, sharply defining the limits of their ambition, of their lives. A place like Dickens, with its paved roads, hotel, Coca-Cola signs, and pianos for cash at good prices, had no right to be here. Yet Lou suddenly realized that the time period her father had written about had been well over twenty years ago.

She sighed. Everything, even the mountains and its people, apparently, changed. Now Lou assumed her great-grandmother probably lived in a quite ordinary neighborhood with quite ordinary neighbors. Perhaps she had a cat and went to have her hair done every Saturday at a shop that smelled of chemicals and cigarette smoke. Lou and Oz would drink orange soda pop on the front porch and go to church on Sunday and wave to people as they passed in their cars, and life would not be all that much different than it had been in New York. And while there was absolutely nothing wrong with that, it was not the dense, breathtaking wilderness Lou had been expecting. It was not the life her father had experienced and then written about, and Lou was clearly disappointed.

The car passed through more miles of trees, soaring rock and dipping valleys, and then Lou saw another sign. This town was named Tremont. This was probably it, she thought. Tremont appeared roughly one-third the size of Dickens. About fifteen cars were slant-parked in front of shops similar to those in the larger town, only there was no high-rise building, no courthouse, and the asphalt road had given way to macadam and gravel. Lou also spotted the occasional horse rider, and then Tremont was behind them, and the ground moved higher still. Her great-grandmother, Lou surmised, must live on the outskirts of Tremont.

The next place they passed had no sign naming its location, and the scant number of buildings and few people they saw didn't seem enough to justify a name. The road was now dirt, and the Hudson swayed from side to side over this humble pack of shifting earth. Lou saw a shallow post office building, and next to that was a leaning pile of boards with no sign out front, and steps that had the rot. And finally there was a good-sized general store with the name "McKenzie's" on the wall; crates of sugar, flour, salt, and pepper were piled high outside. In one window of McKenzie's hung a pair of blue overalls, harnesses, and a kerosene lamp. And that was about all there was of the nameless stop along the poor road.

As they drifted over the soft dirt, they passed silent, sunken-eyed men, faces partially covered by wispy beards; they wore dirty one-piece overalls, slouch hats, and lumpy brogans, and traveled on foot, mule, or horse. A woman with vacant eyes, a droopy face, and bony limbs, clothed in a gingham blouse and a homespun woolen skirt bunched at the waist with pins, rocked along in a small schooner wagon pulled by a pair of mules. In the back of the wagon was a pile of children riding burlap seed bags bigger than they were. Running parallel to the road here a long coal train was stopped under a water tower and taking in big gulps, steam belching out from its throat with each greedy swallow. On another mountain in the distance Lou could see a coal tipple on wooden stilts, and another line of coal cars passing underneath this structure, like a column of obedient ants.

They passed over a large bridge. A tin sign said this

was the McCloud River flowing thirty feet underneath them. In the reflection of the rising sun the water looked pink, like a miles-long curvy tongue. The mountain peaks were smoke-blue, the mists of fog right below them forming a gauzy kerchief.

With no more towns apparent, Lou figured it was time to get acquainted with the gentleman up front.

"What's your name?" she asked. She had known many Negroes, mostly writers, poets, musicians, and those who acted on the stage, all her parents' friends. But there had been others too. During her excursions through the city with her mother, Lou had met colored people who loaded the trash, flagged down the cabs, heaved the bags, scooted after others' children, cleaned the streets, washed the windows, shined the shoes, cooked the food, and did the laundry, and took, in amicable measures, the insults and tips of their white clientele.

This fellow driving, he was different, because he apparently didn't like to talk. Back in New York Lou had befriended one kindly old gentleman who worked a lowly job at Yankee Stadium, where she and her father would sometimes steal away to games. This old man, only a shade darker than the peanuts he sold, had told her that a colored man would talk your ear off every day of the week except the Sabbath, when he'd let God and the women have their shot.

The big fellow just continued to drive; his gaze didn't even creep to the rearview mirror when Lou spoke. A lack of curiosity was something Lou could not tolerate in her fellow man.

"My parents named me Louisa Mae Cardinal, after my great-grandmother. I go by Lou, though, just Lou.

My dad is John Jacob Cardinal. He's a very famous writer. You've probably heard of him."

The young man didn't grunt or even wiggle a finger. The road ahead apparently held fascination for him that a dose of Cardinal family history simply could not compete with.

Getting into his sister's spirited attempt at conversation, Oz said, "He's dead, but our mom's not."

This indelicate comment drew an immediate scowl from Lou, and just as quickly Oz looked out the window, ostensibly to admire the countryside.

They were thrown forward a little when the Hudson came to an abrupt stop.

The young boy standing there was a little older than Lou, but about the same height. His red hair was all crazy-angled cowlicks, which still failed to cover conical ears that could easily have caught on a nail. He wore a stained long john shirt and dirty overalls that didn't manage to hide bony ankles. His feet were bare even though the air wasn't warm. He carried a long, hand-whittled cane fishing pole and a dented tackle box, which appeared to have once been blue. There was a black-and-tan mutt of a dog next to him, its lumpy pink tongue hanging out. The boy put his pole and box through the Hudson's open rear window and climbed in the front seat like he owned it, his dog following his relaxed lead.

"Howdy-howdy, Hell No," the stranger boy said amiably to the driver, who acknowledged this newcomer with an ever-so-slight nod of the head.

Lou and Oz looked at each other in puzzlement over this very odd greeting.

Like a pop-up toy, the visitor poked his head over the

seat and stared at them. He had more than an adequate crop of freckles on his flat cheeks, a small mound of nose that carried still more freckles, and out of the sun his hair seemed even redder. His eyes were the color of raw peas, and together with the hair they made Lou think of Christmas wrapping paper.

"I bet I knowed me what, y'all Miss Louisa's people, ain'tcha?" he said in a pleasant drawl, his smile endearingly impish.

Lou nodded slowly. "I'm Lou. This is my brother, Oz," she said, with an easy courtesy, if only to show she wasn't nervous.

Swift as a salesman's grin, the boy shook hands with them. His fingers were strong, with many fine examples of the countryside imbedded in each of them. Indeed, if he'd ever had fingernails, it was difficult to tell under this remarkable collection of dirt. Lou and Oz both couldn't help but stare at those fingers.

He must have noted their looks, because he said, "Been to digging worms since afore light. Candle in one hand, tin can in the other. Dirty work, y'all know." He said this matter-of-factly, as though for years they all had knelt side by side under a hot sun hunting skinny bait.

Oz looked at his own hand and saw there the transfers of rich soil from the handshake. He smiled because it was as though the two had just undertaken the blood brother ritual. A brother! Now that was something Oz could get excited about.

The red-haired young man grinned good-naturedly, showing that most of his teeth were where they were supposed to be, though not many of them were what one could call either straight or white.

"Name's Jimmy Skinner," he said by way of modest introduction, "but folk call me Diamond, 'cause my daddy say that how hard my head be. This here hound's Jeb."

At the sound of his name Jeb poked his fluffy head over the seat and Diamond gave each of the dog's ears a playful tug. Then he looked at Oz.

"That a right funny name fer a body. Oz."

Now Oz looked worried under the scrutiny of his blood brother. Was their partnership not to be?

Lou answered for him. "His real name is Oscar. As in Oscar Wilde. Oz is a nickname, like in the Wizard of."

His gaze on the ceiling of the Hudson, Diamond considered these facts, obviously searching his memory.

"Never tell of no Wildes up here." He paused, thinking hard again, the wrinkles on his brow crazy-lined. "And wizard'a what 'xactly?"

Lou could not hide her astonishment. "The book? The movie? Judy Garland?"

"The Munchkins? And the Cowardly Lion?" added Oz.

"Ain't never been to no pitcher show." Diamond glanced at Oz's bear and a disapproving look simmered on his face. "You right big fer that, now ain'tcha, son?"

This sealed it for Oz. He sadly wiped his hand clean on the seat, annulling his and Diamond's solemn covenant.

Lou leaned forward so close she could smell Diamond's breath. "That's none of your business, is it?"

A chastened Diamond slumped in the front seat and let Jeb idly lick dirt and worm juice from his fingers. It was as though Lou had spit at the boy using words.

The ambulance was far ahead of them, driving slowly.

"I sorry your ma hurt," said Diamond, in the manner of passing the peace pipe.

"She's going to get better," said Oz, always nimbler on the draw than was Lou with matters concerning their mother.

Lou stared out the window, arms across her chest.

"Hell No," said Diamond, "just plop me off over to the bridge. Catch me anythin' good, I bring it fer supper. Tell Miss Louisa?"

Lou watched as Hell No edged his blunt chin forward, apparently signaling a big, happy "Okay, Diamond!"

The boy popped up over the seat again. "Hey, y'all fancy good lard-fried fish fer supper?" His expression was hopeful, his intentions no doubt honorable; however, Lou was unwilling just now to make friends.

"We all shore would, Diamond. Then maybe we can find us a pitcher show in this one-horse town."

As soon as Lou said this, she regretted it. It wasn't just the disappointed look on Diamond's face; it was also the fact that she had just blasphemed the place where her father had grown up. She caught herself looking to heaven, watching for grim lightning bolts, or maybe sudden rains, like tears falling.

"From some big city, ain'tcha?" Diamond said.

Lou drew her gaze from the sky. "The biggest. New York," she said.

"Huh, well, y'all don't be telling folks round here that."

Oz gaped at his ex–blood brother. "Why not?"

"Right chere's good, Hell No. Come on now, Jeb."

Hell No stopped the car. Directly in front of them

was the bridge, although it was the puniest such one
Lou had ever seen. It was a mere twenty feet of warped
wooden planks laid over six-by-six tarred railroad ties,
with an arch of rusted metal on either side to prevent
one from plummeting all of five feet into what looked
to be a creek full of more flat rock than water. Suicide
by bridge jumping did not appear to be a realistic option here. And, judging from the shallow water, Lou did
not hold out much hope for a lard-fried fish dinner, not
that such a meal sounded particularly appealing to her
anyway.

As Diamond pulled his gear from the back of the Hudson, Lou, who was a little sorry for what she had said,
but more curious than sorry, leaned over the seat and
whispered to him through the open rear window.

"Why do you call him Hell No?"

Her unexpected attention brought Diamond back to
good spirits and he smiled at her. " 'Cause that be his
name," he said in an inoffensive manner. "He live with
Miss Louisa."

"Where did he get that kind of a name?"

Diamond glanced toward the front seat and pretended
to fiddle with something in his tackle box. In a low voice
he said, "His daddy pass through these parts when Hell
No ain't no more'n a baby. Plunked him right on the
dirt. Well, a body say to him, 'You gonna come back,
take that child?' And he say, 'Hell no.' Now, Hell No,
he never done nobody wrong his whole life. Ain't many
folk say that. And no rich ones."

Diamond grabbed his tackle box and swung the pole
to his shoulder. He walked to the bridge, whistling a tune,
and Hell No drove the Hudson across, the structure groan-

ing and complaining with each turn of the car wheels. Diamond waved and Oz returned it with his stained hand, hope welling back for maybe a friendship of enduring degree with Jimmy "Diamond" Skinner, crimson-crowned fisherboy of the mountain.

Lou simply stared at the front seat. At a man named Hell No.

CHAPTER SEVEN

THE DROP WAS A GOOD THREE THOUSAND FEET IF it was an inch. The Appalachians might pale in size if leveled against the upstart Rockies, but to the Cardinal children they seemed abundantly tall enough.

After leaving the small bridge and Diamond behind, the ninety-six horses of the Hudson's engine had started to whine, and Hell No had dropped to a lower gear. The car's protest was understandable, for now the uneven dirt road headed up at almost a forty-five-degree angle and wound around the mountain like a rattler's coils. The road's supposed twin lanes, by any reasonable measurement, were really only a single pregnant one. Fallen rock lay along the roadside, like solid tears from the mountain's face.

Oz looked out only once at this potential drop to heaven, and then he chose to look no more. Lou stared off, their rise to the sky not really bothering her any.

Then, suddenly flying around a curve at them was a farm tractor, mostly rust and missing pieces and held together with coils of rusty wire and other assorted trash.

It was almost too big for the narrow road all by itself, much less with a lumbering Hudson coming at it. Children were hanging and dangling every which way on the bulky equipment, as if it were a mobile jungle gym. One young boy about Lou's age was actually suspended over nothing but air, hanging on only by his own ten fingers and God's will, and he was laughing! The other children, a girl of about ten and a boy about Oz's age, were clamped tight around whatever they could find to hold, their expressions seized with terror.

The man piloting this contraption was far more frightening even than the vision of out-of-control machinery holding flailing children hostage. A felt hat covered his head, years of sweat having leached to all points of the material. His beard was bristly rough, and his face was burnt dark and heavily wrinkled by the unforgiving sun. He seemed to be short, but his body was thick and muscular. His clothes, and those of the children, were almost rags.

The tractor was almost on top of the Hudson. Oz covered his eyes, too afraid even to attempt a scream. But Lou cried out as the tractor bore down on them.

Hell No, with an air of practiced calm, somehow drove the car out of the tractor's path and stopped to let the other vehicle safely pass. So close were they to the edge that a full third of the Hudson's tires were gripping nothing but the chilly brace of mountain air. Displaced rock and dirt dribbled over the side and were instantly scattered in the swirl of wind. For a moment Lou was certain they were going over, and she gripped Oz with all her strength, as though that would make a difference.

As the tractor roared by, the man glared at them all before settling on Hell No and shouting, "Stupid nig—"

The rest, thankfully, was covered by the whine of the tractor and the laughter and whoops of the suspended-in-air boy. Lou looked at Hell No, who didn't flinch at any of this. Not the first time, she imagined—the near fatal collision and the awful name calling.

And then like a strike of hail in July, this rolling circus was gone. Hell No drove on.

As she got her nerves settled down, Lou could see loaded coal trucks far below them inching down one side of a road, while on the other side empty trucks flew hell-bent back up, like honeybees, to gorge some more. All around here the face of the mountains had been gashed open in places, exposing rock underneath, the topsoil and trees all gone. Lou watched as coal trolleys emerged from these wounds in the mountains, like drips of blackened blood, and the coal was tippled into the truck beds.

"Name's Eugene."

Lou and Oz both stared toward the front seat. The young man was looking at them in the mirror.

"Name's Eugene," he said again. "Diamond, he fergit sometime. But he a good boy. My frien'."

"Hi, Eugene," said Oz. And then Lou said hello too.

"Ain't see folks much. Words ain't come easy for me. I sorry for that."

"That's okay, Eugene," said Lou. "Meeting strangers is hard."

"Miss Louisa and me, we real glad you come. She a good woman. Take me in when I ain't got no home. You lucky she your kin."

"Well, that's good because we haven't been very lucky lately," said Lou.

"She talk 'bout y'all much. And your daddy and momma. She care for your momma. Miss Louisa, she heal the sick."

Oz looked at Lou with renewed hope, but she shook her head.

More miles went by, and then Eugene turned the car down a lane that wasn't much more than twin ruts in the dirt spread over with still dormant grass and bracketed by thick wild brush. As they were obviously drawing near to their destination, Oz and Lou exchanged a glance. Excitement, nervousness, panic, and hope competed for space on the small landscapes of their faces.

The dirt lane nudged over to the north as it cleared a rise. Here the land splayed out into a broad valley of simple beauty. Green meadows were bracketed by vast forests of every wood the state boasted. Next to the meadows were cleared patchwork fields that yielded to split-rail corrals, weathered gray and wrapped with naked rambler rose vines. Anchoring the corrals was a large two-story plank barn, topped by a gambrel roof with rain hood, all covered by cedar shingles fashioned with froe and maul. It had large double doors at each end, with a set of hay doors above. A projecting timber was immediately above this portal and used to support the hay fork dangling from it. Three cows lay in the grass in one protected space, while a roan horse grazed alone in a small snake-rail corral. Lou counted a half dozen sheared sheep in another pen. And behind that was another fenced space where enormous hogs rolled in a wallow of mud, like giant babies at play. A pair of mules were doubletreed to a large wagon that sat by the barn, the sun reflecting off its tin-wrapped wooden wheels. Near the barn was a farmhouse of modest proportion.

There were other buildings and lean-tos, large and small, scattered here and there, most of plank. One structure situated in an overhang of maple trees looked to be formed from logs chinked with mud and seemed half-buried in the earth. The cleared fields, which sloped at their ends like the curl of hair, sprang outward from the central farm buildings like spokes on a wheel. And rising high behind all of this were the Appalachians, making this good-sized farm property seem but a child's model by comparison.

Lou was finally here, the place her father had spent much of his life writing about yet had never returned to. She drew in several quick breaths, and sat very erect as they drove on to the house, where Louisa Mae Cardinal, the woman who had helped to raise their father, awaited them.

CHAPTER EIGHT

❧

I NSIDE THE FARMHOUSE THE NURSE WAS ADVISING THE
woman as to Amanda's condition and other essen-
tials, while the woman listened intently and asked
pointed questions.

"And we might as well get *my* requirements out of
the way," said the nurse finally. "I suffer from animal
and pollen allergies, and you need to make sure that their
presence here is kept to a minimum. Under no circumstances should animals be allowed in the house. I have
certain specific dietary needs. I will provide you with a
list. I will also require a free reign in overseeing the children. I know that falls outside my formal duties, but those
two obviously need discipline, and I intend to so provide it. That girl, in particular, is a real piece of work.
I'm sure you can appreciate my frankness. Now you can
show me to my room."

Louisa Mae Cardinal said to the nurse, "I *appreciate*
you coming out. Fact is, we ain't got room for you."

The tall nurse stood as erect as she could, but she was
still shorter than Louisa Mae Cardinal. "Excuse me?" she
said with indignation.

"Tell Sam out there to take you on back to the train station. Another train north be coming through. Rare place for a walk while you wait."

"I was retained to come here and look after my patient."

"I look after Amanda just fine."

"You are not qualified to do so."

"Sam and Hank, they need get on back, honey."

"I need to call somebody about this." The nurse was so red-faced that she looked as though *she* might become a patient.

"Nearest phone on down the mountain in Tremont. But you can call the president of these United States, still my home." Louisa Mae gripped the woman's elbow with a strength that made the nurse's eyes flutter. "And we ain't got to bother Amanda with this." She guided the woman from the room, closing the door behind them.

"Do you seriously expect me to believe that you don't have a telephone?" the nurse said.

"Don't have that electricity thing neither, but I hear they right fine. Thank you agin, and you have a good trip back." She placed three worn dollar bills in the nurse's hand. "I wish it was more, honey, but it all the egg money I got."

The nurse stared down at the cash for a moment and said, "I'm staying until I'm satisfied that my patient—"

Louisa Mae once more gripped her elbow and led her to the front door. "Most folk here got rules 'bout trespassing. Warning shot's fired right close to the head. Get they's attention. Next shot gets a lot more personal. Now, I'm too old to waste time firing a warning shot, and I

ain't never once used salt in my gun. And now I can't
give it no straighter'n that."

※

When the Hudson pulled up, the ambulance was still
parked in front of the farmhouse, which had a deep, cool
porch and shadows elongating across it as the sun rose
higher. Lou and Oz got out of the car and confronted
their new home. It was smaller than it had appeared from
a distance. And Lou noted several sets of uneven add-
ons to the sides and back, all of which were set on a
crumbling fieldstone base with stepstone rock leading
from ground to porch. The unshingled roof had what
looked to be black tar paper across it. A picket-fence railing ran along the porch, which also sagged in places.
The chimney was made of hand-formed brick, and the
mortar had leached over parts of it. The clapboard was
in need of painting, heat pops were fairly numerous, and
wood had buckled and warped in places where moisture
had crawled inside.

Lou accepted it for what it clearly was: an old house,
having gone through various reincarnations and situated
in a place of unforgiving elements. But the front-yard
grass was neatly cut, the steps, windows, and porch floor
were clean, and she tallied the early bloom of flowers in
glass jars and wooden buckets set along the porch rail
and in window boxes. Climbing rose vines ran up the
porch columns, a screen of dormant maypops covered
part of the porch, and a husky vine of sleeping honeysuckle spread against one wall. There was a rough-hewn

workbench on the porch with tools scattered across its
surface and a split-bottom hickory chair next to it.

Brown hens started singing around their feet, and a
couple of mean-looking geese came calling, sending the
hens off screeching for their lives. And then a yellow-
footed rooster stomped by and scared the geese off,
cocked its head at Lou and Oz, gave a crow, and stomped
back from whence it had come. The mare whinnied a
greeting from its corral, while the pair of mules just stared
at nothing. Their hairy skin was cave black, their ears
and snouts not quite balanced with each other. Oz took
a step toward them for a better look and then retreated
when one of the mules made a noise Oz had never heard
before yet which clearly sounded threatening.

Lou's and Oz's attention shifted to the front door when
it was thrown open with far more thrust than was necessary. Their mother's nurse came clomping out. She
stalked past them, her long arms and legs cocking and
firing off rounds of silent fury.

"Never in all my life," she wailed to the Appalachians. Without another word or grimace, flap of arm or
kick of leg, she climbed into the ambulance, closed the
doors, which made two modest thunks as metal hit metal,
and the volunteer brigade beat a timid retreat.

Beyond perplexed, Lou and Oz turned back to the
house for answers and found themselves staring at her.

Standing in the doorway was Louisa Mae Cardinal.
She was very tall, and though also very lean, she looked
strong enough to strangle a bear, and determined enough
to do so. Her face was leathern, the lines creasing it the
etch of wood grain. Although she was approaching her
eightieth year, the balls of her cheeks still rode high. The

jaw was also strong, though her mouth drooped some. Her silver hair was tied with a simple cord at the nape, and then plunged to her waist.

Lou was heartened to see that she wore not a dress, but instead baggy denim trousers faded to near white and an indigo shirt patched in various places. Old brogans covered her feet. She was statue-like in her majesty, yet the woman had a remarkable pair of hazel eyes that clearly missed nothing in their range.

Lou boldly stepped forward while Oz did his best to melt into his sister's back. "I'm Louisa Mae Cardinal. This is my brother, Oscar." There was a tremble to Lou's voice. She stood her ground, though, only inches from her namesake, and this proximity revealed a remarkable fact: Their profiles were almost identical. They seemed twins separated by a mere three generations.

Louisa said nothing, her gaze trailing the ambulance.

Lou noted this and said, "Wasn't she supposed to stay and help look after our mother? She has a lot of needs, and we have to make sure that she's comfortable."

Her great-grandmother shifted her focus to the Hudson.

"Eugene," Louisa Mae said in a voice possessed of negligible twang, yet which seemed undeniably southern still, "bring the bags in, honey." Only then did she look at Lou, and though the stare was rigid, there was something prowling behind the eyes that gave Lou a reason to feel welcome. "We take good care of your mother."

Louisa Mae turned and went back in the house. Eugene followed with their bags. Oz was fully concentrating on his bear and his thumb. His wide, blue eyes were blinking rapidly, a sure indication that his nerves were racing at a feverish pitch. Indeed, he looked like he wanted to run all the way back to New York City right that minute. And Oz very well might have, if only he had known in which direction it happened to be.

CHAPTER NINE

THE BEDROOM GIVEN TO LOU WAS SPARTAN AND ALSO the only room on the second floor, accessed by a rear staircase. It had one large window that looked out over the farmyard. The angled walls and low ceiling were covered with old newspaper and magazine pages pasted there like wallpaper. Most were yellowed, and some hung down where the paste had worn away. There was a simple rope bed of hickory and a pine wardrobe scarred in places. And there was a small desk of rough-hewn wood by the window, where the morning light fell upon it. The desk was unremarkable in design, yet it drew Lou's attention as though cast from gold and trimmed by diamonds.

Her father's initials were still so vivid: "JJC." John Jacob Cardinal. This had to be the desk at which he had first started writing. She imagined her father as a little boy, lips set firm, hands working precisely, as he scored his initials into the wood, and then set out upon his career as a storyteller. As she touched the cut letters, it was as though she had just put her hand on top of her father's.

For some reason Lou sensed that her great-grandmother had deliberately given her this room.

Her father had been reserved about his life here. However, whenever Lou had asked him about her namesake, Jack Cardinal had been effusive in his answer. "A finer woman never walked the earth." And then he would tell about some of his life on the mountain, but only some. Apparently, he left the intimate details for his books, all but one of which Lou would have to wait until adulthood to read, her father had told her. Thus she was left with many unanswered questions.

She reached in her suitcase and pulled out a small, wood-framed photograph. Her mother's smile was wide, and though the photograph was black and white, Lou knew the swell of her mother's amber eyes was near hypnotic. Lou had always loved that color, even sometimes hoping that the blue in hers would disappear one morning and be replaced with this collision of brown and gold. The photo had been taken on her mother's birthday. Toddler Lou was standing in front of Amanda, and mother had both arms around her child. In the photo their smiles were suspended together for all time. Lou often wished she could remember something of that day.

Oz came into the room and Lou slipped the photograph back into her bag. As usual, her brother looked worried.

"Can I stay in your room?" he asked.

"What's wrong with yours?"

"It's next to hers."

"Who, Louisa?" Oz answered yes very solemnly, as though he was testifying in court. "Well, what's wrong with that?"

"She scares me," he said. "She really does, Lou."

"She let us come live with her."

"And I'm right glad you did come."

Louisa came forward from the doorway. "Sorry I was short with you. I was thinking 'bout your mother." She stared at Lou. "And her needs."

"That's okay," Oz said, as he flitted next to his sister. "I think you spooked my sister a little, but she's all right now."

Lou studied the woman's features, seeing if there was any of her father there. She concluded that there wasn't.

"We didn't have anyone else," Lou said.

"Y'all always have me," Louisa Mae answered back. She moved in closer, and Lou suddenly saw fragments of her father there. She also now understood why the woman's mouth drooped. There were only a few teeth there, all of them yellowed or darkened.

"Sorry as I can be I ain't made the funeral. News comes slowly here when it bothers to come a'tall." She looked down for a moment, as though gripped by something Lou couldn't see. "You're Oz. And you're Lou." Louisa pointed to them as she said the names.

Lou said, "The people who arranged our coming, I guess they told you."

"I knew long afore that. Y'all call me Louisa. They's chores to be done each day. We make or grow 'bout all we need. Breakfast's at five. Supper when the sun falls."

"Five o'clock in the morning!" exclaimed Oz.

"What about school?" asked Lou.

"Called Big Spruce. No more'n couple miles off. Eugene take you in the wagon first day, and then y'all walk after that. Or take the mare. Ain't spare the mules, for they do the pulling round here. But the nag will do."

Oz paled. "We don't know how to ride a horse."

"Y'all will. Horse and mule bestest way to get by up here, other than two good feet."

"What about the car?" asked Lou.

Louisa shook her head. "T'ain't practical. Take money we surely ain't got. Eugene know how it works and built a little lean-to for it. He start it up every now and agin, 'cause he say he have to so it run when we need it. Wouldn't have that durn thing, 'cept William and Jane Giles on down the road give it to us when they moved on. Can't drive it, no plans to ever learn."

"Is Big Spruce the same school my dad went to?" asked Lou.

"Yes, only the schoolhouse he went to ain't there no more. 'Bout as old as me, it fall down. But you got the same teacher. Change, like news, comes slowly here. You hungry?"

"We ate on the train," said Lou, unable to draw her gaze from the woman's face.

"Fine. Your momma settled in. Y'all g'on see her."

Lou said, "I'd like to stay here and look around some."

Louisa held the door open for them. Her voice was gentle but firm. "See your momma first."

The room was comfortable—good light, window open. Homespun curtains, curled by the damp and bleached by the sun, were lightly flapping in the breeze. As Lou looked around, she knew it had probably taken some effort to make this into what amounted to a sickroom. Some of the furniture looked worked on, the floor freshly scrubbed, the smell of paint still lingering; a chipped rocking chair sat in one corner with a thick blanket across it.

On the walls were ancient ferrotypes of men, women, and children, all dressed in what was probably their finest clothing: stiff white-collared shirts and bowler hats for the men; long skirts and bonnets for the women; lace frills for the young girls; and small suits and string ties for the boys. Lou studied them. Their expressions ran the gamut from dour to pleased, the children being the most animated, the grown women appearing the most suspicious, as though they believed their lives were to be taken, instead of simply their photographs.

Amanda, in a bed of yellow poplar, was propped up on fat feather pillows, and her eyes were shut. The mattress was feather-filled too, lumpy but soft, housed in a striped ticking. A patchwork quilt covered her. A faded drugget lay next to the bed so bare feet wouldn't have to touch a cold wood floor first thing in the morning. Lou knew her mother would not be needing that. On the walls were pegs with items of clothing hung from them. An old dresser was in one corner, a painted china pitcher and bowl resting on it. Lou wandered around the room idly, looking and touching. She noted that the window frame was slightly crooked, the panes of glass filmy, as though a fog had infiltrated the material somehow.

Oz sat next to his mother, leaned over, and kissed her. "Hi, Mom."

"She can't hear you," Lou muttered to herself as she stopped her wandering and looked out the window, smelling air purer than any she had before; in the draft were a medley of trees and flowers, wood smoke, long bluegrass, and animals large and small.

"It sure is pretty here in . . ." Oz looked at Lou.

"Virginia," Lou answered, without turning around.

"Virginia," Oz repeated. Then he took out the necklace.

From the doorway, Louisa watched this exchange.

Lou turned and saw what he was doing. "Oz, that stupid necklace doesn't work."

"So why'd you get it back for me then?" he said sharply.

This stopped Lou dead, for she had no ready answer. Oz turned back and began his ritual over Amanda. But with each swing of the quartz crystal, with each softly spoken utterance by Oz, Lou just knew he was trying to melt an iceberg with a single match; and she wanted no part of it. She raced past her great-grandmother and down the hall.

Louisa stepped into the room and sat down next to Oz. "What's that for, Oz?" she asked, pointing to the jewelry.

Oz cupped the necklace in his hand, eyed it closely, like it was a timepiece and he was checking what o'clock it was. "Friend told me about it. Supposed to help Mom. Lou doesn't believe it will." He paused. "Don't know if I do either."

Louisa ran a hand through his hair. "Some say believing a person get better is half the battle. I'm one who subscribes to that notion."

Fortunately, with Oz, a few seconds of despair were usually followed by replenished hope. He took the necklace and slid it under his mother's mattress. "Maybe it'll keep oozing its power this way. She'll get well, won't she?"

Louisa stared at the little boy, and then at his mother lying so still there. She touched Oz's cheek with her hand—very old against very new skin, and its mix seemed pleasing to both. "You keep right on believing, Oz. Don't you never stop believing."

CHAPTER TEN

✿

THE KITCHEN SHELVES WERE WORN, KNOTHOLED PINE, floors the same. The floorboards creaked slightly as Oz swept with a short-handled broom, while Lou loaded lengths of cut wood into the iron belly of the Sears catalogue cookstove that took up one wall of the small room. Fading sunlight came through the window and also peered through each wall crevice, and there were many. An old coal-oil lamp hung from a peg. Fat black iron kettles hung from the wall. In another corner was a food safe with hammered metal doors; a string of dried onions lay atop it and a glass jug of kerosene next to that.

As Lou examined each piece of hickory or oak, it was as though she was revisiting each facet of her prior life, before throwing it in the fire, saying good-bye as the flames ate it away. The room was dark and the smells of damp and burnt wood equally pungent. Lou stared over at the fireplace. The opening was large, and she guessed that the cooking had been done there before the Sears cookstove had come. The brick ran to the ceiling, and iron nails were driven through the mortar all over; tools and kettles, and odd pieces of other things Lou couldn't identify but that looked well-used, hung from them. In the center of the brick wall was a long rifle resting on twin braces angled into the mortar.

The knock on the door startled them both. Who would expect visitors so far above sea level? Lou opened the door and Diamond Skinner stared back at her with a vast smile. He held up a mess of smallmouth bass, as though he was offering her the crowns of dead kings. Loyal Jeb was beside him, his snout wrinkling as he drew in the fine fishy aroma.

Louisa came striding in from outside, her brow glistening with sweat, her gloved hands coated with rich dirt, as were her brogans. She slipped off her gloves and dabbed at her face with a sweat rag pulled from her pocket. Her long hair was pulled up under a cloth scarf, wisps of silver peeking out in spots.

"Well, Diamond, I believe that's the nicest mess of smallmouth I ever seen, son." She gave Jeb a pat. "How you doing, Mr. Jeb? You help Diamond catch all them fish?"

Diamond's grin was so wide Lou could almost count all his teeth. "Yes'm. Did Hell No—"

Louisa held up a finger and politely but firmly corrected, "Eugene."

Diamond looked down, collecting himself after this blunder. "Yes'm, sorry. Did Eugene tell you—"

"That you'd be bringing supper? Yes. And you'll be staying for it seeing you caught it. And get to know Lou and Oz here. Sure y'all be good friends."

"We've already met," Lou said stiffly.

Louisa looked between her and Diamond. "Well, that's

right good. Diamond and you close in years. And be good for Oz to have another boy round."

"He's got me," Lou said bluntly.

"Yes, he does," Louisa agreed. "Well, Diamond, you gonna stay for the meal?"

He considered the matter. "I ain't got me no more 'pointments today, so yep, I set myself down." Diamond glanced at Lou, and then he wiped at his dirty face and attempted to tug down one of a dozen cowlicks. Lou had turned away, however, completely unaware of his effort.

The table was set with Depression glass plates and cups, collected over the years by Louisa, she told them, from Crystal Winter oatmeal boxes. The dishes were green, pink, blue, amber, and rose. However pretty they might be, no one was really focusing on the dishes. Instead, tin fork and knife clashed as they all dug into the meal. When Louisa had said the meal prayer, Lou and Oz crossed themselves, while Diamond and Eugene looked on curiously but said nothing. Jeb lay in the corner, surprisingly patient with his portion. Eugene sat at one end of the table, methodically chewing his food. Oz absorbed his entire meal so fast Lou seriously considered checking to make sure his fork had not disappeared down his throat. Louisa dished Oz the last piece of lard-fried fish, the rest of the cooked vegetables, and another piece of cooked-in-grease cornbread, which, to Lou, tasted better than ice cream.

Louisa had not filled her plate.

"You didn't have any fish, Louisa," Oz said, as he stared guiltily at his second helping. "Aren't you hungry?"

"Meal by itself seeing a boy eating his way up to a growed man. Et while I cooked, honey. Always do."

Eugene glanced questioningly at Louisa when she said this and then went back to his meal.

Diamond's gaze kept sliding between Lou and Oz. He seemed eager to make friends again, yet seemed unsure how to accomplish it.

"Can you show me some of the places my dad would go around here?" Lou asked Louisa. "The things he liked to do? See, I'm a writer too."

"I know that," she said, and Lou gave her a surprised look. Louisa put her cup of water down and studied Lou's face. "Your daddy he like to tell 'bout the land. But afore he done that he done something real smart." She paused as Lou considered this.

"Like what?" the girl finally asked.

"He come to unnerstand the land."

"Understand . . . dirt?"

"It got lots of secrets, and not all good ones. Things up here hurt you bad if you ain't careful. Weather so fickle, like it break your heart 'bout the time it do your back. Land don't help none who don't never bother to learn it." On this she glanced at Eugene. "Lord knows Eugene could use help. This farm ain't going one minute more without his strong back."

Eugene swallowed a piece of fish and washed it down with a gulp of water he had poured directly into his glass from a bucket. As Lou watched him, Eugene's mouth trembled. She interpreted that as a big smile.

"Fact is," Louisa continued, "you and Oz coming here

:s a blessing. Some folk might say I helping you out, but that ain't the truth. You helping me a lot more'n I can you. For that I thank you."

"Sure," said Oz gallantly. "Glad to do it."

"You mentioned there were chores," Lou said.

Louisa looked over at Eugene. "Better to show, not tell. Come morning, I commence showing."

Diamond could contain himself no longer.

"Johnny Booker's pa said some fellers been looking round his place."

"What fellers?" asked Louisa sharply.

"Ain't know. But they's asking questions 'bout the coal mines."

"Get your ears on the ground, Diamond." Louisa looked at Lou and Oz. "And you too. God put us on this earth and he take us away when he good and ready. Meantime, family got to look out for each other."

Oz smiled and said he'd keep his ears so low to the ground, they'd be regularly filled with dirt. Everyone except Lou laughed at that. She simply stared at Louisa and said nothing.

The table was cleared, and while Louisa scraped dishes, Lou worked the sink hand pump hard, the way Louisa had shown her, to make only a very thin stream of water come out. No indoor plumbing, she had been told. Louisa had also explained to them the outhouse arrangement and shown them the small rolls of toilet paper stacked in the pantry. She had said a lantern would be needed after dark if the facilities were required, and she had shown Lou how to light one. There was also a chamberpot under each of their beds if the call of nature was of such urgency that they couldn't make it to the outhouse in time. However, Louisa informed them that the cleaning of the chamberpot was strictly the responsibility of the one using it. Lou wondered how timid Oz, a champion user of the bathroom in the middle of the night, would get along with this accommodation. She imagined she would be standing outside this outhouse many an evening while he did his business, and that was a weary thought.

Right after supper Oz and Diamond had gone outside with Jeb. Lou now watched as Eugene lifted the rifle off its rack above the fireplace. He loaded the gun and went outside.

Lou said to Louisa, "Where's he going with that gun?"

Louisa scrubbed plates vigorously with a hardened corncob. "See to the livestock. Now we done turned out the cows and hogs, Old Mo's coming round."

"Old Mo?"

"Mountain lion. Old Mo, he 'bout as old as me, but that durn cat still be a bother. Not to people. Lets the mare and the mules be too, 'specially the mules, Hit and Sam. Don't never cross no mule, Lou. They's the toughest things God ever made, and them durn critters keep grudges till kingdom come. Don't never forget one smack of the whip, or slip of a shoeing nail. Some folks say mules 'bout as smart as a man. Mebbe that why they get so mean." She smiled. "But Mo does go after the sheep, hogs, and cows. So we got to protect 'em. Eugene gonna fire the gun, scare Old Mo off."

"Diamond told me about Eugene's father leaving him."

Louisa glanced at her sternly. "A lie! Tom Randall were a good man."

"What happened to him then?" Lou prompted when it appeared Louisa was not inclined to go on.

Louisa finished with a plate first and set it down to dry. "Eugene's mother die young. Tom left the baby with his sister here and went on over to Bristol, Tennessee, for work. He a coal miner here, but lot of folks started coming round to do that too, and they always let the Negroes go first. He got kilt in an accident afore he could send for Eugene. When Eugene's aunt passed on, I took him in. The other's just lies by folks who have hate in their hearts."

"Does Eugene know?"

"Course he does! I told him when he were old enough."

"So why don't you tell people the truth?"

"People don't want'a listen, ain't no good what you try tell 'em." She shot Lou a glance. "Unnerstand me?"

Lou nodded, but in truth she wasn't convinced she did.

CHAPTER ELEVEN

WHEN LOU WENT OUTSIDE, SHE SAW DIAMOND and Oz over by the split-rail corral where the horse was grazing. When Diamond saw Lou, he pulled a sheet of paper and a tin of tobacco out of his pocket, rolled the smoke, licked it closed, struck a match against a rail, and lit up.

Oz and Lou both gaped, and she exclaimed, "You're too young to do that."

Diamond casually waved off her protest, a pleased smile on his face. "Aww, I all growed up. Man a man."

"But you're not much older than me, Diamond."

"Different up here, you see."

"Where do you and your family live?" asked Lou.

"On down the road a piece afore you get somewhere."

Diamond pulled a cover-less baseball from his pocket and tossed it. Jeb raced after the ball and brought it back.

"Man give me that ball 'cause I tell him his future."

"What was his future?" asked Lou.

"That he gonna give a feller named Diamond his old ball."

"It's getting late," Lou said. "Won't your parents be getting worried?"

Diamond stubbed out the homemade smoke on his overalls and stuck it behind his ear as he wound up to throw again. "Naw, like I say, all growed up. Ain't got to do nothing if'n don't want to."

Lou pointed to something dangling on Diamond's overalls. "What's that?"

Diamond looked down and grinned. "Left hind foot of a graveyard rabbit. Aside fur heart'a calf, luckiest thing they is. Shoot, don't they school you nuthin' in the city?"

"A graveyard rabbit?" Oz said.

"Yessir. Caught and kilt in graveyard in black of night." He slipped the foot off its string and gave it to Oz. "Here, son, I always get me 'nuther, anytime I want I can."

Oz held it reverently. "Gosh, thanks, Diamond."

Oz watched Jeb race after the ball. "Jeb sure is a good dog. Gets that ball every time."

When Jeb brought the ball and dropped it in front of Diamond, he picked it up and tossed it over to Oz. "Prob'ly ain't much room to throw nuthin' in the city, but give it a whirl, son."

Oz stared at the ball as though he'd never held one. Then he glanced at Lou.

"Go ahead, Oz. You can do it," she said.

Oz wound up and threw the ball, his arm snapping like a whip, and that ball sprang forth from his small hand like a freed bird, soaring higher and higher. Jeb raced after it, but the dog wasn't gaining any ground. An astonished Oz just stared at what he'd done. Lou did the same.

The cigarette fell off a startled Diamond's ear. "God
dog, where'd you learn to toss like that?"

Oz could only offer up the wonderful smile of a boy
who had just realized he might be athletically gifted. Then
he turned and raced after the ball. Lou and Diamond were
silent for a bit and then the ball came sailing back. In the
gathering darkness they couldn't even see Oz yet, but they
could hear him and Jeb coming, a total of six spirited
legs flying at them.

"So what do you do for excitement in this place,
Diamond?" asked Lou.

"Fishing mostly. Hey, you ever skinny-dip in a gravel
pit?"

"There are no gravel pits in New York City. Anything
else?"

"Well"—he paused dramatically—"course, there's the
haunted well."

"A haunted well?" exclaimed Oz, who had just run
up, Jeb at his heels.

"Where?" asked Lou.

"Come on now."

Captain Diamond and his company of infantry cleared
the tree line and plunged across an open field of tall grass
so fine and uniformly placed, it looked like combed hair.
The wind was chilly, but they were much too excited to
be bothered by that slight discomfort.

"Where is it?" asked Lou, running beside Diamond.

"Shhh! Getting close, so's we got to be real quiet. Spooks round."

They kept moving forward. Suddenly Diamond called out, "Hit the ground!"

They all dropped as though attached by taut rope.

Oz said in a trembling voice, "What is it, Diamond?"

Diamond hid a smile. "Thought mebbe I hear something, is all. Can't never be too careful round spooks." They all rose.

"What y'all doing here?"

The man had stepped from behind a stand of hickory trees, the shotgun in his right hand. Under the moonlight Lou could make out the glow of an evil pair of eyes staring dead at them. The three stood frozen as the fellow approached. Lou recognized him as the crazy man on the tractor recklessly flying down the mountain. He stopped in front of them and his mouth delivered a shot of chew spit near their feet.

"Got no bizness round here," the man said, as he lifted up the shotgun and rested the barrel on his left forearm such that the muzzle was pointed at them, his forefinger near the trigger.

Diamond stepped forward. "Ain't doing nuthin', George Davis, 'cept running round, and ain't no law agin that."

"You shet your mouth, Diamond Skinner, afore I put my fist to it." He peered over at quaking Oz, who drew back and clutched his sister's arm.

"You 'em chillin Louisa take in. Got the crippled ma. Ain'tcha?" He spit again.

Diamond said, "You ain't got no bizness with 'em, so leave 'em be."

Davis moved closer to Oz. "Mountain cat round, boy," he said, his voice low and taunting. And then he cried out, "You want it *git* you!" At the same time he said this, Davis feigned a lunge at Oz, who threw himself down and huddled in the high grass. Davis cackled wickedly at the terrified boy.

Lou stood between her brother and the man. "You stay away from us!"

"Gawd damn you, girl," Davis said. "Telling a man what to do?" He looked at Diamond. "You on my land, boy."

"T'ain't your land!" said Diamond, his hands making fists, his anxious gaze fixed on that shotgun. "Don't belong nobody."

"Calling me a liar?" snapped Davis, in a fearsome voice.

Then the scream came. It rose higher and higher until Lou figured the trees must surely topple from the force, or the rocks would work loose and slide down the mountain and maybe, with luck, crush their antagonist. Jeb came around growling, his hackles up. Davis stared off anxiously into the trees.

"You got you a gun," said Diamond, "then go git your old mountain cat. 'Cept mebbe you scared."

Davis's gaze burned into the boy, but then the scream came again, and hit them all just as hard, and Davis took off at a half-trot toward the trees.

"Come on now!" cried out Diamond, and they ran as fast as they could between trees and along more open fields. Owls hooted at them, and a bobwhite bobwhited at them. Things they couldn't see ran up and down tall oaks, or flitted in front of them, yet none of it came close to scaring them as much as they already had been by George Davis and his shotgun. Lou was a blur, faster even than Diamond. But when Oz tripped and fell, she rounded back and helped him.

They finally stopped and squatted in the high grass, breathing heavy and listening for a crazy man or a wildcat coming after them.

"Who is that awful man?" asked Lou.

Diamond checked behind him before answering. "George Davis. He got a farm next Miss Louisa's. He a hard man. A bad man! Dropped on his head when he were a baby, or mebbe mule kicked him, don't know which. He got a corn liquor still up here in one of the hollows, so's he don't like people coming round. I wish somebody just shoot him."

They soon reached another small clearing. Diamond held up his hand for them to stop and then proudly pointed up ahead, as though he had just discovered Noah's Ark on a simple mountaintop in Virginia.

"There she is."

The well was moss-crusted brick, crumbling in places, and yet undeniably spooky. The three glided up to it; Jeb guarded their rear flank while hunting small prey in the high grass.

They all peered over the edge of the well's opening. It was black, seemingly without bottom; they could have been staring at the other side of the world. All sorts of things could have been peering back.

"Why do you say it's haunted?" Oz asked breathlessly.

Diamond sprawled in the grass next to the well and they joined him.

" 'Bout a thousand million years ago," he began in a

thick and thrilling voice that made Oz's eyes widen, fast-blink, and water all at the same time, "they was a man and woman live up chere. Now, they was in love, ain't no denying that. And so's they wanted to get hitched o'-course. But they's family hated each other, wouldn't let 'em do it. No sir. So they come up with a plan to run off. Only somethin' went bad and the feller thought the woman had done got herself kilt. He was so broke up, he came to this here well and jumped in. It's way deep, shoot, you seed that. And he drowned hisself. Now the girl found out what was what, and she come and jumped in herself too. Never found 'em 'cause it was like they was plopped on the sun. Not a durn thing left."

Lou was completely unmoved by this sad tale. "That sounds a lot like Romeo and Juliet."

Diamond looked puzzled. "That kin of yours?"

"You're making this up," she said.

All around them sounds of peculiar quality started up, like millions of tiny voices all trying to jabber at once, as though ants had suddenly acquired larynxes.

"What's that?" Oz said, clinging to Lou.

"Don't be doubting my words, Lou," Diamond hissed, his face the color of cream. "You riling the spirits."

"Yeah, Lou," said Oz, who was looking everywhere for demons of hell coming for them. "Don't be riling the spirits."

The noises finally died down, and Diamond, regaining his confidence, stared triumphantly at Lou. "Shoot, any fool can see this well's magic. You see a house anywhere round? No, and I tell you why. This well growed up right out of the earth, that's why. And it ain't just a haunted well. It what you call a wishing well."

Oz said, "A wishing well? How?"

"Them two people lost each other, but they's still in love. Now, people die, but love don't never die. Made the well magic. Anybody done got a wish, they come here, wish for it, and it'll happen. Ever time. Rain or shine."

Oz clutched his arm. "Any wish? You're sure?"

"Yep. 'Cept they's one little catch."

Lou spoke up, "I thought so. What is it?"

" 'Cause them folks died to make this here a wishing well, anybody want a wish, they's got to give up somethin' too."

"Give up what?" This came from Oz, who was so excited the boy seemed to float above the supple grass like a tethered bubble.

Diamond lifted his arms to the dark sky. "Like just the most grandest, importantest thing they got in the whole dang world."

Lou was surprised he didn't take a bow. She knew what was coming now, as Oz tugged at her sleeve.

"Lou, maybe we can—"

"No!" she said sharply. "Oz, you have got to understand that dangling necklaces and wishing wells won't work. Nothing will."

"But, Lou."

The girl stood and pulled her brother's hand free. "Don't be stupid, Oz. You'll just end up crying your eyes out again."

Lou ran off. After a second's hesitation Oz followed her.

Diamond was left with the spoils of something, surely not victory, judging by his disappointed face. He looked around and whistled, and Jeb came running. "Let's get on home, Jeb," he said quietly.

The pair ran off in the opposite direction from Lou and Oz, as the mountains headed for sleep.

CHAPTER TWELVE

✿

THERE WAS NO TRACE OF OUTSIDE LIGHT AS YET, when Lou heard the creak of foot on stair. The door to her room opened and Lou sat up in bed. The glow of lantern light eased into the space, followed by Louisa, already fully dressed. With her flow of silver hair and the gentle illumination around her, the woman seemed a messenger from heaven to Lou's sleepy mind. The air in the room was chilly; Lou thought she could see her own breath.

"Thought I'd let you and Oz sleep in," Louisa said softly as she came and sat next to Lou.

Lou stifled a yawn and looked out the window at the blackness. "What time is it?"

"Nearly five."

"Five!" Lou dropped back against her pillow and pulled the covers over her head.

Louisa smiled. "Eugene's milking the cows. Be good you learn how."

"I can't do it later?" Lou asked from under the blanket.

"Cows don't care to wait round for us people," Louisa

said. "They moan till the bag's dry." She added, "Oz is already dressed."

Lou jolted upright. "Mom couldn't get him out of bed before eight, and even that was a fight."

"He's right now having a bowl of molasses over cornbread and fresh milk. Be good if you'd join us."

Lou threw off the covers and touched the cold floor, which sent a shiver directly to her brain. Now she was convinced she could see her breath. "Give me five minutes," she said bravely.

Louisa noted the girl's obvious physical distress. "Had us a frost last night," Louisa said. "Stays cold up here longer. Works into your bones like a little knife. Be warm afore long, and then when winter comes, we move you and Oz down to the front room, right by the fire. Fill it with coal, keep you warm all night. We'll make it right good for you here." She paused and looked around the room. "Can't give you what you had in the city, but we do our best." She rose and went to the door. "I put hot water in the washbowl earlier so's you can clean up."

"Louisa?"

She turned back, the arc of lantern light throwing and then magnifying her shadow against the wall. "Yes, honey?"

"This was my dad's room, wasn't it?"

Louisa looked around slowly before coming back to the girl, and the question. "From time he was four till he gone away. Ain't nobody use this room since."

Lou pointed to the covered walls. "Did my dad do that?"

Louisa nodded. "He'd walk ten miles to get ahold of a paper or a book. Read 'em all a dozen times and then stuck them newspapers up there and kept right on reading. Never saw a boy that curious in all my life." She looked at Lou. "Bet you just like him."

"I want to thank you for taking Oz and me in."

Louisa looked toward the door. "This place be good for your mother too. We all pitch in, she be fine."

Lou looked away, started to fumble with her nightdress. "I'll be down in a minute," she said abruptly.

Louisa accepted this change in the girl's manner without comment and softly closed the door behind her.

❧

Downstairs, Oz was just finishing the last of his breakfast when Lou appeared, dressed, as he was, in faded overalls, long john shirt, and lace-up boots Louisa had laid out for them. A lantern hanging on a wall hook, and the coal fire, gave the room its only light. Lou looked at the grandmother clock on the fireplace mantel, itself a six-by-six timber of planed oak. It was indeed a little past five. Who would have thought cows would be up so early? she thought.

"Hey, Lou," Oz said. "You've got to taste this milk. It's great."

Louisa looked at Lou and smiled. "Those clothes fit real good. Said a prayer they would. If'n the boots too big, we fill 'em with rags."

"They're fine," said Lou, though they were actually too small, pinching her feet some.

Louisa brought over a bucket and a glass. She put the glass on the table, draped a cloth over it, and poured the milk from the bucket into it, foam bubbling up on the cloth. "Want molasses on your cornbread?" she asked. "Real good that way. Line your belly."

"It's great," gushed Oz as he swallowed the last bite of his meal and washed it down with the rest of his milk.

Lou looked at her glass. "What's the cloth for?"

"Take things out the milk you don't need in you," answered Louisa.

"You mean the milk's not pasteurized?" Lou said this in such a distressed tone that Oz gaped at his empty glass, looking as though he might drop dead that very instant.

"What's pastures?" he asked anxiously. "Can it get me?"

"The milk's fine," Louisa said in a calm tone. "I've had it this way all my life. And your daddy too."

At her words, a relieved Oz sat back and commenced breathing again. Lou sniffed at her milk, tasted it gingerly a couple of times, and then took a longer swallow.

"I told you it was good," Oz said. "Putting it out to pasture probably makes it taste bad, I bet."

Lou said, "Pasteurization is named after Louis Pasteur, the scientist who discovered a process that kills bacteria and makes milk safe to drink."

"I'm sure he were a smart man," said Louisa, as she set down a bowl of cornbread and molasses in front of Lou. "But we boil the cloth in between, and we get by just fine." The way she said this made Lou not want to wrestle the issue anymore.

Lou took a forkful of the cornbread and molasses. Her eyes widened at the taste. "Where do you buy this?" she asked Louisa.

"Buy what?"

"This food. It's really good."

"Told you," said Oz again smugly.

Louisa said, "Don't buy it, honey. Make it."

"How do you do that?"

"Show, remember? A lot better'n telling. And best way of all is doing. Now, hurry up and you get yourself together with a cow by the name of Bran. Old Bran's got trouble you two can help Eugene fix."

With this enticement, Lou quickly finished her breakfast, and she and Oz hurried to the door.

"Wait, children," Louisa said. "Plates in the tub here, and you gonna need this." She picked up another lantern and lit it. The smell of working kerosene filled the room.

"This house really doesn't have electricity?" Lou asked.

"Know some folks down Tremont got the dang thing. It go off sometimes and they got no idea what to do with theirselves. Like they forgot how to light kerosene. Just give me a good lantern in hand and I be fine."

Oz and Lou carried their plates to the sink.

"After you done in the barn, I show you the springhouse. Where we get our water. Haul it up twice a day. Be one of your chores."

Lou looked confused. "But you have the pump."

"That just for dishes and such. Need water for lots of things. Animals, washing, tool grinder, bathing. Pump ain't got no pressure. Take you a day to fill up a good-sized lard bucket." She smiled. "Sometimes seems we spend most our breath hauling wood and water. First ten years'a my life, I thought my name was 'git.' "

They were about to go out the door again, Lou carrying the lantern, when she stopped. "Uh, which one's the cow barn?"

"How's 'bout I *show* you?"

The air was bone-hurting cold and Lou was grateful for the thick shirt, but still wedged her bare hands under her armpits. With Louisa and her lantern leading the way, they went past the chicken coop and corrals and over to the barn, a big A-frame building with a wide set of double doors. These doors stood open and a solitary light was on inside. From the barn Lou heard the snorts and calls of animals, the shuffling of restless hoofs on dirt, and from the coop came the flapping of skittish wings. The sky was curiously darker in some places than in others, and then Lou realized these ebony patches were the Appalachians.

She had never encountered night such as this. No streetlights, no lights from buildings, no cars, no illumination of any kind granted by battery or electricity. The only lights were the few stars overhead, the kerosene lamp Louisa was carrying, and the one Eugene presumably had on in the barn. The darkness didn't frighten Lou at all, though. In fact she felt oddly safe here as she followed the tall figure of her great-grandmother. Oz trailed close, and Lou could sense he was not nearly so comfortable right now. She well knew that, given time to think about it, her brother could imagine unspeakable terror in just about anything.

The barn smelled of stacked hay, wet earth, large animals and their warm manure. The floor was dirt covered with straw. On the walls hung bridles and harnesses, some cracked and worn out, others well oiled and supple. There were single- and doubletrees stacked on top of each other. A hayloft was reached by a wooden ladder with a broken second step. The loft took up most of the upper level and was filled with both loose and baled hay. There were center poles of poplar, which Lou assumed helped hold up the building. The barn had small wings built onto it on the sides and rear. Stalls and pens had been constructed there, and the mare, mules, hogs, and sheep loitered in their respective areas. Lou could see clouds of cold air erupting from warm animal nostrils.

In one stall, Eugene sat on a small three-legged stool that was barely visible under his bulk. Right next to him was a cow, white with black patches. Her tail twitched back and forth, her head dipping into the manger box.

Louisa left them there with Eugene and returned to the farmhouse. Oz crowded close to Lou as the cow in the next stall bumped into the partition and let out a moo. Eugene looked up at them.

"Old Bran got the milk fever," he said. "Got to hep Old Bran out." He pointed to a rusty tire pump in one corner of the stall. "Hand me that there pump, Miss Lou."

Lou gave it to him, and Eugene held the hose tightly against one of Bran's teats.

"Now g'on pump."

Oz pumped while Eugene went about holding the hose end against each of the four teats and rubbing the cow's udder, which was inflating like a ball.

"That a good girl, never held your milk afore. We take care of you," Eugene said soothingly to Bran. "Okay, that's right good," he said to Oz, who stopped pumping and stepped back, waiting. Eugene set the pump aside and motioned for Lou to take his place on the stool. He guided her hands to Bran's teats and showed her how to grip them properly and also how to rub them to get them supple to help the flow.

"We done pumped her up, now we got to get her dry. You pull hard, Miss Lou, Old Bran ain't caring none. Got to get her milk to run. That what be hurting her bad."

Lou pulled tentatively at first, and then started to hit her stride. Her hands worked efficiently, and they all heard the air escaping from the udder. It made small, warm clouds in the cold air.

Oz stepped forward. "Can I try?"

Lou got up and Eugene moved Oz in, set him up. Soon he was pulling as well as Lou, and finally drips of milk appeared at the ends of the teats.

"You doing good, Mr. Oz. You done pulled cow teat up there in the city?"

They all laughed over that one.

Three hours later, Lou and Oz were no longer laughing. They had milked the other two cows—one heavy with calf, Louisa told them—which had taken half an hour each; carried four large buckets of water into the house; and then lugged four more from the springhouse for the animals. That was followed by two loads of wood and three of coal to fill the house's wood and coal bins. Now they were slopping the hogs, and their chore list only seemed to be growing.

Oz struggled with his bucket and Eugene helped him get it over the top rail. Lou dumped hers and then stepped back.

"I can't believe we have to feed pigs," she said.

"They sure eat a lot," added Oz, as he watched the creatures attack what appeared to be liquid garbage.

"They're disgusting," said Lou, as she wiped her hands on her overalls.

"And they give us food when we need it."

They both turned and saw Louisa standing there, a full bucket of corn feed for the chickens in hand, her brow already damp with sweat, despite the coolness. Louisa picked up Lou's empty slop bucket and handed it to her. "Snow come there's no going down the mountain. Have to store up. And they're *hogs*, Lou, not pigs." Lou and Louisa held a silent stare-down for a half dozen heartbeats, until the sound of the car coming made them look toward the farmhouse.

It was an Oldsmobile roadster, packing all of forty-seven horsepower and a rumble seat. The car's black paint was chipped and rusted in numerous places, fenders dented, skinny tires near bald; and it had a convertible top that was open on this cold morning. It was a beautiful wreck of a thing.

The man stopped the car and got out. He was tall, with a lanky body that both foretold a certain fragility and also promised exceptional strength. When he took off his hat, his hair was revealed as dark and straight, cutting a fine outline around his head. A nicely shaped nose and jawline, pleasant light blue eyes, and a mouth that had an abundance of laugh lines shimmying around it gave him a face that would prompt a smile even on a trying day. He appeared closer to forty than thirty. His suit was a two-piece gray, with a black vest and a gentleman's watch the size of a silver dollar hanging from a heavy chain riding across the front of the vest. The pants were baggy at the knee, and the man's shoes had long since given back their shine for good. He started to walk toward them, stopped, went back to his car, and pulled out a fat and battered briefcase.

Absentminded, Lou thought to herself as she watched him closely. After meeting the likes of Hell No and Diamond, she wondered what odd moniker this stranger might have.

"Who's that?" Oz asked.

Louisa said in a loud voice, "Lou, Oz, this here's Cotton Longfellow, the finest lawyer round."

The man smiled and shook Louisa's hand. "Well, since I'm also one of the very few lawyers round here, that's a dubious distinction at best, Louisa."

His voice, a mixture of southern drawl and a New England rhythm, was unique to Lou. She could not place him to a particular area, and she was usually quite good at that. *Cotton Longfellow!* Lord, she had not been disappointed with the name.

Cotton put down his briefcase and shook their hands solemnly, though there was an easy twinkle in his eye as he did so. "Very honored to meet you both. I feel like I know you from all that Louisa has told me. I've always hoped to meet you one day. And I'm right sorry it has to be under these circumstances." He said the last with a gentleness that not even Lou could fault.

"Cotton and I got things to talk about. After you slop the hogs, you help Eugene turn the rest of the livestock out and drop hay. Then you can finish gathering the eggs."

As Cotton and Louisa walked off, Oz picked up his bucket and happily went for some more slop. But Lou stared after Cotton and Louisa, clearly not thinking of hogs. She was wondering about a man with the strange name of Cotton Longfellow, who spoke sort of oddly and seemed to know so much about them. Finally, she eyed a four-hundred-pound hog that would somehow keep them from all starving come winter, and trudged after her brother. The walls of mountains seemed to close around the girl.

CHAPTER THIRTEEN

COTTON AND LOUISA ENTERED THE HOUSE THROUGH the back door. As they headed down the hallway to the front room, Cotton stopped, his gaze holding through the partially opened door and into the room where Amanda lay in bed.

Cotton said, "What do the doctors say?"

"Men . . . tal trau . . . ma." Louisa formed the strange words slowly. "That what the nurse call it."

They went to the kitchen and sat down in stump-legged chairs of hand-planed oak worn so smooth the wood felt like glass. Cotton pulled some papers from his briefcase and slid a pair of wire-rimmed spectacles from his pocket. He slipped them on and studied the papers for a moment, and then settled back, prepared to discuss them. Louisa poured out a cup of chicory coffee for him. He took a swallow and smiled. "If this don't get you going, then you must be dead."

Louisa poured herself a cup and said, "So what'd you find out from them fellers?"

"Your grandson didn't have a will, Louisa. Not that it mattered much, because he also didn't have any money."

Louisa looked bewildered. "With all his fine writing?"

Cotton nodded. "As wonderful as they were, the books didn't sell all that well. He had to take on other writing assignments to make ends meet. Also, Oz had some health problems when he was born. Lot of expenses. And New York City is not exactly cheap."

Louisa looked down. "And that ain't all," she said. He looked at her curiously. "Jack sent me money all these years, he did. I wrote him back once, told him it weren't right for him to be doing it. Got his own family and all. But he say he were a rich man. He told me that! Wanted me to have it, he say, after all I done for him. But I ain't really done nothing."

"Well, it seems Jack was planning to go write for a movie studio in California when the accident happened."

"California?" Louisa said the word like it was a malignancy, and then sat back and sighed. "That little boy always run circles round me. But giving me money when he ain't got it. And curse me for taking it." She stared off for a bit before speaking again. "I got me a problem, Cotton. Last three years of drought and ain't no crops come in. Down to five hogs and gotta butcher me one purty soon. Got me three sows and one boar left over. Last litter more runts than anythin'. Three passable milking cows. Had one studded out, but she ain't dropped her calf yet and I getting right worried. And Bran got the fever. Sheep getting to be more bother than anything. And that old nag ain't do a lick of work no more, and eats me out of house and home. And yet that old girl done worked herself to death all these years for me." She paused and drew a breath. "And McKenzie on down at the store, he ain't giving no more credit to us folk up here."

"Hard times, Louisa, no denying that."

"I know I can't complain none, this old mountain give me all it can over the years."

Cotton hunched forward. "Well, the one thing you do have, Louisa, is land. Now, there's an asset."

"Can't sell it, Cotton. When time comes, it'll go to Lou and Oz. Their daddy loved this place as much as me. And Eugene too. He my family. He work hard. He getting some of this land so's he can have his own place, raise his own family. Only fair."

Cotton said, "I think so too."

"When them folks wrote to see if'n I'd take the children, how could I not? Amanda's people all gone, I'm all they got left. And a sorry savior I am, long past being worth a spit for farming." Her fingers clustered nervously together, and she stared anxiously out the window. "I been thinking 'bout them all these years, wondering what they was like. Reading Amanda's letters, seeing them pictures she sent. Just busting with pride over what Jack done. And them beautiful children." She let out a troubled sigh, the deeply cut wrinkles on her long forehead like tiny furrows in a field.

Cotton said, "You'll get by, Louisa. You need me for anything, come up and help with the planting, the children, you just let me know. I'd be beyond proud to help you."

"G'on now, Cotton, you a busy lawyer."

"Folks up here don't have much need for the likes of me. And maybe that's not such a bad thing. Got a problem, go down to Judge Atkins over the courthouse and just talk it out. Lawyers just make things complicated." He smiled and patted her hand. "It'll be okay, Louisa.

Those children being here with you is the right thing. For everybody."

Louisa smiled, and then her expression slowly changed to a frown. "Cotton, Diamond said some men coming round folks' coal mines. Don't like that."

"Surveyors, mineral experts, so I've heard."

"Ain't they cutting the mountains up fast enough? Make me sick ever' time I see another hole. I never sell out to the coal folk. Rip all that's beautiful out."

"I've heard these folks are looking for oil, not coal."

"Oil!" she said in disbelief. "This ain't Texas."

"Just what I've heard."

"Can't worry about that nonsense." She stood. "You right, Cotton, it'll be just fine. Lord'll give us rain this year. If not, well, I figger something out."

As Cotton rose to leave, he looked back down the hallway. "Louisa, do you mind if I stop in and pay my respects to Miss Amanda?"

Louisa thought about this. "Another voice might do her good. And you got a nice way about you, Cotton. How come you ain't never married?"

"I've yet to find the good woman who could put up with the sorry likes of me."

In Amanda's room, Cotton put down his briefcase and hat and quietly approached the bed. "Miss Cardinal, I'm Cotton Longfellow. It's a real pleasure to meet you. I feel like I know you already, for Louisa has read me some of the letters you sent." Amanda of course moved not one muscle, and Cotton looked over at Louisa.

"I been talking to her. Oz too. But she ain't never say nothing back. Don't never even wiggle a finger."

"And Lou?" asked Cotton.

Louisa shook her head. "That child's gonna bust one day, all she keep inside."

"Louisa, it might be a good idea to have Travis Barnes from Dickens come up and look at Amanda."

"Doctors cost money, Cotton."

"Travis owes me a favor. He'll come."

Louisa said quietly, "I thank you."

He looked around the room and noted a Bible on the dresser. "Can I come back?" he asked. Louisa looked at him curiously. "I thought I might, well, that I might read to her. Mental stimulation. I've heard of such. There are no guarantees. But if I can do nothing else well, I can read."

Before Louisa could answer, Cotton looked at Amanda. "It'll be my real privilege to read to you."

CHAPTER FOURTEEN

A S DAWN BROKE, LOUISA, EUGENE, LOU, AND OZ
stood in one of the fields. Hit, the mule, was har-
nessed on a singletree to a plow with a turnover
blade.

Lou and Oz had already had their milk and cornbread
in gravy for breakfast. The food was good, and filling,
but eating by lantern light had already grown old. Oz had
gathered chicken eggs while Lou had milked the two
healthy cows under Louisa's watchful eye. Eugene had
split wood, and Lou and Oz had hauled it in for the cookstove and then carried buckets of water for the animals.
Livestock had been turned out and hay dropped for them.
And now, apparently, the real work was about to begin.

"Got to plow unner this whole field," said Louisa.

Lou sniffed the air. "What's that awful smell?"

Louisa bent down, picked up some earth, and crum-
bled it between her fingers. "Manure. Muck the stalls ever
fall, drop it here. Makes rich soil even better."

"It stinks," said Lou.

Louisa let the bits of dirt in her hand swirl away in

the morning breeze as she stared pointedly at the girl. "You'll come to love that smell."

Eugene handled the plow while Louisa and the children walked beside him.

"This here's a turnover blade," Louisa said, pointing to the oddly shaped disc of metal. "You run it down one row, turn mule and plow round, kick the blade over, go down the row again. Throws up same furrows of dirt on both sides. It kicks up big clods of earth too. So's after we plow, we drag the field to break up the clods. Then we harrow, makes the dirt real smooth. Then we use what's called a laid-off plow. Gives you fine rows. Then we plant."

She had Eugene plow one row to show them how, and then Louisa kicked at the plow. "You look purty strong, Lou. You want'a give it a go?"

"Sure," she said. "It'll be easy."

Eugene set her up properly, put the guide straps around her waist, handed her the whip, and then stepped back. Hit apparently summed her up as an easy mark, because he took off unexpectedly fast. Strong Lou very quickly got a taste of the rich earth.

As Louisa pulled her up and wiped her face, she said, "That old mule had the best of you this time. Bet it won't next go round."

"I don't want to do this anymore," Lou said, hiding her face with her sleeve, spitting up chunks of things she didn't want to think about. Her cheeks were red, and tears edged from under her eyelids.

Louisa knelt in front of her. "First time your daddy tried to plow, he your age. Mule took him on a ride ended in the crick. Took me the better part of a day to get him and that durn animal out. Your daddy said the same thing you did. And I decided to let him be about it."

Lou stopped brushing at her face, her eyes drying up. "And what happened?"

"For two days he wouldn't go near the fields. Or that mule. And then I come out here to work one morning and there he was."

"And he plowed the whole field?" Oz guessed.

Louisa shook her head. "Mule and your daddy ended up in the hog pen with enough slop on both choke a bear." Oz and Lou laughed, and then Louisa continued, "Next time, boy and mule reached an unnerstanding. Boy had paid his dues, and mule had had his fun, and them two made the best plow team I ever saw."

From across the valley there came the sound of a siren. It was so loud that Lou and Oz had to cover their ears. The mule snorted and jerked against its harness. Louisa frowned.

"What is that?" Lou shouted.

"Coal mine horn," said Louisa.

"Was there a cave-in?"

"No, hush now," Louisa said, her eyes scanning the slopes. Five anxious minutes passed by and the siren finally stopped. And then from all sides they heard the low rumbling sound. It rose around them like an avalanche coming. Lou thought she could see the trees, even the mountain, shaking. She gripped Oz's hand and was thinking of fleeing, but she didn't because Louisa hadn't budged. And then the quiet returned.

Louisa turned back to them. "Coal folks sound the horn afore they blast. They use dynamite. Sometimes too much and they's hill slides. And people get hurt. Not miners.

Farmers working the land." Louisa scowled once more in
the direction where the blast seemed to have come from,
and then they went back to farming.

At supper, they had steaming plates of pinto beans
mixed with cornbread, grease, and milk, and washed down
with springwater so cold it hurt. The night was chilly, the
wind howling fiercely as it attacked the structure, but the
walls and roof withstood this charge. The coal fire was
warm, and the lantern light gentle on the eye. Oz was so
tired he almost fell asleep in his Crystal Winters Oatmeal
plate the color of the sky.

After supper Eugene went out to the barn, while Oz
lay in front of the fire, his little body so obviously sore
and spent. Louisa watched as Lou went over to him, put
his head in her lap, and stroked his hair. Louisa slid a
pair of wire-rimmed spectacles over her eyes and worked
on mending a shirt by the firelight. After a while, she
stopped and sat down beside the children.

"He's just tired," Lou said. "He's not used to this."

"Can't say a body ever gets used to hard work." Louisa
rubbed at Oz's hair too. It seemed the little boy just had
a head people liked to touch. Maybe for luck.

"You doing a good job. Real good. Better'n me when
I your age. And I ain't come from no big city. Make it
harder, don't it?"

The door opened and the wind rushed in. Eugene
looked worried. "Calf coming."

In the barn the cow called Purty lay on her side in a

wide birthing stall, pitching and rolling in agony. Eugene
knelt and held her down, while Louisa got in behind her
and pried with her fingers, looking for the slicked pack-
age of a fresh calf emerging. It was a hard-fought battle,
the calf seeming not to want to enter the world just yet.
But Eugene and Louisa coaxed it out, a slippery mass of
limbs, eyes scrunched tight. The event was bloody, and
Lou's and Oz's stomach took another jolt when Purty ate
the afterbirth, but Louisa told them that was natural. Purty
started licking her baby and didn't stop until its hair was
sticking out all over. With Eugene's help, the calf rose on
tottering stick legs, while Louisa got Purty ready for the
next step, which the calf took to as the most natural en-
deavor of all: suckling. Eugene stayed with the mother
and her calf while Louisa and the children went back inside.

Lou and Oz were both excited and exhausted, the
grandmother clock showing it was nearing midnight.

"I've never seen a cow born before," said Oz.

"You've never seen anything born before," said his sister.

Oz thought about this. "Yes, I did. I was there when
I was born."

"That doesn't count," Lou shot back.

"Well, it should," countered Oz. "It was a lot of work.
Mom told me so."

Louisa put another rock of coal on the fire, drove it
into the flames with an iron poker, and then sat back
down with her mending. The woman's dark-veined and
knotted hands moved slowly yet with precision.

"You get on to bed, both of you," she said.

Oz said, "I'm going to see Mom first. Tell her about

the cow." He looked at Lou. "My *second* time." He walked off.

His sister made no move to leave the fire's warmth.

"Lou, g'on see your mother too," said Louisa.

Lou stared into the depths of the coal fire. "Oz is too young to understand, but I do."

Louisa put down her mending. "Unnerstand what?"

"The doctors in New York said that each day there was less chance Mom would come back. It's been too long now."

"But you can't give up hope, honey."

Lou turned to look at her. "You don't understand either, Louisa. Our dad's gone. I saw him die. Maybe"— Lou swallowed with difficulty—"maybe I was partly the reason he did die." She rubbed at her eyes and then Lou's hands curled to fists. "And it's not like she's laying in there healing. I listened to the doctors. I heard everything all the grown-ups said about her, even though they tried to hide it from me. Like it wasn't my business! They let us take her home, because there was nothing more they could do for her." She paused, took a long breath, and slowly grew calm. "And you just don't know Oz. He gets his hopes up so high, starts doing crazy things. And then . . ." Lou's voice trailed off, and she looked down. "I'll see you in the morning."

In the fade of lantern light and the flickering coal fire, Louisa could only stare after the young girl as she trudged off. When her footsteps faded away, Louisa once more picked up her sewing, but the needle did not move. When Eugene came in and went to bed, she was still there, the fire having died down low, as thoughts as humbling as the mountains outside consumed her.

After a bit, though, Louisa rose and went into her bedroom, where she pulled out a short stack of letters from her dresser. She went up the stairs to Lou's room and found the girl wide awake, staring out the window.

Lou turned and saw the letters.

"What are those?"

"Letters your mother wrote to me. I want you to read 'em."

"What for?"

" 'Cause words say a lot about a person."

"Words won't change anything. Oz can believe if he wants to. But he doesn't know any better."

Louisa placed the letters on the bed. "Sometime older folks do right good to follow the young'uns. Might learn 'em something."

After Louisa left, Lou put the letters in her father's old desk and very firmly shut the drawer.

CHAPTER FIFTEEN

LOU GOT UP ESPECIALLY EARLY AND WENT INTO HER mother's room, where she watched for a bit the even rise and fall of the woman's chest. Perched on the bed, Lou pulled back the covers and massaged and moved her mother's arms. Then she spent considerable time exercising her mother's legs the way the doctors back in New York City had shown her. Lou was just about finished when she caught Louisa watching her from the doorway.

"We have to make her comfortable," explained Lou. She covered her mother and went into the kitchen. Louisa trailed her.

When Lou put on a kettle to boil, Louisa said, "I can do that, honey."

"I've got it." Lou mixed some oat flakes in the hot water and added butter taken from a lard bucket. She took the bowl back into her mother's room and carefully spooned the food into her mother's mouth. Amanda ate and drank readily enough, with just a tap of spoon or cup against her lips, though she could only manage soft food. Yet that was all she could do. Louisa sat with them, and Lou pointed to the ferrotypes on the wall. "Who are those people?"

"My daddy and momma. That me with 'em when I just a spit. Some of my momma's folks too. First time I ever had my pitcher took. I liked it. But Momma scared." She pointed to another ferrotype. "That pitcher there my brother Robert. He dead now. They all dead now."

"Your parents and brother were tall."

"Run in the line. Funny how that get passed down. Your daddy, he were already six feet when he weren't more'n fourteen. I still tall, but I growed down some from what I was. You gonna be big too."

Lou cleaned the bowl and spoon and afterward helped Louisa make breakfast for everyone else. Eugene was in the barn now, and they both heard Oz stirring in his room.

Lou said, "I need to show Oz how to move Mom's arms and legs. And he can help feed her too."

"That right fine." She laid a hand on Lou's shoulder. "Now, did you read any of them letters?"

Lou looked at her. "I didn't want to lose my mother and father. But I have. Now I've got to look after Oz. And I have to look ahead, not back." She added with firmness, "You may not understand that, but it's what I have to do."

After morning chores, Eugene took Lou and Oz by mule and wagon to the school and then left to continue his work. In old burlap seed bags, Lou and Oz carried their worn books, a few sheets of precious paper tucked inside the pages. They each had one fat lead pencil, with dire orders from Louisa to trim it down only when absolutely necessary, and to use a sharp knife when doing so. The books were the same ones their father had learned with, and Lou hugged hers to her chest like it was a present direct from Jesus. They also carried a dented lard bucket with some cornbread chunks, a small jar of apple butter jelly, and a jug of milk for their lunch.

The Big Spruce schoolhouse was only a few years old. It had been built with New Deal dollars to replace the log building that had stood on the same spot for almost eighty years. The structure was white clapboard with windows down one side, and was set on cinder blocks. Like Louisa's farmhouse, the roof had no shingles, just a "roll of roofing" that came in long sheets and was tacked down in overlapping sections like shingles. The school had one door, with a short overhang. A brick chimney rose through the A-frame roof.

On any given day school attendance was roughly half of the number of students who should have been there, and that was actually a high number compared to the attendance figures in the past. On the mountain, farming always trumped book learning.

The schoolyard was dirt, a split-trunk walnut tree in the center of it. There were about fifty children milling about outside, ranging in age from Oz's to Lou's. Most were dressed in overalls, though a few girls wore floral dresses made from Chop bags, which were hundred-pound sacks of feed for animals. The bags were beautiful and of sturdy material, and a girl always felt extra special having a Chop bag outfit. Some children were in bare feet, others in what used to be shoes but were now sandals of sorts. Some wore straw hats, others were bare-headed; a few of the older boys had already upgraded to dirty felt, no doubt hand-me-downs from their daddies. Some girls favored pigtails, others wore their hair straight, and still others had the sausage curl at the end.

The children all stared at the newcomers with what Lou perceived as unfriendly eyes.

One boy stepped forward. Lou recognized him as the one who had dangled on the tractor over the side of the mountain their first day here. Probably the son of George Davis, the crazy man who had threatened them with the shotgun in the woods. Lou wondered if the fellow's off-spring also suffered from insanity.

"What's the matter, y'all can't walk by yourselves? Hell No got to bring you?" the boy said.

"His name is Eugene," said Lou right to the boy's face. Then she asked, "Can anybody tell me where the second- and sixth-grade classes are?"

"Why sure," the same boy said, pointing. "They's both right over there."

Lou and Oz turned and saw the listing wooden outhouse behind the school building.

"Course," the boy added with a sly grin, "that's just for you Yankees."

This set all the mountain children to whooping and laughing, and Oz nervously took a step closer to Lou.

Lou studied the outhouse for a moment and then looked back at the boy.

"What's your name?" she asked.

"Billy Davis," he said proudly.

"Are you always that scintillating, Billy Davis?"

Billy frowned. "What's that mean? You call me a name, girl?"

"Didn't you just call us one?"

"Ain't said nuthin' 'cept the truth. Yankee once is a Yankee for life. Coming here ain't changing that."

The crowd of rebels voiced their complete agreement with this point of view, and Lou and Oz found themselves encircled by the enemy. They were saved only by the ringing of the school bell, which sent the children dashing for the door. Lou and Oz looked at each other and then trudged after this mob.

"I don't think they like us much, Lou," Oz said.

"I don't think I much care," his sister said back.

The number of classrooms was one, they immediately discovered, which served all grades from first to seventh, the students separated in discrete clusters by age. The number of teachers matched the number of classrooms. Her name was Estelle McCoy, and she was paid eight hundred dollars a school year. This was the only job she had ever had, going on thirty-nine years now, which explained why her hair was far more white than mousey brown.

Wide blackboards covered three walls. A potbellied stove sat in one corner, a long pipe from it running to the ceiling. And, seeming very much out of place in the simple confines, a beautifully crafted maple bookcase with an arched top took up another corner of the room. It had glass-paned doors, and inside Lou could see a number of books. A handwritten sign on the wall next to the cabinet read: "Library."

Estelle McCoy stood in front of them all with her

apple cheeks, canyon smile, and chubby figure draped in a bright floral dress.

"I have a real treat for y'all, today. I'd like to introduce two new students: Louisa Mae Cardinal and her brother, Oscar. Louisa Mae and Oscar, will you stand up please?"

As someone who routinely bowed to the slightest exercise of authority, Oz immediately leapt to his feet. However, he stared down at the floor, one foot shifting over the other, as though he had to pee really badly.

Lou, however, remained sitting.

"Louisa Mae," Estelle McCoy said again, "stand up and let them see you, honey."

"My name is Lou."

Estelle McCoy's smile went down a bit in wattage. "Yes, um, their father was a very famous writer named Jack Cardinal."

Here, Billy Davis piped in loudly, "Didn't he die? Somebody say that man's dead."

Lou glared at Billy, who made a face right back at her.

Their teacher now looked completely flustered. "Billy, please. Uh, as I was saying, he was famous, and I helped teach him. And in my own humble way, I hope that I had some influence over his development as a writer. And they do say the early years are the most important. Anyway, did you know that Mr. Jack Cardinal even signed one of his books in Washington, for the president of these United States?"

As Lou looked around the room, she could tell this meant absolutely nothing to the children of the mountain. In fact, mentioning the capital of the Yankee nation was probably not a smart thing to do. It didn't make her angry that they were not properly in awe of her father's accomplishments; instead it made Lou pity their ignorance.

Estelle McCoy was ill-prepared for the prolonged silence. "Uh, well, we welcome you, Louisa Mae, and you too, Oscar. I'm sure you'll do your father proud here, at his . . . alma mater."

Now Lou stood, even as Oz hastily dropped back into his seat, his face down, his eyes scrunched closed. One could tell he was afraid of whatever it was his sister was about to do. Lou never did anything in a small way, Oz well knew. It was either both barrels of the shotgun in your face, or you got to live another day. There was rarely any middle ground with the girl.

And yet all she said was "My name is Lou." And then she took her seat.

Billy leaned over and said, "Welcome to the mountain, Miss Louisa Mae."

※

The school day ended at three, and the children didn't rush to go home, since it was certain only more chores awaited them there. Instead, they milled about in small packs in the schoolyard, the boys swapping pocket knives, hand-whittled yo-yos, and homemade burley chew. The girls exchanged local gossip and cooking and sewing secrets, and talked about boys. Billy Davis did pull-ups on a sapling that had been laid across the low branches of the walnut tree, to the admiring look of one wide-hipped girl with crooked teeth, but also rosy cheeks and pretty blue eyes.

As Lou and Oz came outside, Billy stopped his workout and strolled over to them.

"Why, it's Miss Louisa Mae. You been up see the president, Miss Louisa Mae?" he said in a loud, mocking voice.

"Keep walking, Lou, please," said Oz.

Billy spoke even louder. "Did he get you to sign one of your daddy's books, him being dead and all?"

Lou stopped. Oz, sensing that further pleading was futile, stepped back. Lou turned to look at her tormentor.

"What's the matter, you still sore because us Yankees kicked your tail, you dumb hillbilly?"

The other children, sensing blood, quietly formed a circle to shield from the eyes of Mrs. McCoy a potentially good fight.

Billy scowled. "You best take that back."

Lou dropped her bag. "You best make me, if you think you can."

"Shoot, I ain't hitting no girl."

This made Lou angrier than ever a thrown fist could have. She grabbed Billy by his overall straps and threw him to the dirt, where he lay stunned, probably both at her strength and at her audacity. The crowd moved closer.

"I'll kick your tail if you don't take *that* back," Lou said, and she leaned down and dug a finger in his chest.

Oz pulled at her as the crowd closed even tighter, as though a hand becoming a fist. "Come on, Lou, please don't fight. Please."

Billy jumped up and proceeded to commit a major offense. Instead of swinging at Lou, he grabbed Oz and threw him down hard.

"No-good stinking northerner."

His look of triumph was short-lived because it ran smack into Lou's bony right fist. Billy joined Oz on the ground, blood spurting from his nose. Lou was straddling Billy before the boy could take a breath, both her fists pounding away. Billy, howling like a whipped dog, swung his arms wildly back. One blow caught Lou on the lip, but she kept slugging until Billy finally stopped swinging and just covered his face.

Then the seas parted, and Mrs. McCoy poured through this gap. She managed to pull Lou off Billy, but not without an effort that left her breathing hard.

"Louisa Mae! What would your daddy think?" she said.

Lou's chest rose and fell hard, her hands still balled into mighty, boy-bashing instruments.

Estelle McCoy helped Billy up. The boy covered his face with his sleeve, quietly sobbing into his armpit. "Now, you tell Billy you're sorry," she said.

Lou's response was to lunge and take another furious swing at him. Billy jumped back like a rabbit cornered by a snake intent on eating it.

Mrs. McCoy pulled hard on Lou's arm. "Louisa Mae, you stop that right now and tell him you're sorry."

"He can go straight on to hell."

Estelle McCoy looked ready to keel over in the face of such language from the daughter of a famous man.

"Louisa Mae! Your mouth!"

Lou jerked free and ran like the wind down the road.

Billy fled in the other direction. And Estelle McCoy stood there empty-handed on the field of battle.

Oz, forgotten in all this, quietly got off the ground, picked up his sister's burlap bag, brushed it off, and went and tugged on his teacher's dress. She looked down at him.

"Excuse me, ma'am," Oz said. "But her name is Lou."

CHAPTER SIXTEEN

LOUISA CLEANED THE CUT ON LOU'S FACE WITH WATER and lye soap, and applied some homemade tincture that stung like fire, but Lou made herself not even flinch.

"Glad you got yourself off to such a good start, Lou."

"They called us Yankees!"

"Well, good Lord," Louisa said with mock indignity. "Ain't that evil!"

"And he hurt Oz."

Louisa's expression softened. "You got to go to school, honey. You got to learn to get along."

Lou scowled. "Why can't they get along with us?"

" 'Cause this their home. They act like that 'cause you're not like nobody they ever seen."

Lou stood. "You don't know what it's like to be an outsider." She ran out the door, while Louisa looked after her, shaking her head.

Oz was waiting for his sister on the front porch.

"I put your bag in your room," he told her.

Lou sat on the steps and rested her chin on her knees.

"I'm okay, Lou." Oz stood and spun in a circle to show

her and almost fell off the porch. "See, he didn't hurt me any."

"Good thing, or I really would've pounded him."

Oz closely studied her cut lip. "Does it hurt much?"

"Don't feel a thing. Shoot, they might be able to milk cows and plow fields, but mountain boys sure can't hit worth anything."

They looked up as Cotton's Oldsmobile pulled into the front yard. He got out, a book cradled under one arm.

"I heard about your little adventure over at the school today," he said, walking up.

Lou looked surprised. "That was fast."

Cotton sat next to them on the steps. "Up here when a good fight breaks out people will move heaven and earth to get the word around."

"Wasn't much of a fight," said Lou proudly. "Billy Davis just curled up and squawked like a baby."

Oz added, "He cut Lou's lip, but it doesn't hurt any."

She said, "They called us Yankees, like it was some kind of disease."

"Well, if it makes you feel any better, I'm a Yankee too. From Boston. And they've accepted me here. Well, at least most of them have."

Lou's eyes widened as she made the connection and wondered why she hadn't before. "Boston? Longfellow. Are you—"

"Henry Wadsworth Longfellow was my grandfather's great-grandfather. I guess that's the easiest way to put it."

"Henry Wadsworth Longfellow. Gosh!"

"Yeah, gosh!" Oz said, though in fact he had no idea who they were talking about.

"Yes, gosh indeed. I wanted to be a writer since I was a child."

"Well, why aren't you?" asked Lou.

Cotton smiled. "While I can appreciate inspired, well-crafted writing better than most, I'm absolutely confounded when attempting to do it myself. Maybe that's why I came here after I got my law degree. As far from Longfellow's Boston as one can be. I'm not a particularly good lawyer, but I get by. And it gives me time to read those who can write well." He cleared his throat and recited in a pleasant voice: "Often I think of the beautiful town, that is seated by the sea; Often in thought go up and down—"

Lou took up the verse: "The pleasant streets of that dear old town. And my youth comes back to me."

Cotton looked impressed. "You can quote Longfellow?"

"He was one of my dad's favorites."

He held up the book he was carrying. "And this is one of *my* favorite writers."

Lou glanced at the book. "That's the first novel my dad ever wrote."

"Have you read it?"

"My dad read part of it to me. A mother loses her only son, thinks she's all alone. It's very sad."

"But it's also a story of healing, Lou. Of one helping another." He paused. "I'm going to read it to your mother."

"Dad already read all his books to her," she said coldly.

Cotton realized what he had just done. "Lou, I'm not trying to replace your father."

She stood. "He was a real writer. He didn't have to go around quoting other people."

Cotton stood too. "I am sure if your father were here he would tell you that there is no shame in repeating the words of others. That it's a show of respect, in fact. And I have the greatest respect for your father's talents."

"You think it might help? Reading to her," said Oz.

"Waste your time if you want." Lou walked off.

"It's okay with me if you read to her," said Oz.

Cotton shook the boy's hand. "Thank you much for your permission, Oz. I'll do my best."

"Come on, Oz, there's chores to do," called Lou.

As Oz ran off, Cotton glanced down at the book and then went inside. Louisa was in the kitchen.

"You here to do your reading?" she asked.

"Well, that was my thinking, but Lou made it very clear she doesn't want me to read from her father's books. And maybe she's right."

Louisa looked out the window and saw Lou and Oz disappear into the barn. "Well, I tell you what, I got lots of letters Jack wrote to me over the years. They's some he sent me from college that I always liked. He use some big words then I ain't know what they mean, but the letters' still nice. Why don't you read those to her? See, Cotton, my thinking is it ain't *what* folks read to her that's important. I think the best thing is for us to spend time with her, to let Amanda know we ain't give up hope."

Cotton smiled. "You are a wise woman, Louisa. I think that's a fine idea."

Lou carried the coal bucket in and filled the bin next to the fireplace. Then she crept to the hallway and listened. Murmurs of a single voice drifted down the hall. She scooted back outside and stared at Cotton's car, the curiosity bug finally getting the better of her. She ran around the side of the house and came up under her mother's bedroom window. The window was open, but it was too high for her to look in. She stood on tiptoe, but that didn't work either.

"Hey there."

She whirled around and saw Diamond. She grabbed his arm and pulled him away from the window. "You shouldn't sneak up on people like that," she said.

"Sorry," he said, smiling.

She noticed he had something behind his back. "What do you have there?"

"Where?"

"Right there behind your back, Diamond."

"Oh, that. Well, you see I was just walking down by the meadow, and, well, they was just sitting there all purty like. And swear to Jesus they was saying your name."

"What was?"

Diamond pulled out a bunch of yellow crocuses and handed them to her.

Lou was touched, but of course she didn't want to show it. She said thank you to Diamond and gave him a hard smack on the back that made him cough.

"I didn't see you at school today, Diamond."

"Oh, well." He pawed the ground with one bare foot, gripped his overalls, and looked everywhere except at Lou. "Hey, what you be doing at that window when I come up?" he finally said.

Lou forgot about school for now. She had an idea, and like Diamond, she wished to defer the explanation behind her actions. "You want to help me with something?"

A few moments later, Diamond fidgeted some, and Lou smacked him on the head to make him be still. This was easy for her to do since she was sitting on his shoulders while peering into her mother's room. Amanda was propped in the bed. Cotton was in the rocking chair next to her, reading. Lou noted with surprise that he was not reading from the novel he had brought, but rather from a letter he was holding. And Lou had to admit, the man had a pleasant voice.

Cotton had selected the letter he was reading from a number Louisa had given him. This letter, he had thought, was particularly appropriate.

"Well, Louisa, you'll be pleased to know the memories of the mountain are as strong right now as the day I left three years ago. In fact, it is rather easy for me to transport myself back to the high rock in Virginia. I simply close my eyes, and I immediately see many examples of reliable friends parceled here and there, like favorite books kept in special places. You know the stand of river birch down by the creek. Well, when their branches pressed together, I always imagined they were imparting secrets to each other. Then right in front of me a wisp of does and fawns creep along the fringe where your plowed fields snuggle up against the hardwood. Then I look to the sky and follow the jagged flight of irascible black crows, and then settle upon a solitary hawk tacked against a sky of cobalt blue.

"*That sky. Oh, that sky. You told me so many times that up on the mountain it seems you can just reach up and take it, hold it in your hand, stroke it like a dozing cat, admire its abundant grace. I always found it to be a generous blanket I just wanted to wrap myself in, Louisa, take a long nap on the porch with as I settled under its cool warmth. And when night came, I would always hold the memory of that sky tight and fast, as though an honored dream, right up to the smoldering pink of sunrise.*

"*I also remember you telling me that you often looked out upon your land knowing full well that it never truly belonged to you, no more than you could hold deed to the sunlight or save up the air you breathed. I sometimes imagine many of our line standing at the door of the farmhouse and staring out at that same ground. But, at some point, the Cardinal family will all be gone. After that, my dear Louisa, you take heart, for the sweep of open land across the valley, the race of busy rivers, and the gentle bumps of green-shrouded hills, with little beads of light poking out here and there, like bits of sly gold—they all will continue on. And they won't be worse off either, for our mortal dabbling in their forever existence, seeing that God made them to last forever, as you've also told me so many times.*

"*Though I have a new life now, and am enjoying the city for the most part, I will never forget that the passing down of memories is the strongest link in the gossamer bridge that binds us as people. I plan to devote my life to doing just that. And if you taught me anything, it's that what we hold in our hearts is truly the fiercest component of our humanity."*

Cotton heard a noise, glanced toward the window, and saw a glimpse of Lou right before she ducked down. Cotton silently read the last part of the letter and then decided to read it in a very loud voice. He would be speaking as much to the daughter, who the man knew lurked right outside the window, as to the mother lying in bed.

"And from watching you all those years conduct your life with honesty, dignity, and compassion, I know that there is nothing so powerful as the emboldened kindness of one human being reaching out to another, who is held only by despair. I think of you every day, Louisa, and so I will, as long as my heart continues to beat. With much love, Jack."

Lou poked her head over the sill again. Inch by inch she turned until she was looking at her mother. But there was no change in the woman, none at all. Lou angrily pushed away from the window. Poor Diamond was teetering mightily now, for her shove against the windowsill had done his balancing efforts no kindness. Diamond finally lost the battle, and both he and Lou went tumbling over, their plummet ending in a series of grunts and groans as they sprawled on the ground.

Cotton rushed to the window in time to see the pair race around the house. He turned back to the woman in bed. "You really must come and join us, Miss Amanda," he said, and then added quietly, as though afraid that anyone other than himself would hear, "for a lot of reasons."

CHAPTER SEVENTEEN

THE HOUSE WAS DARK, THE SKY A MESS OF CLOUDS that promised a good rain come morning. However, when skittish clouds and fragile currents bumped over high rock, the weather often changed quickly: snow became rain and clear became foul, and a body got wet or cold when he least expected to. The cows, hogs, and sheep were safely in the barn, for Old Mo, the mountain lion, had been seen around, and there had been talk of the Tyler farm losing a calf, and the Ramseys a pig. All those on the mountain handy with a shotgun or rifle were keeping their eyes peeled for the old scavenger.

Sam and Hit stood silently in their own corral. Old Mo would never prey on the pair. An ornery mule could kick just about anything to death in a matter of minutes.

The front door of the farmhouse opened. Oz made not a sound when he closed the door behind him. The boy was fully dressed and had his bear clutched tight. He looked around for a few seconds and then took off past the corral, cleared the fields, and plunged into the woods.

The night was a bucket of coal, the wind rattled tree limbs, the underbrush was thick with sounds of stealthy movement, and the tall grass seemed to clutch at Oz's pant legs. The little boy was certain that regiments of hobgoblins were roaming nearby in full terrifying splendor, he their sole target on earth. Yet something inside Oz had clearly risen superior to these horrors, for he did not once think of turning back. Well, maybe once, he admitted to himself. Or perhaps twice.

He ran hard for a while, making his way over knolls, navigating crisscross gullies, and stumbling through the jumble of dense woods. He cleared one last grove of trees, stopped, stooped low, waited a bit, and then eased out into the meadow. Up ahead he saw what he had come for: the well. He took one last deep breath, gripped his bear, and boldly walked right up to it. But Oz was no fool, so just in case, he whispered, "It's a wishing well, not a haunted well. It's a wishing well, not a haunted well."

He stopped and stared at the brick-and-mortar beast, then spit on one hand and rubbed it on his head for luck. He next looked at his beloved bear for a long time, and then laid it gently down against the base of the well and backed away.

"Good-bye, bear. I love you, but I've got to give you up. You understand."

Now Oz was unsure of how to proceed. Finally, he crossed himself and put his hands together as though in prayer, figuring that would satisfy even the most demanding of spirits who granted wishes to little boys desperately in need of them. Staring at the sky he said, "I wish that my mother will wake up and love me again." He paused and then added solemnly, "And Lou too."

He stood there with the wind slicing into him and with

peculiar sounds emerging from a thousand hidden crevices, all potent with evil, he was sure. And yet with all that, Oz was unafraid; he had done what he came to do.

He concluded with "Amen, Jesus."

Moments after Oz turned and ran off, Lou stepped from the trees and looked after her little brother. She walked up to the well, reached down, and picked up his bear.

"Oz, you are so dumb." But she didn't have her heart in the insult, and her voice broke. And ironically it was iron-tough Lou and not open-souled Oz who knelt there on the damp ground and sobbed. Finally wiping her face on her sleeve, Lou rose and turned her back to the well. With Oz's bear held tightly to her chest, she started to walk away. Something made her stop though—she wasn't exactly sure what. But, yes, the fierce wind truly seemed to be blowing her backward, toward the thing Diamond Skinner had so foolishly called a wishing well. She turned and looked at it, and on a night when the moon seemed to have totally abandoned her and the well, the brick seemed to glow as though afire.

Lou wasted no time. She set the bear back down, reached in the pocket of her overalls, and pulled it out: the photo of her and her mother, still in the frame. Lou placed the precious photograph next to the beloved bear, stepped back, and taking a page from her brother's book, clasped her hands together and looked to the sky. Unlike Oz, though, she did not bother to cross herself, or to speak loud and clear to that well or to the heavens above. Her mouth moved, but no words could be heard, as though her faith in what she was doing were lacking still.

Finished, she turned and ran after her brother, though

she would be careful to keep her distance. She didn't want Oz to know he'd been followed, even though she had come along only to watch over him. Behind her the bear and the photo lay forlornly against the brick, resembling nothing so much as a temporary shrine to the dead.

As Louisa had predicted, Lou and Hit finally reached middle ground. Louisa had proudly watched as Lou rose each time Hit knocked her down, the girl growing not more afraid through each tussle with the wily beast, but rather more determined. And smarter. Now plow, mule, and Lou moved with a fluid motion.

For his part Oz had become an expert at riding the big sled that Sam the mule dragged through the fields. Since Oz was lacking in girth, Eugene had piled rocks all around him. The big clods of dirt gave way and broke up under the constant dragging, and the sled eventually smoothed the field like icing on a cake. After weeks of work, sweat, and tired muscles, the four of them stood back and took stock of good ground that was ready now to accept seed.

Dr. Travis Barnes had come up from Dickens to check on Amanda. He was a burly man—red hammy face, short legs—with gray side whiskers, dressed all in black. To Lou, he looked more like an undertaker coming to bury a body than a man trained in preserving life. However, he turned out to be kindly, with a sense of humor designed to make them all comfortable in light of his bleak mission. Cotton and the children waited in the front room while Louisa stayed with Travis during his examination.

He was shaking his head and clutching his black bag when he joined them in the front room. Louisa trailed him, trying to look cheerful. The doctor sat at the kitchen table and fingered the cup of coffee Louisa had poured. He stared into his cup for a bit, as though looking for some comforting words floating among the strains of beans and chicory root.

"Good news," he began, "is that far as I can tell, your momma's fine physically. Her injuries all healed up. She's young and strong and can eat and drink, and so long as you keep exercising her arms and legs, the muscles won't get too weak." He paused and set his cup down. "But I'm afraid that's also the bad news, for that means the problem lies here." He touched his forehead. "And there's not much we can do about that. Certainly beyond me. We can only hope and pray that she comes out of it one day."

Oz took this in stride, his optimism barely tarnished. Lou absorbed this information simply as further validation of what she already knew.

※

School had been going more smoothly than Lou had thought it would. She and Oz found the mountain children to be far more accepting of them now than before Lou had thrown her punches. Lou didn't feel she would ever be close to any of them, but at least the outright hostility had waned. Billy Davis did not return to school for several days. By the time he did, the bruises she had inflicted were mostly healed, though there were fresh ones which Lou suspected had originated with the awful George

Davis. And that was enough to make her feel a certain guilt. For his part, Billy avoided her like she was a water moccasin looking to get the jump on him, yet Lou was still on her guard. She knew by now: It was right when you least expected it that trouble tended to smack you in the head.

Estelle McCoy, too, was subdued around her. It was apparent that Lou and Oz were well ahead of the others in terms of book learning. They did not flaunt this advantage, though, and Estelle McCoy seemed appreciative of that. And she never again referred to Lou as Louisa Mae. Lou and Oz had given the school library a box of their own books, and the children had slipped by one after the other to thank them. It was a steady if not spectacular truce all around.

Lou rose before dawn, did her chores, then went to school and did her work there. At lunchtime she ate her cornbread and drank her milk with Oz under the walnut tree, which was scored with the initials and names of those who had done their learning here. Lou never felt an urge to carve her name there, for it suggested a permanency she was far from willing to accept. They went back to the farm to work in the afternoon, and then went to bed, exhausted, not long after the sun set. It was a steady, uninspired life much appreciated by Lou right now.

Head lice had made their way through Big Spruce, though, and both Lou and Oz had endured shampoos in kerosene. "Don't get near the fire," Louisa had warned.

"This is disgusting," said Lou, fingering the coated strands.

"When I was at school and got me the lice, they put sulfur, lard, and gunpowder on my hair," Louisa told them.

"I couldn't bear to smell myself, and I was terrible afraid somebody'd strike a match and my head would blow."

"They had school when you were little?" Oz asked.

Louisa smiled. "They had what was called subscription school, Oz. A dollar a month for three month a year, and I were a right good student. We was a hunnerd people in a one-room log cabin with a puncheon floor that was splintery on hot days and ice on cold. Teacher quick with the whip or strap, some bad child standing on tippy-toe a good half hour with his nose stuck in a circle the teacher drawed on the board. I ain't never had to stand on tippy-toe. I weren't always good, but I ain't never got caught neither. Some were growed men not long from the War missing arms and legs, come to learn they's letters and numbers. Used to say our spelling words out loud. Got so the durn noise spooked the horses." Her hazel eyes sparkled. "Had me one teacher who used the markings on his cow to learn us geography. To this day, I can't never look at no map without thinking of that durn animal." She looked at them. "I guess you can fill up your head just about anywhere. So you learn what you got to. Just like your daddy done," she added, mostly for Lou's benefit, and the girl finally stopped complaining about her kerosene hair.

CHAPTER EIGHTEEN

LOUISA FELT SORRY FOR THEM ONE MORNING AND GAVE
Lou and Oz a much needed Saturday off to do as
they pleased. The day was fine, with a clean breeze
from the west across a blue sky, trees flushed with green
swaying to its touch. Diamond and Jeb came calling that
morning, because Diamond said there was a special place
in the woods he wanted to show them, and they started
off.

His appearance was little changed: same overalls, same
shirt, no shoes. The bottoms of his feet must have had
every nerve deadened like hoofs, Lou thought, because
she saw him run across sharp rocks, over briars, and even
through a thorny thicket, and never once did she see blood
drawn or face wince. He wore an oily cap pulled low on
his forehead. She asked him if it was his father's, but received only a grunt in response.

They came to a tall oak set in a clearing, or at least
where underbrush had been cut away some. Lou noted
that pieces of sawed wood had been nailed into the tree's
trunk, forming a rough ladder. Diamond put a foot up on
the first rung and started to climb.

"Where are you going?" asked Lou, as Oz kept a grip on Jeb because the hound was acting as though he too wanted to head up the tree behind his master.

"See God," Diamond hollered back, pointing straight up. Lou and Oz looked to the sky.

Far up a number of stripped scrub pines were laid side by side on a couple of the oak's massive branches, forming a floor. A canvas tarp had been flung over a sturdy limb above, and the sides had been tied down to the pines with rope to form a crude tent. While promising all sorts of pleasant times, the tree house looked a good puff of wind away from hitting the ground.

Diamond was already three-quarters up, moving with an easy grace. "Come on now," he said.

Lou, who would have preferred to die a death of impossible agony rather than concede that anything was beyond her, put a hand and a foot on two of the pieces of wood. "You can stay down here if you want, Oz," she said. "We probably won't be long." She started up.

"I got me neat stuff up here, yes sir," Diamond said enticingly. He had reached the summit, his bare feet dangling over the edge.

Oz ceremoniously spit on his hands, gripped a wood piece, and clambered up behind his sister. They sat cross-legged on the laid pines, which formed about a six-by-six square, the canvas roof throwing a nice shade, and Diamond showed them his wares. First out was a flint arrowhead he said was at least one million years old and had been given to him in a dream. Then from a cloth bag rank with outside damp he pulled the skeleton of a small bird that he said had not been seen since shortly after God put the universe together.

"You mean it's extinct," Lou said.

"Naw, I mean it ain't round no more."

Oz was intrigued by a hollow length of metal that had a thick bit of glass fitted into one end. He looked through it, and while the sights were magnified some, the glass was so dirty and scratched, it started giving him a headache.

"See a body coming from miles away," proclaimed Diamond, sweeping a hand across his kingdom. "Enemy or friend." He next showed them a bullet fired from what he said was an 1861 U.S. Springfield rifle.

"How do you know that?" said Lou.

" 'Cause my great-granddaddy five times removed passed it on down and my granddaddy give it to me afore he died. My great-granddaddy five times removed, he fought for the Union, you know."

"Wow," Oz said.

"Yep, turned his pitcher to the wall and everythin', they did. But he weren't taking up a gun for nobody owning nobody else. T'ain't right."

"That's admirable," said Lou.

"Look here now," said Diamond. From a small wooden box, he pulled forth a lump of coal and handed it to Lou. "What d'ya think?" he asked. She looked down at it. The rock was all chipped and rough.

"It's a lump of coal," she said, giving it back and wiping her hand clean on her pants leg.

"No, it ain't just that. You see, they's a diamond in there. A diamond, just like me."

Oz inched over and held the rock. "Wow" was again all he could manage.

"A diamond?" Lou said. "How do you know?"

" 'Cause the man who gimme it said it was. And he

ain't ask for not a durn thing. And man ain't even know my name was Diamond. So there," he added indignantly, seeing the disbelief on Lou's features. He took the coal lump back from Oz. "I chip me off a little piece ever day. And one time I gonna tap it and there it'll be, the biggest, purtiest diamond anybody's ever saw."

Oz eyed the rock with the reverence he usually reserved for grown-ups and church. "Then what will you do with it?"

Diamond shrugged. "Ain't sure. Mebbe nothing. Mebbe keep it right up here. Mebbe give it to you. You like that?"

"If there is a diamond in there, you could sell it for a lot of money," Lou pointed out.

Diamond rubbed at his nose. "Ain't need no money. Got me all I need right here on this mountain."

"Have you ever been off this mountain?" Lou asked.

He stared at her, obviously offended. "What, you think I'a hick or somethin'? Gone on down to McKenzie's near the bridge lots of times. And over to Tremont."

Lou looked out over the woods below. "How about Dickens? You ever been there?"

"Dickens?" Diamond almost fell out of the tree. "Take a day to walk it. 'Sides, why'd a body want'a go there?"

"Because it's different than here. Because I'm tired of dirt and mules and manure and hauling water," said Lou. She patted her pocket. "And because I've got twenty dollars I brought with me from New York that's burning a hole in my pocket," she added, staring at him.

This gigantic sum staggered Diamond, yet even he seemed to understand the possibilities. "Too fer to walk," he said, fingering the coal lump, as though trying to hurry the diamond into hatching.

"Then we *don't* walk," replied Lou.

He glanced at her. "Tremont right closer."

"No, Dickens. I want to go to Dickens."

Oz said, "We could take a taxi."

"If we get to the bridge at McKenzie's," Lou ventured, "then maybe we can hitch a ride to Dickens with somebody. How far is the bridge on foot?"

Diamond considered this. "Well, by road it a good four hour. Time git down there, got to come back. And that be a tiring way to spend a day off from farming."

"What way is there other than the road?"

"You really want'a get on down there?" he said.

Lou took a deep breath. "I really want to, Diamond."

"Well, then, we going. I knowed me a shortcut. Shoot, get us there quick as a sneeze."

Since the mountains had been formed, water had continued eroding the soft limestone, carving thousand-foot-deep gullies between the harder rocks. The line of finger ridges marched next to the three of them as they walked along. The ravine they finally came to was wide and seemed impassable until Diamond led them over to the tree. The yellow poplars here grew to immense proportion, gauged by a caliper measured in feet instead of inches. Many were thicker than a man was tall, and rose up to a hundred and fifty feet in height. Fifteen thousand board feet of lumber could be gotten from a single poplar. A healthy specimen lay across this gap, forming a bridge.

"Going 'cross here cuts the trip way down," Diamond said.

Oz looked over the edge, saw nothing but rock and water at the end of a long fall, and backed away like a spooked cow. Even Lou looked uncertain. But Diamond walked right up to the log.

"Ain't no problem. Thick and wide. Shoot, walk 'cross with your eyes closed. Come on now."

He made his way across, never once looking down. Jeb scooted easily after him. Diamond reached safe ground and looked back. "Come on now," he said again.

Lou put one foot up on the poplar but didn't take another step.

Diamond called out from across the chasm. "Just don't look down. Easy."

Lou turned to her brother. "You stay here, Oz. Let me make sure it's okay." Lou clenched her fists, stepped onto the log, and started across. She kept her eyes leveled on nothing but Diamond and soon joined him on the other side. They looked back at Oz. He made no move toward the log, his gaze fixed on the dirt.

"You go on ahead, Diamond. I'll go back with him."

"No, we ain't gonna do that. You said you want'a go to town? Well, dang it, we going to town."

"I'm *not* going without Oz."

"Ain't got to."

Diamond jogged back across the poplar bridge after telling Jeb to stay put. He got Oz to climb on his back and Lou watched in admiration as Diamond carried him across.

"You sure are strong, Diamond," said Oz as he gingerly slid down to the ground with a relieved breath.

"Shoot, that ain't nuthin'. Bear chased me 'cross that tree one time and I had Jeb *and* a sack of flour on my back. And it were nighttime too. And the rain was pouring so hard God must've been bawling 'bout somethin'. Couldn't see a durn thing. Why, I almost fell twice."

"Well, good Lord," said Oz.

Lou hid her smile well. "What happened to the bear?" she asked in seemingly honest excitement.

"Missed me and landed in the water, and that durn thing never bothered me no mo'."

"Let's go to town, Diamond," she said, pulling on his arm, "before that bear comes back."

They crossed one more bridge of sorts, a swinging one made from rope and cedar slats with holes bored in them so the hemp could be pulled through and then knotted. Diamond told them that pirates, colonial settlers, and later on, Confederate refugees had made the old bridge and added to it at various points in time. And Diamond said he knew where they were all buried, but had been sworn to secrecy by a person he wouldn't name.

They made their way down slopes so steep they had to hang on to trees, vines, and each other to stop from tumbling down head-first. Lou stopped every once in a while to gaze out as she clutched a sapling for support. It was something to stand on steep ground and look out at land of even greater angles. When the land became flatter and Oz grew tired, Lou and Diamond took turns carrying him.

At the bottom of the mountain, they were confronted with another obstacle. The idling coal train was at least a hundred cars long, and it blocked the way as far as they could see in either direction. Unlike those of a passenger train, the coal train's cars were too close together to step between. Diamond picked up a rock and hurled it at one of the cars. It struck right at the name emblazoned across it: Southern Valley Coal and Gas.

"Now what?" said Lou. "Climb over?" She looked at the fully loaded cars and the few handholds, and wondered how that would be possible.

"Shoot naw," said Diamond. "Unner." He stuck his hat in his pocket, dropped to his belly, and slid between the car wheels and under the train. Lou and Oz quickly followed, as did Jeb. They all emerged on the other side and dusted themselves off.

"Boy got hisself cut in half last year doing that very thing," said Diamond. "Train start up when he were unner it. Now, I ain't see it, but I hear it were surely not purty."

"Why didn't you tell us that *before* we crawled under the train?" demanded a stunned Lou.

"Well, if I'd done that, you ain't never crawled unner, now would you?"

On the main road they caught a ride in a Ramsey Candy truck and each was given a Blue Banner chocolate bar by the chubby, uniformed driver. "Spread the word," he told them. "Good stuff."

"Sure will," said Diamond as he bit into the candy. He chewed slowly, methodically, as though suddenly a connoisseur of fine chocolate testing a fresh batch. "You give me 'nuther one and I get the word out *twice* as fast, mister."

After a long, bumpy ride the truck dropped them off in the middle of Dickens proper. Diamond's bare toes had hardly touched asphalt when he quickly lifted first one foot and then the other. "Feels funny," he said. "Ain't liking it none."

"Diamond, I swear, you'd walk on nails without a

word," Lou said as she looked around. Dickens wasn't even a bump in the road compared to what she was used to, but after their time on the mountain it seemed like the most sophisticated metropolis she had ever seen. The sidewalks were filled with people on this fine Saturday morning, and small pockets of them spilled onto the streets. Most were dressed in nice clothes, but the miners were easy enough to spot, lumbering along with their wrecked backs and the loud, hacking coughs coming from their ruined lungs.

A huge banner had been stretched across the street. It read "Coal Is King" in letters black as the mineral. Directly under where the banner had been tied off to a beam jutting from one of the buildings was a Southern Valley Coal and Gas office. There was a line of men going in, and a line of them coming out, all with smiles on their faces, clutching either cash, or, presumably, promises of a good job.

Smartly dressed men in fedoras and three-piece suits chucked silver coins to eager children in the streets. The automobile dealership was doing a brisk business, and the shops were filled with both quality goods and folks clamoring to purchase them. Prosperity was clearly alive and well at the foot of this Virginia mountain. It was a happy, energetic scene, and it made Lou homesick for the city.

"How come your parents have never brought you down here?" Lou asked Diamond as they walked along.

"Ain't never had no reason to come here, that's why." He stuffed his hands in his pockets and stared up at a telephone pole with wires sprouting from it and smacking into one building. Then he eyed a droop-shouldered man in a suit and a little boy in dark slacks and a dress shirt as they came out of a store with a big paper bag of something. The two went over to one of the slant-parked cars that lined both sides of the street, and the man opened the car door. The boy stared over at Diamond and asked him where he was from.

"How you know I ain't from right here, son?" said Diamond, glaring at the town boy.

The child looked at Diamond's dirty clothes and face, his bare feet and wild hair, then jumped in the car and locked the door.

They kept walking and passed the Esso gas station with its twin pumps and a smiling man in crisp company uniform standing out front as rigidly as a cigar store Indian. Next they peered through the glass of a Rexall drugstore. The store was running an "all-in-the-window" sale. The two dozen or so varied items could be had for the sum of three dollars.

"Shoot, why? You can make all that stuff yourself. Ain't got to buy it," Diamond pointed out, apparently sensing that Lou was tempted to go inside and clean out the display.

"Diamond, we're here to spend money. Have fun."

"I'm having fun," he said with a scowl. "Don't be telling me I ain't having no fun."

They headed past the Dominion Café with its Chero Cola and "Ice Cream Here" signs, and then Lou stopped.

"Let's go in," she said. Lou gripped the door, pulled it open, setting a bell to tinkling, and stepped inside. Oz followed her. Diamond stayed outside for a long enough time to show his displeasure with this decision and then hurried in after them.

The place smelled of coffee, wood smoke, and baking

fruit pies. Umbrellas for sale hung from the ceiling. There was a bench down one wall, and three swivel chrome barstools with padded green seats were bolted to the floor in front of a waist-high counter. Glass containers filled with candy rested on the display cabinets. There was a modest soda and ice cream fountain machine, and through a pair of saloon doors they could hear the clatter of dishes and smell the aromas of food cooking. In one corner was a potbellied stove, its smoke pipe supported by wire and cutting through one wall.

A man dressed in a white shirt with sleeves rolled to the elbows, a short wide tie, and wearing an apron passed through the saloon doors and stood behind the counter. He had a smooth face and hair parted equally to either side, held down with what appeared to Lou to be a slop bucket of grease.

He looked at them as though they were a brigade of Union troops sent directly from General Grant to rub the good Virginians' noses in it a little more. He edged back a bit as they moved forward. Lou got up on one of the stools and looked at the menu neatly written in loopy cursive on a blackboard. The man moved back farther. His hand glided out and one of his knuckles rapped against a glass cabinet set against the wall. The words "No Credit" had been written in thick white strokes on the glass.

In response to this not-so-subtle gesture, Lou pulled out five one-dollar bills and aligned them neatly on the counter. The man's eyes went to the folding cash and he smiled, showing off a gold front tooth. He came forward, now their good friend for all time. Oz scooted up on another of the barstools, leaned on the counter, and sniffed the wonderful smells coming through those saloon doors.

Diamond hung back, as though wanting to be nearest the door when they had to make a run for it.

"How much for a slice of pie?" Lou asked.

"Nickel," the man said, his gaze locked on the five Washingtons on his counter.

"How about a whole pie?"

"Fifty cents."

"So I could buy ten pies with this money?"

"Ten pies?" exclaimed Diamond. "God dog!"

"That's right," the man said quickly. "And we can make 'em for you too." He glanced over at Diamond, his gaze descending from the boy's explosion of cowlicks to his bare toes. "He with you?"

"Naw, they with me," said Diamond, ambling over to the counter, fingers tucked around his overall straps.

Oz was staring at another sign on the wall. "Only Whites Served," he read out loud, and then glanced in confusion at the man. "Well, our hair's blond, and Diamond's is red. Does that mean only old people can get pie?"

The fellow looked at Oz like the boy was "special" in the head, stuck a toothpick between his teeth, and eyed Diamond. "Shoes are required in my establishment. Where you from, boy? Mountain?"

"Naw, the moon." Diamond leaned forward and flashed an exaggerated smile. "Want'a see my green teeth?"

As though brandishing a tiny sword, the man waved the toothpick in front of Diamond's face. "You smart mouth. Just march yourself right outta here. Go on. Git back up that mountain where you belong and stay there!"

Instead, Diamond went up on his toes, grabbed an umbrella off the ceiling rack, and opened it.

The man came around from behind the counter.

"Don't you do that now. That's bad luck."

"Why, I doing it. Mebbe a chunk of rock'll fall off the mountain and squash you to poultice!"

Before the man reached him, Diamond tossed the opened umbrella into the air and it landed on the soda machine. A stream of goo shot out and painted one cabinet a nice shade of brown.

"Hey!" the man yelled, but Diamond had already fled.

Lou scooped up her money, and she and Oz stood to leave.

"Where y'all going?" the man said.

"I decided I didn't want pie," Lou said amiably and shut the door quietly behind her and Oz.

They heard the man yell out, "Hicks!"

They caught up with Diamond, and all three bent over laughing while people walked around them, staring curiously.

"Nice to see you having a good time," a voice said.

They turned and saw Cotton standing there, wearing vest, tie, and coat, briefcase in hand, yet with a clear look of mirth in his eyes.

"Cotton," Lou said, "what are you doing here?"

He pointed across the street. "Well, I happen to work here, Lou."

They all stared at where he was pointing. The courthouse loomed large before them, beautiful brick over ugly concrete.

"Now, what are y'all doing here?" he asked.

"Louisa gave us the day off. Been working pretty hard," said Lou.

Cotton nodded. "So I've seen."

Lou looked at the bustle of people. "It surprised me when I first saw this place. Really prosperous."

Cotton glanced around. "Well, looks can be deceiving. Thing about this part of the state, we're generally one industry-moving-on from total collapse. Lumber folks did it, and now most jobs are tied to the coal and not just the miners. And most of the businesses here rely on those people spending those mining dollars. If that goes away, then it might not seem so prosperous anymore. A house of cards falls swiftly. Who knows, in five years' time this place might not even be here." He eyed Diamond and grinned. "But the mountain folk will. They always get by." He looked around. "I tell you what, I've got some things to do over to the courthouse. Court's not in session today of course, but always some work to be done. Suppose you meet me there in two hours. Then I'd be proud to buy you some lunch."

Lou looked around. "Where?"

"A place I think you'd like, Lou. Called the New York Restaurant. Open twenty-four hours, breakfast, lunch, or supper any time of the day or night. Now, there aren't many folk in Dickens who stay up past nine o'clock, but I suppose it's comforting to have the option of eggs, grits, and bacon at midnight."

"Two hours," repeated Oz, "but we don't have anything to tell time with."

"Well, the courthouse has a clock tower, but it tends to run a little slow. I tell you what, Oz, here." Cotton took off his pocket watch and handed it to him. "You use this. Take good care of it. My father gave it to me."

"When you left to come here?" Lou asked.

"That's right. He said I'd have plenty of time on my

hands, and I guess he wanted me to keep good track of it." He tipped his hat to them. "Two hours." And then he walked away.

"So what we gonna do for two hours?" said Diamond.

Lou looked around and her eyes lit up.

"Come on," she said and took off running. "You're finally going to see yourself a picture show, Mr. Diamond."

For almost two hours they were in a place far removed from Dickens, Virginia, the mountains of Appalachia, and the troublesome concerns of real life. They were in the breathtaking land of *The Wizard of Oz*, which was having a long run at movie houses across the land. When they came out, Diamond peppered them with dozens of questions about how any of what they had just seen was possible.

"Had God done it?" he asked more than once in a hushed tone.

Lou pointed to the courthouse. "Come on, or we'll be late."

They dashed across the street and up the wide steps of the courthouse. A uniformed deputy sheriff with a thick mustache stopped them.

"Whoa, now, where you think y'all going?"

"It's all right, Howard, they're with me," Cotton said, coming out the door. "They all might be lawyers one day. Coming to check out the halls of justice."

"God forbid, Cotton, we ain't needing us no more fine lawyers," Howard said, smiling, and then moved on.

"Having a good time?" Cotton asked.

"I just seen a lion, a durn scarecrow, and a metal man on a big wall," said Diamond, "and I still ain't figgered out how they done it."

"Y'all want to see where I do my daily labor?" asked Cotton.

They all clamored that they did indeed. Before they went inside, Oz solemnly handed the pocket watch back to Cotton.

"Thanks for taking such good care of it, Oz."

"It's been two hours, you know," said the little boy.

"Punctuality is a virtue," replied the lawyer.

They went inside the courthouse while Jeb lay down outside. There were doorways up and down the broad hall, and hanging above the doors various brass plates that read: "Marriage Registrar," "Tax Collections," "Births and Deaths," "Commonwealth's Attorney," and so on. Cotton explained their various functions and then showed them the courtroom, which Diamond said was the largest such space he had ever seen. They were introduced to Fred the bailiff, who had popped out of some room or other when they had come in. Judge Atkins, he explained, had gone home for lunch.

On the walls were portraits of white-haired men in black robes. The children ran their hands along the carved wood and took turns sitting in the witness and jury boxes. Diamond asked to sit in the judge's chair, but Cotton didn't think that was a good idea, and neither did Fred. When they weren't looking, Diamond grabbed a sit anyway and came away puff-chested like a rooster, until Lou, who had seen this offense, poked him hard in the ribs.

They left the courthouse and went next door to a building that housed a small number of offices, including Cotton's. His place was one large room with creaky oak flooring that had shelves on three sides which held worn law books, will and deed boxes, and a fine set of the

Statutes of Virginia. A big walnut desk sat in the middle of the room, along with a telephone and drifts of papers. There was an old crate for a wastebasket, and a listing hat and umbrella stand in one corner. There were no hats on the hooks, and where the umbrellas should have been was an old fishing pole. Cotton let Diamond dial a single number on the phone and talk to Shirley the operator. The boy nearly jumped out of his skin when her raspy voice tickled his ear.

Next, Cotton showed them the apartment where he lived at the top of this same building. It had a small kitchen that was piled high with canned vegetables, jars of molasses and bread and butter pickles, sacks of potatoes, blankets, and lanterns, among many other items.

"Where'd you get all that stuff?" asked Lou.

"Folks don't always have cash. Pay their legal bills in barter." He opened the small icebox and showed them the cuts of chicken, beef, and bacon in there. "Can't put none of it in the bank, but it sure tastes a lot better'n money." There was a tiny bedroom with a rope bed and a reading light on a small nightstand, and one large front room utterly buried under books.

As they stared at the mounds, Cotton took off his glasses. "No wonder I'm going blind," he said.

"You read all them books?" Diamond asked in awe.

"I plead guilty to that. In fact I've read many of them more than once," Cotton answered.

"I read me a book one time," Diamond said proudly.

"What was the title?" Lou asked.

"Don't recall 'xactly, but it had lots of pictures. No, I take that back, I read me two books, if you count the Bible."

"I think we can safely include that, Diamond," said Cotton, smiling. "Come over here, Lou." Cotton showed her one bookcase neatly filled with volumes, many of them fine leatherbound ones of notable authors. "This is reserved for my favorite writers."

Lou looked at the titles there and immediately saw every novel and collection of short stories her father had written. It was nice, conciliatory bait Cotton was throwing out, only Lou was not in a conciliatory mood. She said, "I'm hungry. Can we eat now?"

The New York Restaurant served nothing remotely close to New York fare but it was good food nonetheless, and Diamond had what he said was his first bottle of "soder" pop. He liked it so much he had two more. Afterward they walked down the street, peppermint candy rolling in their mouths. They went into the five-and-dime and 25-cent store and Cotton showed them how because of the land grade all six stories of the place opened out onto ground level, a fact that had actually been discussed in the national media at one point. "Dickens's claim to fame," he chuckled, "unique angles of dirt."

The store was stacked high with dry goods, tools, and foodstuffs. The aromas of tobacco and coffee were strong and seemed to have settled into the bones of the place. Horse collars hung next to racks of spooled thread, which sat alongside fat barrels of candies. Lou bought a pair of socks for herself and a pocketknife for Diamond, who was reluctant to accept it until she told him that in return he had to whittle something for her. She purchased a stuffed bear for Oz and handed it to him without commenting on the whereabouts of the old one.

Lou disappeared for a few minutes and returned with

an object which she handed to Cotton. It was a magnifying glass. "For all that reading," she said and smiled, and Cotton smiled back. "Thank you, Lou. This way I'll think of you every time I open a book." She bought a shawl for Louisa and a straw hat for Eugene. Oz borrowed some money from her and went off with Cotton to browse. When they came back, he held a parcel wrapped in brown paper and steadfastly refused to reveal what it was.

After wandering the town, Cotton showing them things that Lou and Oz had certainly seen before, but Diamond never had, they piled into Cotton's Oldsmobile, which sat parked in front of the courthouse. They headed off, Diamond and Lou squeezed into the rumble seat while Oz and Jeb rode with Cotton in front. The sun was just beginning its descent now and the breeze felt good to all. There didn't seem to be anything so pretty as sun setting over mountain.

They passed through Tremont and a while later crossed the tiny bridge near McKenzie's and started up the first ridge. They came to a railroad crossing, and instead of continuing on the road, Cotton turned and drove the Oldsmobile on down the tracks.

"Smoother than the roads up here," he explained. "We'll pick it back up later on. They've got asphalt and macadam at the foothills, but not up here. These mountain roads were built by hands swinging picks and shovels. Law used to be every able-bodied man between sixteen and sixty had to help build the roads ten days a year and bring his own tools and sweat to do it. Only teachers and preachers were exempt from having to do it, although I imagine those workers could've used some powerful prayers every now and again. They did a right good job, built eighty miles of road over forty years, but it's still hard on one's bottom to travel across the results of all that fine work."

"What if a train comes?" asked an anxious Oz.

"Then I suspect we'll have to get off," Cotton said.

They eventually did hear the whistle and Cotton pulled the car to safety and waited. A few minutes later a fully loaded train rolled past, looking like a giant serpent. It was moving slowly, for the track was curvy here.

"Is that coal?" Oz said, eyeing the great lumps of rock visible in the open train cars.

Cotton shook his head. "Coke. Made from slack coal and cooked in the ovens. Ship it out to the steel mills." He shook his head slowly. "Trains come up here empty and leave full. Coal, coke, lumber. Don't bring anything here except more bodies for labor."

On a spur off the main line, Cotton showed them a coal company town made up of small, identical homes, with a train track dead center of the place and a commissary store that had goods piled floor to ceiling, Cotton informed them, because he had been inside before. A long series of connected brick structures shaped like beehives were set along one high road. Each one had a metal door and a chimney with fill dirt packed around it. Smoke belched from each stack, turning the darkening sky ever blacker. "Coke ovens," Cotton explained. There was one large house with a shiny new Chrysler Crown Imperial parked out front. The mine superintendent's home, Cotton told them. Next to this house was a corral with a few grazing mares and a couple of energetic yearlings leaping and galloping around.

"I got to take care of some personal business," said Diamond, already pulling his overall straps down. "Too much soder pop. Won't be one minute, just duck behind that shed."

Cotton stopped the car and Diamond got out and ran off. Cotton and the children talked while they waited, and the lawyer pointed out some other things of interest.

"This is a Southern Valley coal mining operation. The Clinch Number Two mine, they call it. Coal mining pays pretty good, but the work is terribly hard, and with the way the company stores are set up the miners end up owing more to the company than they earn in wages." Cotton stopped talking and looked thoughtfully in the direction of where Diamond had gone, a frown easing across his face. He continued, "And the men also get sick and die of the black lung, or from cave-ins, accidents, and such."

A whistle sounded and they watched as a group of charcoal-faced, probably bone-tired men emerged from the mine entrance. A group of women and children ran to greet them, and they all walked toward the copycat houses, the men swinging metal dinner pails and pulling out their smokes and liquor bottles. Another group of men, looking as tired as the other, trudged past them to take their place under the earth.

"They used to run three shifts here, but now they only have two," said Cotton. "Coal's starting to run out."

Diamond returned and vaulted into the rumble seat.

"You all right, Diamond?" asked Cotton.

"Am now," said the boy, a smile pushing against his cheeks, his feline green eyes lighted up.

Louisa was upset when she learned they had gone to town. Cotton explained that he should not have kept the children as long as he had, therefore she should blame him. But then Louisa said she recalled that their daddy had done the very same thing, and the pioneer spirit was a hard one to dodge, so it was okay. Louisa accepted the shawl with tears in her eyes, and Eugene tried on the hat and proclaimed it the nicest gift he had ever gotten.

After supper that night Oz excused himself and went to his mother's room. Curious, Lou followed him, spying on her brother as usual from the narrow opening between door and wall. Oz carefully unwrapped the parcel he had purchased in town and held the hairbrush firmly. Amanda's face was peaceful, her eyes, as always, shut. To Lou, her mother was a princess reclining in a deathlike state, and none of them possessed the necessary antidote. Oz knelt on the bed and began brushing Amanda's hair and telling his mother of their wonderfully fine day in town. Lou watched him struggle with the brushing for a few moments and then went in to help. She held out her mother's hair and showed Oz how to properly perform the strokes. Their mother's hair had grown out some, but it was still short.

Later that night Lou went to her room, put away the socks she had bought, lay on the bed fully dressed down to her boots, thinking about their trip to town, and never once closed her eyes until it was time to milk the cows the next morning.

CHAPTER NINETEEN

T HEY ALL WERE SITTING DOWN TO DINNER A FEW
nights later while the rain poured down outside.
Diamond had come for supper, wearing a tattered
piece of worn canvas with a hole cut out for his head, his
homegrown mackintosh of sorts. Jeb had shaken himself
off and headed for the fire as though he owned the place.
When Diamond freed himself from the canvas coat, Lou
saw something tied around his neck. And it wasn't particularly sweet-smelling.

"What is *that*?" Lou asked, her fingers pinching her
nose, for the stench was awful.

"Asafetida," Louisa answered for the boy. "A root. Ward
off sickness. Diamond, honey, I think if you warm yourself by the fire, you can give that to me. I thank you."
While Diamond wasn't looking, she carried the root out
to the back porch and flung the foul thing away into the
darkness.

Louisa's frying pan held the dual aromas of popping
lard and ribs cut thick with so much fat they didn't dare
curl. The meat had come from one of the hogs they had
had to slaughter. Usually a winter task, they had been com-

pelled, by a variety of circumstances, to perform the deed in spring. Actually, Eugene had done the killing while the children were at school. But at Oz's insistence Eugene had agreed to let him help scrape down the hog and get off the ribs, middle meat, bacon, and chitlins. However, when Oz saw the dead animal strung up on a wooden tripod, a steel hook through its bloody mouth, and a cauldron of boiling water nearby—just waiting, he no doubt believed, for the hide of a little boy to give it the right spice, he had run off. His screams echoed back and forth across the valley, as though from a careless giant who had stubbed his toe. Eugene had admired both the boy's speed and lung capacity and then gone on to work the hog himself.

They all ate heartily of the meat, and also of canned tomatoes and green beans that had marinated for the better part of six months in brine and sugar, and the last of the pinto beans.

Louisa kept all plates full, except her own. She nibbled on some of the tomato chunks and beans, and dipped cornbread into heated lard, but that was all. She sipped on a cup of chicory coffee and looked around the table where all were enjoying themselves, laughing hard at something silly Diamond had said. She listened to the rain on the roof. So far so good, though rain now meant nothing; if none fell in July and August, the crop would still be dust, blown off in a gentle breeze, and dust had never lined anyone's belly. Very soon they would be laying in their food crops: corn, pole beans, tomatoes, squash, rutabaga, late potatoes, cabbage, sweet potatoes, and string beans. Irish potatoes and onions were already in the ground, and duly hilled over, frost not bothering them any. The land would be good to them this year; it was their due this time around.

Louisa listened to the rain some more. *Thank you, Lord, but be sure to send us some more of your bounty come summer. Not too much so's the tomatoes burst and rot on the vines, and not too little that the corn only grows waist high. I know it's asking a lot, but it'd be much appreciated.* She said a silent amen and then did her best to join in the festivities.

There came a rap on the door and Cotton walked in, his outer coat soaked through even though the walk from car to porch was a quick one. He was not his usual self; the man did not even smile. He accepted a cup of coffee, a bit of cornbread, and sat next to Diamond. The boy stared up at him as though he knew what was coming.

"Sheriff came by to see me, Diamond."

Everyone looked at Cotton first and then they all stared at Diamond. Oz's eyes were open so wide the boy looked like an owl without feathers.

"Is that right?" Diamond said, as he took a mouthful of beans and stewed onions.

"Seems a pile of horse manure got in the mine superintendent's brand-new Chrysler at the Clinch Number Two. The man sat in it without knowing, it still being dark and all, and he had the bad cold in the nose and couldn't smell it. He was understandably upset by the experience."

"Durn, how 'bout that," said Diamond. "Wonder how the horse done got that in there? Pro'bly just backed itself up to the window and let fly." That said, Diamond went right on eating, though none of the others did.

"I recall I dropped you off to do some personal business right around there on our drive back from Dickens."

"You tell the sheriff that?" Diamond asked quickly.

"No, my memory curiously abandoned me about the time he asked." Diamond looked relieved as Cotton continued. "But I spent a sorry hour over at the courthouse with the superintendent and a coal company lawyer who were all-fire sure that you had done it. Now upon my careful cross-examination I was able to demonstrate that there were no eyewitnesses and no other evidence tying you to the scene of this . . . little situation. And, fortunately, one can't take fingerprints from horse manure. Judge Atkins held with my side of things, and so there we are. But those coal folk have long memories, son, you know that."

"Not so long as mine," countered Diamond.

"Why would he do something like that?" said Lou.

Louisa looked at Cotton and he looked at her, and then Cotton said, "Diamond, my heart's with you on this, son, it really is. You know that. But the law's not. And next time, it might not be so easy to get out of it. And folk might start taking matters into their own hands. So my advice to you is to get on with things. I'm saying it for your own good, Diamond, you know that I am."

With that Cotton rose and put his hat back on. He refused all further questions from Lou and declined an invitation to stay. He paused and looked at Diamond, who was considering the rest of his meal without enthusiasm.

Cotton said, "Diamond, after those coal folk left the courtroom, me and Judge Atkins had us a long laugh. I'd say that was a right good one to end your career on, son. Okay?"

Diamond finally smiled at the man and said, "Okay."

CHAPTER TWENTY

L OU ROSE EARLY ONE MORNING, EVEN BEFORE LOUISA and Eugene, she believed, for she heard no stirring below. She had grown used to dressing in the dark now and her fingers moved swiftly, arranging her clothes and lacing her boots. She stepped to the window and looked out. It was so dark she had a vague feeling of being deep underwater. She flinched, for Lou thought she had seen something slip out from the barn. And then, like a frame of spent lightning, it was gone. She opened the window for a better look, but whatever it was wasn't there anymore. It must have been her imagination.

She went down the stairs as quietly as she could, started toward Oz's room to wake him, but stopped at the door of her mother's instead. It was partially open, and Lou just stood there for a moment, as though something blocked her passage. She leaned against the wall, squirmed a bit, slid her hands along the door frame, pushed herself away, and then leaned back. Finally, Lou edged her head into the bedroom.

Lou was surprised to see two figures on the bed. Oz was lying next to their mother. He was dressed in his long johns, a bit of his thin calves visible where the bottoms had inched up, his feet in thick wool socks he had brought with him to the mountain. His tiny rear end was stuck up in the air, his face turned to the side so Lou could see it. A tender smile was on his lips, and he was clenching his new bear.

Lou crept forward and laid a hand on his back. He never stirred, and Lou let her hand slide down and gently touch her mother's arm. When she exercised her mother's limbs, a part of Lou would always be feeling for her mother to be pushing back just a little. But it was always just dead weight. And Amanda had been so strong during the accident, keeping her and Oz from being hurt. Maybe in saving her children, Lou thought, she had used up all she had. Lou left the two and went to the kitchen.

She loaded the coal in the front-room fireplace, got the flame going, then sat in front of the fire for a time, letting the heat melt the chill from her bones. At dawn she opened the door and felt the cool air on her face. There were corpulent gray clouds loitering about from a passed storm, their underbellies outlined in flaming reddish-pink. Right below this was the broad sweep of mountainous green forest that stepped right to the sky. It was one of the most glorious breakups of night she could ever recall. Lou certainly had never seen dawns like this in the city.

Though it had not been that long ago, it seemed like many years since Lou had walked the concrete pavement of New York City, ridden the subway, raced for a cab with her father and mother, pushed through the crowds of shoppers at Macy's the day after Thanksgiving, or gone to Yankee Stadium to lunge for white leather balls and gobble hot dogs. Several months ago all of that had been replaced by steep land, dirt and trees, and animals that smelled and made you earn your place. Corner grocers had been exchanged for crackling bread and strained milk, tap water for water pumped or in bucket hauled, grand public libraries for a pretty cabinet of few books, tall buildings for taller mountains. And for a reason she couldn't quite get at, Lou did not know if she could stay here for long. Maybe there was a good reason her father had never come back.

She went to the barn and milked the cows, carrying a full bucket into the kitchen and the rest to the spring-house, where she laid it in the cool stream of water. The air was already growing warmer.

Lou had the cookstove hot and the pan with lard fired up when her great-grandmother walked in. Louisa was fretting that she and Eugene had slept late. Then Louisa eyed the full buckets on the sink, and Lou told her she had already milked the cows. When she saw the rest of the work Lou had done, Louisa smiled appreciatively. "Next thing I know you'll be running this place without me."

"I doubt that will ever happen," said the girl in a way that made Louisa stop smiling.

❧

Cotton showed up unannounced a half hour later dressed in patched work pants, an old shirt, and worn bro-gans. He didn't wear his wire-rim glasses, and his fedora had been replaced with a straw hat, which, Louisa said, was foresight on his part because it looked like the sun would burn a bright one today.

They all said their hellos to the man, though Lou had mumbled hers. He had come to read to her mother regularly, as promised, and Lou was resenting it more each time. However, Lou appreciated his gentle ways and courtly manners. It was a conflicted, troubling situation for the girl.

The temperature, though cold the night before, had not come close to freezing. Louisa didn't have a thermometer, but, as she said, her bones were just as accurate as bottled mercury. The crops were going in, she declared to all. Late to plant often meant never to harvest.

They trucked over to the first field to be sown, a sloped rectangle of ten acres. The vigilant wind had chased the malingering gray clouds over the ridgeline, leaving the sky clear. The mountains, though, looked markedly flat this morning, as if they were props only. Louisa carefully passed out bags of seed corn from the season before, shelled and then kept in the corncrib over the winter. She instructed the troops carefully as to their usage. "Thirty bushels of corn an acre is what we want," she said. "More, if we can."

For a while things went all right. Oz walked his rows, meticulously counting out three seeds per hill as Louisa had told them. Lou, though, was letting herself become sloppy, dropping two at some places, four at others.

"Lou," Louisa said sharply. "Three seeds per hill, girl!"

Lou stared at her. "Like it really makes a difference."

Louisa rested fists on her haunches. "Difference twixt eating and not!"

Lou stood there for a moment and then started up again,

at a clip of three seeds per hill about nine inches apart. Two hours later, with the five of them working steadily, only about half the field had been laid. Louisa had them spend another hour using hoes to hill the planted corn. Oz and Lou soon had purple blood blisters in the crooks of their hands, despite the gloves they wore. And Cotton too had done the same to his.

"Lawyering is poor preparation for honest work," he explained, showing off his twin sore prizes.

Louisa's and Eugene's hands were so heavily callused that they wore no gloves at all, hilled twice as much as the others, and came away with palms barely reddened by the tools' coarse handles.

With the last dropped seed hilled, Lou, far more bored than tired, sat on the ground, slapping her gloves against her leg. "Well, that was fun. What now?"

A curved stick appeared in front of her. "Before you get on to school, you and Oz gonna find some wayward cows."

Lou looked up into Louisa's face.

Lou and Oz tramped through the woods. Eugene had let the cows and the calf out to graze in the open field, and, as cows, like people, were wont to do, they were wandering the countryside looking for better prospects.

Lou smacked a lilac bush with the stick Louisa had given her to scare off snakes. She had not mentioned the threat of serpents to Oz, because she figured if he knew, she'd end up carrying her brother on her back. "I can't believe we have to find some stupid cows," she said angrily. "If they're dumb enough to get lost, they should stay lost."

They pushed through tangles of dogwood and mountain laurel. Oz swung on the lower branch of a scraggly pine, and then gave out a whistle as a cardinal flitted by, though most folks from the mountain would have certainly called it a redbird.

"Look, Lou, a cardinal, like us."

Keeping an eye out more for birds than cows, they quickly saw many varieties, most of which they did not know. Hummingbirds twitted over beds of morning glories and wood violets; the children scared up a mess of field larks from thick ground-cover. A sparrow hawk let them know it was around, while a pack of nasty blue jays bothered everybody and everything. Wild, bushy rhododendrons were beginning to bloom in pink and red, as were the lavender-tipped white flowers of Virginia thyme. On the sides of steep slopes they could see trailing arbutus and wolfsbane among the stacked slate and other protrusions of rocks. The trees were in full, showy form, and the sky a cap of blue to finish it off. And here they were, hunting aimless bovines, thought Lou.

A cowbell clunked to the east of them.

Oz looked excited. "Louisa said to follow the bell the cows wear."

Lou chased Oz through groves of beech, poplar, and basswood, the strong vines of wisteria clutching at them like irksome hands, their feet tripping over bumps of shallow roots clinging to uneven, shifting ground. They came to a small clearing ringed with hemlock and gum and heard the bell again, but saw no cows. A goldfinch darted past, startling them.

"Moo. Moooo!" came the voice, and the bell clunked.

The pair looked around in bewilderment until Lou glanced up in the crook of a maple and saw Diamond swinging the bell and speaking cow. He was barefoot, same clothes as always, cigarette behind his ear, hair reaching to the sky, as though a mischievous angel was tugging at the boy's red mop.

"What are you doing?" Lou demanded angrily.

Diamond gracefully swung from branch to branch, dropped to the ground, and clunked the bell once more. Lou noted that he had used a piece of twine to tie the pocketknife she had given him to a loop on his overalls.

"Believing I were a cow."

"That's not funny," Lou said. "We have to find them."

"Shoot, that's easy. Cows ain't never really lost, they just mosey round till somebody come get 'em." He whistled and Jeb broke through the tangle of brush to join them.

Diamond led them through a swath of hickory and ash; on the trunk of the latter a pair of squirrels were having an argument, apparently over some division of spoils. They all stopped and stared in reverence at a golden eagle perched on a limb of a ruler-straight eighty-foot poplar. In the next clearing, they saw the cows grazing in a natural pen of fallen trees.

"I knowed they was Miss Louisa's right off. Figger you'd probably come traipsing through after 'em."

With Diamond's and Jeb's help, they drove the cows back to their farm pen. Along the way, Diamond showed them how to hold on to the animals' tails, let the cows pull them uphill, to make them pay back a little, he said, for wandering off. When they shut the corral gate, Lou said, "Diamond, tell me why you put horse manure in that man's car."

"Can't tell you, 'cause I ain't do it."

"Diamond, come on. You as good as admitted you did to Cotton."

"Got me oak ears, can't hear nuthin' you saying."

A frustrated Lou drew circles in the dirt with her shoe. "Look, we have to get to school, Diamond. You want to come with us?"

"Don't go to no school," he said, slipping the unlit cigarette between his lips and becoming an instant adult.

"How come your parents don't make you go?"

In response to this Diamond whistled for Jeb and the pair took off running.

"Hey, Diamond," Lou called after him.

Boy and dog only ran faster.

CHAPTER TWENTY-ONE

LOU AND OZ RACED PAST THE EMPTY YARD AND INside the schoolhouse. Breathless, they hustled to their seats.

"I'm sorry we're late," Lou said to Estelle McCoy, who was already chalking something on the board. "We were working in the fields and . . ." She looked around and noted that fully half the seats were empty.

"Lou, it's all right," said her teacher. "Planting time's starting, I'm just glad you made it in at all."

Lou sat down in her seat. From the corner of her eye she saw that Billy Davis was there. He looked so angelic that she told herself to be cautious. When she lifted up her desk top to put away her books, she could not stifle the scream. The snake coiled in her desk—a three-foot brown and yellow-banded copperhead—was dead. However, the piece of paper tied around the serpent, with the words "Yankee Go Home" scrawled upon it, was what really made Lou angry.

"Lou," called Mrs. McCoy from the blackboard, "is anything wrong?"

Lou closed the desk and looked at Billy, who pursed his lips and attended to his book. "No," said Lou.

It was lunchtime, and the air was cool, but with a warming sun, and the children gathered outside to eat, lard buckets and other like containers in hand. Just about everyone had something to line his or her stomach, even if it was just scraps of cornbread or biscuit, and many a hand cradled a small jug of milk or jar of springwater. Children settled back on the ground to do their eating, drinking, and talking. Some of the younger ones ran around in circles until they were so dizzy they fell down, and then older siblings picked them up and made them eat.

Lou and Oz sat under the deep shade of the walnut tree, the breeze slowly lifting the ends of Lou's hair. Oz bit heartily into his buttered biscuit and drank down the cold springwater they had brought in a canning jar. Lou, though, did not eat. She seemed to be waiting for something, and stretched her limbs as though preparing for a race.

Billy Davis strutted through the small clumps of eaters, prominently swinging his wooden lunch pail made from a small nail keg with a wire driven through it for a handle. He stopped at one group, said something, laughed, glanced over at Lou, and laughed some more. He finally climbed into the lower branches of a silver maple and opened his lunch pail. He screamed out, fell backward out of the tree, and landed mostly on his head. The snake was on him, and he rolled and pitched trying to get the serpent off. Then he realized it was his own dead copperhead that had been tied to the lid of the pail, which he still clutched in his hand. When he stopped squealing like a stabbed pig, he realized everyone in the schoolyard was belly-laughing at him.

All except Lou, who just sat there with her arms crossed pretending to ignore this spectacle. Then she broke out into a smile so wide it threatened to block the sun. When Billy stood, so did she. Oz pushed the biscuit into his mouth, gulped down the rest of the water, and scooted to safety behind the walnut tree. Fists cocked, Lou and Billy met in the very center of the schoolyard. The crowd closed around them, and Yankee girl and mountain boy went for round two.

Lou, the other side of her lip cut this time, sat at her desk. She stuck her tongue out at Billy, who sat across from her, his shirt torn and his right eye a nice purplish black. Estelle McCoy stood in front of them, arms crossed, a scowl on her face. Right after stopping the championship bout, the angry teacher had ended school early and sent word to the fighters' respective families.

Lou was in high spirits, for she had clearly licked Billy again in front of everybody. He didn't look too comfortable, though, fidgeting in his chair and glancing nervously at the door. Lou finally understood his anxiety when the schoolhouse door crashed open and George Davis stood there.

"What in the hell's going on here?" he roared loud enough to make even Estelle McCoy cower.

As he stalked forward, the teacher drew back. "Billy was in a fight, George," Mrs. McCoy said.

"You called me in here on 'count of a damn fight?" he snarled at her, and then towered menacingly over Billy. "I were out in the field, you little bastard, ain't got time for this crap." When George saw Lou, his wild eyes grew even more wicked, and then the man threw a backhand that caught Billy on the side of his head and knocked him to the floor.

Father stood over the fallen son. "You let a damn girl do that to you?"

"George Davis!" Estelle McCoy cried out. "You let your son be."

He held up a menacing hand to her. "Now on, boy works the farm. No more this damn school."

"Why don't you let Billy decide that?"

Louisa said this as she walked into the room, Oz following closely behind her clutching at the woman's pants leg.

"Louisa," the teacher said with great relief.

Davis stood his ground. "He a boy, he damn well do what I say."

Louisa helped Billy into his seat and comforted him, before turning to the father. "You see a boy? I see me a fine young man."

Davis snorted. "He ain't no growed man."

Louisa took a step toward him and spoke in a quiet voice, but her look was so fierce Lou forgot to breathe. "But *you* are. So don't you never hit him agin."

Davis pointed right in her face with a nail-less finger.

"Don't you go telling me how to handle my boy. You had yourself one child. Had me nine, 'nuther on the way."

"Number of children fathered got little enough to do with being a good daddy."

"You got that big nigger Hell No livin' with you. God'll strike you down for that. Must be that Cherokee blood. You don't belong here. Never did, Injun woman."

A stunned Lou looked at Louisa. Yankee. And Indian.

"His name is Eugene," said Louisa. "And my daddy were part Apache, not Cherokee. And the God I know punishes the wicked. Like men who beat their children." Louisa took one more step forward. "You ever lay a hand on that child agin, best pray to whatever god *you* counsel with I ain't find you."

Davis laughed nastily. "You scaring me, old woman."

"Then you smarter than I thought."

Davis's hand curled to a fist and he looked ready to swing until he saw big Eugene filling the doorway, and his courage seemed to peter away.

Davis grabbed Billy. "Boy, you git on home. Git!" Billy raced out of the room. Davis followed slowly, taking his time. He looked back at Louisa. "This ain't over. No sir." He banged the door shut on his way out.

CHAPTER TWENTY-TWO

SCHOOL HAD ENDED FOR THE YEAR, AND THE HARD work of farming had begun. Each day Louisa rose particularly early, before the night even seemed to have settled in, and made Lou get up too. The girl did both her and Oz's chores as punishment for fighting with Billy, and then they all spent the day working the fields. They ate simple lunches and drank cold springwater under the shade of a cucumber magnolia, none of them saying much, the sweat seeping through their clothes. During these breaks Oz threw rocks so far the others would smile and clap their hands. He was growing taller, the muscles in his arms and shoulders becoming more and more pronounced, the hard work fashioning in him a lean, hard strength. As it did in his sister. As it seemed to in most who struggled to survive here.

The days were warm enough now that Oz wore only his overalls and no shirt or shoes. Lou had on overalls and was barefoot as well, but she wore an old cotton undershirt. The sun was intense at this elevation and they were becoming blonder and darker every day.

Louisa kept teaching the children things: She explained

how blue lake beans have no strings, but pole beans, grown around the cornstalks, do, and they'll choke you if you don't first string them. And that they could raise most of their crop seed, except for oats, which required machinery to thresh them, machinery that simple mountain farmers would never have. And how to wash the clothes using the washboard and just enough soap made from lye and pig fat—but not too much—keeping the fire hot, rinsing the clothes properly, and adding bluing on the third rinse to get everything good and white. And then at night, by firelight, how to darn with needle and thread. Louisa even talked of when would be a good time for Lou and Oz to learn the fine arts of mule shoeing and quilting by frame.

Louisa also finally found time to teach Lou and Oz to ride Sue the mare. Eugene would hoist them, by turns, up on the mare, bareback, without even a blanket.

"Where's the saddle?" Lou asked. "And the stirrups?"

"Your saddle's your rump. A pair of strong legs your stirrups," Louisa answered.

Lou sat up on Sue while Louisa stood beside the mare.

"Now, Lou, hold the reins in your right hand like I done showed you, like you mean it now!" said Louisa. "Sue'll let you get by with some, but you got to let her know who's boss."

Lou flicked the reins, prodded the horse's sides, generally kicked up a good row, and Sue remained absolutely motionless, as though she were sound asleep.

"Dumb horse," Lou finally declared.

"Eugene," Louisa called out to the field. "Come give me a boost up, please, honey."

Eugene limped over and helped Louisa up on the horse, and she settled in behind Lou and took the reins.

"Now, the problem ain't that Sue's dumb, it's that you ain't speaking her way yet. Now, when you want Sue to go, you give her a nice punch in the middle and make a little *chk-chk* noise. To her that means go. When you want her to turn, you don't jerk on the reins, you just glide them like. To stop, a little quick tug back."

Lou did as Louisa had shown her, and Sue started moving. Lou glided the reins to the left and the horse actually went that way. She fast-tugged back on the reins and Sue came to a slow stop.

Lou broke into a big smile. "Hey, look at me. I'm riding."

From Amanda's bedroom window, Cotton leaned his head out and watched. Then he looked to the beautiful sky, and then over at Amanda in the bed.

A few minutes later, the front door opened and Cotton carried Amanda outside and put her in the rocking chair there, next to a screen of maypops that were in full bloom of leathery purple.

Oz, who was now up on Sue with his sister, looked over, saw his mother, and almost fell off the horse. "Hey, Mom, look at me. I'm a cowboy!" Louisa stood next to the horse, staring over at Amanda. Lou finally looked, but she didn't seem very excited to see her mother outside. Cotton's gaze went from daughter to mother, and even Cotton had to admit, the woman looked pitifully out of place in the sunshine, her eyes closed, the breeze not lifting her short hair, as though even the elements had abandoned her. He carried her back inside.

It was a bright summer's morning a few days later, and Lou had just finished milking the cows and was coming out of the barn with full buckets in her arms. She stopped dead as she stared across at the fields. She ran so fast to the house that the milk splashed around her feet. She set the buckets on the porch and ran into the house, past Louisa and Eugene and down the hall yelling at the top of her lungs. She burst into her mother's room, and there was Oz sitting next to her, brushing her hair.

Lou was breathless. "It's working. It's green. Everything. The crops are coming up. Oz, go see." Oz raced out of the room so fast he forgot he only had on his underwear. Lou stood there in the middle of the room, her chest heaving, her smile wide. As her breathing calmed, Lou went over to her mother and sat down, took up a limp hand. "I just thought you'd like to know. See, we've been working really hard." Lou sat there in silence for a minute more, and then put the hand down and left, her excitement spent.

In her bedroom that night, as on so many other evenings, Louisa worked the Singer pedal sewing machine she had bought for ten dollars on installment nine years back. She wouldn't reveal to the children what she was making, and wouldn't even let them guess. Yet Lou knew it must be something for her and Oz, which made her feel even guiltier about the fight with Billy Davis.

After supper the next evening, Oz went to see his mother, and Eugene went to work on some scythes in the corncrib. Lou washed the dishes, and then sat on the front porch next to Louisa. For a while, neither ventured to talk. Lou saw a pair of titmice fly out of the barn and land on the fence. Their gray plumage and pointed crests were glorious, but the girl wasn't much interested.

"I'm sorry about the fighting," Lou said quickly, and let out a relieved breath that her apology was finally done.

Louisa stared at the two mules in the pen. "Good to know," she said, and then said no more. The sun was starting its fall and the sky was fairly clear, with not many clouds worth noting. A big crow was sky-surfing alone, catching one drift of wind and then another, like a lazily falling leaf.

Lou cupped some dirt and watched a battalion of ants trail across her hand. The honeysuckle vine was in full, scented morning glory, filling the air along with the fragrances of cinnamon rose and clove pinks, and the purple wall of maypops dutifully shaded the porch. Rambling rose had twisted itself around most of the fence posts and looked like bursts of still fire.

"George Davis is an awful man," said Lou.

Louisa leaned her back against the porch railing. "Work his children like mules and treats his mules better'n his children."

"Well, Billy didn't have to be mean to me," Lou said, and then grinned. "And it was funny to see him fall out of that tree when he saw the dead snake I put in his lunch pail."

Louisa leaned forward and looked at her curiously. "You see anythin' else in that pail?"

"Anything else? Like what?"

"Like food."

Lou appeared confused. "No, the pail was empty."

Louisa slowly nodded, settled back against the railing once more, and looked to the west, where the sun was commencing its creep behind the mountains, kindling the sky pink and red.

Louisa said, "You know what I find funny? That children believe they should be shamed 'cause their daddy don't see fit to give them food. So shamed they'd haul an empty pail to school and pretend to eat, so's nobody catch on they ain't got nothing to eat. You find that funny?"

Lou shook her head, her gaze at her feet. "No."

"I know I ain't talked to you 'bout your daddy. But my heart goes out to you and Oz, and I love both of you even more, on 'count of I want to make up for that loss, even though I know I can't." She put a hand on Lou's shoulder and turned the girl to her. "But you had a fine daddy. A man who loved you. And I know that makes it all the harder to get by, and that's both a blessing and a curse that we all just got to bear in this life. But thing is, Billy Davis got to live with his daddy ever day. I'd ruther be in your shoes. And I know Billy Davis would. I pray for all them children ever day. And you should too."

CHAPTER TWENTY-THREE

THE GRANDMOTHER CLOCK HAD JUST STRUCK MID-
night when the pebbles hit Lou's window. The girl
was in the middle of a dream that disintegrated
under the sudden clatter. Lou stepped to the window and
looked out, seeing nothing at first. Then she spotted her
caller and opened the window.

"What do you think you're doing, Diamond Skinner?"

"Come get you," said the boy, standing there next to
his faithful hound.

"For what?"

In answer he pointed at the moon. It glowed more
brightly than Lou had ever seen before. So fine was her
view, she could see dark smudges on its surface.

"I can see the moon all by myself, thank you very
much," she said.

Diamond smiled. "Naw, not just that. Fetch your
brother. Come on, now, it be fun where we going. You
see."

Lou looked unsure. "How far is it?"

"Not fer. Ain't scared of the dark, are ya?"

"Wait right there," she said and shut the window.

In five minutes' time Lou and Oz were fully dressed and had crept out of the farmhouse and joined Diamond and Jeb.

Lou yawned. "This better be good, Diamond, or *you* should be scared for waking us up."

They set out at a good pace to the south. Diamond kept up an animated chatter the whole way, yet absolutely refused to divulge where they were going. Lou finally quit trying and looked at the boy's bare feet as he stepped easily over some sharp-edged rocks. She and Oz were wearing their shoes.

"Diamond, don't your feet ever get sore or cold?" she asked as they paused on a small knoll to catch their breath.

"Snow comes, then mebbe y'all see something on my feet, but only if it drifts to more'n ten foot or so. Come on now."

They set off again, and twenty minutes later, Lou and Oz could hear the quickened rush of water. A minute later Diamond put up his hand and they all stopped. "Got to go real slow here," he said. They followed him closely as they moved over rocks that were becoming more slippery with each step; and the sound of the rushing water seemed to be coming at them from all quarters, as though they were about to be confronted by a tidal wave. Lou gripped Oz's hand for it was all a little unnerving to her, and thus she assumed her brother must be suffering stark terror. They cleared a stand of towering birch and weeping willow heavy with water, and Lou and Oz looked up in awe.

The waterfall was almost one hundred feet high. It poured out from a crop of worn limestone and plummeted straight down into a pool of foamy water, which then snaked off into the darkness. And then Lou suddenly realized what Diamond had meant about the moon. It glowed so brightly, and the waterfall and pool were placed so perfectly, that the trio were surrounded by a sea of illumination. The reflected light was so strong, in fact, that night seemed to have been turned into day.

They moved back farther, to a place where they could still see everything but the noise of the falls wasn't as intense and they could speak without having to shout over the thunder of the water.

"Feeder line for the McCloud River is all," said Diamond. "Right higher'n most though."

"It looks like it's snowing upwards," said Lou, as she sat, amazed, upon a moss-covered rock. And with the frothing water kicking high and then seized by the powerful light, it did look like snow was somehow returning to the sky. At one corner of the pool the water was especially brilliant. They gathered at this place.

Diamond said very solemnly, "Right there's where God done touched the earth."

Lou leaned forward and examined the spot closely. She turned to Diamond and said, "Phosphorus."

"What?" he said.

"I think it's phosphorus rock. I've studied it in school."

"Say that word agin," said Diamond.

And she did, and Diamond said it over and over until it slipped quite easily out of his mouth. He proclaimed it a grand and pleasing word to say, yet still defined it as a thing God had touched, and Lou did not have the heart to say otherwise.

Oz leaned forward and dipped his hand into the pool, then pulled it back immediately and shivered.

"Always that way," said Diamond, "even on the hottest durn day." He looked around, a smile on his lips. "But it sure purty."

"Thanks for bringing us," said Lou.

"Tote all my friends here," he said amiably and then looked to the sky. "Hey, y'all knowed your stars good?"

"Some of them," Lou said. "The Big Dipper, and Pegasus."

"Ain't never heard'a none of them." Diamond pointed to the northern sky. "Turn your head a little and right there's what I call the bear what missing one leg. And over to there's the stone chimbly. And right there"—he stabbed his finger more to the south—"now right there is Jesus a'sitting next to God. Only God ain't there, 'cause he off doing good. 'Cause he God. But you see the chair." He looked back at them. "Ain'tcha' now? See it?"

Oz said that he could see them all, clear as day though it was night. Lou hesitated, wondering whether it was better to instruct Diamond on proper constellations or not. She finally smiled. "You know a lot more about stars than we do, Diamond. Now that you pointed them out, I can see them all too."

Diamond grinned big. "Well, up here on the mountain, we a lot closer to 'em than down to the city. Don't worry, I teach you good."

They spent a pleasant hour there and then Lou thought it would be best if they got back.

They were about halfway home when Jeb started growling and making slow circles in the tall grass, his snout wrinkled and his teeth bared.

"What's wrong with him, Diamond?" asked Lou.

"Just smells something. Lotta critters round. Don't pay him no mind."

Suddenly Jeb took off running hard and howling so loud it hurt their ears.

"Jeb!" Diamond called after him. "You come back here now." The dog never slowed, though, and they finally saw why. The black bear was moving in long strides across the far fringe of the meadow.

"Dang it, Jeb, leave that bear be." Diamond raced after the dog, and Lou and Oz ran after Diamond. But dog and bear soon left the two-legs in the dust. Diamond finally stopped, gasping for air, and Lou and Oz ran up to him and fell on the ground, their lungs near bursting.

Diamond smacked his fist into his palm. "Dang that dog."

"Will that bear hurt him?" asked Oz anxiously.

"Shoot, naw. Jeb pro'bly tree the durn thing and then get tired and go on home." Diamond didn't look convinced though. "Come on now."

They walked briskly for some minutes, until Diamond slowed, looked around, and held up his hand for them to stop. He turned, put a finger to his lips, and motioned for them to follow, but to keep low. They scooted along for about thirty feet, and then Diamond went down on his belly and Lou and Oz did too. They crawled forward and were soon on the rim of a little hollow. It was surrounded by trees and underbrush, the limbs and vines overhanging the place and forming a natural roof, but the shafts of moonlight had broken through in places, leaving the space well illuminated.

"What is it?" Lou wanted to know.

"Shh," Diamond said, and then cupped his hand around her ear and whispered. "Man's still."

Lou looked again, and picked up on the bulky contraption with its big metal belly, copper tubing, and wooden block legs. Jugs to be filled with the corn whiskey sat on boards placed over stacked stone. A lit kerosene lamp was hooked to a slender post thrust into the moist ground. Steam rose from the still. They heard movement.

Lou flinched as George Davis appeared next to the still and flopped down a forty-pound burlap bag. The man was intent on his work and apparently never heard them. Lou looked at Oz, who was shaking so hard Lou was afraid George Davis might feel the ground vibrating. She tugged at Diamond and pointed to where they had come from. Diamond nodded in agreement and they began to slither backward. Lou glanced back at the still, but Davis had disappeared. She froze. And then she nearly screamed because she heard something coming and feared the worst.

The bear flashed by her line of sight first and into the hollow. Then came Jeb. The bear cut a sharp corner, and the dog skidded into the post holding the lamp and knocked it over. The lamp hit the ground and smashed. The bear careened into the still, and metal gave way under three hundred pounds of black bear and fell over, breaking open and tearing loose the copper tubing. Diamond raced into the hollow, yelling at his dog.

The bear apparently was weary of being chased and turned and rose up on its hind legs, its claws and teeth now quite prominent. Jeb stopped dead at the sight of the six-foot black wall that could bite him in half, and backed up, growling. Diamond reached the hound and pulled at his neck.

"Jeb, you fool thing!"

"Diamond!" Lou called out as she too jumped up and saw the man coming at her friend.

"What the hell!" Davis had emerged from the darkness, shotgun in hand.

"Diamond, look out!" screamed Lou again.

The bear roared, the dog barked, Diamond hollered, and Davis pointed his shotgun and swore. The gun fired twice, and bear, dog, and boy took off running like the holy hell. Lou ducked as the buckshot tore through leaves and imbedded in bark. "Run, Oz, run," screamed Lou. Oz jumped up and ran, but the boy was confused, for he headed into the hollow instead of away from it. Davis was reloading his shotgun when Oz came upon him. The boy realized his mistake too late, and Davis snagged him by the collar. Lou ran toward them. "Diamond!" screamed Lou once more. "Help!"

Davis had Oz pinned against his leg with one hand and was trying to reload his gun with the other.

"Gawd damn you," the man thundered at the cowering boy.

Lou flung her fists into him but didn't do any damage, for though he was short, George Davis was hard as brick.

"You let him go," Lou yelled. "Let him go!"

Davis did let go of Oz, but only so he could strike Lou. She crumpled to the ground, her mouth bleeding. But the man never saw Diamond. The boy picked up the fallen post, swung it, and clipped Davis's legs out from under him, sending the man down hard. Then Diamond conked Davis on the head with the post for good measure. Lou grabbed Oz, and Diamond grabbed Lou, and the three were more than fifty yards from the hollow by the time George Davis regained his legs in a lathered fury. A few seconds after that, they heard one more shotgun blast, but they were well out of range by then.

They heard running behind them and picked up their pace. Then Diamond looked back and said that it was okay, it was only Jeb. They ran all the way back to the farmhouse, where they collapsed on the front porch, their breathing tortured, their limbs shaking from both fatigue and fright.

When they sat up, Lou considered taking up the run once more because Louisa was standing there in her night-dress looking at them and holding a kerosene lamp. She wanted to know where they'd been. Diamond tried to answer for them, but Louisa told him to hush in a tone so sharp it struck the always chatty Diamond mute.

"The truth, Lou," ordered the woman.

And Lou told her, including the almost deadly run-in with George Davis. "But it wasn't our fault," she said. "That bear—"

Louisa snapped, "Get yourself to the barn, Diamond. And take that dang dog with you."

"Yes'm," said Diamond, and he and Jeb slunk away.

Louisa turned back to Lou and Oz. Lou could see she was trembling. "Oz, you get yourself to bed. Right now."

Oz glanced once at Lou and fled inside. And then it was just Lou and Louisa.

Lou stood there as nervous as she had ever been.

"You could'a got yourself kilt tonight. Worse'n that you could'a got you *and* your brother kilt."

"But, Louisa, it wasn't our fault. You see—"

"Is your fault!" Louisa said fiercely, and Lou felt the tears rush to her eyes at the woman's tone.

"I didn't have you come to this mountain to die at the sorry hands of George Davis, girl. You gone off on your own bad enough. But taking your little brother too—and he follow you cross *fire,* not knowing no better—I'm ashamed of you!"

Lou bowed her head. "I'm sorry. I'm really sorry."

Louisa stood very erect. "I ain't never raised my hand to a child, though my patience run sore over the years. But if you ever do somethin' like that agin, you gonna find my hand 'cross your skin, missy, and it be some-thin' you ain't never forget. You unnerstand me?" Lou nodded dumbly. "Then get to bed," said Louisa. "And we speak no more of it."

The next morning George Davis rode up on his wagon pulled by a pair of mules. Louisa came outside to face him, her hands behind her back.

Davis spit chew onto the ground next to the wagon wheel. "Them devils broke up my propity. Here to get paid."

"You mean for busting up your *still.*"

Lou and Oz came outside and stared at the man.

"Devils!" he roared. "Gawd damn you!"

Louisa stepped off the porch. "If you gonna talk that way, git yourself off my land. Now!"

"I want my money! And I want them beat bad for what they done!"

"You fetch the sheriff and go show him what they done to your still, and then *he* can tell me what's fair."

Davis stared at her dumbly, the mule whip clenched in one hand. "You knowed I can't do that, woman."

"Then you know the way off my land, George."

"How 'bout I put the torch to your farm?"

Eugene came outside, a long stick in his big hand.

Davis held up the whip. "Hell No, you keep your nigger self right there afore I put the whip to you just like your granddaddy had 'cross his back!" Davis started to get down from the wagon. "Mebbe I'll just do it anyway, boy. Mebbe all'a you!"

Louisa pulled the rifle from behind her back and leveled it at George Davis. The man stopped halfway off his wagon when he saw the Winchester's long barrel pointed at him.

"Get off my land," Louisa said quietly, as she cocked the weapon and rested its butt against her shoulder, her finger on the trigger. "Afore I lose my patience, and you lose some blood."

"I pay you, George Davis," Diamond called out as he came out of the barn, Jeb trailing him.

Davis visibly shook, he was so angry. "My damn head's still ringing from where you done walloped me, boy."

"You durn lucky then, 'cause I could'a hit you a lot harder if'n I wanted to."

"Don't you smartmouth me!" Davis roared.

"You want'a git your money or not?" said Diamond.

"What you got? You ain't got nuthin'."

Diamond put his hand in his pocket and drew out a coin. "Got me this. Silver dollar."

"Dollar! You wreck my still, boy. Think a damn dollar gonna fix that? Fool!"

"It done come from my great-granddaddy five times removed. A hunnerd year old it is. Man down Tremont say he gimme twenty dollar for it."

Davis's eyes lighted up at this. "Lemme see it."

"Naw. Take it or leave it. I telling the truth. Twenty dollar. Man named Monroe Darcy. He run the store down Tremont. You knowed him."

Davis was silent for a bit. "Gimme it."

"Diamond," Lou called out, "don't do it."

"Man got to pay his debts," said Diamond. He sauntered over to the wagon. When Davis reached out for the coin, Diamond pulled it back. "Look here, George Davis, this means we square. You ain't coming round to Miss Louisa for nuthin' if'n I give you this. You got to swear."

Davis looked like he might put the whip to Diamond's back instead, but he said, "I swear. Now gimme it!"

Diamond flipped the coin to Davis, who caught it, studied it, bit on it, and then stashed it in his pocket.

"Now git yourself gone, George," said Louisa.

Davis glared at her. "Next time, *my* gun don't miss."

He turned mules and wagon around and left in a whirl of dust. Lou stared at Louisa, who held the rifle on Davis until the man was out of sight. "Would you really have shot him?" she asked.

Louisa uncocked the rifle and went inside without answering the question.

CHAPTER TWENTY-FOUR

LOU WAS CLEANING UP THE SUPPER DISHES TWO NIGHTS later while Oz carefully wrote out his letters on a piece of paper at the kitchen table. Louisa sat next to him, helping. She looked tired, Lou thought. She was old, and life up here wasn't easy; Lou had certainly experienced that firsthand. One had to fight for each little thing. And Louisa had been doing this all her life. How much longer could she?

By the time Lou had dried the last plate, there came a knock on the door. Oz ran to open it.

Cotton was standing at the front door, wearing his suit and tie, a large box cradled in his arms. Behind him was Diamond. The boy was dressed in a clean white shirt, face scrubbed, hair pounded down with water and maybe sticky sap, and Lou almost gasped, because the boy was wearing *shoes*. It was true she could see his toes, but still most of the boy's feet were covered. Diamond nodded shyly to all, as though being scrubbed and shod made him a circus spectacle of sorts.

Oz eyed the box. "What's in there?"

Cotton set the box on the table and took his time opening it. "While there is much to be said for the written word," he told them, "we must never forget that other great creative body of work." With a flourish to rival the best of vaudeville performances, he unveiled the gramophone.

"Music!"

Cotton took a record out of a slipcase and carefully placed it on the gramophone. Then he vigorously turned the crank and set the needle in place. It scratched the wobbly record for a moment, and then the room was filled with what Lou recognized as the music of Beethoven. Cotton looked around the room and then moved a chair against the wall. He motioned to the other men. "Gentlemen, if you please." Oz, Diamond, and Eugene pitched in, and they soon had an open space in the middle of the room.

Cotton went down the hallway and opened Amanda's door. "Miss Amanda, we have a variety of popular tunes for your listening pleasure tonight."

Cotton came back to the front room.

"Why did you move the furniture?" Lou asked.

Cotton smiled and removed his suit coat. "Because you can't simply listen to music, you must become one with it." He bowed deeply to Lou. "May I have this dance, ma'am?"

Lou found herself blushing at this formal invitation. "Cotton, you're crazy, you really are."

Oz said, "Go ahead, Lou, you're a good dancer." He added, "Mom taught her."

And they danced. Awkwardly at first, but then they picked up their pace and soon were spinning around the room. All smiled at the pair, and Lou found herself giggling.

Overcome with excitement, as he so often was, Oz ran to his mother's room. "Mom, we're dancing, we're dancing." And then he raced back to see some more.

Louisa was moving her hands to the music, and her foot was tapping against the floor. Diamond came up.

"Care to stroll the floor, Miss Louisa?"

She took his hands. "Best offer I had me in years."

As they joined Lou and Cotton, Eugene stood Oz on the tops of his shoes, and they clomped around with the others.

The music and laughter drifted down the hall and into Amanda's room. Since they had been here, winter had turned to spring and spring had given way to summer. And during all that time, Amanda's condition had not changed. Lou interpreted that as positive proof that her mother would never rejoin them, while Oz, ever the optimist, saw it as a good thing, because his mother's condition had not become any worse. Despite her bleak opinion of her mother's future, Lou helped Louisa spongebathe Amanda every day and also wash her hair once a week. And both Lou and Oz changed their mother's resting positions frequently and exercised her arms and legs daily. Yet there was never any reaction from their mother; she was just there, eyes closed, limbs motionless. She was not "dead," but what her mother was could surely not be called "living" either, Lou had often thought. However, something was a little odd now with the music and laughter filtering into her room. Perhaps if it was possible to smile without moving one facial muscle, Amanda Cardinal had just accomplished it.

Back in the front room a few records later, the music had changed to tunes designed to make one kick up his heels. The partners had also changed: Lou and Diamond jumped and spun with youthful energy; Cotton twirled Oz; and Eugene—bad leg and all—and Louisa were doing a modest jitterbug.

Cotton left the dance floor after a while and went to Amanda's bedroom and sat next to her. He spoke to her very quietly, relaying news of the day, how the children were doing, the next book he intended to read to her. All just normal conversation, really, and Cotton hoping that she could hear him and be encouraged by it. "I have enjoyed the letters you wrote to Louisa immensely. Your words show a beautiful spirit. However, I look forward to getting to know you personally, Amanda." He took her hands very gently and moved them slowly to the music.

The sounds drifted outside, and the light spilled into the darkness. For one stolen moment, all in the house seemed happy and secure.

The small coal mine on Louisa's land was about two miles from the house. There was a matted-down path leading to it, and that connected with a dirt road that snaked back to the farm. The opening of the mine was broad and tall enough for sled and mule to enter easily, which they did each year to bring out coal for the winter's heat. With the moon now shielded by high clouds, the entrance to the mine was invisible to the naked eye.

Off in the distance there was a wink of light, like a

firefly. Then came another flash and then another. Slowly
the group of men emerged from the darkness and came
toward the mine, the blinks of light now revealed as lit
kerosene lamps. The men wore hard hats with carbide
lamps strapped to them. In preparation for entering the
mine, each man took off his hat, filled the lamp pouch
with moistened carbide pellets, turned the handle, which
adjusted the wick, struck a match, and a dozen lamps together ignited.

A man bigger than all the others called the workers
around, and they formed a tight huddle. His name was
Judd Wheeler, and he had been exploring dirt and rock
looking for things of value most of his adult life. In one
big hand he held a long roll of paper which he spread
open, and one of the men shone a lantern upon it. The
paper held detailed markings, writing and drawings. The
caption on the paper was printed boldly across the top:
"Southern Valley Coal and Gas Geological Survey."

As Wheeler instructed his men on tonight's duties, from
out of the darkness another man joined them. He wore
the same felt hat and old clothes. George Davis also held
a kerosene lamp and appeared quite excited at all the activity. Davis spoke animatedly with Wheeler for a few
minutes, and then they all headed inside the mine.

CHAPTER TWENTY-FIVE

LOU WOKE EARLY THE NEXT MORNING. THE SOUNDS of music had stayed with her through the night, and her dreams had been pleasant ones. She stretched, gingerly touched the floor, and went to look out the window. The sun had already begun its rise and she knew she had to get to the barn to milk, a task she had rapidly taken as her own, for she had grown to like the coolness of the barn in the morning, and also the smell of the cows and the hay. She would sometimes climb to the loft, push open the hay doors, and sit on the edge there, gazing out at the land from her high perch, listening to the sounds of birds and small animals darting through trees, crop field, and high grass and catching the breeze that always seemed to be there.

This was just such another morning of flaming skies, brooding mountains, the playful lift of birds, the efficient business of animals, trees, and flowers. However, Lou was not prepared for the sight of Diamond and Jeb slipping out of the barn and heading off down the road.

Lou dressed quickly and went downstairs. Louisa had food on the table, though Oz had not yet appeared.

"That was fun last night," Lou said, sitting at the table.

"You prob'ly laugh now, but when I's younger, I could do me some stompin'," remarked Louisa, as she put a biscuit covered with gravy and a glass of milk on the table for Lou.

"Diamond must have slept in the barn," said Lou as she bit into her biscuit. "Don't his parents worry about him?" She gave Louisa a sideways glance and added, "Or I guess I should be asking if he has any parents."

Louisa sighed and then stared at Lou. "His mother passed when he was born. Happen right often up here. Too often. His daddy joined her four year ago."

Lou put down her biscuit. "How did his father die?"

"No business of ours, Lou."

"Does this have anything to do with what Diamond did to that man's car?"

Louisa sat and tapped her fingers against the table.

"Please, Louisa, please. I really want to know. I care about Diamond. He's my friend."

"Blasting at one of the mines," Louisa said bluntly. "Took down a hillside. A hillside Donovan Skinner was farming."

"Who does Diamond live with then?"

"He a wild bird. Put him in a cage, he just shrivel up and die. He need anythin', he know to come to me."

"Did the coal company have to pay for what happened?"

Louisa shook her head. "Played legal tricks. Cotton tried to help but weren't much he could do. Southern Valley's a powerful force hereabouts."

"Poor Diamond."

"Boy sure didn't take it lying down," Louisa said. "One time the wheels of a motorman's car fell off when it come out the mine. And then a coal tipple wouldn't open and they had to send for some people from Roanoke. Found a rock stuck in the gears. That same coal mine boss, he was in an outhouse one time got tipped over. Durn door wouldn't open, and he spent a sorry hour in there. To this day nobody ever figgered out who tipped it over or how that rope got round it."

"Did Diamond ever get in trouble?"

"Henry Atkins the judge. He a good man, know what was what, so's nothing ever come of it. But Cotton kept talking to Diamond, and the mischief finally quit." She paused. "Least it did till the horse manure got in that man's car."

Louisa turned away, but Lou had already seen the woman's broad smile.

※

Lou and Oz rode Sue every day and had gotten to the point where Louisa had proclaimed them good, competent riders. Lou loved riding Sue. She could see forever, it seemed, from that high perch, the mare's body wide enough that falling off seemed impossible.

After morning chores, they would go swimming with Diamond at Scott's Hole, a patch of water Diamond had introduced them to, and which he claimed had no bottom. As the summer went along Lou and Oz became dark brown, while Diamond simply grew larger freckles.

Eugene came with them as often as he could, and Lou was surprised to learn he was only twenty-one. He did not know how to swim, but the children remedied that, and

Eugene was soon performing different strokes, and even flips, in the cool water, his bad leg not holding him back any in that environment.

They played baseball in a field of bluegrass they had scythed. Eugene had fashioned a bat from an oak plank shaved narrow at one end. They used Diamond's coverless ball and another made from a bit of rubber wound round with sheep's wool and knitted twine. The bases were pieces of shale set in a straight line, this being the proper way according to Diamond, who termed it straight-town baseball. New York Yankees' fan Lou said nothing about this, and let the boy have his fun. It got so that none of them, not even Eugene, could hit a ball that Oz threw, so fast and tricky did it come.

They spent many afternoons running through the adventures of the Wizard of Oz, making up parts they had forgotten, or which they thought, with youthful confidence, could be improved upon. Diamond was quite partial to the Scarecrow; Oz, of course, had to be the cowardly lion; and, by default, Lou was the heartless tin man. They unanimously proclaimed Eugene the Great and Mighty Wizard, and he would come out from behind a rock and bellow out lines they had taught him so loud and with such a depth of feigned anger that Oz, the Cowardly Lion, asked Eugene, the Mighty Wizard, if he could please tone it down a bit. They fought many pitched battles against flying monkeys and melting witches, and with a little ingenuity and some luck at just the right moments, good always triumphed over evil on the glorious Virginia mountain.

Diamond told them of how in the winter he would skate on the top of Scott's Hole. And how using a short-handled ax he would cleave off a strip of bark from an oak and use that as his sled to go sailing down the iced slopes of the mountains at speeds never before achieved by a human being. He said he would be glad to show them how he did it, but would have to swear them to secrecy, lest the wrong sort of folks found out and maybe took over the world with such valuable knowledge.

Lou did not once let on that she knew about Diamond's parents. After hours of fun, they would say their good-byes and Lou and Oz would ride home on Sue or take turns with Eugene when he came with them. Diamond would stay behind and swim some more or hit the ball, doing, as he often said, just as he pleased.

On the ride back home after one of these outings, Lou decided to take a different way. A fine mist hung over the mountains as she and Oz approached the farmhouse from the rear. They cleared a rise, and on top of a little knoll about a half-mile from the house, Lou reined Sue to a halt. Oz squirmed behind her.

"Come on, Lou, we need to get back. We've got chores."

Instead, the girl clambered off Sue, leaving Oz to grab at the reins, which almost made him fall off the animal. He called crossly after her, but she seemed not to hear.

Lou went over to the little cleared space under the dense shade of an evergreen and knelt down. The grave markers were simple pieces of wood grayed by the weather. And clearly much time had passed. Lou read the names of the dead and the bracket dates of their existence, which were carved deeply into the wood and were probably about as distinct as the day they were chiseled.

The first name was Joshua Cardinal. The date of his birth and death made Lou believe that he must have been Louisa's husband, Lou and Oz's great-grandfather. He had passed in his fifty-second year—not that long of a life, Lou thought. The second grave marker was a name that Lou knew from her father. Jacob Cardinal was her father's father, her and Oz's grandfather. As she recited the name, Oz joined her and knelt down in the grass. He pulled off his straw hat and said nothing. Their grandfather had died far younger than even his father. Was there something about this place? Lou wondered. But then she thought of how old Louisa was, and the wondering stopped there.

The third grave marker looked to be the oldest. It only had a name on it, no dates of birth or death.

"Annie Cardinal," Lou said out loud. For a time the two just knelt there and stared at the pieces of board marking the remains of family they had never known. Then Lou rose, went over to Sue, gripped the horse's bushy mane, climbed up, and then helped Oz on board. Neither spoke all the way back.

At supper that night, more than once Lou was about to venture a question to Louisa about what they had seen, but then something made her not. Oz was obviously just as curious, yet, like always, he was inclined to follow his sister's lead. They had time, Lou figured, for all of their questions to be answered. Before she went to sleep that night, Lou went out on the back porch and looked up to that knoll. Even with a nice slice of moon she could not see the graveyard from here, yet now she knew where it was. She had never much been interested in the dead, particularly since losing her father. Now she knew that she would go back soon to that burying ground and look once more at those bits of plain board set in dirt and engraved with the names of her flesh and blood.

CHAPTER TWENTY-SIX

COTTON SHOWED UP WITH DIAMOND A WEEK LATER and handed out small American flags to Lou, Oz, and Eugene. He had also brought a five-gallon can of gas, which he put in the Hudson's fuel tank. "We all can't fit in the Olds," he explained. "And I handled an estate problem for Leroy Meekins who runs the Esso station. Leroy doesn't like to pay in cash, though, so one could say I'm flush with oil products right now."

With Eugene driving, the five went down to Dickens to watch the parade. Louisa stayed behind to keep watch over Amanda, but they promised to bring her back something.

They ate hot dogs with great splotches of mustard and ketchup, swirls of cotton candy, and enough soda pop to make the children run to the public toilet with great frequency. There were contests of skill at booths set up wherever space was available, and Oz cleaned up on all those that involved throwing something in order to knock something else down. Lou bought a pretty bonnet for Louisa, which she let Oz carry in a paper bag.

The town was done up in red, white, and blue, and

both townfolk and those from the mountain lined both sides of the street as the floats came down. These barges on land were pulled by horse, mule, or truck and displayed the most important moments in America's history, which, to most native Virginians, had naturally all occurred in the Commonwealth. There was a group of children on one such float representing the original thirteen colonies, with one boy carrying the Virginia colors, which were far bigger than the flags the other children carried, and he wore the showiest costume as well. A regiment of decorated war veterans from the area trooped by, including several men with long beards and shriveled bodies who claimed to have served with both the honorable Bobby Lee and the fanatically pious Stonewall Jackson.

One float, sponsored by Southern Valley, was devoted to the mining of coal and was pulled by a customized Chevrolet truck painted gold. There wasn't a black-faced, wrecked-back miner in sight, but instead, smack in the center of the float, on a raised platform simulating a coal tipple, stood a pretty young woman with blond hair, a perfect complexion, and brilliant white teeth, wearing a sash that read "Miss Bituminous Coal 1940" and waving her hand as mechanically as a windup doll. Even the most dense in the crowd could probably grasp the implied connection between lumps of black rock and the pot of gold pulling it. And the men and boys gave the expected reaction of cheers and some catcalls to the passing beauty. There was one old and humpbacked woman standing next to Lou who told her that her husband and three sons all labored in the mines. The old woman watched the beauty queen with scornful eyes and then commented that that young gal had obviously never been near a coal mine in her entire life. And she wouldn't know a lump of coal if it jumped up and grabbed her in the bituminous.

High-ranking representatives of the town made important speeches, motivating the citizens into bursts of enthusiastic applause. The mayor held forth from a temporary stage, with smiling, expensively dressed men next to him, who, Cotton told Lou, were Southern Valley officials. The mayor was young and energetic, with slicked hair, wearing a nice suit and fashionable watch and chain, and carrying boundless enthusiasm in his beaming smile and hands reaching to the sky, as though ready to snag on any rainbows trying to slip by.

"Coal is king," the mayor announced into a clunky microphone almost as big as his head. "And what with the war heating up across the Atlantic and the mighty United States of America building ships and guns and tanks for our friends fighting Hitler, the steel mill's demands for coke, our good, patriotic Virginia coke, will skyrocket. And some say it won't be long before we join the fighting. Yes, prosperity is here in fine abundance and here it will stay," said the mayor. "Not only will our children live the glorious American dream, but their children will as well. And it will be all due to the good work of folks like Southern Valley and their unrelenting drive to bring out the black rock that is driving this town to greatness. Rest assured, folks, we will become the New York City of the south. One day some will look back and say, 'Who knew the outstanding things that destiny held for the likes of Dickens, Virginia?' But y'all already know, because I'm telling you right now. Hip-hip hooray for Southern Valley and Dickens, Virginia." And the exuberant mayor threw his straw boater hat high into the air. And the crowd joined him in the cheer, and more hats were catapulted into the swirling breeze. And though Diamond, Lou, Oz, Eugene, and Cotton all applauded too, and the children grinned happily at each other, Lou noticed that Cotton's expression wasn't one of unbridled optimism.

As night fell, they watched a display of fireworks color the sky, and then the group climbed in the Hudson and headed out of town. They had just passed the courthouse when Lou asked Cotton about the mayor's speech and his muted reaction to it.

"Well, I've seen this town go boom and bust before," he said. "And it usually happens when the politicians and the business types are cheering the loudest. So I just don't know. Maybe it'll be different this time, but I just don't know."

Lou was left to ponder this while the cheers of the fine celebration receded and then those sounds were gone entirely, replaced with wind whistling through rock and tree, as they headed back up the mountain.

❧

There had not been much rain, but Louisa wasn't worried yet, though she prayed every night for the skies to open up and bellow hard and long. They were weeding the cornfield, and it was a hot day and the flies and gnats were particularly bothersome. Lou scraped at the dirt, something just not seeming right. "We already planted the seeds. Can't they grow by themselves?"

"Lot of things go wrong in farming and one or two

most always do," Louisa answered. "And the work don't never stop, Lou. Just the way it is here."

Lou swung the hoe over her shoulder. "All I can say is, this corn better taste good."

"This here's field corn," Louisa told her. "For the animals."

Lou almost dropped her hoe. "We're doing all this work to feed the animals?"

"They work hard for us, we got to do the same for them. They got to eat too."

"Yeah, Lou," said Oz as he attacked the weeds with vigorous strokes. "How can hogs get fat if they don't eat? Tell me that."

They worked the hills of corn, side by side under the fierce sun, which was so close it almost seemed to Lou that she could reach up and pocket it. The katydids and crickets scraped tunes at them from all corners. Lou stopped hoeing and watched Cotton drive up to the house and get out.

"Cotton coming every day and reading to Mom is making Oz believe that she's going to get better," said Lou to Louisa, taking care that her brother did not hear her.

Louisa wielded the hoe blade with the energy of a young person and the skill of an old. "You right, it's so terrible bad having Cotton helping your momma."

"I didn't mean it like that. I like Cotton."

Louisa stopped and leaned on her hoe. "You should, because Cotton Longfellow's a good man, none better. He's helped me through many a hard time since he come here. Not just with his lawyering, but with his strong back. When Eugene hurt his leg bad, he was here ever day for a month doing field work when he could've been in Dickens making himself good money. He's helping your ma 'cause he wants her to get better. He wants her to be able to hold you and Oz agin."

Lou said nothing to this, but was having trouble getting the hoeing down, chopping instead of slicing. Louisa took a minute to show her again, and Lou picked up the proper technique quickly.

They worked for a while longer in silence, until Louisa straightened up and rubbed at her back. "Body's telling me to slow down a bit. But my body wants to eat come winter."

Lou stared out at the countryside. The sky looked painted in oils today, and the trees seemed to fill every spare inch with alluring green.

"How come Dad never came back?" Lou asked quietly.

Louisa followed Lou's gaze. "No law say a person got to come back to his home," she said.

"But he wrote about it in all his books. I know he loved it here."

Louisa stared at the girl and then said, "Let's go get us a cool drink." She told Oz to rest some, and they would bring him back some water. He immediately dropped his hoe, picked up some rocks, and started heaving and whooping at each toss, in a manner it seemed only little boys could successfully accomplish. He had taken to placing a tin can on top of a fence post and then throwing rocks at it until he knocked it off. He had become so good that one hard toss would now send the can flying.

They left him to his fun and went to the springhouse, which clung to one side of a steep slope below the house and was shaded by leaning oak and ash trees and a wall of giant rhododendrons. Next to this shack was a split poplar stump, the tip of a large honeycomb protruding from it, a swell of bees above that.

They took metal cups from nails on the wall and dipped them in the water, and then sat outside and drank. Louisa picked up the green leaves of a mountain spurge growing next to the springhouse, which revealed beautiful purple blossoms completely hidden underneath. "One of God's little secrets," she explained. Lou sat there, cup cradled between her dimpled knees, watching and listening to her great-grandmother in the pleasant shade as Louisa pointed out other things of interest. "Right there's an oriole. Don't see them much no more. Don't know why not." She pointed to another bird on a maple branch. "That's a chuck's-will-widder. Don't ask me how the durn thing got its name, 'cause I don't know." Finally, her face and tone grew serious.

"Your daddy's momma was never happy here. She from down the Shenandoah Valley. My son Jake met her at a cakewalk she come up for. They got married, way too fast, put up a little cabin near here. But I know she was all set for the city, though. The Valley was backward for her. Lord, these mountains must've seemed like the birth of the world to the poor girl. But she had your daddy, and for the next few years we had us the worst drought I ever seen. The less rain there was, the harder we worked. My boy soon lost his stake, and they moved in with us. Still no rain. Went through our animals. Went through durn near everything we had." Louisa clenched her hands and then released them. "But we still got by. And then the rains come and we fine after that. But when your daddy was seven, his momma had had enough of this life and she left. She ain't never bothered to learn the farm, and even the way round a frying pan, so's she weren't much help to Jake a'tall."

"But didn't Jake want to go with her?"

"Oh, I 'xpect he did, for she was a real purty little thing, and a young man is a young man. They ain't 'xactly made'a wood. But she didn't want him along, if you unnerstand me right, him being from the mountains and all. And she didn't want her own child neither." Louisa shook her head at this painful remembrance.

"Course, Jake never got over that. Then his daddy died soon after, which didn't help matters none for any of us." Louisa smiled. "But your father were the shiny star in our days. Even with that, though, we watched a man we loved die a little more each day, and there weren't nothing we could do. Two days after your daddy was ten years old, Jake died. Some say heart attack. I say heartbreak. And then it was just me and your daddy up here. We had us good times, Lou, lot of love twixt us. But your daddy suffered a lotta pain too." She stopped and took a drink of the cool water. "But I still wonder why he never come back not once."

"Do I remind you of him?" Lou asked quietly.

Louisa smiled. "Same fire, same bullheadedness. Big heart too. Like how you are with your brother. Your daddy always made me laugh twice a day. When I got up and right afore I went to bed. He say he want me begin and end my day with a smile."

"I wish Mom had let us write you. She said she would one day, but it never happened."

"Like to knock me over with a stick when the first letter come. I wrote her back some, but my eyes ain't that good no more. And paper and stamp scarce."

Lou looked very uncomfortable. "Mom asked Dad to move back to Virginia."

Louisa looked surprised. "And what'd your daddy say?"

Lou could not tell her the truth. "I don't know."

"Oh" was all Louisa offered in response.

Lou found herself growing upset with her father, something she could never remember doing before.

"I can't believe he just left you here by yourself."

"I *made* him go. Mountain no place for somebody like him. Got to share that boy with the world. And your daddy wrote to me all these years. And he give me money he ain't got. He done right by me. Don't you never think badly of him for that."

"But didn't it hurt, that he never came back?"

Louisa put an arm around the girl. "He *did* come back. I got me the three people he loved most in the whole world."

It had been a hard trek along a narrow trail that often petered out to harsh tangles, forcing Lou to dismount and walk the mare. It was a nice ride, though, for the birds were in full warbling splendor, and flowering horsemint poked up from piles of slate. She had passed secret coves overhung with willow and corralled by rock. Many of the coves were graced with cups of frothing springwater. There were neglected fields of long-vanished homesteads, the broomsedge flourishing there around the rock bones of chimneys without houses.

Finally, following the directions Louisa had given her, Lou found herself at the small house in the clearing. She looked over the property. It appeared likely that in another couple of years this homestead would also surrender to the wild that pressed against it on all sides. Trees stretched over the roof that had almost as many holes as shingles. Window glass was missing at various spots; a sapling was growing up through an opening in the front porch, and wild sumac clung to the splintered porch rails. The front door was hanging by a single nail; in fact it had been tied back so that the door always stood open. A horseshoe was nailed over the doorway, for luck, Lou assumed, and the place looked like it could use some. The surrounding fields, too, were all overgrown. And yet the dirt yard was neatly swept, there was no trash about, and a bed of peonies sat next to the house, with a lilac behind that, and a large snowball bush flourished by a small hand-crank well. A rosebush ran up a trellis on one side of the house. Lou had heard that roses thrived on neglect. If true, this was the most ignored rosebush Lou had ever seen, since it was bent over with the weight of its deep red blooms. Jeb came around the corner and barked at rider and horse. When Diamond came out of the house, he stopped dead and looked around, seemingly for a place to hide quick, but coming up empty.

"What you doing here?" he finally said.

Lou slid off the horse and knelt to play with Jeb. "Just came to pay a visit. Where are your folks?"

"Pa working. Ma went down to McKenzie's."

"Tell 'em I said hello."

Diamond thrust his hands in his pockets, bent one bare toe over the other. "Look, I got things to do."

"Like what?" asked Lou, rising.

"Like fishing. I got to go fishing."

"Well, I'll go with you."

He cocked his head at her. "You know how to fish?"

"They have lots of fishing holes in Brooklyn."

They stood on a makeshift pier built from a few planks of rough-hewn oak not even nailed together but merely wedged into the rocks that stuck out from the bank of the wide stream. Diamond strung the line with a squirmy pink worm while Lou looked on in disgust. A tomboy was a tomboy, but apparently a worm was a worm. He handed the extra pole to her.

"G'on cast your line out there."

Lou took the pole and hesitated.

"You want hep?"

"I can do it."

"See this here's a southern pole, and I 'xpect you prob'ly used to them newfangled northern poles."

"You're right, that's all I use. Northern pole."

To his credit, Diamond never cracked a smile, but just took the pole, showed her how to hold it, and then threw a near perfect cast.

Lou watched his technique carefully, took a couple of practice tosses, and then sailed a pretty cast herself.

"Why, that was 'bout good as any I throwed," Diamond said with all due southern modesty.

"Give me a couple more minutes and I'll do better than you," she said slyly.

"You still got to catch the fish," Diamond gamely replied.

A half hour later Diamond had hooked his third small-mouth and worked it to shore with steady motions. Lou looked at him, properly in awe of his obvious skill, but her competitive streak ran long, and she redoubled her efforts to trump her fish-mate.

Finally, without warning, her line went tight and she was pulled toward the water. With a whiplike effort, she reared the pole back, and a thick catfish came halfway out of the stream.

"Holy Lord," said Diamond as he saw this creature rise and then fall back into the water. "Biggest catfish I ever seed." He reached for the pole.

Lou cried out, "I got it, Diamond." He stepped back and watched girl and fish fighting it out on roughly equal terms. Lou appeared to be winning at first, the line going taut and then slacking, while Diamond called out words of advice and encouragement. Lou slipped and slid all over the unsteady pier, once more almost going in the water, before Diamond yanked on her overalls and pulled her back.

Finally, though, Lou grew weary and gasped out, "I need some help here, Diamond."

With both pulling on pole and line, the fish quickly was dragged to shore. Diamond reached down, hauled it out of the water, and dropped it on the boards, where it flopped from side to side. Fat and thick, it would be good eating, he said. Lou squatted down and looked proudly at her conquest, aided though it had been. Right as she peered really closely, the fish shimmied once more, then jumped in the air, and spat water, the hook working free from its mouth at the same time. Lou screamed and jumped back, knocked into Diamond, and they both went tumbling into the water. They came up sputtering and watched as the catfish flopped itself over to the edge of the pier, fell in the water, and was gone in a blink. Diamond and Lou looked at each other for a tortured moment and then commenced a titanic splashing battle. Their peals of laughter could probably be heard on the next mountain.

Lou sat in front of the fireplace while Diamond built up the flames so they could dry off. He went and got an old blanket that smelled to Lou of either Jeb, mildew, or both, but she told Diamond thank you as he put it around her shoulders. The inside of Diamond's house surprised her because it was neat and clean, though the pieces of furniture were few and obviously handmade. On the wall was an old photo of Diamond and a man Lou assumed was his father. There were no photos Lou could see of his mother. While the fire picked up, Jeb lay down next to her and started attending to some fleas in his fur.

Diamond expertly scaled the bass, ran a hickory stick through each, mouth to tail, and cooked them over the fire. Next he cut up an apple and rubbed the juice into the meat. Diamond showed Lou how to feel the rib cage of the fish and pry thick white meat from tiny bones. They ate with their fingers, and it was good. "Your dad was real nice-looking," Lou said, pointing to the picture.

Diamond looked over at the photo. "Yep, he was." He caught a breath and glared at Lou.

"Louisa told me," she said.

Diamond rose and poked the fire with a crooked stick. "Ain't right playing no tricks on me."

"Why didn't you tell me on your own?"

"Why should I?"

"Because we're friends."

This took the sting out of Diamond and he sat back down.

"You miss your mom?" Lou asked.

"Naw, how could I? Never knowed the woman." He ran his hand along the crumpling brick, mud, and horsehair of the fireplace, and his features grew troubled. "See, she died when I's born."

"That's okay, Diamond. You can still miss her, even if you didn't know her."

Diamond nodded, his thumb now idly scratching at a dirty cheek. "I do think 'bout what my momma were like. Ain't got no pitchers. My daddy told me course, but it ain't the same." He stopped, nudged a piece of firewood with a stick, and then said, "I think mostly 'bout what her voice was like. And how she smelled. The way her eyes and hair could'a catch the light just so. But I miss my daddy too, 'cause he were a good man. Schooled me all's I need to know. Hunting, fishing." He looked at her. "I bet you miss your daddy too."

Lou looked uncomfortable. She closed her eyes for a moment and nodded. "I miss him."

"Good thing you got your momma."

"No, I don't. I don't, Diamond."

"Looks bad now, but it be okay. Folks don't never leave out, less we fergit 'em. I ain't knowed much, but I knowed that."

Lou wanted to tell him that he didn't understand. His

mother was gone from him, without question. Lou sat atop quicksand with her mother. And Lou had to be there for Oz.

They sat listening to the sounds of the woods, as trees, bugs, animals, and birds went about their lives.

"How come you don't go to school?" Lou asked.

"I's fourteen year old, and doing just fine."

"You said you had read the Bible."

"Well, some folks read parts of it to me."

"Do you even know how to sign your name?"

"Why, everybody up here knowed who I is." He stood and pulled out the pocketknife and carved an "X" in a bare wall stud. "That's how my daddy done it all his life, and it be good enough fer him, it be good enough fer me."

Lou wrapped the blanket around her and watched the dance of flames, a wicked chill eating into her.

CHAPTER TWENTY-SEVEN

ONE ESPECIALLY WARM NIGHT THERE CAME A POUND-
ing on the door about the time Lou was thinking
of going upstairs to bed. Billy Davis almost fell
into the room when Louisa opened the door.

Louisa gripped the shaking boy. "What's wrong,
Billy?"

"Ma's baby coming."

"I knew she were getting on. Midwife got there?"

The boy was wild-eyed, his limbs twitching like he
was heatstroked. "Ain't none. Pa won't let 'em."

"Lord, why not?"

"Say they charge a dollar. And he ain't paying it."

"That a lie. No midwife up here ever charge a dime."

"Pa said no. But Ma say baby ain't feel right. Rode
the mule come get you."

"Eugene, get Hit and Sam doubletreed to the wagon.
Quick now," she said.

Before Eugene went out, he took the rifle off the rack
and held it out to Louisa. "Better be taking this, you got
to deal with that man."

Louisa, though, shook her head as she looked at a nervous Billy, finally smiling at the boy. "I'll be watched over, Eugene. I feel it. It be fine."

Eugene held on to the gun. "I go with you, then. That man crazy."

"No, you stay with the children. Go on now, get the wagon ready." Eugene hesitated for a moment, and then did as she told him.

Louisa grabbed some things and put them in a lard bucket, slipped a small packet of cloths in her pocket, bundled together a number of clean sheets, and started for the door.

"Louisa, I'm coming with you," said Lou.

"No, ain't a good place for you."

"I'm coming, Louisa. Whether in the wagon or on Sue, but I'm coming. I want to help you." She glanced at Billy. "And them."

Louisa thought for a minute and then said, "Prob'ly could use another set of hands. Billy, your pa there?"

"Gotta mare gonna drop its foal. Pa said he ain't coming out the barn till it born."

Louisa stared at the boy. Then, shaking her head, she headed for the door.

They followed Billy in the wagon. He rode an old mule, its muzzle white, part of its right ear torn away. The boy swung a kerosene lamp in one hand to help guide them. It was so dark, Louisa said, a hand right in front of your face could still get the drop on you.

"Don't whip up the mules none, Lou. Ain't do no good for Sally Davis we end up in a ditch."

"That's Billy's mother?"

Louisa nodded, as the wagon swayed along, the woods close on either side of them, their only light that arcing lamp. To Lou it appeared either as a beacon, true and reliable, or as a Siren of sorts, leading them to shipwreck.

"First wife die in childbirth. His children by that poor woman got away from George fast as they could, afore he could work or beat or starve 'em to death."

"Why did Sally marry him if he was so bad?"

" 'Cause he got his own land, livestock, and he were a widower with a strong back. Up here, 'bout all it takes. And weren't nothing else for Sally. She were only fifteen."

"Fifteen! That's only three years older than me."

"People get married quick up here. Start birthing, raising a family to help work the land. How it goes. I was in front of the preacher at fo'teen."

"She could have left the mountain."

"All she ever know. Scary thing leave that."

"Did you ever think of leaving the mountain?"

Louisa thought about this for a number of turns of the wagon wheel. "I could'a if'n I wanted. But I ain't believe in my heart I be happier anywhere else. Went down the Valley one time. Wind blow strange over flat land. Ain't liked it too much. Me and this mountain get along right fine for the most part." She fell silent, her eyes watching the rise and fall of the light up ahead.

Lou said, "I saw the graves up behind the house."

Louisa stiffened a bit. "Did you?"

"Who was Annie?"

Louisa stared at her feet. "Annie were my daughter."

"I thought you only had Jacob."

"No. I had me my little Annie."

"Did she die young?"

"She lived but a minute."

Lou could sense her distress. "I'm sorry. I was just curious about my family."

Louisa settled back against the hard wood of the wagon seat and stared at the black sky as though it was the first time she'd ever gazed upon it.

"I always had me a hard time carrying the babies. Wanted me a big family, but I kept on losing 'em long afore they ready to be born. Longest time I thought Jake be it. But then Annie were born on a cool spring evening with a full mane'a black hair. She come quick, no time for midwife. It were a terrible hard birth. But oh, Lou, she were so purty. So warm. Her little fingers wrapped tight round mine, tips not even touching." Here Louisa stopped. The sounds of the mules trotting along and the turn of wagon wheel were the only noises. Louisa finally continued in a low voice, as she eyed the depthless sky. "And her little chest rose and fell, rose and fell, and then it just forgit to rise agin. It t'were amazing how quick she took cold, but then she were so tiny." Louisa took a number of quick breaths, as though still trying to breathe for her child. "It were like a bit of ice on your tongue on a hot day. Feel so good, and then it gone so fast you ain't sure it was ever there."

Lou put her hand over Louisa's. "I'm sorry."

"Long time ago, though it don't never seem it." Louisa slid a hand across her eyes. "Her daddy made her coffin, no more'n a little box. And I stayed up all night and sewed her the finest dress I ever stitched in my whole life. Come morning I laid her out in it. I would'a give all I had to see her eyes looking at me just one time. It ain't seem right that a momma don't get to see her baby's eyes just one time. And then her daddy put her in that little box, we carried her on up to that knoll, and laid her to rest and prayed over her. And then we planted an evergreen on the south end so she'd have her shade all year round." Louisa closed her eyes.

"Did you ever go up there?"

Louisa nodded. "Ever day. But I ain't been back since I buried my other child. It just got to be too long a walk."

She took the reins from Lou and, despite her own earlier warning, Louisa whipped up the mules. "We best get on. We got a child to help into the world this night."

Lou could not make out much of the Davis farmyard or the buildings because of the darkness, and she prayed that George Davis would stay in the barn until the baby was born and they were gone.

The house was surprisingly small. The room they entered was obviously the kitchen, because the stove was there, but there were also cots with bare mattresses lined up here. In three of the beds were a like number of children, two of them, who looked to be twin girls about five, lying naked and asleep. The third, a boy Oz's age, had on a man's undershirt, dirty and sweat-stained, and he watched Lou and Louisa with frightened eyes. Lou recognized him as the other boy from the tractor coming down the mountain. In an apple crate by the stove a baby barely a year old lay under a stained blanket. Louisa went to the sink, pumped water, and used the bar of lye soap she had brought to thoroughly clean her hands and forearms. Then Billy led them down a narrow hallway and opened a door.

Sally Davis lay in the bed, her knees drawn up, low moans shooting from her. A thin girl of ten, dressed in what looked like a seed sack, her chestnut hair hacked short, stood barefoot next to the bed. Lou recognized her too from the wild tractor encounter. She looked just as scared now as she had then.

Louisa nodded at her. "Jesse, you heat me up some water, two pots, honey. Billy, all the sheets you got, son. And they's got to be real clean."

Louisa put the sheets she had brought on a wobbly oak slat chair, sat next to Sally, and took her hand. "Sally, it's Louisa. You be just fine, honey."

Lou looked at Sally. Her eyes were red-rimmed, her few teeth and her gums stained dark. She couldn't be thirty yet, but the woman looked twice that old, hair gray, skin drawn and wrinkled, blue veins throbbing through malnourished flesh, face sunken like a winter potato.

Louisa lifted the covers and saw the soaked sheet underneath. "How long since your water bag broke?"

Sally gasped, "After Billy gone fer you."

"How far apart your pains?" Louisa asked.

"Seem like just one big one," the woman groaned.

Louisa felt around the swollen belly. "Baby feel like it want'a come?"

Sally gripped Louisa's hand. "Lord I hope so, afore it kill me."

Billy came in with a couple of sheets, dropped them on the chair, looked once at his ma, and then fled.

"Lou, help me move Sally over so we can lay clean sheets." They did so, maneuvering the suffering woman as gently as they could. "Now go help Jesse with the water. And take these." She handed Lou a number of cloth pads that were layered one over the top of the other, along with some narrow bobbin string. "Wrap the string in the middle of the cloths, and put it all in the oven and cook it till the outside part be scorched brown."

Lou went into the kitchen and assisted Jesse. Lou had never seen her at school, nor the seven-year-old boy who watched them with fearful eyes. Jesse had a wide scar that looped around her left eye, and Lou didn't even want to venture to guess how the girl had come by it.

The stove was already hot, and the kettle water came to a boil in a few minutes. Lou kept checking the outside of the cloth that she placed in the oven drawer, and soon it was sufficiently brown. Using rags, they carried the pots and the ball of cloths into the bedroom and set them next to the bed.

Louisa washed Sally with soap and warm water where the baby would be coming and then drew the sheet over her.

She whispered to Lou, "Baby taking its last rest now, and so can Sally. Ain't tell 'xactly how it lies yet, but it ain't a cross birth." Lou looked at her curiously. "Where the baby lie crossways along the belly. I call you when I need you."

"How many babies have you delivered?"

"Thirty-two over fifty-seven years," she said. " 'Member ever one of 'em."

"Did they all live?"

"No," Louisa answered quietly, and then told Lou to go on out, that she would call her.

Jesse was in the kitchen, standing against a wall, hands clasped in front of her, face down, a side of her hacked hair positioned over the scar and part of her eye.

Lou glanced at the boy in the bed.

"What's your name?" Lou asked him. He said nothing. When Lou stepped toward him, he yelled and threw the blanket over his head, his little body shaking hard under the cover. Lou retreated all the way out of the crazy house.

She looked around until she saw Billy over at the barn peering in the open double doors. She crossed the yard quietly and looked over his shoulder. George Davis was no more than ten feet from them. The mare was on the straw floor. Protruding from her, and covered in the cocoonish white birth sac, was one foreleg and shoulder of the foal. Davis was pulling on the slicked leg, cursing. The barn floor was plank, not dirt. In the blaze of a number of lanterns, Lou could see rows of shiny tools neatly lining the walls.

Unable to stand Davis's coarse language and the mare's suffering, Lou went and sat on the front porch. Billy came and slumped next to her. "Your farm looks pretty big," she said.

"Pa hire men to help him work it. But when I get to be a man, he ain't need 'em. I do it."

They heard George Davis holler from the barn, and they both jumped. Billy looked embarrassed and dug at the dirt with his big toe.

"I'm sorry for putting that snake in your pail."

He looked at her, surprised. "I done it to you first."

"That still doesn't make it right."

"Pa kill a man if he done that to him."

Lou could see the terror in the boy's eyes, and her heart went out to Billy Davis.

"You're not your pa. And you don't have to be."

Billy looked nervous. "I ain't tell him I was fetching Miss Louisa. Don't know what he say when he sees y'all."

"We're just here to help your mother. He can't have a problem with that."

"That right?"

They looked up into the face of George Davis, who stood before them, equine blood and slime coating his shirt and dripping down both arms. Dust swirled around his legs like visible heat, as though mountain had been shucked to desert.

Billy stood in front of Lou. "Pa. How's the foal?"

"Dead." The way he said it made every part of Lou shake. He pointed at her. "What the hell is this?"

"I got them to come help with the baby. Miss Louisa's in with Ma."

George looked over at the door and then back at Billy. The look in his eye was so terrible that Lou was sure the man was going to kill her right there.

"That woman in my house, boy?"

"It's time." They all looked toward the door where Louisa now stood. "Baby's coming," she said.

Davis shoved his son aside, and Lou jumped out of the way as he stalked up to the door.

"Gawd damnit, you got no business here, woman. Get the hell off my land afore you get the butt of my shotgun agin your head, and that damn girl too."

Louisa took not one step back. "You can help with the baby coming, or not. Up to you. Come on, Lou, and you too, Billy. Gonna need both y'all."

It was clear though that George wasn't going to let them go. Louisa was very strong for her age, and taller than Davis, but still, it would not be much of a fight.

And then from the woods they heard the scream. It was the same sound Lou had heard the first night at the well, but even more horrifying somehow, as though whatever it was, was very close and bearing down on them. Even Louisa stared out apprehensively into the darkness.

George Davis took a step back, his hand clenched, as though hoping for a gun to be there. Louisa clutched the children and pulled them in with her. Davis made no move to stop them, but he did call out, "You just make sure it's a damn boy this time. If'n it's a girl, you just let it die. You hear me? Don't need me no more gawd damn girls!"

As Sally pushed hard, Louisa's pulse quickened when she first saw the buttocks of the baby, followed by one of its feet. She knew she didn't have long to get the child out before the cord was crushed between the baby's head and Sally's bone. As she watched, the pains pushed the other foot out.

"Lou," she said, "over here, quick, child." Louisa caught the baby's feet in her right hand and lifted the body up so that the contractions would not have to carry the weight of the baby, and so as to better the angle of the head coming through. She knew they were fortunate that after so many births, Sally Davis's bones would be spread wide. "Push, Sally, push, honey," Louisa called out.

Louisa took Lou's hands and directed them to a spot on Sally's lower abdomen. "Got to get the head out fast," she told Lou, "push right there, hard as you can. Don't worry, ain't hurt the baby none, belly wall hard."

Lou bore down with all her weight while Sally pushed and screamed and Louisa lifted the baby's body higher.

Louisa called out like she was marking water depth on a riverboat. Neck showing, she said, and then she could see hair. And then the entire head showed, and then she was holding the child, and telling Sally to rest, that it was over.

Louisa said a prayer of thanks when she saw it was a boy. It was awfully small, though, and its color poor. She had Lou and Billy heat up cans of water while she tied off the cord in two spots with the bobbin string and then cut the cord in between these points with a pair of boiled scissors. She wrapped the cord in one of the clean, dry cloths that Lou had baked in the oven and tied another of the baked cloths snugly against the baby's left side. She used sweet oil to clean the baby off, washed him with soap and warm water, and then wrapped him in a blanket and gave the boy to his mother.

Louisa placed a hand on Sally's belly and felt to see if the womb was hard and small, which is what she wanted. If it was large and soft, that might mean bleeding inside, she told Lou in a small voice. However, the belly was small and tight. "We fine," she told a relieved Lou.

Next, Louisa took the newborn and laid it on the bed. She took a small wax ampule from her lard bucket and from it took out a small glass vial. She had Lou hold the baby's eyes open while Louisa placed two drops inside each one, while the child squirmed and cried out.

She told Lou, "So baby ain't go blind. Travis Barnes gimme it. Law say you got to do this."

Using the hot cans and some blankets, Louisa fashioned a crude incubator and placed the baby in it. His breathing was so shallow she kept sticking a goose feather under his mouth to see the ripple of air graze it.

Thirty minutes later the last contractions pushed the afterbirth out and Louisa and Lou cleaned that up, changing the sheets once more and scrubbing the mother down for the final time using the last of the baked cloths.

The last things Louisa took out from her bucket were a pencil and a slip of paper. She gave them to Lou and told her to write down the day's date and time. Louisa pulled an old windup pocket watch from her trousers and told Lou the time of birth.

"Sally, what you be calling the baby?" Louisa asked.

Sally looked over at Lou. "She call you Lou, that be your name, girl?" she asked in a weak voice.

"Yes. Well, sort of," said Lou.

"Then it be Lou. After you, child. I thank you."

Lou looked astonished. "What about your husband?"

"He ain't care if'n it got name or ain't got one. Only if'n it a boy and it work. And I ain't seed him in here hepping. Name's Lou. Put it down now, girl."

Louisa smiled as Lou wrote down the name Lou Davis.

"We give that to Cotton," Louisa said. "He take it on down the courthouse so's everybody know we got us another beautiful child on this mountain."

Sally fell asleep and Louisa sat there with mother and

son all night, rousing Sally to nurse when Lou Davis cried and smacked his lips. George Davis never once entered the room. They could hear him stomping around in the front for some time, and then the door slammed shut.

Louisa slipped out several times to check on the other children. She gave Billy, Jesse, and the other boy, whose name Louisa didn't know, a small jar of molasses and some biscuits she had brought with her. It pained her to see how fast the children devoured this simple meal. She also gave Billy a jar of strawberry jelly and some corn-bread to save for the other children when they woke.

They left in the late morning. Mother was doing fine, and the baby's color had improved greatly. He was nursing feverishly, and the boy's lungs seemed strong.

Sally and Billy said their thanks, and even Jesse managed a grunt. But Lou noticed that the stove was cold and there was no smell of food.

George Davis and his hired men were in the fields. But before Billy joined them, Louisa took the boy aside and talked with him about things Lou could not hear.

As they drove the wagon out, they passed corrals filled with enough cattle to qualify as a herd, and hogs and sheep, a yard full of hens, four fine horses, and double that number of mules. The crop fields extended as far as the eye could see, and dangerous barbed wire encircled all of it. Lou could see George and his men working the fields with mechanized equipment, clouds of dirt being thrown up from the swift pace of the machines.

"They have more fields and livestock than we do," Lou said. "So how come they don't have anything to eat?"

" 'Cause their daddy want it that way. And his daddy

were the same way with George Davis. Tight with a dollar. Didn't let none go till his feet wedged agin root."

They rattled by one building and Louisa pointed out a sturdy padlock on the door. "Man'll let the meat in that smokehouse *rot* afore he give it up to his children. George Davis sells every last bit of his crop down at the lumber camp, and to the miners, and hauls it to Tremont and Dickens." She pointed to a large building that had a line of doors all around the first floor. The doors were open, and plainly visible inside were large green plant leaves hanging from hooks. "That's burley tobacco curing. It weakens the soil, and what he don't chew hisself, he sells. He got that still and ain't never drunk a drop of the corn whiskey, but sells that wicked syrup to other men who ought be spending their time and money on they's families. And he goes round with a fat roll of dollar bills, and got this nice farm, and all them fancy machines, and man let his family starve." She flicked the reins. "But I got to feel sorry for him in a way, for he be the most miserable soul I ever come across. Now, one day God'll let George Davis know 'xactly what He thinks of it all. But that day ain't here yet."

CHAPTER TWENTY-EIGHT

EUGENE WAS DRIVING THE WAGON PULLED BY THE mules. Oz, Lou, and Diamond were in the back, sitting on sacks of seed and other supplies purchased from McKenzie's Mercantile using egg money and some of the dollars Lou had left over from her shopping excursion in Dickens.

Their path took them near a good-sized tributary of the McCloud River, and Lou was surprised to see a number of automobiles and schooner wagons pulled up near the flat, grassy bank. Folks were hanging about by the river's edge, and some were actually in the brown water, its surface choppy from an earlier rain and good wind. A man with rolled-up sleeves was just then submerging a young woman in the water.

"Dunking," Diamond exclaimed. "Let's have a look."

Eugene pulled the mules to a stop and the three children jumped off. Lou looked back at Eugene, who was making no move to join them.

"Aren't you coming?"

"You g'on, Miss Lou, I gonna rest my bones here."

Lou frowned at this, but joined the others.

Diamond had made his way through a crowd of on-lookers and was peering anxiously at something. As Oz and Lou drew next to him and saw what it was, they both jumped back.

An elderly woman, dressed in what looked to be a turban made from pinned-together homespun sheets and a long piece of hemp with a tie at the waist, was moving in small, deliberate circles, unintelligible chants drifting from her, her speech that of the drunk, insane, or fanatically religious in full, flowering tongues. Next to her a man was in a T-shirt and dress slacks, a cigarette dangling like a fall leaf from his mouth. A serpent was in either of the man's hands, the reptiles rigid, unmoving, like bent pieces of metal.

"Are they poisonous?" whispered Lou to Diamond.

"Course! Don't work lessen use viper."

A cowering Oz had his gaze fixed on the motionless creatures and seemed prepared to leap for the trees once they started swaying. Lou sensed this, and when the snakes did start to move, she gripped Oz's hand and pulled him away. Diamond grudgingly followed, till they were off by themselves.

"What stuff are they doing with those snakes, Diamond?" asked Lou.

"Scaring off bad spirits, making it good for dunking." He looked at them. "You two been dunked?"

"Christened, Diamond," Lou answered. "We were christened in a Catholic Church. And the priest just sprinkles water on your head." She looked to the river where the woman was emerging and spitting up mouthfuls of the tributary. "He doesn't try to drown you."

"Catolick? Ain't never heard'a that one. It new?"

Lou almost laughed. "Not quite. Our mom is Catholic. Dad never really cared for church all that much. They even have their own schools. Oz and I went to one in New York. It's really structured and you learn things like the Sacraments, the Creed, the Rosary, the Lord's Prayer. And you learn the Mortal Sins. And the Venial Sins. And you have First Confession and First Communion. And then Confirmation."

"Yeah," said Oz, "and when you're dying you get the . . . what that's thing, Lou?"

"The Sacrament of Extreme Unction. The Last Rites."

"So you won't rot in hell," Oz informed Diamond.

Diamond pulled at three or four of his cowlicks and looked truly bewildered. "Huh. Who'd thunk believing in God be such hard work? Prob'ly why ain't no Catolicks up this way. Tax the head too much."

Diamond nodded at the group near the river. "Now, them folk Primitive Baptists. They got some right funny beliefs. Like you ain't go and cut your hair, and women ain't be putting on no face paint. And they got some 'ticular ideas on going to hell and such. People break the rules, they ain't too happy. Live and die by the Scriptures. Prob'ly ain't as 'ticular as you Catolicks, but they still be a pain where the sun don't shine." Diamond yawned and stretched his arms. "See, that why I ain't go to church. Figger I got me a church wherever I be. Want'a talk to God, well I say, 'Howdy-howdy, God,' and we jaw fer a bit."

Lou just stared at him, absolutely dumbstruck in the face of this outpouring of ecclesiastical wisdom from Professor of Religion Diamond Skinner.

Diamond suddenly stared off in wonder. "Well, will you look at that."

They all watched as Eugene walked down to the water's edge and spoke with someone, who in turn called to the preacher out in the river, as he was pulling up a fresh victim.

The preacher came ashore, spoke with Eugene for a minute or two, and then led him out into the water, dunked him so that nothing was showing of his person, and then preached over him. The man kept Eugene down so long, Lou and Oz started to worry. But when Eugene came up, he smiled, thanked the man, and then went back to the wagon. Diamond set off on a dead run toward the preacher, who was looking around for other takers of divine immersion.

Lou and Oz crept closer as Diamond went out in the water with the holy man and was fully plunged under too. He finally surfaced, talked with the man for a minute, slipped something in his pocket, and, soaking wet and smiling, rejoined them, and they all headed to the wagon.

"You've never been baptized before?" said Lou.

"Shoot," said Diamond, shaking the water from his hair, the cowlick of which had not been disturbed in the least, "that's my ninth time dunked."

"You're only supposed to do it *once*, Diamond!"

"Well, ain't hurt keep doing it. Plan to work me up to a hunnerd. Figger I be a lock for heaven then."

"That's not how it works," exclaimed Lou.

"Is so," he shot back. "Say so in the Bible. Ever time you get dunked it means God's sending an angel to come look after you. I figger I got me a right good regiment by now."

"That is *not* in the Bible," insisted Lou.

"Maybe you ought'n read your Bible agin."

"Which part of the Bible is it in? Tell me that."

"Front part." Diamond whistled for Jeb, ran the rest of the way to the wagon, and climbed on.

"Hey, Eugene," he said, "I let you knowed next time they's dunking. We go swimming together."

"You were never baptized, Eugene?" asked Lou as she and Oz clambored onto the wagon.

He shook his head. "But sitting here I got me a hankering to do just that. 'Bout time, I 'xpect."

"I'm surprised Louisa never had you baptized."

"Miz Louisa, she believe in God with all her soul. But she don't subscribe to church much. She say the way some folk run they's churches, it take God right out cha heart."

As the wagon pulled off, Diamond slid from his pocket a small glass jar with a tin screw cap. "Hey, Oz, I got me this from the preacher. Holy dunking water." He handed it to Oz, who looked down at it curiously. "I figger you put some on your ma from time to time. Bet it hep."

Lou was about to protest, when she received the shock of her life. Oz handed the jar back to Diamond.

"No, thanks," he said quietly and looked away.

"You sure?" asked Diamond. Oz said he was real sure, and so Diamond tipped the bottle over and poured out the blessed water. Lou and Oz exchanged a glance, and the sad look on his face stunned her again. Lou looked to the sky, because she figured if Oz had given up hope, the end of the world must not be far behind. She turned her back to them all and pretended to be admiring the sweep of mountains.

It was late afternoon. Cotton had just finished reading to Amanda and it was apparent that he was experiencing a growing sense of frustration.

At the window, Lou watched, standing on an overturned lard bucket.

Cotton looked at the woman. "Amanda, now I just know you can hear me. You have two children who need you badly. You *have* to get out of that bed. For them if for no other reason." He paused, seeming to select his words with care. "Please, Amanda. I would give all I will ever have if you would get up right now." An anxious few moments went by, and Lou held her breath, yet the woman didn't budge. Cotton finally bowed his head in despair.

When Cotton came out of the house later and got in his Olds to leave, Lou hurried up carrying a basket of food.

"Reading probably gives a man an appetite."

"Well, thank you, Lou."

He put the basket of food in the seat next to him. "Louisa tells me you're a writer. What do you want to write about?"

Lou stood on the roadster's running board. "My dad wrote about this place, but nothing's really coming to me."

Cotton looked out over the mountains. "Your daddy was actually one of the reasons I came here. When I was in law school at the University of Virginia, I read his very first novel and was struck by both its power and beauty. And then I saw a story in the newspaper about him. He talked about how the mountains had inspired him so. I thought coming here would do the same for me. I walked all over these parts with my pad and pencil, waiting for beautiful phrases to seep into my head so I could put them down on the paper." He smiled wistfully. "Didn't exactly work that way."

Lou said quietly, "Maybe not for me either."

"Well, people seem to spend most of their lives chasing something. Maybe that's part of what makes us human." Cotton pointed down the road. "You see that old shack down there?" Lou looked at a mud-chinked, falling-down log cabin they no longer used. "Louisa told me about a story your father wrote when he was a little boy. It was about a family that survived one winter up here in that little house. Without wood, or food."

"How'd they do it?"

"They believed in things."

"Like what? Wishing wells?" she said with scorn.

"No, they believed in each other. And created something of a miracle. Some say truth is stranger than fiction. I think that means that whatever a person can imagine really does exist, somewhere. Isn't that a wonderful possibility?"

"I don't know if my imagination is that good, Cotton. In fact, I don't even know if I'm much of a writer. The things I put down on paper don't seem to have much life to them."

"Keep at it, you might surprise yourself. And rest assured, Lou, miracles *do* happen. You and Oz coming here and getting to know Louisa being one of them."

Lou sat on her bed later that night, looking at her mother's letters. When Oz came in, Lou hurriedly stuffed them under her pillow.

"Can I sleep with you?" asked Oz. "Kind'a scary in my room. Pretty sure I saw a troll in the corner."

Lou said, "Get up here." Oz climbed next to her.

Oz suddenly looked troubled. "When you get married, who am I going to come get in bed with when I'm scared, Lou?"

"One day you're gonna get bigger than me, then I'm going to be running to you when *I* get scared."

"How do you know that?"

"Because that's the deal God makes between big sisters and their little brothers."

"Me bigger than you? Really?"

"Look at those clodhoppers of yours. You grow into those feet all the way, you'll be bigger than Eugene."

Oz snuggled in, happy now. Then he saw the letters under the pillow.

"What are those?"

"Just some old letters Mom wrote," Lou said quickly.

"What did she say?"

"I don't know, I haven't read them."

"Will you read them to me?"

"Oz, it's late and I'm tired."

"Please, Lou. Please."

He looked so pitiful Lou took out a single letter and turned up the wick on the kerosene lamp that sat on the table next to her bed.

"All right, but just one."

Oz settled down as Lou began to read.

"Dear Louisa, I hope you are doing well. We all are. Oz is over the croup and is sleeping through the night."

Oz jumped up. "That's me! Mom wrote about me!" He paused and looked confused. "What's croup?"

"You don't want to know. Now, do you want me to read it or not?" Oz lay back down while his sister commenced reading again. "Lou won first place in both the spelling bee and the fifty-yard dash at May Day. The latter included the boys! She's something, Louisa. I've seen a picture of you that Jack had, and the resemblance is remarkable. They're both growing up so fast. So very fast it scares me. Lou is so much like her father. Her mind is so quick, I'm afraid she finds me a little boring. That thought keeps me up nights. I love her so much. I try to do so much with her. And yet, well, you know, a father and his daughter. . . . More next time. And pictures too. Love to you. Amanda. P.S. My dream is to bring the children to the mountain, so that we can finally meet you. I hope that dream comes true one day."

Oz said, "That was a good letter. Night, Lou."

As Oz drifted off to sleep, Lou slowly reached for another letter.

CHAPTER TWENTY-NINE

LOU AND OZ WERE FOLLOWING DIAMOND AND JEB through the woods on a glorious day in early fall, the dappled sunlight in their faces, a cool breeze tracking them along with the fading scents of summer's honeysuckle and wild rose.

"Where are we going?" asked Lou.

Diamond would only say mysteriously, "You see."

They went up a little incline and stopped. Fifty feet away and on the path was Eugene, carrying an empty coal bucket and a lantern. In his pocket was a stick of dynamite.

Diamond said, "Eugene headed to the coal mine. Gonna fill up that bucket. Afore winter come, he'll take a drag down there with the mules and get out a big load'a coal."

"Gee, that's about as exciting as watching somebody sleep," was Lou's considered opinion.

"Huh! Wait till that dynamite blows," countered Diamond.

"Dynamite!" Oz said.

Diamond nodded. "Coal deep in that rock. Pick can't git to it. Gotta blast it out."

"Is it dangerous?" asked Lou.

"Naw. He knowed what he doing. Done it myself."

As they watched from a distance, Eugene pulled the dynamite out of his pocket and attached a long fuse to it. Then he lit his lantern and went inside the mine. Diamond sat back against a redbud, took out an apple, and cut it up. He flicked a piece to Jeb, who was messing around some underbrush. Diamond noted the worried looks on the faces of Lou and Oz.

"That fuse slow-burning. Walk to the moon and back afore it go off."

A while later Eugene came out of the mine and sat down on a rock near the entrance.

"Shouldn't he get away from there?"

"Naw. Don't use that much dynamite for a bucketful. After it blow and the dust settles, I show you round in there."

"What's to see in some old mine?" asked Lou.

Diamond suddenly hunched forward. "I tell you what. I seed some fellers down here late one night poking round. 'Member Miss Louisa told me to keep my eyes open? Well, I done that. They had lanterns and carrying boxes into the mine. We go in and see what they's up to."

"But what if they're in the mine now?"

"Naw. I come by just a bit ago, looked round, threw a rock inside. And they's fresh footprints in the dirt heading out. 'Sides, Eugene would'a seed 'em." He had a sudden idea. "Hey, mebbe they running shine, using the mine to store the still and corn and such."

"More likely they're just hobos using the mine to keep dry at night," said Lou.

"Ain't never heard tell of no hobos up here."

"So why didn't you tell Louisa?" Lou challenged him.

"She got enough to worry 'bout. Check it out first. What a man do."

Jeb flushed out a squirrel and chased it around a tree while they all watched and waited for the explosion.

Lou said, "Why don't you come live with us?"

Diamond stared at her, clearly troubled by this question. He turned to his hound. "Cut it out, Jeb. That squirrel ain't doing nuthin' to you."

Lou added, "I mean, we could use the help. Another strong man around. And Jeb too."

"Naw. I a feller what needs his freedom."

"Hey, Diamond," said Oz, "you could be my big brother. Then Lou wouldn't have to beat up everybody by herself."

Lou and Diamond smiled at each other.

"Maybe you should think about it," said Lou.

"Mebbe I will." He looked at the mine. "Ain't be long now."

They sat back and waited. Then the squirrel broke free from the woods and flashed right into the mine. Jeb plunged in after it.

Diamond leapt to his feet. "Jeb! Jeb! Git back here!" The boy charged out of the woods. Eugene made a grab for him, but Diamond dodged him and ran into the mine.

Lou screamed, "Diamond! Don't!"

She ran for the mine entrance.

Oz shouted, "Lou, no! Come back!"

Before she could reach the entrance, Eugene grabbed her. "Wait here. I git him, Miss Lou."

Eugene fast-limped into the mine, screaming, "Diamond! Diamond!"

Lou and Oz looked at each other, terrified. Time ticked by. Lou paced in nervous circles near the entrance. "Please, please. Hurry." She went to the entrance, heard something coming. "Diamond! Eugene!"

But it was Jeb that came racing out of the mine after the squirrel. Lou grabbed at the dog, and then the concussive force of the explosion knocked Lou off her feet. Dust and dirt poured out of the mine, and Lou coughed and gagged in this maelstrom. Oz raced to help her while Jeb barked and jumped.

Lou got her bearings and her breath and stumbled to the entrance. "Eugene! Diamond!"

Finally, she could hear footsteps coming. They drew closer and closer, and they seemed unsteady. Lou said a silent prayer. It seemed to take forever, but then Eugene appeared, dazed, covered with dirt, bleeding. He looked at them, tears on his face.

"Damn, Miss Lou."

Lou took one step back, then another, and then another. Then she turned and ran down the trail as fast as she could, her wails covering them all.

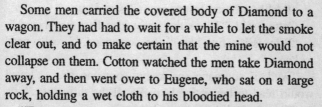

Some men carried the covered body of Diamond to a wagon. They had had to wait for a while to let the smoke clear out, and to make certain that the mine would not collapse on them. Cotton watched the men take Diamond away, and then went over to Eugene, who sat on a large rock, holding a wet cloth to his bloodied head.

"Eugene, sure you don't need anything else?"

Eugene looked at the mine like he expected to see Diamond walk out with his stuck-up hair and silly smile. "All I need, Mr. Cotton, is this be a bad dream I wake myself up from."

Cotton patted his big shoulder and then glanced at Lou sitting on a little hump of dirt, her back to the mine. He went to her and sat down.

Lou's eyes were raw from crying, her cheeks stained with tears. She was hunched over in a little ball, like every part of her was in wrenching pain.

"I'm sorry, Lou. Diamond was a fine boy."

"He was a *man*. A *fine man*!"

"I suppose you're right. He was a man."

Lou eyed Jeb, who sat mournfully at the mine entrance. "Diamond didn't have to go in that mine after Jeb."

"Well, that dog was all Diamond had. When you love something, you can't just sit by and not do anything."

Lou picked up some pine needles and then let a few trickle out between her fingers. Minutes passed before she spoke again. "Why do things like this happen, Cotton?"

He sighed deeply. "I suppose it may be God's way of telling us to love people while they're here, because tomorrow they may be gone. I guess that's a pretty sorry answer, but I'm afraid it's the only one I've got."

They were silent for a bit longer.

"I'd like to read to my mom," said Lou.

Cotton said, "That's the finest idea I've ever heard."

"Why is it a fine idea?" she demanded. "I really need to know."

"Well, if someone she knew, someone she . . . loved would read to her, it might make all the difference."

"Do you really think she knows?"

"When I carried your mother outside that day, I was holding a living person fighting like the devil to get out. I could feel it. And she will one day. I believe it with all my heart, Lou."

She shook her head. "It's hard, Cotton. To let yourself love something you know you may never have."

Cotton nodded slowly. "You're wise beyond your years. And what you say makes perfect sense. But I think when it comes to matters of the heart, perfect sense may be the last thing you want to listen to."

Lou let the rest of the needles fall and wiped her hands clean. "You're a good man too, Cotton."

He put his arm around her and they sat there together, neither one of them willing to look at the blackened, swollen cavity of the coal mine that had taken their friend from them forever.

CHAPTER THIRTY

THERE WAS ENOUGH STEADY RAIN, AND SOME THUNDERstorms added to the plenty, such that virtually all the crops came in healthy and in abundance. One fierce hailstorm damaged some of the corn, but not to any great extent. A stretch of powerful rain did wash a gully out of a hill, like a scoop of ice cream, but no person, animal, or crop was hurt by it.

Harvesting time was full upon them, and Louisa, Eugene, Lou, and Oz worked hard and long, which was good, because it gave them little time to think about Diamond not being with them anymore. Occasionally they would hear the mine siren, and then a bit later the slow rumbling of the explosion would come. And each time Louisa would lead them all in a song to take their minds off Diamond's having been killed by such an awful thing.

Louisa did not speak much of Diamond's passing. Yet Lou noted that she read her Bible a lot more often by the firelight, and her eyes swelled with tears whenever his name was mentioned, or when she looked at Jeb. It was hard for all of them, yet all they could do was keep going, and there was much to do.

They harvested the pinto beans, cast them in Chop bags, stomped them to get the husks off, and had them for dinner every night with gravy and biscuits. They picked the pole beans, which had grown up around the cornstalks, careful, as Louisa schooled them, to avoid the green stinger worms that lived under the leaves. They scythed the cornfield and bundled the cornstalks into shocks, which they stood in the field, and which would later be used for livestock feed. They shucked the corn, hauled it by sled to the corncrib, and filled it to almost overflowing. From a distance the tumble of cobs looked like yellowjackets at frenzied play.

The potatoes came in thick and fat, and with churned butter were a meal by themselves. The tomatoes came in too, plump and blood red, eaten whole or sliced, and also cut up and canned in jars in a great iron kettle on the stove, along with beans and peppers and many other vegetables. They stacked the jars in the foodsafe and under the stairs. They filled lard buckets with wild strawberries and gooseberries, and apples by the bushel, made jams and pies, and canned the rest. They ground down the cane stalks and made molasses, and shelled some of the corn and made cornmeal and fried crackling bread.

It seemed to Lou that nothing was wasted; it was an efficient process and she admired it, even as she and Oz worked themselves to near death from before sunup to long after sundown. Everywhere they turned with tool or hand, food was flying at them. This made Lou think of Billy Davis and his family having nothing to eat. She thought about it so much she talked to Louisa about it.

"You stay up tomorrow night, Lou, and you'll find that you and me thinking on the same line."

All of them were waiting by the barn late that night when they heard a wagon coming down the road. Eugene held up a lantern and the light fell upon Billy Davis as he pulled the mules to a halt and nervously stared at Lou and Oz.

Louisa approached the wagon. "Billy, I thought we might need some help. I want'a make sure you get a good load. Land been real fine to us this year."

Billy looked embarrassed for a moment, but then Lou said, "Hey, Billy, come on, I'm going to need your muscle to lift this bucket."

Thus encouraged, Billy jumped down to help. They all spent a solid hour loading bags of cornmeal, canning jars full of beans and tomatoes, and buckets of rutabagas, collards, cucumbers, potatoes, apples, plump cabbages, pears, sweet potatoes, onions, and even some cuts of salted hog meat on that wagon.

While Lou was loading, she saw Louisa take Billy to a corner of the barn and look at his face with a lantern. Then she had him raise his shirt, and she did an examination there and came away apparently satisfied.

When Billy turned the wagon around and left, the mules strained under the new weight, and the boy carried a big smile as he flicked the whip and disappeared into the night.

"They can't hide all that food from George Davis," Lou said.

"I been doing this many a year now. Man never once fretted about where the bounty come from."

Lou looked angry. "That's not fair. He sells his crop and makes money, and *we* feed his family."

"What's fair is a momma and her children eating good," answered Louisa.

"What were you checking for under his shirt?" asked Lou.

"George is smart. Most times hits where the clothing covers."

"Why didn't you just ask Billy if he had hit him?"

"Just like an empty lunch pail, children will lie when they shamed."

With all their surplus, Louisa decided the four would drive the wagon laden with crops down to the lumber camp. On the day of the trip Cotton came over to look after Amanda. The lumber folks were expecting them, for quite a crowd had gathered by the time they arrived. The camp was large, with its own school, store, and post office. Because the camp was forced to move frequently when forests had been exhausted, the entire town was on rails, including the workers' homes, the school, and the store. They were laid out on various spurs like a neighborhood. When a move was called for, the locomotives hooked up to the cars and off the entire town went in short order.

The lumber camp families paid for the crops either with cash money or with barter items, such as coffee, sugar, toilet paper, stamps, pencils and paper, some throw-off clothes and shoes, and old newspapers. Lou had ridden Sue down, and she and Oz took turns giving the camp children rides free of charge, but the patrons could "donate" peppermint sticks and other delicacies if they saw fit, and many did.

Later, from atop the sharp spine of a ridge, they looked down where a shaft of the McCloud River flowed. A splashdam of stone and wood had been created downriver, artificially backing the water up and covering boulders and other obstructions that made log transport by river difficult. Here the water was filled bank to bank with trees, mostly mighty poplar, the bottoms of the trunks scored with the lumber company's brand. They looked like pencils from this great height, but then Oz and Lou noted that the small specks on each of them were actually full-grown men riding the logs. They would float down to the splashdam, where a vital wedge would be kicked out, and the thundering water would carry the trees downriver, where they would be tied off and Virginia logs would ride on to Kentucky markets.

As Lou surveyed the land from this high perch, something seemed to be missing. It took her a moment to realize that what was absent was the trees. As far as she could see, there were just stumps. When they went back down to the camp, she also noted that some of the rail lines were empty.

"Sucked just 'bout all the wood we can from here," one of the lumberjacks proudly explained. "Be heading out soon." He didn't seem bothered by this at all. Lou figured he was probably used to it. Conquer and move on, the only trace of their presence the butts of wood left behind.

On the trip home they tied Sue to the wagon and Lou and Oz rode in the back with Eugene. It had been a good day for everyone, but Oz was the happiest of them all, for he had "won" an official baseball from one of the camp boys by throwing it farther than any of them. He told them it was his proudest possession behind the graveyard rabbit's foot Diamond Skinner had given him.

CHAPTER THIRTY-ONE

IN READING TO HER MOTHER, LOU CHOSE NOT BOOKS, but rather *Grit* newspapers, and some copies of the *Saturday Evening Post* they had gotten from the lumber camp. Lou would stand against the wall of her mother's room, the paper or magazine held in front of her, and read of the economy, world catastrophes, Hitler's bludgeoning war across Europe, politics, the arts, movies, and the latest news of writing and writers, which made Lou realize how long it had been since she had actually read a book. School would start again very soon; even so, she had ridden Sue over to Big Spruce a few days before and borrowed some reading material for her and Oz from the "lending library," with Estelle McCoy's permission of course.

Louisa had taught Eugene to read when he was a child, and so Lou brought a book for him too. He was concerned he would find no time to read it, and yet he did, late at night under lamplight, his moistened thumb slowly turning the pages as he concentrated. Other times Lou helped him with his words as they worked the fields in preparation for the coming winter, or when milking the cows by kerosene lamp. Lou would take him through the *Grit*s and the *Post*s and Eugene particularly liked saying "Rooooosevelt, President Rooooosevelt," a name that appeared often in the *Grit* pages. The cows looked at him strangely whenever he said "Rooooosevelt," as though they thought he was actually mooing at them in a peculiar way. And Lou couldn't help but gape when Eugene asked her why somebody would name their child President.

"You ever think about living somewhere else?" Lou asked him one morning while they were milking.

He said, "Mountain all I seed, but I knowed they a lot mo' to this world."

"I could take you to the city one day. Buildings so tall you can't walk up them. You ride in an elevator." He looked at her curiously. "A little car that pulls you up and down," she explained.

"Car? What, like'n the Hudson?"

"No, more like a little room you stand in."

Eugene thought that interesting, but said he'd probably just stick to farming on the mountain. "Want'a get hitched, have me a family, raise the chillin good."

"You'd make a good dad," she said.

He grinned. "Well, you'd be a fine ma. How you is with your brother and all."

Lou stared at him and said, "My mother was a great mom." Lou tried to recall if she had ever actually told her mother that. Lou knew she had spent most of her adoration on her father. It was a very troubling thought to her, since it was now beyond remedy.

A week after her ride to the school library, Lou had just finished reading to Amanda, when she went out to the barn to be by herself. She climbed to the hayloft and sat in the opening of the double doors and looked across the valley to the mountains beyond. Pondering her mother's depressing future, Lou finally turned her thoughts to the loss of Diamond. She had tried to put it out of her mind, but she realized she never really could.

Diamond's funeral had been a strange yet heartfelt affair. People had emerged from slivers of farms and crevices of homesteads that Lou was unaware even existed, and all these people came to Louisa's home by horse, ox, mule, foot, and tractor, and even one battered Packard with all its doors missing. Folks trooped through with plates of good food and jugs of cider. There were no formal preachers in attendance, but a number of folks stood and with shy voices offered comfort for the friends of the deceased. The cedar coffin sat in the front room, its lid securely nailed down, for no one had a desire to see what dynamite had done to Diamond Skinner.

Lou was not sure that all the older folks were really Diamond's friends, yet she assumed they had been friends of his father. In fact she had heard one old gent by the name of Buford Rose, who had a head of thick white hair and few teeth, mutter about the blunt irony of both father and son having been done in by the damn mines.

They laid Diamond to rest next to the graves of his parents, their mounds long since pulled back into the earth. Various people read from the Bible and there were more than a few tears. Oz stood in the center of them all and boldly announced that his often-baptized friend was a lock for heaven. Louisa laid a bundle of dried wildflowers in the grave, stepped back, started to talk but then couldn't.

Cotton offered up a fine eulogy to his young friend and recited a few examples from a storyteller he said he much admired: Jimmy "Diamond" Skinner. "In his own way," said Cotton, "he would put to shame many of the finest taletellers of the day."

Lou said a few quiet words, addressing them really to her friend in the box under the freshly turned dirt that smelled sweet yet sickened her. But he was not between those planks of cedar, Lou knew. He had gone on to a place higher even than the mountains. He was back with his father, and was seeing his mother for the very first time. He must surely be happy. Lou raised her hand to the sky and waved good-bye once again to a person who had come to mean so much to her, and who was now gone forever.

A few days after the burial, Lou and Oz had ventured to Diamond's tree house and took an accounting of his belongings. Lou said Diamond would naturally want Oz to have the bird skeleton, the Civil War bullet, the flint arrowhead, and the crude telescope.

"But what do you get?" asked Oz, as he examined his inherited spoils.

Lou picked up the box and took out the lump of coal, the one allegedly containing the diamond. She would make it her mission to chip carefully away at it, for as long as it took, until the brilliant center was finally revealed, and then she would go and bury it with Diamond. When she noted the small piece of wood lying on the floor in the back of the tree house, she sensed what it was before ever she picked it up. It was a whittled piece, not yet finished.

It was cut from hickory, shape of a heart, the letter L carved on one side, an almost finished D on the other. Diamond Skinner *had* known his letters. Lou pocketed the wood and coal, climbed down the tree, and didn't stop running until she was back home.

They had, of course, adopted the loyal Jeb, and he seemed comfortable around them, though he would sometimes grow depressed and pine for his old master. Yet he too seemed to enjoy the trips Lou and Oz took to see Diamond's grave, and the dog, in the mysterious way of the canine pet, would start to yip and do spins in the air when they drew near to it. Lou and Oz would spread fall leaves over the mound and sit and talk to Diamond and to each other and retell the funny things the boy had done or said, and there was no short supply of either. Then they would wipe their eyes and head home, sure in their hearts that his spirit was roaming freely on his beloved mountain, his hair just as stuck up, his smile just as wide, his feet just as bare. Diamond Skinner had had no material possessions to his name and yet had been the happiest creature Lou had ever met. He and God would no doubt get along famously.

They prepared for winter by sharpening tools with the grinder and rattail files, mucking out the stalls and spreading the manure over the plowed-under fields. Louisa had been wrong about that, though, for Lou never grew to love the smell of manure. They brought the livestock in, kept them fed and watered, milked the cows, and did their other chores, which now all seemed as natural as breathing. They carried jugs of milk and butter, and jars of mixed pickles in vinegar and brine, and canned sauerkraut and beans down to the partially underground dairy house, which had thick log walls, daubed and chinked, and paper stuffed where mud had fallen away. And they repaired everything on the farm that called for it.

School started, and, true to his father's words, Billy Davis never came back. No mention was made of his absence, as though the boy had never existed. Lou found herself thinking of him from time to time, though, and hoped he was all right.

After chores were done one late fall evening, Louisa sent Lou and Oz down to the creek that ran on the south side of the property to fetch balls from the sycamore trees that grew in abundance there. The balls had sharp stickers, but Louisa told them they would be used for Christmas decorations. Christmas was still a ways off, but Lou and Oz did as they were told.

When they got back, they were surprised to see Cotton's car in front. The house was dark and they cautiously opened the door, unsure of what they would find. The lights flew up as Louisa and Eugene took the black cloths from around the lanterns and they and Cotton called out "Happy Birthday," in a most excited tone. And it was their birthday, both of them, for Lou and Oz had been born on the same day, five years apart, as Amanda had informed Louisa in one of her letters. Lou was officially a teenager now, and Oz had survived to the ripe old age of eight.

A wild-strawberry pie was on the table, along with cups of hot cider. Two small candles were in the pie and

Oz and Lou together blew them out. Louisa pulled out the presents she had been working on all this time, on her Singer sewing machine: a Chop bag dress for Lou that was a pretty floral pattern of red and green, and a smart jacket, trousers, and white shirt for Oz that had been created from clothes Cotton had given her.

Eugene had carved two whistles for them that gave off different tunes, such that they could communicate when apart in the deep woods or across acres of field. The mountains would send an echo to the sun and back, Louisa told them. They gave their whistles a blast, which tickled their lips, making them giggle.

Cotton presented Lou with a book of poems by Walt Whitman. "My ancestor's superior in the arena of the poem, if I may so humbly admit," he said. And then he pulled from a box something that made Oz forget to breathe. The baseball mitts were things of beauty, well-oiled, worn to perfection, smelling of fine leather, sweat, and summer grass, and no doubt holding timeless and cherished childhood dreams. "They were mine growing up," Cotton said. "But I'm embarrassed to admit that while I'm not that good of a lawyer, I'm a far better lawyer than I ever was a ballplayer. Two mitts, for you and Lou. And me too, if you'll put up with my feeble athletic skills from time to time."

Oz said he would be proud to, and he hugged the gloves tight to his chest. Then they ate heartily of the pie and drank down the cider. Afterward Oz put on his suit, which fit very nicely; he looked almost like a tiny lawyer. Louisa had wisely tucked extra material under the hems to allow for the boy's growth, which seemed now to occur daily. So dressed, Oz took his baseball gloves and his whistle and went to show his mother. A little while later Lou heard strange sounds coming from Amanda's bedroom. When she went to check, she saw Oz standing on a stool, a sheet around his shoulders, a baseball glove on his head like a crown, and brandishing a long stick.

"And the great Oz the brave, and not cowardly lion anymore, killed all the dragons and saved all the moms and they all lived happily ever after in Virginia." He took off his crown of oiled leather and gave a series of sweeping bows. "Thank you, my loyal subjects, no trouble a'-tall."

Oz sat next to his mother, lifted a book off the nightstand, and opened it to a place marked by a slip of paper. "Okay, Mom," said Oz, "this is the scary part, but just so you know, the witch doesn't eat the children." He inched close to her, draped one of her arms around his waist, and with big eyes started to read the scary part.

Lou went back to the kitchen, sat at the table in her Chop bag dress, which also well suited her, and read the brilliant words of Whitman by the glow of reliable kerosene. It became so late that Cotton stayed, and slept curled up in front of the coal fire. And another fine day had passed on the mountain.

CHAPTER THIRTY-TWO

WITHOUT EITHER LOUISA OR EUGENE KNOWING, Lou took a lantern and a match and she and Oz rode Sue down to the mine. Lou jumped down, but Oz sat on the horse and stared at the mouth of that cave as though it were the direct portal to hell. "I'm not going in there," he declared.

"Then wait out here," said his sister.

"Why do you want to go in there? After what happened to Diamond? The mountain might fall in on you. And I bet it'd hurt bad."

"I want to know what the men Diamond saw were up to."

Lou lit the lantern and went in. Oz waited near the entrance, pacing nervously, and then he ran in, quickly catching up to his sister.

"I thought you weren't coming," Lou said.

"I thought you might get scared," Oz answered, even as he clutched at her shirt.

They moved along, shivering from the cool air and their tender nerves. Lou looked around and saw what appeared to be new support beams along the walls and ceiling of the shaft. On the walls she also saw various markings in what looked to be white paint. A loud hissing sound reached out to them from up ahead.

"A snake?" asked Oz.

"If it is, it's about the size of the Empire State Building. Come on." They hurried ahead and the hissing sound grew louder with each step. They turned one corner, and the sound became even louder, like steam escaping. They cleared one more turn, ran forward, edged around a final bend in the rock, and stopped. The men wore hard hats and carried battery-powered lights, and their faces were covered with masks. In the floor of the mine was a hole, with a large metal pipe inserted in it. A machine that looked like a pump was attached by hoses to the pipe and was making the hissing sound they had heard. The masked men were standing around the hole, but didn't see the children. Lou and Oz backed up slowly and then turned and ran. Right into Judd Wheeler. Then they dodged around him and kept right on running.

A minute later Lou and Oz burst out of the mine. Lou stopped next to Sue and scrambled on, but Oz, apparently unwilling to trust his survival to something as slow as a horse, flew by sister and mare like a rocket. Lou punched Sue in the ribs with her shoes and took off after her brother. She didn't gain any ground on the boy, however, as Oz was suddenly faster than a car.

※

Cotton, Louisa, Lou, and Oz were having a powwow around the kitchen table.

"You crazy to go in that mine," said Louisa angrily.

"Then we wouldn't have seen those men," replied Lou.

Louisa struggled with this and then said, "G'on now. Me and Cotton need to talk."

After Lou and Oz left, she looked at Cotton.

"So what you think?" she asked.

"From how Lou described it, I think they were looking for natural gas instead of oil. And found it."

"What should we do?"

"They're on your property without your permission, and they know that we know. I think they'll come to you."

"I ain't selling my land, Cotton."

Cotton shook his head. "No, what you can do is sell the mineral rights. And keep the land. And gas isn't like coal mining. They won't have to destroy the land."

She shook her head stubbornly. "Had us a good harvest. Don't need no help from nobody."

Cotton looked down and spoke slowly. "Louisa, I hope you outlive all of us. But the fact is, if those children come into the farm while they're still under age, it'd be right difficult for them to get along." He paused and then added quietly, "And Amanda may need special care."

Louisa nodded slightly at his words but said nothing.

Later, she watched Cotton drive off, while Oz and Lou playfully chased his convertible down the road, and Eugene diligently worked on some farm equipment. This was the sum total of Louisa's world. Everything seemed to move along smoothly, yet it was all very fragile, she well knew. The woman leaned against the door with a most weary face.

The Southern Valley men came the very next afternoon.

Louisa opened the door and Judd Wheeler stood there, and beside him was a little man with snake eyes and a slick smile, dressed in a well-cut three-piece suit.

"Miss Cardinal, my name's Judd Wheeler. I work for Southern Valley Coal and Gas. This is Hugh Miller, the vice president of Southern."

"And you want my natural gas?" she said bluntly.

"Yes, ma'am," replied Wheeler.

"Well, it's a right good thing my lawyer's here," she said, glancing at Cotton, who had come into the kitchen from Amanda's bedroom.

"Miss Cardinal," said Hugh Miller as they sat down, "I don't believe in beating around the bush. I understand that you've inherited some additional family responsibilities, and I know how trying that can be. So I am most happy to offer you . . . a hundred thousand dollars for your property. And I've got the check, and the paperwork for you to sign, right here."

Louisa had never held more than five dollars cash money in her whole life, so "My goodness!" was all she could manage.

"Just so we all understand," Cotton said, "Louisa would just be selling the underlying mineral rights."

Miller smiled and shook his head. "I'm afraid for that kind of money, we expect to get the land too."

"I ain't gonna do that," said Louisa.

Cotton said, "Why can't she just convey the mineral rights? It's a common practice up here."

"We have big plans for her property. Gonna level the mountain, put in a good road system, and build an extraction, production, and shipping facility. And the longest durn pipeline anybody's seen outside of Texas. We've spent a while looking. This property is perfect. Don't see one negative."

Louisa scowled at him. " 'Cept I ain't selling it to you. You ain't scalping this land like you done everywhere else."

Miller leaned forward. "This area is dying, Miss Cardinal. Lumber gone. Mines closing. Folks losing their jobs. What good are the mountains unless you use them to help people? It's just rock and trees."

"I got me a deed to this land says I own it, but nobody really own the mountains. I just watching over 'em while I here. And they give me all I need."

Miller looked around. "All you need? Why, you don't even have electricity or phones up here. As a God-fearing woman I'm sure you realize that our creator gave us brains so that we can take advantage of our surroundings. What's a mountain compared to people making a good living? Why, what you're doing is going against the Scriptures, I do believe."

Louisa stared at the little man and looked as though she might laugh. "God made these mountains so's they last forever. Yet he put us people here for just a little-bitty time. Now, what does that tell you?"

Miller looked exasperated. "Look here now, my company is looking to make a substantial investment in bringing this place back to life. How can you stand in the way of all that?"

Louisa stood. "Just like I always done. On my own two feet."

Cotton followed Miller and Wheeler to their car.

"Mr. Longfellow," said Miller, "you ought to talk your client into accepting our proposal."

Cotton shook his head. "Once Louisa Mae Cardinal makes up her mind, changing it is akin to trying to stop the sun from rising."

"Well, the sun goes *down* every night too," said Miller.

Cotton watched as the Southern Valley men drove off.

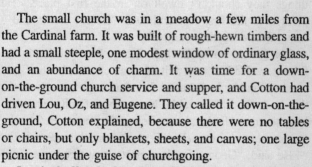

The small church was in a meadow a few miles from the Cardinal farm. It was built of rough-hewn timbers and had a small steeple, one modest window of ordinary glass, and an abundance of charm. It was time for a down-on-the-ground church service and supper, and Cotton had driven Lou, Oz, and Eugene. They called it down-on-the-ground, Cotton explained, because there were no tables or chairs, but only blankets, sheets, and canvas; one large picnic under the guise of churchgoing.

Lou had offered to stay home with her mother so Louisa could go, but the woman wouldn't hear of it. "I read me my Bible, I pray to my Lord, but I ain't needing to be sitting and singing with folks to prove my faith."

"Why should I go then?" Lou had asked.

" 'Cause after church is supper, and that food ain't to be beat, girl," Louisa answered with a smile.

Oz had on his suit, and Lou wore her Chop bag dress and thick brown stockings held up by rubber bands, while Eugene wore the hat Lou had given him and a clean shirt. There were a few other Negroes there, including one petite young woman with remarkable eyes and beautifully smooth skin with whom Eugene spent considerable time talking. Cotton explained that there were so few Negroes up this way, they didn't have a separate church. "And I'm right glad of that," he said. "Not usually that way down south, and in the towns the prejudice is surely there."

"We saw the 'Whites Only' sign in Dickens," said Lou.

"I'm sure you did," said Cotton. "But mountains are different. I'm not saying everybody up here is a saint, because they're surely not, but life is hard and folks just trying to get by. Doesn't leave much time to dwell on things they shouldn't dwell on in the first place." He pointed to the first row and said, "George Davis and a few others excepted, that is."

Lou looked on in shock at George Davis sitting in the front pew. He had on a suit of clean clothes, his hair was combed, and he had shaved. Lou had to grudgingly admit that he looked respectable. None of his family was with him, though. His head was bowed in prayer. Before the service started, Lou asked Cotton about this spectacle.

He said, "George Davis almost always comes to services, but he never stays for the meal. And he never brings his family because that's just the way he is. I would hope he comes and prays because he feels he has much to atone for. But I think he's just hedging his bets. A calculating man, he is."

Lou looked at Davis there praying like God was in his heart and home, while his family remained behind in rags and fear and would have starved except for the kindness of Louisa Cardinal. She could only shake her head. Then she said to Cotton, "Whatever you do, don't stand next to that man."

Cotton looked at her, puzzled. "Why not?"

"Lightning bolts," she answered.

For too many hours they listened to the circuit minister, their rumps worn sore by hard oak benches, their noses tickled by the scents of lye soap, lilac water, and grittier smells from those who had not bothered to wash before coming. Oz nodded off twice, and Lou had to kick him each time to rouse him. Cotton offered up a special prayer for Amanda, which Lou and Oz very much appreciated. However, it seemed they were all doomed to hell according to this fleshy Baptist minister. Jesus had given his life for them, and a sorry lot they were, he said, himself included. Not good for much other than sinning and similar lax ways. Then the holy man really got going and reduced every human being in the place to near tears, or to at least the shakes, at their extreme uselessness and at the guilt dwelling in their awful sinned-out souls. And then he passed the collection plate and asked very politely for the cold hard cash of all the fine folks there today, their awful sin and extreme uselessness notwithstanding.

After services they all headed outside. "My father's a pastor in Massachusetts," said Cotton, as they walked down the church steps. "And he's also right partial to the fire and brimstone method of religion. One of his heroes was Cotton Mather, which is where I got my rather curious name. And I know that my father was greatly upset when I did not follow him on to the pulpit, but such is life. I had no great calling from the Lord, and didn't want to do the ministry any disservice just to please my father. Now, I'm no expert on the subject, yet a body does get weary of being dragged through the holy briar patch only to have his pocket regularly picked by a pious hand." Cotton smiled as he surveyed the folks gathering around the food. "But I guess it's a fair price to pay to sample some of these good vittles."

The food indeed was some of the best Lou and Oz had ever had: baked chicken, sugar-cured Virginia ham, collard greens and bacon, fluffy grits heaped with churned butter, fried crackling bread, vegetable casseroles, many-kind beans, and warm fruit pies—all no doubt created with the most sacred and closely guarded of family recipes. The children ate until they could eat no more, and then lay under a tree to rest.

Cotton was sitting on the church steps, working on a chicken leg and a cup of hot cider, and enjoying the peace of a good church supper, when the men approached. They were all farmers, with strong arms and blocky shoulders, a forward lean to all of them, their fingers curled tight, as though they were still working the hoe or scythe, toting buckets of water or pulling udder teats.

"Evening, Buford," said Cotton, inclining his head at one of the men who stepped forward from the pack, felt hat in hand. Cotton knew Buford Rose to be a toiler in dirt and seed of long standing here, and a good, decent man. His farm was small, but he ran it efficiently. He was not so old as Louisa, but he had said so long to middle age years ago. He made no move to talk, his gaze fixed on his crumbling brogans. Cotton looked at the other men, most of whom he knew from helping them with some legal problem, usually to do with their deeds, wills, or land taxes. "Something on your minds?" he prompted.

Buford said, "Coal folk come by to see us all, Cotton. Talk 'bout the land. Selling it, that is."

"Hear they're offering good money," said Cotton.

Buford glanced nervously at his companions, his fingers digging into his hat brim. "Well, they ain't got that fer yet. See, thing is, they ain't a'wanting to buy our land 'less Louisa sell. Say it got to do with how the gas lie and all. I ain't unnerstand it none, but that what they say."

"Good crops this year," said Cotton. "Land generous to all. Maybe you don't need to sell."

"What 'bout next year?" said a man who was younger than Cotton but looked a good ten years older. He was a third-generation farmer up here, Cotton knew, and he didn't look all that happy about it right now. "One good year ain't make up fer three bad."

"Why ain't Louisa want'a sell, Cotton?" asked Buford. "She way older'n me even, and I done all worked out, and my boy he ain't want to do this no more. And she got them chillin, and the sick woman care for. Ain't make no sense to me she ain't partial to sell."

"This is her home, Buford. Just like it is yours. And it doesn't have to make sense to us. It's her wishes. We have to respect that."

"But can't you talk to her?"

"She's made up her mind. I'm sorry."

The men stared at him in silence, clearly not a single one of them pleased with this answer. Then they turned and walked away, leaving a very troubled Cotton Longfellow behind.

Oz had brought his ball and gloves to the church supper, and he threw with Lou and then with some of the other boys. The men gawked at his prowess and said Oz had an arm like they had never seen before. Then Lou happened upon a group of children talking about the death of Diamond Skinner.

"Stupid as a mule, getting hisself blowed up like that," said one fat-cheeked boy Lou didn't know.

"Going in a mine with dynamite lit," said another. "Good Lord, what a fool."

"Course, he never went to school," said a girl with dark hair rolled in sausage curls who wore an expensive wide-brimmed hat with a ribbon around it and a frilly dress of similar cost. Lou knew her as Charlotte Ramsey, whose family didn't farm but owned one of the smaller coal mines, and did well with it. "So poor thing probably didn't know any better."

After listening to this, Lou pushed her way into the group. She had grown taller in the time she had been living on the mountain, and she towered over all of them, though they were all close in age to her.

"He went in that mine to save his dog," said Lou.

The fat-cheeked boy laughed. "Risk his life to save a hound. Boy *was* dumb."

Lou's fist shot out, and the boy was on the ground holding one of those fat cheeks that had just grown a little plumper. Lou stalked away and kept right on walking.

Oz saw what had happened and he collected his ball and gloves and caught up with her. He said nothing but walked silently beside her, letting her anger cool, surely nothing new for him. The wind was picking up and the clouds were rolling in as a storm front cleared the mountain tops.

"Are we walking all the way home, Lou?"

"You can go back and ride with Cotton and Eugene if you want."

"You know, Lou, as smart as you are, you don't have to keep hitting people. You can beat 'em with words."

She glanced at him and couldn't help but smile at his comment. "Since when did you get so mature?"

Oz thought about this for a few moments. "Since I turned eight."

They walked on.

Oz had strung his gloves around his neck with a piece of twine, and he idly tossed the ball in the air and caught it behind his back. He tossed it again but did not catch it, and the ball dropped to the ground, forgotten.

George Davis had stepped from the woods quiet as a fog. For Lou, his nice clothes and clean face did nothing to soften the evil in the man. Oz was instantly cowed by him, but Lou said fiercely, "What do you want?"

"I know 'bout them gas people. Louisa gonna sell?"

"That's her business."

"My bizness! I bet I got me gas on my land too."

"Then why don't you sell your property?"

"Road to my place goes cross her land. They can't git to me 'less she sell."

"Well, that's your problem," said Lou, hiding her smile, for she was thinking that perhaps God had finally turned his attention to the man.

"You tell Louisa if she knowed what's good for her she better sell. You tell her, she better damn well sell."

"And you better get away from us."

Davis raised his hand. "Smart-mouthed cuss!"

Quick as a snake, a hand grabbed Davis's arm and

stopped it in midair. Cotton stood there, holding on to that powerful arm and staring at the man.

Davis jerked his arm free and balled his fists. "You gonna get hurt now, lawyer."

Davis threw a punch. And Cotton stopped the fist with his hand, and held on. And this time Davis couldn't break the man's grip, though he tried awfully hard.

When Cotton spoke, it was in a tone that was quiet and sent a delicious chill down Lou's back. "I majored in American literature in college. But I was also captain of the boxing team. If you ever raise your hand to these children again, I'll beat you within an inch of your life."

Cotton let go of the fist and Davis stepped back, obviously intimidated by both the calm manner and strong hands of his opponent.

"Cotton, he wants Louisa to sell her property so he can too. He's kind of insisting on it," said Lou.

"She doesn't want to sell," said Cotton firmly. "So that's the end of it."

"Lot of things happen, make somebody want'a sell."

"If that's a threat, we can take it up with the sheriff. Unless you'd like to address it with me right now."

With a snarl, George Davis stalked off.

As Oz picked up his baseball, Lou said, "Thank you, Cotton."

CHAPTER THIRTY-THREE

LOU WAS ON THE PORCH TRYING HER HAND AT DARN-ing socks, but not enjoying it much. She liked working outside better than anything else and looked forward to feeling the sun and wind upon her. There was an orderliness about farming that much appealed to her. In Louisa's words, she was quickly coming to understand and respect the land. The weather was getting colder every day now, and she wore a heavy woolen sweater Louisa had knitted for her. Looking up, she saw Cotton's car coming down the road, and she waved. Cotton saw her, waved back, and, leaving his car, joined her on the porch. They both looked out over the countryside. "Sure is beautiful here this time of year," he remarked. "No other place like it, really."

"So why do you think my dad never came back?"

Cotton took off his hat and rubbed his head. "Well, I've heard of writers who have lived somewhere while young and then wrote about it the rest of their lives without ever once going back to the place that inspired them. I don't know, Lou, it may be they were afraid if they ever returned and saw the place in a new light, it would rob them of the power to tell their stories."

"Like tainting their memories?"

"Maybe. What do you think about that? Never coming back to your roots so you can be a great writer?"

Lou did not have to ponder this long. "I think it's too big a price to pay for greatness."

Before going to bed each night, Lou tried to read at least one of the letters her mother had written Louisa. One night a week later, as she pulled out the desk drawer she'd put them in, it slid crooked and jammed. She put her hand on the inside of the drawer to gain leverage to right it, and her fingers brushed against something stuck to the underside of the desk top. She knelt down and peered in, probing farther with her hand as she did so. A few seconds later she pulled out an envelope that had been taped there. She sat on her bed and gazed down at the packet. There was no writing on the outside, but Lou could feel the pieces of paper inside. She drew them out slowly. They were old and yellowed, as was the envelope. Lou sat on her bed and read through the precise handwriting on the pages, the tears creeping down her cheeks long before she had finished. Her father had been fifteen years old when he wrote this, for the date was written at the top of the page.

Lou went to Louisa and sat with her by the fire, explained to her what she had found and read the pages to her in as clear a voice as she could:

"My name is John Jacob Cardinal, though I'm called Jack for short. My father has been dead five years now, and my mother, well, I hope that she is doing fine wherever she is. Growing up on a mountain leaves its mark upon all those who share both its bounty and its hardship. Life here is also well known for producing stories that amuse and also exact tears. In the pages that follow I recount a tale that my own father told me shortly before he passed on. I have thought about his words every day since then, yet only now am I finding the courage to write them down. I remember the story clearly, yet some of the words may be my own, rather than my father's, though I feel I have remained true to the spririt of his telling.

"The only advice I can give to whoever might happen upon these pages is to read them with care, and to make up your own mind about things. I love the mountain almost as much as I loved my father, yet I know that one day I will leave here, and once I leave I doubt I will ever come back. With that said, it is important to understand that I believe I could be very happy here for the rest of my days."

Lou turned the page and began reading her father's story to Louisa.

"It had been a long, tiring day for the man, though as a farmer he had known no other kind. With crop fields dust, hearth empty, and children hungry, and wife not happy about any of it, he set out on a walk. He had not gone far when he came upon a man of the cloth sitting upon a high rock overlooking stagnant water. 'You are a man of the soil,' said he in a voice gentle and seeming wise. The farmer answered that indeed he did make his living with dirt, though he would not wish such a life upon his children or even his dearest enemy. The preacher invited the farmer to join him upon the high rock, so he settled himself next to the man. He asked the farmer why he would not wish his children to carry on after their father. The farmer looked to the sky pretending thought, for his mind well knew what his mouth would say. 'For it is the most miserable life of all,' he said. 'But it is so beautiful here,' the preacher replied. 'Think of the wretched of the city living in squalor. How can a man of the open air and the fine earth say such a thing?' The farmer answered that he was not a learned man such as the preacher, yet he had heard of the great poverty in the cities where the folks stayed in their hovels all day, for there was no work for them to do. Or they got by on the dole. They starved— slowly, but they starved. Was that not true? he asked. And the preacher nodded his great and wise head at him. 'So that is starvation without effort,' said the farmer. 'A miserable existence if ever I heard of one,' said the holy man. And the farmer agreed with him, and then said, 'And I have also heard that in other parts of the country there are farms so grand, on land so flat that the birds cannot fly over them in one day.' 'This too is true,' replied the other man. The farmer continued. 'And that when crops come in on such farms, they can eat like kings for years from a single harvest, and sell the rest and have money in their pockets.' 'All true,' said the preacher. 'Well, on the mountain there are no such places,' said the farmer. 'If the crops come fine we eat, nothing more.' 'And your point?' said the preacher. 'Well, my plight is this, preacher: My children, my wife, myself, we all break our backs every year, working from before the rise of sun till past dark. We work hard coaxing the land to feed us. Things may look good, our hopes may be high. And then it so often comes to naught. And we still starve. But you see, we starve with great effort. Is that not more miserable?' 'It has indeed been a hard year,' said the other man. 'But did you know that corn will grow on rain and prayer?' 'We pray every day,' the farmer said, 'and the corn stands at my knee, and it is September now.' 'Well,' the preacher said, 'of course the more rain the better. But you are greatly blessed to be a servant of the earth.' The farmer said that his marriage would not stand much more blessing, for his good wife did not see things exactly that way. He bowed his head and said, 'I'm sure I am a miserable one to complain.' 'Speak up, my son,' the holy man said, 'for I am the ears of God.' 'Well,' the farmer said, 'it creates discomfort in the marriage, pain between husband and wife, this matter of hard work and no reward.' The other man raised a pious finger and said, 'But hard work can be its own reward.' The farmer smiled. 'Praise the Lord then, for I have been richly rewarded all my life.' And the preacher seconded that and said, 'So your marriage is having troubles?' 'I am a wretch to complain,' the farmer said. 'I am the eyes of the Lord,' the preacher replied. They both looked at a sky of blue that had not a drop of what the farmer needed in it. 'Some *people are not cut out for a life of such rich rewards,'* he said. *'It is your wife you are speaking of now,'* the preacher stated. *'Perhaps it is me,'* the farmer said. *'God will lead you to the truth, my son,'* the preacher said. *Can a man be afraid of the truth?* the farmer wanted to know. *A man can be afraid of anything,* the preacher told him. *They rested there a bit, for the farmer had run clear out of words. Then he watched as the clouds came, the heavens opened, and the water rushed to touch them. He rose, for there was work to be done now. 'You see,' said the holy man, 'my words have come true. God has shown you the way.' 'We will see,' the farmer said. 'For it is late in the season now.' As he moved off to return to his land, the preacher called after him. 'Son of the soil,' he said, 'if the crops come fine, remember thy church in thy bounty.' The farmer looked back and touched his hand to the brim of his hat. 'The Lord does work in mysterious ways,' he told the other man. And then he turned and left the eyes and ears of God behind."*

Lou folded the letter and looked at Louisa, hoping she had done the right thing by reading the words to her. Lou wondered if the young Jack Cardinal had noticed that the story had become far more personal when it addressed the issue of a crumbling marriage.

Louisa stared into the fire. She was silent for a few minutes and then said, "It be a hard life up here, 'specially for a child. And it hard on husband and wife, though I ain't never suffered that. If my momma and daddy ever said a cross word to the other, I ain't never heard it. And me and my man Joshua get along to the minute he took his last breath. But I know it not that way for your daddy up here. Jake and his wife, they had their words."

Lou took a quick breath and said, "Dad wanted you to come and live with us. Would you have?"

She looked at Lou. "You ask me why I don't never leave this place? I love this land, Lou, 'cause it won't never let me down. If the crops don't come, I eat the apples or wild strawberries that always do, or the roots that's there right under the soil, if'n you know where to look. If it snow ten-foot deep, I can get along. Rain or hail, or summer heat that melt tar, I get by. I find water where there ain't supposed to be none, I get on. Me and the land. Me and this mountain. That ain't prob'ly mean nothing to folks what can have light by pushing a little knob, or talk to people they can't even see." She paused and drew a breath. "But it means everything to me." She looked into the fire once more. "All your daddy say is true. High rock be beautiful. High rock be cruel." She gazed at Lou and added quietly, "And the mountain is my home."

Lou leaned her head against Louisa's chest. The woman stroked Lou's hair very gently with her hand as they sat there by the fire's warmth.

And then Lou said something she thought she never would. "And now it's my home too."

CHAPTER THIRTY-FOUR

FLAKES OF SNOW WERE DROPPING FROM THE BELLIES of bloated clouds. Near the barn there came a whooshing sound and then a spark of harsh light that kept right on growing.

Inside the farmhouse Lou groaned in the throes of a nightmare. Her and Oz's beds had been moved to the front room, by the coal fire, and they were bundled under crazy quilts Louisa had sewn over the years. In Lou's tortured sleep she heard a noise, but couldn't tell what it was. She opened her eyes, sat up. There came a scratching at the door. In an instant Lou was alert. She opened the door and Jeb burst in, yipping and jumping.

"Jeb, what is it? What's wrong?"

Then she heard the screams of the farm animals.

Lou ran out in her nightshirt. Jeb followed her, barking, and Lou saw what had spooked him: The barn was fully ablaze. She ran back to the house, screamed out what was happening, and then raced to the barn.

Eugene appeared at the front door of the farmhouse, saw the fire, and hurried out, Oz at his heels.

When Lou threw open the big barn door, smoke and flames leapt out at her.

"Sue! Bran!" she screamed as the smoke hit her lungs; she could feel the hairs on her arms rise from the heat.

Eugene fast-limped past her, plunged into the barn, and then came right back out, gagging. Lou looked at the trough of water by the corral and a blanket hanging over the fence. She grabbed the blanket and plunged it into the cold water.

"Eugene, put this over you."

Eugene covered himself with the wet blanket and then lunged back into the barn.

Inside a beam dropped down and barely missed Eugene. Smoke and fire were everywhere. Eugene was as familiar with the insides of this barn as he was with anything on the farm, yet it was as though he had been struck blind. He finally got to Sue, who was thrashing in her stall, threw open the door, and put a rope around the terrified mare's neck.

Eugene stumbled out of the barn with Sue, threw the rope to Lou, who led the horse away with assistance from Louisa and Oz, and then Eugene went back into the barn. Lou and Oz hauled buckets of water from the springhouse, but Lou knew it was like trying to melt snow with your breath. Eugene drove out the mules and all the cows except one. But they lost every hog. And all their hay, and most of their tools and harnesses. The sheep were wintered outside, but the loss was still a devastating one.

Louisa and Lou watched from the porch as the barn, bare studs now, continued to burn. Eugene stood by the corral where he had driven the livestock. Oz was next to him with a bucket of water to dump on any creep of fire.

Then Eugene called out, "She coming down," and he pulled Oz away. The barn collapsed in on itself, the flames leaping skyward and the snow gently falling into this inferno.

Louisa stared in obvious agony at this ruin, as though she were caught in the flames herself. Lou tightly held her hand and was quick to notice when Louisa's fingers began to shake, the strong grip suddenly becoming impossibly weak.

"Louisa?"

The woman dropped to the porch without a word.

"Louisa!"

The girl's anguished cries echoed across the stark, cold valley.

Cotton, Lou, and Oz stood next to the hospital bed where Louisa lay. It had been a wild ride down the mountain in the old Hudson, gears thrashed by a frantic Eugene, engine whining, wheels slipping and then catching in the snowy dirt. The car almost went over the edge twice. Lou and Oz had clung to Louisa, praying that she would not leave them. They had gotten her to the small hospital in Dickens, and then Lou had run and rousted Cotton from his bed. Eugene had gone back up to look after Amanda and the animals.

Travis Barnes was attending her, and the man looked worried. The hospital was also his home, and the sight of a dining room table and a General Electric refrigerator had not comforted Lou.

"How is she, Travis?" asked Cotton.

Barnes looked at the children and then pulled Cotton to the side. "She's had a stroke," he said in a low voice. "Looks to be some paralysis on the left side."

"Is she going to recover?" This came from Lou, who had heard everything.

Travis delivered a woeful shrug. "There's not much we can do for her. The next forty-eight hours are critical. If I thought she could make the trip, I'd have sent her on to the hospital in Roanoke. We're not exactly equipped for this sort of thing. You can go on home. I'll send word if her condition changes."

Lou said, "I'm not leaving." And then Oz said the same.

"I think you've been overruled," said Cotton quietly.

"There's a couch right outside," Travis said kindly.

They were all asleep there, each holding the others up, when the nurse touched Cotton's shoulder.

She said softly, "Louisa's awake."

Cotton and the children eased the door open and went in. Louisa's eyes were open, but not much more than that. Travis stood over her.

"Louisa?" said Cotton. There was no answer, not even a hint of recognition. Cotton looked at Travis.

"She's still very weak," Travis said. "I'm amazed she's even conscious."

Lou just stared at her, more scared than she'd ever been. She just couldn't believe it. Her father, her mother.

Diamond. Now Louisa. Paralyzed. Her mother had not moved a muscle for longer than Lou cared to think about. Was that to be Louisa's fate too? A woman who loved the earth? Who cherished her mountain? Who had lived as good a life as one could live? It was almost enough to make Lou stop believing in a God who could do such a terrible thing. Leaving a person with no hope. Leaving a person with nothing at all really.

Cotton, Oz, Lou, and Eugene had just started their meal at the farmhouse.

"I can't believe they haven't caught whoever burned the barn down," Lou said angrily.

"There's no proof anybody burned it down, Lou," replied Cotton, as he poured the milk and then passed the biscuits.

"I know who did it. George Davis. Probably that gas company paid him to."

"You can't go around saying that, Lou, that's slander."

"I know the truth!" the girl shot back.

Cotton took off his glasses. "Lou, believe me—"

Lou leapt up from the table, her knife and fork clattering down and making them all jump. "Why should I believe anything you say, Cotton? You said my mom was going to come back. Now Louisa's gone too. Are you going to lie and say she's going to get better? Are you?"

Lou ran off. Oz started to go after her, but Cotton stopped him. "Let her be for now, Oz," he said. Cotton got up and went out on the porch, looking at the stars and contemplating the collapse of all he knew.

Flashing across in front of him was Lou on the mare. A startled Cotton could only stare after her, and then horse and girl were gone.

Lou rode Sue hard through the moonlit trails, tree limbs and brush poking and slapping at her. She finally came to Diamond's house and slid down, running and falling until she reached the doorway and plunged inside.

Tears streaming down her face, Lou stumbled around the room. "Why'd you have to leave us, Diamond? Now Oz and I have nobody. Nobody! Do you hear me? Do you, Diamond Skinner!"

A scuffling sound came from the front porch. Lou turned, terrified. Then Jeb raced through the open door and jumped into her arms, licking her face and breathing heavy from his long run. She hugged him. And then the tree branches started rattling against the glass, and an anxious moan came down the chimney, and Lou held especially tight to that dog. A window banged open, and the wind swirled around the room, and then things grew calm, and, finally, so did Lou.

She went outside, mounted Sue, and headed back, unsure of why she had even come here. Jeb trailed behind, tongue hanging low. She came to a fork in the road and turned left, toward the farm. Jeb started howling before Lou heard the noises herself. The throaty growls and ominous thrashing of underbrush were close upon them. Lou whipped up the horse, but before Sue could get rolling faster, the first of the wild dogs cleared the woods and came straight into their path. Sue reared up on her hind legs as the hideous creature, more wolf than dog, bared its teeth, its hackles straight up. Then another and another came from the woods, until a half dozen circled them. Jeb had his fangs bared and his hackles up too, yet he didn't stand a chance against so many, Lou knew. Sue kept rearing and neighing, and spinning in little circles until Lou felt herself slipping, as the wide body of the mare seemed to grow as narrow as a tightrope, and was also slicked, for the horse was lathered heavily after the long run.

One of the pack made a lunge for Lou's leg, and she pulled it up; the animal collided with one of Sue's hoofs and was temporarily stunned. There were too many of them, though, circling and snarling, ribs showing. Jeb went on the attack, but one of the brutes threw him down and he retreated, blood showing on his fur.

And then another beast snapped at Sue's foreleg and she went up again. And when she came down this time, she was riderless, for Lou had finally lost her grip and landed on her back, the wind knocked from her. Sue took off down the trail for home, yet Jeb stood like a stone wall in front of his fallen mistress, no doubt prepared to die for her. The pack moved in, sensing the easy kill. Lou forced herself up, despite the ache in her shoulder and back. There wasn't even a stick within reach, and she and Jeb moved backward until there was nowhere else to go. As she prepared herself to die fighting, the only thing Lou could think of was that Oz would now be all alone, and the tears welled up in her eyes.

The scream was like a net dropped over them, and the half-wolves turned. Even the largest of them, the size of a calf, flinched when it saw what was coming. The panther was big and sleek, muscles flexing under charcoal skin. It had amber eyes, and fangs showing that were double the size of the near-wolves'. And its claws too were fearsome things, like pitchfork hooked to knuckle. It screamed again when it got to the trail and headed for the wild pack with the power of a loaded coal train. The dogs turned and fled the fight, and that cat followed them, screaming with each graceful stride.

Lou and Jeb ran as hard as they could for home. About a half mile from the house they once more heard the crash of the underbrush next to them. Jeb's hackles went north again, and Lou's heart nearly stopped: She beheld the amber eyes of the cat out of the darkness as it ran parallel to them through the woods. That terrifying animal could shred both girl and hound in seconds. And yet all that thing did was run next to them, never once venturing out of the woods. The only reason Lou knew it was still there was the sounds of its paws against the leaves and undergrowth, and the glow of those luminous eyes, which looked free-floating in the darkness, as black skin blended with stark night.

Lou let out a thankful cry when she saw the farmhouse, and she and Jeb ran to the porch and then inside to safety. No one else was stirring, and Cotton, she assumed, had probably left long ago. Her chest heaving, Lou looked out the window, but never saw a sign of the beast.

Lou went down the hallway, every nerve still jangling badly. She paused at her mother's door and leaned against it. She had come so close to dying tonight, and it had been awful, more terrible than the car accident even, for she had been alone in her crisis. Lou peered inside the room and was surprised to find the window open. She went in, closed it, and turned to the bed. For one dazed moment she could not find her mother in the covers, and then of course there she was. Lou's breath became normal, the shivers of fear fading as she drew closer to the bed. Amanda was breathing lightly, her eyes closed, fingers actually curled, as though in pain. Lou reached out and touched her and then withdrew her hand. Her mother's skin was moist, clammy. Lou fled the room and bumped into Oz standing in the hall.

"Oz," she said, "you're not going to believe what happened to me."

"What were you doing in Mom's room?"

She took a step back. "What? I—"

"If you don't want Mom to get better, then you should just leave her alone, Lou. Just leave her alone!"

"But Oz—"

"Dad loved you the best, but I'll take care of Mom. Just like she always took care of us. I know Mom will get better, even if you don't."

"But you didn't take the bottle of holy water Diamond got for you."

"Maybe necklaces and holy water won't help Mom, but me believing she'll get better will. But *you* don't believe, so just leave her be."

He had never in his life talked to her this way. He just stood there and glared, his thin, strong arms dangling by his sides, like needles at the end of thread. Her little brother really angry at her! She couldn't believe it. "Oz!" He turned and walked away. "Oz," she called again. "Please, don't be mad at me. Please!" Oz never turned around. He went into his room and shut the door.

Lou stumbled to the back of the house, then went out

and sat on the steps. The beautiful night, the wondrous sight of the mountains, the calls of all kind of wildlife made no impression at all on her. She looked at her hands where the sun had leathered them, the palms rough as oak bark. Her fingernails were jagged and dirty, her hair knotted and lye-soaped to death, her body fatigued beyond her years, her spirit given way to despair after losing almost all those she cared about. And now her precious Oz no longer loved her.

At that moment, the hated mine siren boomed across the valley. It was as though the mountain were shrieking in anticipation of the coming pain. The sound seemed to splinter Lou's very soul. And next the rumble of the dynamite came and finished her off. Lou looked to that Cardinal graveyard knoll and suddenly wished she was there too, where nothing else could ever hurt her.

She bent over and wept quietly into her lap. She hadn't been there long when she heard the door creak open behind her. At first she thought it might be Eugene checking on her, but the tread was too light. The arms wrapped around her and held her tight.

Lou could feel her brother's delicate breaths on her neck. She stayed bent over, yet she reached behind her and wrapped an arm around him. And brother and sister stayed there like that for the longest time.

CHAPTER THIRTY-FIVE

THEY RODE THE WAGON DOWN TO MCKENZIE'S MER-
cantile, and Eugene, Lou, and Oz went inside. Rollie McKenzie stood behind a waist-high counter of
warped maple. He was a little ball of a man, with a shiny,
hairless head and a long grayish white beard that rested
on his slack chest. He wore spectacles of great strength,
yet the man still had to squint to see. The store was filled
to nearly overflowing with farm supplies and building
materials of various kinds. The smell of leather harnesses,
kerosene oil, and burning wood from the corner potbelly
filled the large space. There were glass candy dispensers
and a Chero Cola box against one wall. A few other customers were in the place and they all stopped and gaped
at Eugene and the children as though they were appari-
tions come haunting.

McKenzie squinted and nodded at Eugene, his fingers
picking at his thick beard, like a squirrel worrying a nut.

"Hi, Mr. McKenzie," said Lou. She had been here several times now and found the man gruff but fair.

Oz had his baseball mitts draped around his neck and

was tossing his ball. He was never without them now, and Lou suspected her brother even slept with the things.

"Real sorry to hear 'bout Louisa," McKenzie said.

"She's going to be fine," said Lou firmly, and Oz gave her a surprised look and almost dropped his baseball.

"What can I do for you?" asked McKenzie.

"Got to raise us a new barn," said Eugene. "Got to have us some things."

"Somebody burned our barn down," said Lou, and she glared around at the people staring.

"Use some finished board, posts, nails, hardware for the doors, and such," said Eugene. "Got me a good list right chere." He pulled a piece of paper from his pocket and laid it on the counter. McKenzie did not look at it.

"I'll need cash up front," he said, finally letting his beard alone.

Eugene stared at the man. "But we good on our 'count. All paid up, suh."

Now McKenzie eyed the paper. "Lot of stuff on that list. Can't carry you for that much."

"So's we bring you crop. Barter."

"No. Cash."

"Why can't we get credit?" asked Lou.

"Hard times," replied McKenzie.

Lou looked around at the piles of supplies and goods everywhere. "Times look pretty good to me."

McKenzie slid back the list. "I'm sorry."

"But we's got to have a barn," said Eugene. "Winter come fast and we ain't keep the animals out. They die."

"The animals we have *left*," said Lou, glaring some more at the still staring faces.

A man equal in size to Eugene approached from the

rear of the store. Lou knew him to be McKenzie's son-in-law, who was no doubt looking forward, she figured, to inheriting this good business one day when McKenzie squinted his last.

"Look here, Hell No," said the man, "you got your answer, boy."

Before Lou could say a word, Eugene stepped directly in front of the man. "You knowed that ain't *never* been my name. It be Eugene Randall. And don't you *never* call me nuthin' else." The big man appeared stunned, and he took a step back. Lou and Oz exchanged glances and then looked proudly upon their friend.

Eugene stared down each of the customers in the store, ostensibly, Lou thought, to make clear that this statement applied to all of them as well.

Rollie McKenzie called out, "I'm sorry for that, Eugene. It won't never happen again."

Eugene nodded at McKenzie and then told the children to come on. They went outside and climbed on the wagon. Lou was shaking with anger. "It's that gas company. They've scared everybody. Turned people against us."

Eugene took up the reins. "It be all right. We think'a somethin'."

Oz cried out, "Eugene, wait a minute." He jumped down from the wagon and ran back inside.

"Mr. McKenzie? Mr. McKenzie?" Oz called out, and the old man came back to the counter, blinking and picking at his beard.

Oz plopped his mitts and ball on the curled maple planks. "Will this buy us a barn?"

McKenzie stared at the child, and the old man's lips

trembled some, and his blinking eyes grew moist through
the heft of glass. "You go on home, boy. You go on home
now."

❦

They cleared all the debris from the remains of the
barn and collected all the nails, bolts, and usable wood
that they could from the ruins. Cotton, Eugene, and the
children stood and stared at the meager pile.

"Not much there," said Cotton.

Eugene looked at the surrounding forests. "Well, we
got us lot of wood, and it all free, 'cept the sweat of
felling it."

Lou pointed to the abandoned shack her father had
written about. "And we can use stuff from there," she
said, then looked at Cotton and smiled. They had not spoken since Lou's outburst, and she was feeling badly about
it. "Maybe make us a miracle," she added.

"Well, let's get to work," said Cotton.

They tore down the shack and salvaged what they
could. Over the next several days they cut down trees
with an ax and a crosscut saw that had been in the corncrib and thus had escaped the fire. They pulled out the
felled trees with the mules and chains. Fortunately, Eugene was a first-rate, if self-taught, carpenter. They topped
off the trees and stripped the bark, and using a square
and a measuring tape, Eugene cut marks in the wood
showing where notches needed to be chiseled. "Ain't got
'nough nails, so's we got to make do. Notch and strap

the joints best we can, mud chink 'tween. When we get mo' nails, we do the job right."

"What about the corner posts?" asked Cotton. "We don't have any mortar to set them in."

"Ain't got to. Dig the holes deep, way below the cold line, crack up the rock, pack it in good and hard. It hold. I give us some extra hep at the corners with the braces. You see."

"You're the boss," said Cotton with an encouraging smile.

Using a pick and shovel, Cotton and Eugene dug one hole. It was tough going against the hard ground. Their cold breath filled the air, and their gloved hands ached with the raw. While they were doing this, Oz and Lou chiseled out and hand-drilled the notches and insertion holes on the posts where timber mortise would meet timber tenon. Then they mule-dragged one of the posts to the hole and realized they had no way to get it in there. Try as they might, from every angle, and with every conceivable leverage, and with big Eugene straining every muscle he had, and little Oz too, they could not lift it enough. "We figger that out later," said Eugene finally, his big chest heaving from the failed effort.

He and Cotton laid out the first wall on the ground and started to hammer. Halfway through they ran out of nails. They collected all the scrap metal they could find and Eugene made a roaring coal fire for his forge. Then, using his smithy hammer, tongs, and shoeing anvil, he fashioned as many rough nails from the scrap as he could.

"Good thing iron doesn't burn," remarked Cotton, as he watched Eugene working away on the anvil, which still stood in the middle of what used to be the barn.

All of Eugene's hard work netted them enough nails to finish another third of the first wall, and that was all.

They had been at this for many cold days now, and all they had to show for it was one hole and a single finished corner post and no way to allow either to meet, and a wall without enough nails to hold it together.

They collected early one morning around the post and hole to mull this over, and all agreed the situation did not look good. A hard winter was creeping ever closer and they had no barn. And Sue, the cows, and even the mules were showing the ill effects of being out in the freezing air all night. They could not afford to lose any more livestock.

And as bad as this plight was, it was really the least of their problems, for while Louisa had regained consciousness from time to time, she had not spoken a word when awake, and her eyes appeared dead. Travis Barnes was very worried, and fretted that he should send her to Roanoke, but he was afraid she would still not survive the trip, and the fact was, there wasn't much they could do for her there anyway. She had been able to drink and eat a bit, and while it wasn't much, Lou took it as something to hold on to. It was as much as her mother was able to do. At least they were both still alive.

Lou looked around their small, depressed group, then gazed at the naked trees on the angled slopes and wished winter would magically dissolve to summer's warmth, and Louisa would rise fine and healthy from her sickbed. The sounds of the wheels made them all turn and stare. The line of approaching wagons pulled by mule, horse, and oxen teams was a long one. They were filled with cut lumber, large padstones, kegs of nails, ropes, ladders, block and tackle, augers, and all manners of other tools, that Lou suspected came in part from McKenzie's Mercantile. Lou counted thirty men in all, all from the mountain, all of them farmers. Strong, quiet, bearded, they wore coarse clothing and wide-brimmed hats against a winter's sun, and all had large, thick hands severely battered by both the mountain elements and a lifetime of hard work. With them were a half dozen women. They unloaded their supplies. While the women laid out canvas and blankets and used Louisa's cookstove and fireplace to start preparing the meals, the men began to build a barn.

Under Eugene's direction, they constructed supports for the block and tackle. Forgoing the route of post and mortar in hole, they opted to use the large, flat padstones for the barn's foundation. They dug shallow footers, laid the stones, leveled them, and then placed massive hewn timbers across the stones as the sill plates. These plates were secured together all around the foundation. Additional timbers were run down the middle of the barn floor and attached to the sill plates. Later, other posts would be placed here and braced to support the roof framework and hayloft. Using the block and tackle, the mule teams lifted the massive corner posts up and on top of the sill plates. Thick brace timbers were nailed into the corner posts on either side, and then the braces themselves were firmly attached to the plates.

With the barn's foundation set, the wall frames were built on the ground, and Eugene measured and marked and called out instructions on placement. Ladders were put up against the corner posts and holes augured into them. They used the block and tackle to raise other timbers up to be used as the crossbeams. Holes had been hand-drilled through these timbers, and they were attached to the corner posts with long metal bolts.

There was a shout as the first wall was run up, and each time after that as the remaining walls were built and run up. They framed the roof, and then the hammering became relentless as stud walls were further built out. Saws sliced through the air, cold breaths crowded each other, sawdust swirled in the breeze, men held nails in their mouths, and hands moved hammers with practiced motions.

Two meals were rung for, and the men dropped to the ground and ate hard each time. Lou and Oz carried plates of warm food and pots filled with hot chicory coffee to the groups of tired men. Cotton sat with his back against the rail fence, sipping his coffee, resting his sore muscles, and watching with a broad smile as a barn began to emerge out of nothing but the sweat and charity of good neighbors.

As Lou placed a platter of hot bread slathered with butter in front of the men, she said, "I want to thank all of you for helping."

Buford Rose picked up a piece of the bread and took a savage, if near toothless, bite. "Well, got to hep each other up here, 'cause ain't nobody else gonna. Ask my woman, ain't b'lieve me. And Lord knows Louisa's done her share of hepping folks round here." He looked over at Cotton, who tipped his cup of coffee to the man. "I knowed what I said to you 'bout being all worked out, Cotton, but lotta folk got it badder'n me. My brother be a dairy farmer down the Valley. Can't barely walk no more with all that setting on the stool, fingers done curled like some crazy root. And folk say two things dairy farmer ain't never gonna need they's whole lives: suit'a nice clothes and a place to sleep." He tore off another bread chunk.

A young man said, "Hell, Ms. Louisa done borned me. My ma say I aint'a coming to this world what she not there." Other men nodded and grinned at this remark. One of them looked over to where Eugene was standing near the rising structure, chewing on a piece of chicken and figuring out the next tasks to be done.

"And he done help me raise new barn two spring ago. Man good with hammer 'n saw. Ain't no lie."

From under knotted plugs of eyebrows Buford Rose studied Lou's features. "I 'member your daddy good, girl. You done take after him fine. That boy, all the time pestering folk with questions. I had to tell him I done ain't got no more words in my head." He gave a near tooth-less grin, and Lou smiled back.

The work continued. One group planked the roof and then laid out the roll of roofing paper on top. Another team, headed up by Eugene, fashioned the double doors for both ends, as well as the hayloft doors, while yet another group planked and daubed the outside walls. When it got too dark to see what they were hitting and cutting, kerosene lamps lit the night. The hammering and sawing got to be almost pleasing to hear. Almost. None complained, though, when the final board had been laid, the last nail driven. It was well into dark when the work was done and the wagons headed out.

Eugene, Cotton, and the children wearily herded the animals into their new home and laid the floor with hay gathered from the fields and the corncrib. The hayloft, stalls, storage bins, and such still needed to be built out, and the roll of roofing would eventually need to be covered with proper wood shingles, but the animals were inside and warm. With a very relieved smile, Eugene shut the barn doors tight.

CHAPTER THIRTY-SIX

COTTON WAS DRIVING THE CHILDREN DOWN TO VISIT Louisa. Though they were well into winter, heavy snow had not yet come, merely dustings of several inches, though it would only be a matter of time before it fell hard and deep. They passed the coal company town where Diamond had adorned the superintendent's new Chrysler Crown Imperial with horse manure. The town was empty now, the housing abandoned, the store vacant, the tipple sagging, the entrance to the mine boarded up, and the mine superintendent's fancy, horseshitted Chrysler long gone.

"What happened?" said Lou.

"Shut down," answered Cotton grimly. "Fourth mine in as many months. Veins were already petering out, but then they found out the coke they make here is too soft for steel production, so America's fighting machine went looking elsewhere for its raw material. Lot of folks here out of work. And the last lumber company moved on to Kentucky two months ago. A double blow. Farmers on the mountain had a good year, but the people in the towns are hurting bad. It's usually one or the other. Prosperity only seems to come in halves up here." Cotton shook his head. "Indeed, the fine mayor of Dickens resigned his post, sold out his stake at inflated prices before the crash, and headed to Pennsylvania to seek a new fortune. I've often found the ones who talk the best game are the first ones to run at the earliest sign of trouble."

Coming down the mountain, Lou noted that there were fewer coal trucks, and that many of the mountainside tipples weren't even being operated. When they passed Tremont, she saw that half the stores were boarded up, and there were few people on the streets, and Lou sensed it wasn't just because of the chilly weather.

When they got to Dickens, Lou was shocked, for many stores were boarded up here as well, including the one Diamond had opened an umbrella in. Bad luck had reigned there after all, and it was no longer funny to Lou. Ill-clothed men sat on sidewalks and steps, staring at nothing. There weren't many cars slant-parked, and shopkeepers stood, idle hands on hips, nervous looks on faces, in the doorways of their empty stores. The men and women walking the streets were very few in number, and their faces carried an anxious pallor. Lou watched as a bus filled with folks slowly headed out of town. An empty coal train symbolically crept behind the line of buildings and parallel to the main road. The "Coal Is King" banner was no longer flying mighty and proud across the street, and Miss Bituminous Coal of 1940 had probably fled as well, Lou imagined.

As they went along, Lou could see more than one group of people point at them and then talk among themselves.

"Those people don't look very happy," said Oz nervously, as they climbed out of Cotton's Oldsmobile and looked across the street at another collection of men who were watching them closely. At the front of this mob was none other than George Davis.

"Come on, Oz," said Cotton. "We're here to see Louisa, that's all."

He led them into the hospital, where they learned from Travis Barnes that Louisa's condition had not changed. Her eyes were wide open and glassy. Lou and Oz each held one of her hands, but she clearly did not know them. Lou would have thought she had already passed, except for her shallow breathing. She watched the rise and fall of that chest with the deepest intensity, praying with all her soul for it to keep rising, until Cotton told her it was time to go, and Lou was surprised to learn that an hour had passed.

When they walked back to the Oldsmobile, the men were waiting for them. George Davis had his hand on the door of Cotton's car.

Cotton walked boldly up to them. "What can I do for you folks?" he inquired politely, even as he firmly removed Davis's hand from the Olds.

"You get that fool woman in there sell her land, that what!" shouted Davis.

Cotton looked the men over. Other than Davis, they were all men from the town, not the mountain. But he knew that didn't mean they were any less desperate than folks who tethered their survival to dirt, seed, and the fickleness of rain. These folks had just tied their hopes to coal. But coal was unlike corn; once plucked, coal didn't grow back.

"I've already been over this with you, George, and the

answer hasn't changed. Now, if you'll excuse me, I've got to get these children home."

"Whole town gone to hell," said another man.

"And you think that's Louisa's fault?" asked Cotton.

"She dying. She ain't need her land," said Davis.

"She's not dying!" said Oz.

"Cotton," said a well-dressed man about fifty years old who, Cotton knew, ran the automobile dealership in Dickens. He had narrow shoulders, thin arms, and smooth palms that clearly showed he had never hoisted a hay bale, swung a scythe, or plowed a field. "I'm going to lose my business. I'm going to lose everything I've got if something doesn't replace the coal. And I'm not the only one like that. Look around, we're hurting bad."

"What happens when the natural gas runs out?" countered Cotton. "Then what will you be looking for to save you?"

"Ain't got to look that fer ahead. Take care of bizness now, and that bizness be gas," said Davis in an angry voice. "We all git rich. I ain't got no problem selling my place, hep my neighbor."

"Really?" said Lou. "I didn't see you at the barn raising, George. In fact you haven't been back since Louisa ran you off. Unless you had something to do with our barn burning down in the first place."

Davis spit, wiped his mouth, and hitched his britches, and would've no doubt throttled the girl right there if Cotton hadn't been standing next to her.

"Lou," said Cotton firmly, "that's enough."

"Cotton," said the well-dressed man, "I can't believe you're abandoning us for some stupid mountain woman.

Hell, you think you'll have any lawyering to do if the town dies?"

Cotton smiled. "Don't y'all worry about me. You'd be amazed at how little I can get by on. And regarding Miss Cardinal, y'all listen up, because it's the last time I'm going to say it. She does *not* want to sell her land to Southern Valley. That's her right, and y'all better damn well respect it. Now, if you really and truly can't survive here without the gas folks, then I suggest you leave. Because you see, Miss Cardinal doesn't have that problem. Every lick of coal and gas could disappear from this earth tomorrow, and electricity and phones too, and she'd be just fine." He stared pointedly at the well-dressed man. "Now tell me, who's the stupid one?"

Cotton told the children to climb in the car, and he eased himself into the driver's seat, even as the men pushed forward a bit, crowding him. Several of them moved back and blocked the rear of the car. Cotton started the engine of the Olds, rolled down the window, and looked at them. "Now, the clutch on this thing is right peculiar. Sometimes it pops out and this old girl jumps about a country mile. Almost killed a man one time when it did that. Well, here goes. Look out now!"

He popped the clutch, and the Olds jumped backward, and so did all the men. The path cleared, Cotton backed out and they headed off. When the rock banged against the rumble seat of the car, Cotton pushed down on the accelerator and told Lou and Oz to get down and stay down. Several more rocks hit against the car, before they were safely out of range.

"What about Louisa?" asked Lou.

"She'll be fine. Travis is most always around, and he's

a man not to be beat with a shotgun. And when he's not there, his nurse is just about as fine a shot. And I warned the sheriff folks were getting a bit riled. They'll keep close watch. But those people aren't going to do anything to a helpless woman in a bed. They're hurting, but they're not like that."

"Are they going to throw rocks at us every time we come to visit Louisa?" asked Oz fearfully.

Cotton put an arm around the boy. "Well, if they do, I suspect they'll run out of rocks long before we run out of visits."

When they got back to the farmhouse, an anxious-looking Eugene hurried out, a piece of paper in his hand.

"Man from the town come by with this, Mr. Cotton. I ain't knowed what it is. He say give it to you quick."

Cotton opened up the slip of paper and read it. It was a delinquent tax notice. He had forgotten Louisa had not paid her property taxes for the last three years because there had been no crops, and thus no money. The county had carried her over, as it did with all the other farmers in similar circumstances. They were expected to pay of course, but they were always given time. This notice, however, was demanding payment in full immediately. Two hundred dollars' worth of payment. And since she had been in default for so long, they could foreclose and sell the land far more quickly than normal. Cotton could feel Southern Valley's vicious stamp all over the paper.

"Is something wrong, Cotton?" asked Lou.

He looked at her and smiled. "I'll take care of it, Lou. Just paperwork, honey."

Cotton counted out the two hundred dollars to the clerk of the court and was given a stamped receipt. He trudged back to his apartment and boxed up the last pile of books. A few minutes later he looked up to see Lou standing in his doorway.

"How did you get here?" he asked.

"I got a ride with Buford Rose in his old Packard. There are no doors on the thing, so it's a fine view, but you're only one jolt away from flying out, and it's pretty cold." She stared around at the empty room. "Where are all your books, Cotton?"

He chuckled. "They were taking up too much space." He tapped his forehead. "And, leastways, I've got it all right up here."

Lou shook her head. "I went by the courthouse. I figured there was more to that paper we got than you were letting on. Two hundred dollars for all your books. You shouldn't have done it."

Cotton closed up the box. "I still have some left. And I'd like you to have them."

Lou stepped into the room. "Why?"

"Because they're your father's works. And I can't think of a better person to take care of them."

Lou said nothing while Cotton taped the box shut.

"Let's go over and see Louisa now," Cotton said.

"Cotton, I'm getting scared. More stores have closed. And another bus full of people just left. And the looks folks gave me on the street. They're really angry. And Oz got in a fight at school with a boy who said we were ruining people's lives by not selling."

"Is Oz all right?"

She smiled weakly. "He actually won the fight. I think it surprised him more than anybody. He's got a black eye, and he's right proud of it."

"It'll be all right, Lou. Things will work out. We'll weather this."

She took a step closer, her expression very serious. "Things aren't working out. Not since we've come here. Maybe we should sell and leave. Maybe it'll be better for all of us. Get Mom and Louisa the care they need." She paused and could not look at him as she added, "Someplace else."

"Is that what you want to do?"

Lou wearily stared off. "Sometimes what I want to do is go up on the little knoll behind our house, lay on the ground, and never move again. That's all."

Cotton considered this for a few moments and then said, "In the world's broad field of battle, / In the bivouac of Life, / Be not like dumb, driven cattle! / Be a hero in the strife! / Trust no Future, howe'er pleasant! / Let the dead Past bury its dead! / Act—act in the glorious Present! / Heart within, and God o'erhead! / Lives of great men all remind us / We can make *our* lives sublime, / And, departing, leave behind us . . . Footprints on the sands of time."

" 'A Psalm of Life.' Henry Wadsworth Longfellow," said Lou without much enthusiasm.

"There's more to the poem, but I've always considered those lines the essential parts."

"Poetry is beautiful, Cotton, but I'm not sure it can fix real life."

"Poetry needn't fix real life, Lou, it need just be. The fixing is up to us. And laying on the ground and never moving again, or running from trouble, is not the Lou Cardinal I know."

"That's very interesting," said Hugh Miller, as he stood there in the doorway. "I looked for you at your office, Longfellow. I understand you've been over at the courthouse paying the debts of *others*." He flashed a nasty grin. "Right good of you, however misguided."

"What do you want, Miller?" said Cotton.

The little man stepped into the room and looked at Lou. "Well, first I want to say how sorry I am about Miss Cardinal."

Lou crossed her arms and looked away.

"Is that all?" Cotton said curtly.

"I also came by to make another offer on the property."

"It's not my property to sell."

"But Miss Cardinal isn't in a position to consider the offer."

"She already refused you once, Miller."

"That's why I'm cutting right to the chase and raising my offer to five hundred thousand dollars."

Cotton and Lou exchanged startled glances, before Cotton said, "Again, it's not my property to sell."

"I assumed you would have a power of attorney to act on her behalf."

"No. And if I did, I still wouldn't sell to you. Now, is there anything else I *can't* do for you?"

"No, you've told me all I need to know." Miller handed a packet of papers to Cotton. "Consider your client served."

Miller walked out with a smile. Cotton quickly read through the papers, while Lou stood nervously beside him.

"What is it, Cotton?"

"Not good, Lou."

Cotton suddenly grabbed Lou's arm, and they raced down the stairs and over to the hospital. Cotton pushed open the door to Louisa's room. The flashbulb went off right as they came in. The man looked over at them and then he took another picture of Louisa in her bed. There was another man next to him, large and powerfully built. Both were dressed in nice suits and wore creased hats.

"Get out of here!" cried Cotton.

He raced over and tried to grab the camera from the man, but the big fellow pulled him away, allowing his partner to slide out the door. Then the big man backed out of the room, a smile on his lips.

Cotton could only stand there, breathing hard and looking helplessly between Lou and Louisa.

CHAPTER THIRTY-SEVEN

IT WAS A PARTICULARLY COLD, CLOUDLESS DAY WHEN Cotton entered the courtroom. He stopped when he saw Miller and another man there, who was tall, portly, and very well dressed, his fine silver hair combed neatly on a head so massive it seemed hardly natural.

Cotton said to Miller, "I was pretty sure I'd see you today."

Miller inclined his head at the other man. "You probably heard of Thurston Goode, Commonwealth's attorney for Richmond?"

"Indeed I have. You argued a case before the United States Supreme Court recently, didn't you, sir?"

"More precisely," Goode said in a deep, confident baritone, "I *won* the case, Mr. Longfellow."

"Congratulations. You're a long way from home."

"The state was kind enough to allow Mr. Goode to come down here and act on its behalf in this very important matter," explained Miller.

"Since when does a simple suit to declare a person mentally unfit qualify for the expertise of one of the finest lawyers in the state?"

Goode smiled warmly. "As an officer of the Commonwealth I don't have to explain to you why I'm here, Mr. Longfellow. Suffice it to say, that I *am* here."

Cotton put a hand to his chin and pretended to ponder something. "Let's see now. Virginia elects its Commonwealth's attorneys. Might I inquire as to whether Southern Valley has made a donation to your campaign, sir?"

Goode's face flushed. "I don't like what you're implying!"

"I did not mean it as an implication."

Fred the bailiff came in and announced, "All rise. The Court of the Honorable Henry J. Atkins is now in session. All those having business before this court draw near and you shall be heard."

Judge Henry Atkins, a small man with a short beard, thinning silver hair, and clear gray eyes, came into the room from his adjacent chambers and took his seat behind the bench. Before he got up there, he looked too small for his black robe. Once he got there, he looked too large for the courtroom.

It was at this point that Lou and Oz crept in without anyone seeing them. Wearing barter coats and thick socks stuffed into oversized boots, they had retraced their steps across the poplar-log bridge and down the mountain, catching a ride on a truck to Dickens. It had been a much harder trek in cold weather, but the way Cotton had explained it to them, the potential effect of this proceeding on all their lives was very clear. They sat slumped down at the rear, their heads barely visible over the back of the seats in front of them.

"Call the next case," said Atkins. It was his only case today, but the law court had its rituals.

Fred announced the pending matter of *Commonwealth versus Louisa Mae Cardinal.*

Atkins smiled broadly from his judicial perch. "Mr. Goode, I'm honored to have you in my courtroom, sir. Please state the Commonwealth's position."

Goode rose and hooked a finger in his lapel.

"This certainly is not a pleasant task, but one that the Commonwealth has a duty to perform. Southern Valley Coal and Gas has made an offer to purchase property solely owned by Miss Cardinal. We believe that because of her recent stroke she is not legally fit to make an informed decision on that offer. Her only relatives are both underage and thus disqualified from acting for her. And we understand that the surviving parent of these children is herself severely mentally incapacitated. We also have it on good authority that Miss Cardinal has signed no power of attorney allowing others to represent her interests."

On this Cotton cast a sharp glance at Miller, who just looked ahead in his cocksure manner.

Goode continued, "In order to fully protect Miss Cardinal's rights in this matter, we are seeking to have her declared mentally unfit, and to have a guardian appointed so that an orderly disposition of her affairs may be conducted, including this very lucrative offer from Southern Valley."

Atkins nodded as Goode sat down. "Thank you, Mr. Goode. Cotton?"

Cotton rose and stood before the bench. "Your Honor, what we have here is an attempt to circumvent rather than facilitate Miss Cardinal's wishes. She has already rejected an offer from Southern Valley to purchase her land."

"Is that true, Mr. Goode?" queried the judge.

Goode looked confident. "Miss Cardinal rejected one such offer; however, the present offer is for considerably more money, and thus must be separately entertained."

"Miss Cardinal made it very clear that she would not sell her land at any price to Southern Valley," said Cotton. He looped his finger around his coat lapel as Goode had done, then thought better of it and removed it.

"Do you have any witnesses to that effect?" asked Judge Atkins.

"Uh . . . just me."

Goode immediately pounced. "Well, if Mr. Longfellow intends to make himself a material witness in this case, I insist he recuse himself as counsel for Miss Cardinal."

Atkins looked at Cotton. "Is that what you want to do?"

"No, it's not. However, I can represent Louisa's interests until she's better."

Goode smiled. "Your Honor, Mr. Longfellow has expressed a clear prejudice to my client in full view of the court. He can hardly be considered independent enough to *fairly* represent Miss Cardinal's interests."

"I'm inclined to agree with him there, Cotton," said Atkins.

"Well, then we contend that Miss Cardinal is not mentally unfit," countered Cotton.

"Then we have ourselves a dispute, gentlemen," said the judge. "I'm setting this for trial in one week."

Cotton was astonished. "That's not enough time."

"One week's fine with us," said Goode. "Miss Cardinal's affairs deserve to be attended to with all due speed and respect."

Atkins picked up his gavel. "Cotton, I've been over to the hospital to see Louisa. Now, whether she has her senses or not, it seems to me those children are going to at least need a guardian. We might as well get it done as quick as possible."

"We can take care of ourselves."

They all looked to the back of the courtroom, where Lou was now standing. "We can take care of ourselves," she said again. "Until Louisa gets better."

"Lou," said Cotton, "this is not the time or place."

Goode smiled at them. "Well, you two sure are adorable *children*. I'm Thurston Goode. How y'all doing?"

Neither Lou nor Oz answered him.

"Young lady," said Atkins, "come up here."

Lou swallowed the lump in her throat and walked up to the bench, where Atkins peered down at her, like Zeus to mortal.

"Young lady, are you a member of the State Bar?"

"No. I mean . . . no."

"Do you know that only members of the Bar may address the court except in the most extraordinary circumstances?"

"Well, since this concerns me and my brother, I think the circumstances *are* extraordinary."

Atkins looked at Cotton and smiled before looking back at Lou. "You're smart, that's easy to see. And quick. But the law is the law, and children your age can't live by themselves."

"We have Eugene."

"He's not a blood relative."

"Well, Diamond Skinner didn't live with anybody."

Atkins looked over at Cotton. "Cotton, will you explain this to her, please."

"Lou, the judge is right, you're not old enough to live by yourself. You need an adult."

Lou's eyes suddenly filled with tears. "Well, we keep running out of those." She turned and raced down the aisle, pushed open the double doors, and was gone. Oz fled after her.

Cotton looked back up at Judge Atkins.

"One week," said the judge. He smacked his gavel and returned to his chambers, like a wizard resting after throwing a particularly difficult spell.

Outside the courtroom, Goode and Miller waited for Cotton. Goode leaned in close to him. "You know, Mr. Longfellow, you can make this a lot easier on everybody if you'd just cooperate. We all know what a mental examination is going to reveal. Why put Miss Cardinal through the humiliation of a trial?"

Cotton leaned even closer to Goode. "Mr. Goode, you could give a damn whether Louisa's affairs are accorded the respect they deserve. You're here as a hired gun for a big company looking to twist the law so they can take her land."

Goode just smiled. "We'll see you in court."

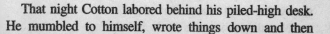

That night Cotton labored behind his piled-high desk. He mumbled to himself, wrote things down and then scratched them out, and paced like an expectant father. The door creaked open, and Cotton stared as Lou came in with a basket of food and a pot of coffee.

"Eugene drove me down in the car to see Louisa," she explained. "I got this over at the New York Restaurant. Figured you probably skipped supper."

Cotton looked down. Lou cleared a place on his desk, laid out the food, and poured the coffee. Finished, she made no move to leave.

"I'm pretty busy, Lou. Thank you for the food."

Cotton went to his desk and sat down, but he moved not one piece of paper, opened not a single book.

"I'm sorry about what I said in court," said Lou.

"It's all right. I guess if I were you, I would've done the same thing."

"You sounded really good."

"On the contrary, I failed utterly."

"But the trial hasn't started yet."

He took off his glasses and rubbed them with his tie. "Truth is I haven't really tried a case in years, and even then I wasn't very good. I just file papers, write up deeds and wills, that sort of thing. And I've never gone up against a lawyer like Goode." He put his glasses back on, seeing clearly for perhaps the first time all day. "And I wouldn't want to promise you something I can't deliver."

This line stood between them like a wall of flames.

"I believe in you, Cotton. Whatever happens, I believe in you. I wanted you to know that."

"Why in the world do you have faith in me? Haven't I done nothing except let you down? Quoted miserable poetry that can't change anything?"

"No, all you've tried to do is help."

"I can never be the man your father was, Lou. In fact, I'm really not good for all that much, it appears."

Lou stood beside him. "Will you promise me one thing, Cotton? Will you promise you won't ever leave us?"

After a few moments Cotton cupped the girl's chin and said in a halting voice that in no way lost its strength, "I will stay for as long as all of you will have me."

CHAPTER THIRTY-EIGHT

OUTSIDE THE COURTHOUSE, FORDS, CHEVYS, AND Chryslers were slant-parked next to wagons pulled by mules and horses. A dusting of snow had given pretty white toppers to just about everything, yet no one was paying any attention to that. They had all hurried into the courthouse to see a much grander show.

The courtroom had never held so many souls. The seats on the main floor were filled. Folks even stood in the back and were sandwiched five deep on the second-floor balcony. There were town men in suits and ties, women in church dresses and boxy hats with veils and fake flowers or dangling fruit. Next to them were farmers in clean overalls and felt hats held in hand, their chew stashed in their pockets. Their women were beside them, Chop dresses to the ankles and wire glasses over worn, creased faces. They looked around the room excitedly as though they were about to see a queen or movie star stroll in.

Children were wedged here and there among the adults like mortar between brick. To get a better look, one boy climbed up on the railing around the balcony and clung to a support column. A man hauled him down and sternly told him that this was a court of law and dignity was required here, not tomfoolery. The ashamed boy trudged off. And then the man climbed up on the railing for a better look-see himself.

Cotton, Lou, and Oz were heading up the steps of the courthouse when a boy in an overcoat, slacks, and shiny black shoes ran up to them.

"My pa says you're doing wrong by the whole town on account of one woman. He said we got to have the gas folks here, any way we can." The little fellow looked at Cotton as though the lawyer had spit on the boy's mother and then laughed about it.

"Is that right?" said Cotton. "Well, I respect your daddy's opinion, though I don't agree with it. Now, you tell him if he wants to discuss it with me in person later, I'd be right glad to do so." Cotton glanced around and saw someone who he was sure was the child's father, for the boy favored the man and he had been staring at them, but quickly looked away. Cotton glanced at all the cars and wagons and then said to the boy, "You and your daddy better get yourselves inside and get a seat. Looks to be a right popular spot today."

When they entered the courtroom, Cotton was still amazed at the numbers in attendance. Yet, the hard work of farming *was* over for now, and people had time on their hands. And for the townsfolk it was an accessible show promising fireworks at a fair price. It seemed they were determined to miss not one legal trick, not one semantical headlock. For many this probably would be the most exciting time of their lives. And wasn't that a sad thing, Cotton thought.

Yet, he knew the stakes here *were* high. A place dying

once more only perhaps to be revitalized by a deep-pocketed company. And all he had to lay against that was an old woman lying in a bed, her senses seemingly struck from her. And there were also two anxious children counting on him; and lying in another bed a woman who maybe he could lose his heart to if only she would awaken. *Lord, how was he ever going to survive this?*

"Find a seat," Cotton told the children. "And keep quiet."

Lou gave him a peck on the cheek. "Good luck." She crossed her fingers for him. A farmer they knew made room for them in one of the rows of seats.

Cotton went up the aisle, nodding at people he recognized in the crowd. Smack in the front row were Miller and Wheeler.

Goode was at the counsel table, seeming as happy as a hungry man at a church supper as he looked around at a crowd that seemed famished to witness this contest.

"You ready to have a go at this?" said Goode.

"As ready as you are," Cotton replied gamely.

Goode chuckled. "With all due respect, I doubt that."

Fred the bailiff appeared and said his official words, and they all rose, and the Court of the Honorable Henry J. Atkins was now in session.

"Send in the jury," the judge said to Fred.

The jury filed in. Cotton looked at them one by one, and almost fell to the floor when he saw George Davis as one of the chosen.

He thundered, "Judge, George Davis wasn't one of the jurors we voir dired. He has a vested interest in the outcome of this case."

Atkins leaned forward. "Now, Cotton, you know we

have a hard enough time getting jurors to serve. I had to drop Leroy Jenkins because he got kicked by his mule. Now, I know he's not the most popular person around, but George Davis has as much right to serve as any other man. Look here, George, can you keep a fair and open mind about this case?"

Davis had his churchgoing clothes on and looked quietly respectable. "Yes, sir," he said politely and looked around. "Why, y'all knowed Louisa's place right next to mine. Get along good." He smiled a black-toothed smile, which he seemed to have difficulty with, as though it were something he'd never before attempted.

"I'm sure Mr. Davis will make a fine juror, Your Honor," said Goode. "No objection here."

Cotton looked at Atkins, and the curious expression on the judge's face made Cotton think twice about what was really going on here.

Lou sat in her seat, silently fuming at this. It was wrong. And she wanted to stand up and say it was, yet for once in her life she was too intimidated. This was a court of law, after all.

"He's lying!" The voice thundered, and every head in the place turned to its source.

Lou looked next to her to find Oz standing on his seat, taller now than all in the courtroom. His eyes were on fire, his finger pointed straight at George Davis. "He's lying," Oz roared again in a voice so deep Lou did not even recognize it as her brother's. "He hates Louisa. It's wrong for him to be here."

Cotton had been struck dumb like all the others. He glanced around the room. Judge Atkins stared at the little boy, none too pleased. Goode was about ready to spring to his feet. And Davis's look was so fierce that Cotton was very grateful that no gun was handy for the man. Cotton raced to Oz and swooped up the boy.

"Apparently, the propensity for public outbursts runs in the Cardinal family," Atkins boomed. "Now, we can't have that, Cotton."

"I know, Judge. I know."

"It's wrong. That man is a liar!" yelled Oz.

Lou was scared. She said, "Oz, please, it's okay."

"No, it's not, Lou," said Oz. "That man is hateful. He starves his family. He's wicked!"

"Cotton, take that child out," roared the judge. "Right now."

Cotton carried out Oz, with Lou trailing in their wake.

They sat on the cold courthouse steps. Oz wasn't crying. He just sat there and smacked his small fists against his slender thighs. Lou felt tears trickle down her cheeks as she watched him. Cotton put an arm around Oz's shoulders.

"It's not right, Cotton," said Oz. "It's just not right." The boy kept punching his legs.

"I know, son. I know. But it'll be okay. Why, having George Davis on that jury might be a good thing for us."

Oz stopped hitting himself. "How can that be?"

"Well, it's one of the mysteries of the law, Oz, but you'll just have to trust me on it. Now I suspect y'all still want to watch the trial." They both said that they would very dearly want to do that.

Cotton glanced around and saw Deputy Howard Walker standing by the door. "Howard, it's a little cold for these children to be waiting out here. If I guarantee no more outbursts, can you find a way to get them back in, 'cause I got to get going. You understand."

Walker smiled and gripped his gunbelt. "Y'all come on with me, children. Let Cotton go work his magic."

Cotton said, "Thank you, Howard, but helping us might cost you some popularity in this town."

"My daddy and brother died in those mines. Southern Valley can go to hell. Now, you get on in there and show them what a fine lawyer you are."

After Cotton went back in, Walker took Lou and Oz in through a rear entrance and got them settled at a spot in the balcony reserved for special visitors, after receiving a solemn promise from Oz that he would not be heard from again.

Lou looked at her brother and whispered. "Oz, you were really brave to do that. I was afraid to." He smiled at her. Then she realized what was missing. "Where's the bear I bought you?"

"Shoot, Lou, I'm too old for bears and thumb sucking."

Lou looked at her brother and suddenly realized that this was true. And a tear clutched at her eye, for she suddenly had an image of her brother grown tall and strong and no longer in need of his big sister.

Down below, Cotton and Goode were having a heated sidebar with Judge Atkins at the bench.

"Now look here, Cotton," said Atkins. "I'm not unmindful of what you're saying about George Davis, and your objection is duly noted for the record, but Louisa delivered two of those jurors into this world, and the Commonwealth didn't object to that." He looked over at Goode. "Mr. Goode, will you excuse us for a minute here?"

The lawyer looked shocked. "Your Honor, an ex parte contact with counsel? We don't do those sorts of things in Richmond."

"Well, damn good thing this ain't Richmond then. Now, just take yourself on over there for a bit." Atkins waved his hand like he was flicking at flies, and Goode reluctantly moved back to his counsel table.

"Cotton," said Atkins, "we both know there's a lot of interest in this case, and we both know why: money. Now, we got Louisa laying over to hospital and most folks thinking she's not going to make it anyway. And then we got us Southern Valley cash staring folks in the face."

Cotton nodded. "So you're thinking the jury is going to go against us despite the merits of the case?"

"Well, I can't really say, but if you do lose here—"

"Then having George Davis on the jury gives me real good grounds for appeal," finished Cotton.

Atkins looked very pleased that Cotton had seized upon this strategy so readily. "Why, I never thought of that. Real glad you did. Now let's get this show on the road."

Cotton moved back to his counsel table while Atkins smacked his gavel and announced, "Jury is hereby impaneled. Be seated."

The jury collectively sat itself down.

Atkins looked them over slowly before his gaze came to rest on Davis. "One more thing now before we start. I've had my backside on this here bench for thirty-four years, and there's never been anything close to jury tampering or messing around along those lines in my courtroom. And there's never going to be such, for if there ever was, the folks that did it will think spending their whole lives in the coal mines a birthday party compared to what I'll do to them." He gave Davis one more good stare, fired similar broadsides at both Goode and Miller, and then said, "Now the parties have waived their opening statements. So Commonwealth, call your first witness."

"Commonwealth calls Dr. Luther Ross," said Goode.

The ponderous Dr. Ross rose and went to the witness stand. He had the gravity lawyers liked, when he was on *their* side; otherwise he was just a well-paid liar.

Fred swore him in. "Raise your right hand, put your left one on the Bible. Do you solemnly swear to tell the truth, the whole truth, and nothing but the truth so help you God?"

Ross said he most certainly would tell the truth and nothing but, and wedged himself into the witness chair.

Fred retreated and Goode approached.

"Dr. Ross, sir, would you state your mighty fine credentials for the jury please?"

"I'm chief of the asylum down over to Roanoke. I've taught courses in mental evaluation at the Medical College in Richmond, and at the University of Virginia. And I've personally handled over two thousand cases like this one."

"Well now, I am sure Mr. Longfellow and this court would agree that you are truly an expert in your field. In fact, you may be the number-one expert in your field, and I would say this jury deserves to hear nothing less."

"Objection, Your Honor!" said Cotton. "I don't believe there's any proof that Mr. Goode is an expert in ranking experts."

"Sustained, Cotton," said Atkins. "Get on with it, Mr. Goode."

Goode smiled benignly, as though this tiny skirmish had been a way for him to evaluate Cotton's mettle. "Now, Mr. Ross," said Goode, "have you had occasion to examine Louisa Mae Cardinal?"

"I have."

"And what is your expert opinion on her mental competence?"

Ross smacked the frame of the witness box with one of his flabby hands. "She is *not* mentally competent. In fact, my considered opinion is she should be institutionalized."

There came a loud buzz from the crowd, and Atkins impatiently pounded his gavel. "Quiet down," said he.

Goode continued. "Institutionalized? My, my. That's some serious business. So you're saying she's in no shape to handle her own affairs? Say, for the sale of her property?"

"Absolutely not. She could be easily taken advantage of. Why, that poor woman can't even sign her own name. Probably doesn't know what her name is." He eyed the jury with a most commanding look. "Institutionalized," he said again in the projected voice of a stage actor.

Goode asked a series of carefully crafted questions, and to each he got the answers he wanted: Louisa Mae was undoubtedly mentally unfit, according to the esteemed expert Dr. Luther Ross.

"No further questions," Goode finally said.

"Mr. Longfellow?" said Atkins. "I suspect you want to have a go."

Cotton got up, took off his glasses, and dangled them by his side as he addressed the witness.

"You say you've examined over two thousand people?"

"That's correct," Ross said with a lift of his chest.

"And how many did you find incompetent, sir?"

Ross's chest immediately deflated, for he clearly hadn't expected that inquiry. "Uh, well, it's hard to say."

Cotton glanced at the jury and moved toward him. "No, it's really not. You just have to *say* it. Let me help you a little. A hundred percent? Fifty percent?"

"Not a hundred percent."

"But not fifty?"

"No."

"Let's whittle it on down now. Eighty? Ninety? Ninety-five?"

Ross thought for a few moments. "Ninety-five percent sounds about right."

"Okay. Let me see now. I think that works out to be nineteen hundred out of two thousand. Lord, that's a lot of crazy people, Dr. Ross."

The crowd laughed and Atkins banged his gavel, but a tiny smile escaped him as well.

Ross glared at him. "I just call 'em like I see 'em, lawyer."

"Dr. Ross, how many stroke victims have you examined to determine whether they're mentally competent?"

"Uh, why, none that I can recall offhand."

Cotton paced back and forth in front of the witness, who kept his gaze on the attorney as an even line of sweat appeared on Ross's brow. "I suppose with most of the people you see, they have some mental disease. Here we have a stroke victim whose *physical* incapacity may make it seem like she's not mentally fit even though she may very well be." Cotton sought out and found Lou in the balcony. "I mean, just because one can't talk or move doesn't mean one can't understand what's going on around her. She may well see, hear, and understand everything. Everything!"

Cotton swung back and looked at his witness. "And given time she may very well fully recover."

"The woman I saw was not likely to recover."

"Are you a medical doctor expert on stroke victims?" Cotton said in a sharp voice.

"Well, no. But—"

"Then I'd like an instruction from the bench for the jury to disregard that statement."

Atkins said to the cluster of men, "You are hereby instructed to take no notice whatsoever of Dr. Ross saying that Miss Cardinal would not recover, for he is most assuredly not *competent* to testify to that."

Atkins and Ross exchanged glares at the judge's choice of words, while Cotton put a hand over his mouth to hide his grin.

Cotton continued. "Dr. Ross, you really can't tell us that today, or tomorrow, or the next day, Louisa Mae Cardinal won't be perfectly capable of handling her own affairs, can you?"

"The woman I examined—"

"Please answer the question I asked, sir."

"No."

"No, what?" Cotton added pleasantly, "For this fine jury."

A frustrated Ross crossed his arms. "No, I cannot say for sure that Miss Cardinal will not recover today or tomorrow or the next day."

Goode heaved himself to his feet. "Your Honor, I see where counsel is going with this and I think I have a resolution. As of right now Dr. Ross's testimony is that Miss Cardinal is not competent. If she gets better, and we all hope she does, then the court-appointed representative can be dismissed and she can handle her own affairs from then on."

Cotton said, "By then, she won't have any land left."

Goode seized upon this opening. "Well, then Miss Cardinal can surely take comfort in the half a million dollars Southern Valley has offered for her property."

An enormous gasp went through the crowd at the mention of this ungodly sum. One man almost toppled over the balcony rail before his neighbors pulled him back to safety. Both dirty and clean-faced children looked at one another, eyes popping. And their mothers and fathers were doing the exact same thing. The jurors too looked at one another in clear astonishment. Yet George Davis just sat there staring straight ahead, not one emotion showing on his features.

Goode continued quickly, "As I'm sure others can when the company makes similar offers to *them*."

Cotton looked around and decided he would much rather be doing anything other than what he was. He saw both mountain dwellers and townsfolk gaping at him: the one man who stood in the way of their rightful fortune. And yet with all that weighing down upon him, he shook his mind clear and roared, "Judge, he's just as good as bribed this jury with that statement. I want a mistrial. My client can't get a fair shake with these people counting Southern Valley dollars."

Goode smiled at the jury. "I withdraw the statement. Sorry, Mr. Longfellow. No harm intended."

Atkins leaned back in his chair. "You're not getting a mistrial, Cotton. Because where else you going to go with this thing? Just about everybody from fifty miles around already's sitting in this courtroom, and the next nearest bench is a day away by train. And the judge there isn't nearly as nice as I am." He turned to the jury. "Now listen here, folks, you're to ignore Mr. Goode's statement about the offer to purchase Miss Cardinal's land. He shouldn't have said it, and you are to forget it. And I mean what I say!"

Atkins next focused on Goode. "I understand you have a fine reputation, sir, and I'd hate to be the one to taint it. But you pull something like that again, and I got me a nice little jail cell in this building where you'll be doing your time for contempt, and I might just forget you're even there. You understand me?"

Goode nodded and said meekly, "Yes, Your Honor."

"Cotton, you have any more questions for Dr. Ross?"

"No, Judge," Cotton said and dropped into his seat.

Goode put Travis Barnes on the stand, and though he did his best, under Goode's artful maneuvering, the good doctor's prognosis for Louisa was rather bleak. Finally, Goode waved a photograph in front of him.

"This is your patient, Louisa Mae Cardinal?"

Barnes looked at the photograph. "Yes."

"Permission to show the jury."

"Go on ahead, but be quick about it," said Atkins.

Goode dropped a copy of the photo in front of Cotton. Cotton didn't even look at it, but ripped the photograph into two pieces and dropped it in the spittoon next to his table while Goode paraded the original in front of the jurors' faces. From the clucks and muted comments and shakes of head, the photo had its intended effect. The only one who didn't look upset was George Davis. He held the photo especially long and seemed to Cotton to have to work awfully hard to hide his delight. The damage done, Goode sat down.

"Travis," said Cotton, rising and coming to stand next to his friend, "have you ever treated Louisa Cardinal for any ailments before this last one?"

"Yes, I have. A couple of times."

"Can you tell us about those instances, please."

"About ten years ago, she was bitten by a rattler. Killed the durn thing herself with a hoe, and then she come down the mountain by horse to see me. Arm swollen to about the size of my leg by that time. She took seriously ill, ran a fever higher'n I'd ever seen. In and out of consciousness for days. But she came out of it, right when we thought she wasn't going to make it. Fought like a durn mule she did."

"And the other time?"

"Pneumonia. That winter four years ago when we had more snow than the South Pole. Y'all remember that one?" he asked the folks in the courtroom and they all nodded back at him.

"No way to get up or down the mountain then. It was four days before they got word to me. I got up there and treated her when the storm ended, but she was already past the worst of it all by herself. Would'a killed a young person *with* medicine, and here she was into her seventies and not a drop of anything except her own will to live. I've never seen anything like it."

Cotton went and stood over near the jury. "So, she sounds like a woman of indomitable spirit. A spirit that cannot be conquered."

"Objection, Your Honor," said Goode. "Is that a question, or a divine pronouncement on your part, Mr. Longfellow?"

"I hope both, Mr. Goode."

"Well, let's put it this way," said Barnes, "if I were a betting man, I wouldn't bet against the woman."

Cotton looked over at the jury. "Neither would I. No further questions."

"Mr. Goode, who you calling next?" asked Atkins.

The Commonwealth's attorney rose and looked around the courtroom. He kept looking and looking until his gaze reached the balcony, moved around its edges, and then came to rest on Lou and Oz. And then finally on Oz alone.

"Young man, why don't you come on down here and talk to us."

Cotton was on his feet. "Your Honor, I see no reason—"

"Judge," broke in Goode, "now, it's the children that's going to have the guardian, and thus I think it reasonable to hear from one of them. And for a little fellow he has a mighty fine voice, since everybody in this courtroom has heard it loud and long already."

There was muted laughter from the crowd, and Atkins absently smacked his gavel while he pondered this request for six rapid beats of Cotton's heart. "I'm going to allow it. But remember, Goode, he's just a little boy."

"Absolutely, Your Honor."

Lou held Oz's hand and they slowly walked down the stairs and passed each of the rows, all eyes in the courtroom upon them. Oz put his hand on the Bible and was sworn in as Lou went back to her seat. Oz perched in the chair, looking so small and helpless that Cotton's heart went out to him, even as Goode moved in.

"Now, Mr. Oscar Cardinal," he began.

"My name's Oz, my sister's name is Lou. Don't call her Louisa Mae or else she'll get mad and punch you."

Goode smiled. "Now, don't you worry about that. Oz and Lou it is." He leaned against the witness stand. "Now, you know the court's right sorry to hear that your momma's doing so poorly."

"She's going to get better."

"Is that right? That what the doctors say?"

Oz looked up at Lou until Goode touched Oz's cheek and pointed his face toward him.

"Now, son, up here on the witness stand you got to speak the truth. You can't look to your big sister for answers. You swore to God to tell the truth."

"I always tell the truth. Cross my heart, stick a needle."

"Good boy. So, again, did the doctors say your mother will get better?"

"No. They said they weren't sure."

"So how do you know she will?"

"Because . . . because I made a wish. At the wishing well."

"Wishing well?" said Goode with an expression for the

jury that clearly spelled out what he thought of that answer. "There's a wishing well round here? I *wish* we had one of them back in Richmond."

The crowd laughed and Oz's face turned pink and he squirmed in his seat. "There *is* a wishing well," he said. "My friend Diamond Skinner told us about it. You make a wish and give up the most important thing you have and your wish will come true."

"Sounds mighty fine. Now, you said you made your wish?"

"Yes, sir."

"And you gave up the most important thing you had. What was that?" Oz looked nervously around the room. "The truth, Oz. Remember what you promised to God, son."

Oz took a long breath. "My bear. I gave up my bear."

There were a few muffled chuckles from the onlookers, until all saw the single tear slide down the little boy's face, and then the snickers ceased.

"Has your wish come true yet?" asked Goode.

Oz shook his head. "No."

"Been a while since you wished?"

"Yes," Oz answered softly.

"And your momma's still real sick, isn't she?"

Oz bowed his head. "Yes," he said in a tiny voice.

Goode put his hands in his pockets. "Well, sad fact is, son, things don't come true just 'cause we wish 'em to. That's not real life. Now, you know your great-grandmother's real sick, don't you?"

"Yes, sir."

"You make a wish for her too?"

Cotton rose. "Goode, leave it be."

"Fine, fine. Now, Oz, you know you can't live by yourself, right? If your great-grandma doesn't get better, under the law, you have to go live with an adult in their home. Or else go to an orphanage. Now, you don't want to go to no old orphanage, do you?"

Cotton jumped to his feet again. "Orphanage? When did that become an issue?"

Goode said, "Well, if Miss Cardinal does not make another miraculous recovery as she did with rattlers and pneumonia, then the children are going to have to go somewhere. Now, unless they've got some money I don't know about, they're going to an orphanage, because that's where children go who don't have blood relatives to take care of them, or other persons of a worthy nature willing to adopt them."

"They can come live with me," said Cotton.

Goode looked about ready to laugh. "You? An unmarried man? A lawyer in a town that's dying? You'd be the last person on earth a court would award those children to." Goode turned back to Oz. "Now, wouldn't you like to go live in your own home with someone who has your best interests at heart? You'd like that, wouldn't you?"

"I don't know."

"Course you would. Orphanages are not the nicest places in the world. Some kids stay there forever."

"Your Honor," said Cotton, "does all this have a point other than to terrify the witness?"

"Why, I was just about to ask Mr. Goode that," declared Atkins.

It was Oz, though, who spoke. "Can Lou come too? I mean, not to the orphanage, but to the other place?"

"Why sure, son, sure," said Goode quickly. "Never break up sister and brother." He added quietly, "But there's no guarantee of that with an orphanage." He paused. "So, that'd be all right with you, Oz?"

Oz hesitated and tried to look at Lou, but Goode was too quick and blocked his view. Oz finally said quietly, "I guess so."

Cotton looked up in the balcony. Lou was on her feet, fingers wrapped around the railing, her anxious gaze fixed on her brother.

Goode went over to the jury and made a show of rubbing his eyes. "That's a fine boy. No further questions."

"Cotton?" said Atkins.

Goode sat down and Cotton rose, but then he stopped, his fingers gripping the table's edge as he stared at the ruin of a boy on the big witness chair; a little boy who, Cotton knew, just wanted to get up and go back to his sister because he was scared to death of orphanages and fat lawyers with big words and embarrassing questions, and huge rooms filled with strangers staring at him.

"No questions," said Cotton very quietly, and Oz fled back to his sister.

After more witnesses had paraded through court, showing that Louisa was utterly incapable of conscious decision, and Cotton only able to slap at bits and pieces of their testimony, the trial was adjourned for the day and Cotton and the children left the courtroom. Outside, Goode and Miller stopped them.

"You're putting up a good fight, Mr. Longfellow," said Goode, "but we all know how this is going to turn out. What say we just put an end to it right now? Save people any further embarrassment." He looked at Lou and

Oz as he said this. He started to pat Oz on the head, but the boy gave the lawyer a fierce look that made Goode pull back his hand before he might have lost it.

"Look, Longfellow," said Miller, pulling a piece of paper out of his pocket, "I've got a check here for half a million dollars. All you got to do is end this nonsense and it's yours."

Cotton looked at Oz and Lou and then said, "I tell you what, Miller, I'll leave it up to the children. Whatever they say, I'll do."

Miller squatted down and smiled at Lou and Oz. "This money will go to you now. Buy anything you want. Live in a big house with a fancy car and people paid to look after you. A right nice life. What do you say, children?"

"We already have a home," said Lou.

"Okay, what about your momma then? People in her condition need a lot of care, and it's not cheap." He dangled the check in front of the girl. "This solves *all* your problems, missy."

Goode squatted down too and looked at Oz. "And it'll keep those nasty orphanages far, far away. You want to stay with your sister, now don't you?"

"You keep your old money," said Oz, "for it's not something we need or want. And Lou and I will always be together. Orphanage or not!"

Oz took his sister's hand and they walked off.

Cotton looked at the men as they rose, and Miller angrily stuffed the check back in his pocket. "From out of the mouths of babes," said Cotton. "We should all be so wise." And then he walked off too.

Back at the farmhouse, Cotton discussed the case with Lou and Oz. "I'm afraid unless Louisa can walk into that courtroom tomorrow, she's going to lose her land." He looked at them both. "But I want you to know that whatever happens, I will be there for all of you. I will take care of all of you. Don't you worry about that. You will *never* go to an orphanage. And you will never be split up. That I swear." Lou and Oz hugged Cotton as tightly as they could, and then he left to prepare for the final day in court. Perhaps their final day on this mountain.

Lou made supper for Oz and Eugene, and then went to feed her mother. After that she sat in front of the fire for a long time while she thought things through. Though it was very cold, she led Sue out of the barn and rode the mare up to the knoll behind the house. She said prayers in front of each grave, taking the longest at the smallest: Annie's. Had she lived, Annie would have been Lou's great-aunt. Lou wished mightily that she could have known what the tiny baby looked like, and she felt miserable that such a thing was now impossible. The stars were fine tonight, and Lou looked around at the mountains painted white, the glitter of ice on branch nearly magical when multiplied as it was ten thousand times. The land could offer Lou no help now, but there was something she could do all on her own. It should have been done long ago, she knew. Yet a mistake was only a mistake if it remained uncorrected.

She rode Sue back, put the mare down for the night, and went into her mother's room. She sat on the bed and took Amanda's hand and didn't move for a bit. Finally, Lou leaned over and kissed her mother's cheek, as the tears started to trickle down the girl's face. "Whatever happens we'll always be together. I promise. You will always have me and Oz. Always." She rubbed at her tears. "I miss you so much." Lou kissed her again. "I love you, Mom." She fled the room, and so Lou never saw the solitary tear leave her mother's eye.

Lou was lying on her bed, quietly sobbing, when Oz came in. Lou did not even make an attempt to stop her weeping. Oz crawled on the bed with her and hugged his sister.

"It'll be okay, Lou, you'll see."

Lou sat up, wiped her face, and looked at him. "I guess all we need is a miracle."

"I could give the wishing well another try," he said.

Lou shook her head. "What do we have to give up for a wish? We've already lost everything."

They sat for some minutes in silence until Oz saw the stack of letters on Lou's desk. "Have you read all of them?" Lou nodded. "Did you like them?" he asked.

Lou looked as though she might start bawling again. "They're wonderful, Oz. Dad wasn't the only writer in the family."

"Can you read some more of them to me? Please?"

Lou finally said all right, she would, and Oz settled in and closed his eyes tightly.

"Why are you doing that?" she asked.

"If I close my eyes when you read the letters it's like Mom is right here talking to me."

Lou looked at the letters as though she held gold. "Oz, you are a genius!"

"I am? Why? What'd I do?"

"You just found our miracle."

Dense clouds had settled over the mountains with no apparent intention to move along anytime soon. Under a freezing rain, Lou, Oz, and Jeb raced along. Chilled to the bone, they reached the clearing, with the old well dead ahead. They ran up to it. Oz's bear and the photo still lay there, soaked and fouled by weather. Oz looked at the photograph and then smiled at his sister. She bent down and took the bear, handing it to Oz.

"Take your bear back," she said tenderly. "Even if you're all grown now."

She put the photo in the bag she carried and then reached inside and pulled out the letters. "Okay, Diamond said we had to give up the most important thing we have in the whole world for the wishing well to work. I can't think of anything more important than Mom's letters. So here goes."

Lou carefully placed the bundle on the edge of the well and set a large rock against it to hold it tight against the wind.

"Now we have to wish."

"For Mom to come back?"

Lou slowly shook her head. "Oz, we have to wish for Louisa to go down to that courthouse. Like Cotton said, it's the only way she'll keep her home."

Oz looked stricken. "But what about Mom? We might not get another chance to wish."

Lou hugged him. "I know, but after all she's done for us, we've got to do this for Louisa. She's our family too. And the mountain means everything to her."

Oz finally nodded sadly in agreement. "You say it then."

Lou held Oz's hand, closed her eyes, and he did too. "We wish that Louisa Mae Cardinal will get up from her bed and show everyone that she's just fine."

Together they said, "Amen, Jesus." And then they ran as fast as they could away from that place, both hoping and praying that there was just one wish left in that pile of old brick and stagnant water.

Late that night Cotton walked along the deserted main street of Dickens, hands stuffed into his pockets, the loneliest man in the world. Cold rain fell steadily, but he was oblivious to it. He sat on a covered bench and eyed the flicker of the street's gas lamps behind the fall of rain. The nameplate on the lamp post was bold and clear: "Southern Valley Coal and Gas." An empty coal truck drifted down the street. A backfire resounded from its tailpipe; the small explosion violently broke the silence of the night.

Cotton watched the truck go by and then slumped down. Yet as his gaze once again caught the flicker of the gas lamp, a flicker of an idea seeped into his mind. He sat up, stared after that coal truck, and then back at that gas lamp. That's when the flicker became a firm idea. And then a rain-soaked Cotton Longfellow stood tall and clapped his hands together, and it sounded like the mighty smack of thunder, for the firm idea had become a miracle of his own.

Minutes later Cotton came into Louisa's room. He stood by the bed and gripped the unconscious woman's hand. "I swear to you, Louisa Mae Cardinal, you will not lose your land."

CHAPTER THIRTY-NINE

THE COURTROOM DOOR SWUNG OPEN AND COTTON
strode in with concentrated purpose. Goode, Miller,
and Wheeler were already there. And along with
this triumvirate, the entire population of the mountain and
town had apparently managed to lever itself into the courtroom. A half-million dollars at stake had stirred feelings
in folks that had not been touched in many years. Even
one elderly gentleman who had long claimed to be the
oldest surviving Rebel soldier of the Civil War had come
to experience the final round of this legal battle. He
clumped in on an oak timber-toe with a capped stump for
a right arm, snowy beard down to his belt, and wearing
the glorious butternut colors of the Confederate soldier.
Those sitting in the front row respectfully made a space
for him.

It was cold and damp outside, though the mountains
had grown weary of the rain and had finally broken up
the clouds and sent them on their way. In the courtroom,
the accumulation of body heat was fierce, the humidity
high enough to fog the windows. And yet every specta-
tor's body was tense against his neighbor, seat or wall.

"I guess it's about time to bring down the curtain on this show," Goode said amiably enough to Cotton. But what Cotton saw was a man with the satisfied look of a professional killer about to blow the smoke off his six-shooter's barrel and then wink at the body lying in the street.

"I think it's just getting started" was Cotton's bludgeoning response.

As soon as the judge was announced and the jury had filed in, Cotton stood. "Your Honor, I would like to make an offer to the Commonwealth."

"Offer? What are you getting at, Cotton?" said Atkins.

"We all know why we're here. It's not about whether Louisa Mae Cardinal is competent or not. It's about gas."

Goode lurched to his feet. "The Commonwealth has a vested interest in seeing that Miss Cardinal's business—"

Cotton interrupted. "The only *business* Miss Cardinal has is deciding whether to sell her land."

Atkins looked intrigued. "What's your offer?"

"I am prepared to concede that Miss Cardinal is mentally unfit."

Goode smiled. "Well, now we're getting somewhere."

"But in return, I want to examine whether Southern Valley is an appropriate party to acquire her land."

Goode looked astonished. "Lord, they're one of the most substantial companies in the state."

Cotton said, "I'm not talking about money. I'm talking about morals."

"Your Honor," Goode said indignantly.

"Approach the bench," said Atkins.

Cotton and Goode hurried forward.

Cotton said, "Judge, there is a long line of Virginia case law that clearly holds that one who commits a wrong shall be barred from profiting from same."

"This is nonsense," said Goode.

Cotton drew close to his adversary. "If you don't agree to let me do it, Goode, I've got my own expert who will contradict everything Dr. Ross has said. And if I lose here, I'll appeal. All the way to the Supreme Court if need be. By the time your client gets to that gas, rest assured, we'll all be dead."

"But I'm a lawyer for the Commonwealth. I have no authority to represent a private company."

"A more ironic statement I have never heard," said Cotton. "But I waive any objection and agree to be bound by the decision of this jury, even with the sorry likes of George Davis sitting on it." Goode was looking toward Miller for a cue, so Cotton gave him a shove. "Oh, Goode, go over there and talk to your client and stop wasting time."

With a sheepish look, Goode slipped over and had a heated discussion with Miller, who looked over repeatedly at Cotton. He finally nodded, and Goode came back.

"No objection."

The judge nodded. "Go ahead, Cotton."

Lou had ridden down to the hospital in the Hudson with Eugene while Oz had stayed behind. He had said he wanted nothing more to do with courts and the law. Buford Rose's wife had come over to look after Oz and his mother. Lou sat in the chair staring at Louisa, waiting for her miracle to take effect. The room was cold and sterile, and it did not seem conducive to anybody's getting well, but Lou was not counting on medicine to make the woman better. Her hopes lay with a stack of old bricks in a grassy meadow and a bundle of letters that might very well be the last words of her mother she would ever have.

Lou rose and drifted to the window. She could see the movie theater from here, where *The Wizard of Oz* was still enjoying a long run. However, Lou had lost her dear Scarecrow, and the Cowardly Lion was no longer afraid. And the Tin Man? Had she finally found her heart? Maybe she had never lost it.

Lou turned and looked at her great-grandmother. The girl stiffened when Louisa opened her eyes and looked at her. There was a strong sense of recognition, a suspicion of a tender smile, and Lou's hopes soared. As though not only their names, but also their spirits, were identical, a tear trickled down the two Louisas' cheeks. Lou went to her, slipped her hand around Louisa's, and kissed it.

"I love you, Louisa," she said, her heart so near to breaking, for she could not recall saying those words before. Louisa's lips moved, and though Lou could not hear the words, she clearly saw on her lips what the woman was saying back: *I love you, Louisa.*

And then Louisa's eyes slowly closed and did not reopen, and Lou wondered if that was to be all of her miracle.

"Miss Lou, they want us down to the courthouse."

She turned and saw a wide-eyed Eugene standing in the doorway. "Mr. Cotton want us both get on the stand."

Lou slowly let go of Louisa's hand, turned, and left.

A minute later Louisa's eyes opened once more. She looked around the room. Her expression was fearful for a moment, but then grew calm. She started pushing herself up, confused at first as to why her left side was not cooperating. She kept her gaze on the window of the room, even as she fought hard to move herself. Inch by precious inch she progressed, until she was half-sitting, her eyes still on that window. Louisa was breathing heavily now, her strength and energy nearly gone after this short struggle. Yet she lay back against her pillow and smiled. For outside the large window her mountain was now boldly visible. The sight was so beautiful to the woman, although winter had taken most of its color. Next year, though, it would surely all return. Like it always did. Family that never really left you. That was what the mountain was. And her eyes remained fixed on the familiar rise of rock and trees, even as Louisa Mae Cardinal grew very still.

※

In the courtroom, Cotton stood before the bench and announced in a strong voice, "I call Miss Louisa Mae Cardinal."

A gasp went up from the crowd. And then the door opened and Lou and Eugene came in. Miller and Goode looked smug once more as they saw it was only the child. Eugene sat while Lou went up to the witness chair.

Fred approached. "Raise your right hand, put your left

on the Bible. You swear to tell the truth, the whole truth, and nothing but the truth, so help you God?"

"I do," she said quietly, looking around at everyone staring at her. Cotton smiled reassuringly. Out of sight of anyone, he showed her that his fingers were crossed for luck too.

"Now, Lou, what I have to ask you is going to be painful, but I need you to answer my questions. Okay?"

"Okay."

"Now, on the day Jimmy Skinner was killed, you were with him, right?"

Miller and Goode exchanged troubled glances. Goode got to his feet.

"Your Honor, what does this have to do with anything?"

"The Commonwealth agreed to let me explore my theory," said Cotton.

"All right," said the judge. "But don't take all day."

Cotton turned back to Lou. "You were at the mine entrance when the explosion occurred?"

"Yes."

"Can you describe for us what happened?"

Lou swallowed, her eyes becoming watery.

"Eugene set the dynamite and came out. We were just going to wait for it to go off. Diamond—I mean, Jimmy—ran into the mine to get Jeb, his dog, who had chased a squirrel in there. Eugene went in to get Jimmy. I was standing in front of the entrance when the dynamite went off."

"Was it a loud explosion?"

"Loudest thing I've heard in my life."

"Could you say whether you heard two explosions?"

She looked confused. "No, I can't."

"Likely as not. Then what happened?"

"Well, this big rush of air and smoke came out and knocked me down."

"Must've been some force."

"It was. It truly was."

"Thank you, Lou. No further questions."

"Mr. Goode?" said Atkins.

"No questions, Your Honor. Unlike Mr. Longfellow, I'm not going to waste the jury's valuable time with this nonsense."

"I next call Eugene Randall," said Cotton.

A nervous Eugene was on the stand. The hat Lou had given him was clutched tightly in his hands.

"Now, Eugene, you went to the mine the day Jimmy Skinner was killed to get some coal, correct?"

"Yes, suh."

"You use dynamite to get the coal out?"

"Yep, most folks do. Coal make good heat. Lot better'n wood."

"How many times you reckon you've used dynamite in that mine?"

Eugene thought about this. "Over the years, thirty times or mo'."

"I think that makes you an expert."

Eugene smiled at this designation. "I reckon so."

"How exactly do you go about using the dynamite?"

"Well, I put the stick'a dynamite in a hole in the wall, cap it, roll out my fuse, and light the fuse with the flame from my lantern."

"Then what do you do?"

"That shaft curves in a couple places, so's I sometimes wait round the curve if I ain't using much dynamite.

Sometime I go outside. Noise's starting to hurt my ears now. And blast kick the coal dust up bad."

"I bet it can. In fact, on the day in question, you did go outside. Right?"

"Yes, suh."

"And then you went back inside to get Jimmy, but were unsuccessful."

"Yes, suh," Eugene answered, looking down.

"Was that the first time you'd been in the mine in a while?"

"Yes, suh. Since the first of the year. Past winter ain't that bad."

"Okay. Now, when the explosion went off, where were you?"

"Eighty feet in. Not to the first curve. Got me the bad leg, ain't moving fast no more."

"What happened to you when the explosion occurred?"

"Throwed me ten féet. Hit the wall. Thought I be dead. Held on to my lantern, though. Ain't know how."

"Good Lord. Ten feet? A big man like you? Now, do you remember where you put the dynamite charge?"

"Don't never forget that, Mr. Cotton. Past the second curve. Three hunnerd feet in. Good vein of coal there."

Cotton feigned confusion. "I'm not getting something here, Eugene. Now, you testified that on occasion you would actually stay in the mine when the dynamite went off. And you weren't injured then. And yet here, how is it that you were over two hundred feet from the dynamite charge, around not just one but *two* shaft curves, and the explosion still knocked you ten feet in the air? If you were any closer, you probably would've been killed. How do you explain that?"

Eugene too was thoroughly bewildered now. "I can't, Mr. Cotton. But it done happened. I swear."

"I believe you. Now, you've heard Lou testify as to being knocked down while she was outside the mine. Whenever you were waiting *outside* the mine, that ever happen to you when the dynamite went off?"

Eugene was shaking his head before Cotton finished his question. "Little bit of dynamite I used ain't have nowhere near that kind'a kick. Just getting me some for the bucket. Use more dynamite come winter when I take the sled and mules down, but even that wouldn't come out the mine like that. Lord, you talking three hunnerd feet in and round two curves."

"You found Jimmy's body. Was there rock and stone on it? Had the mine collapsed?"

"No, suh. But I know he dead. He ain't got no lantern, see. You in that mine with no light, you ain't know which way in or out. Mind play tricks on you. He ain't prob'ly even see Jeb pass him heading out."

"Can you tell us exactly where you found Jimmy?"

" 'Nuther hunnerd twenty feet in. Past the first curve, but not the second."

Farmer and merchant sat and stood side by side as they watched Cotton work. Miller fiddled with his hat and then leaned forward and whispered into Goode's ear. Goode nodded, looked at Eugene, and then smiled and nodded again.

"Well, let's assume," said Cotton, "that Jimmy was close to the dynamite charge when it went off. It could have thrown his body a good ways, couldn't it?"

"If'n he close, sure could."

"But his body wasn't past the second curve?"

Goode stood up. "That's easily explained. The dynamite explosion could have thrown the boy past the second curve."

Cotton looked at the jury. "I fail to see how a body in flight can negotiate a ninety-degree curve and then proceed on before coming to rest. Unless Mr. Goode is maintaining that Jimmy Skinner could fly of his own accord."

Ripples of laughter floated across the courtroom. Atkins creaked back in his chair, yet did not smack his gavel to stop the sounds. "Go on, Cotton. This is getting kind'a interesting."

"Eugene, you remember feeling bad when you were in the mine that day?"

Eugene thought about this. "Hard to recollect. Maybe a little pain in the head."

"Okay, now, in your expert opinion, could the dynamite explosion alone have caused Jimmy Skinner's body to end up where it did?"

Eugene looked over at the jury and took his time in eyeing them one by one. "No, suh!"

"Thank you, Eugene. No further questions."

Goode approached and put the palms of his hands on the witness box and leaned close to Eugene.

"Boy, you live with Miss Cardinal in her house, don't you?"

Eugene sat back a bit, his gaze steady on the man. "Yes, suh."

Goode gave the jury a pointed look. "A colored man and a white woman in the same house?"

Cotton was on his feet before Goode finished his question. "Judge, you can't let him do that."

"Mr. Goode," said Atkins, "y'all might do that sort of

thing on down *Richmond* way, but we don't in my court-room. If you got something to ask the man about this case, then you do it, or else sit yourself down. And last time I checked, his name was Mr. Eugene Randall, not 'boy.'"

"Right, Your Honor, certainly." Goode cleared his throat, stepped back, and slid his hands in his pockets. "Now, *Mister* Eugene Randall, you said in your *expert* opinion that you were two hundred feet or so from the charge, and that Mr. Skinner was about half that distance from the dynamite and such. You remember saying all that?"

"No, suh. I says I was eighty feet in the mine, so's I was two hunnerd and twenty feet from the charge. And I says I *found* Diamond a hunnerd and twenty feet from where I was. That mean he be a hunnerd feet from where I set the dynamite. I ain't got no way to tell how far he got blowed."

"Right, right. Now, you ever been to school?"

"No."

"Never?"

"No, suh."

"So you never took math, never did any adding and subtracting. And yet you're sitting up here testifying under oath to all these *exact* distances."

"Yep."

"So how can that be for an uneducated colored man such as yourself? Who's never even added one plus one under the eye of a teacher? Why should this good jury believe you up here spouting all these big numbers?"

Eugene's gaze never left Goode's confident features. "Knowed my numbers real good. Cipher and all. Take-away. Miss Louisa done taught me. And I right handy with nail and saw. I hepped many a folk on the mountain raise barns. You a carpenter, you got to know numbers. You cut a three-foot board to fill a four-foot space, what 'xactly have you done?"

Laughter floated across the room again, and again Atkins let it go.

"Fine," said Goode, "so you can cut a board. But in a pitch-dark twisting mine how can you be so sure of what you're saying? Come on now, Mister Eugene Randall, tell us." Goode looked at the jury as he said this, a smile playing across his lips.

" 'Cause it be right there on the wall," said Eugene.

Goode stared at him. "Excuse me?"

"I done marked the walls in that mine with whitewash in ten-foot parcels over four hunnerd feet in. Lotta folk up here do that. You blasting in a mine, you better durn sure know how fer you got to go to get out. I knowed I do 'cause I got me the bad leg. And that way I 'member where the good coal veins are. You get yourself on down to the mine right now with a lantern, mister lawyer, you see them marks clear as the day. So's you can put down what I done said here as the word of the Lord."

Cotton glanced at Goode. To him the Commonwealth's attorney looked as though someone had just informed him that heaven did not admit members of the legal Bar.

"Any further questions?" Atkins asked Goode. The man said nothing in response but merely drifted back to his table like an errant cloud and collapsed in the chair.

"Mr. Randall," said Atkins, "you're excused, sir, and the court wants to thank you for your *expert* testimony."

Eugene stood and walked back to his seat. From the

balcony Lou observed that his limp was hardly noticeable.

Cotton next called Travis Barnes to the stand.

"Dr. Barnes, at my request you examined the records pertaining to Jimmy Skinner's death, didn't you? Including a photograph taken outside the mine."

"Yes, I did."

"Can you tell us the cause of death?"

"Massive head and body injuries."

"What was the condition of the body?"

"It was literally torn apart."

"You ever treated anybody injured by a dynamite explosion?"

"In coal mining country? I say I have."

"You heard Eugene testify. In your opinion, under those circumstances, could the dynamite charge have caused the injuries you saw on Jimmy Skinner?"

Goode did not bother to rise to offer his objection. "Calls for speculation from the witness," he said gruffly.

"Judge, I think Dr. Barnes is fully competent to answer that question as an expert witness," said Cotton.

Atkins was already nodding. "Go on ahead, Travis."

Travis eyed Goode with contempt. "I well know the sorts of dynamite charges folks up here use to get a bucket of coal out. That distance from the charge and around a shaft curve, there is no way that dynamite caused the injuries I saw on that boy. I can't believe nobody figured that out before now."

Cotton said, "I guess a person goes in a mine and dynamite goes off, they just believe that's what killed him. You ever seen such injuries before?"

"Yes. Explosion at a manufacturing plant. Killed a dozen men. Same as Jimmy. Literally blown apart."

"What was the cause of that explosion?"

"Natural gas leak."

Cotton turned and looked dead-on at Hugh Miller.

"Mr. Goode, unless you care to take a shot, I'm calling Mr. Judd Wheeler to the stand."

Goode looked at Miller, betrayed. "No questions."

A nervous Wheeler fidgeted in the witness box as Cotton approached.

"You're Southern Valley's chief geologist?"

"I am."

"And you headed up the team that was exploring possible natural gas deposits on Miss Cardinal's property?"

"I did."

"Without her permission or knowledge?"

"Well, I don't know about—"

"Did you have her permission, Mr. Wheeler?" Cotton snapped.

"No."

"You found natural gas, didn't you?"

"That's right."

"And it was something your company was right interested in, wasn't it?"

"Well, natural gas is getting to be very valuable as a heating fuel. We mostly use manufactured gas, town gas they call it. You get that from heating coal. That's what fuels the streetlights in this town. But you can't make much money with town gas. And we have seamless steel pipe now, which allows us to send gas in pipelines a long way. So yes, we were very interested."

"Natural gas is explosive, right?"

"If properly used—"

"Is it, or isn't it?"

"It is."

"Exactly what did you do in that mine?"

"We took readings and did tests and located what appeared to be a huge field of gas in a trap not too far underneath the surface of that mine shaft and about six hundred feet in the mine. Coal, oil, and gas are often found together because all three result from similar natural processes. The gas always lies on top because it's lighter. That's why you have to be careful when you're mining coal. Methane gas buildup is a real danger to the miners. Anyway, we drilled down and hit that gas field."

"Did the gas come up in the mine shaft?"

"Yes."

"On what date did you hit the gas field?"

When Wheeler told them the day, Cotton said loud and clear to the jury, "One week before Jimmy Skinner's death! Would somebody be able to smell the gas?"

"No, in its natural state gas is colorless and odorless. When companies process it, they add a distinct smell so that if there's a leak people can detect it before it overcomes them."

"Or before something ignites it?"

"That's right."

"If someone set off a dynamite charge in a mine shaft where there was natural gas present, what would happen?"

"The gas would explode." Wheeler looked like he wanted to be blown up himself.

Cotton faced the jury. "I guess Eugene was real lucky he was so far away from the hole where the gas was pouring through and his lamp flame didn't ignite the gas. And he was even luckier he didn't strike a match to light that fuse. But the dynamite going off sure did the trick." He turned back to Wheeler. "What sort of explosion? Big enough to cause Jimmy Skinner's death, in the manner described by Dr. Barnes?"

"Yes," Wheeler conceded.

Cotton put his hands on the frame of the witness box and leaned in. "Didn't you ever think about posting warning signs telling people that there was gas there?"

"I didn't know they dynamited in there! I didn't know they used that old mine for anything."

Cotton thought he caught Wheeler shooting an angry look at George Davis, but he couldn't be sure.

"But if anyone went in, they might be overcome by the gas alone. Wouldn't you want to warn people?"

Wheeler spoke fast. "The ceilings in that mine shaft are real high, and there's some natural ventilation through the rock too, so the buildup of the methane wouldn't be so bad. And we were going to cap the hole, but we were waiting on some equipment we needed. We didn't want anybody to get hurt. That's the truth."

"The fact is, you couldn't post warning signs because you were there illegally. Isn't that right?"

"I was just following orders."

"You took great pains to hide the fact that you were working in that mine, didn't you?"

"Well, we only worked at night. Whatever equipment we carried in, we took out with us."

"So nobody would know you'd been there?"

"Yes."

"Because Southern Valley was hoping to buy Miss Cardinal's farm for a lot less money if she didn't know she was sitting on an ocean of gas?"

"Objection!" Goode said.

Cotton steamed right on. "Mr. Wheeler, you knew Jimmy Skinner died in that mine explosion. And you had to know the gas played some role in it. Why didn't you come forward and tell the truth then?"

Wheeler fidgeted with his hat. "I was told not to."

"And who told you not to?"

"Mr. Hugh Miller, company vice president."

Everyone in the courtroom looked at Miller. Cotton stared at Miller when he asked his next questions.

"You have any children, Mr. Wheeler?"

Wheeler looked surprised, but answered: "Three."

"They all doing well? Healthy?"

Wheeler's gaze dropped to his lap before he responded. "Yes."

"You're a lucky man."

Goode was addressing the jury with his closing argument.

"Now, we've heard far more evidence than is necessary for you to find that Louisa Mae Cardinal is mentally unfit. In fact, her own lawyer, Mr. Longfellow, has conceded that she is. Now, all this talk about gas and explosions and such, well what does it really have to do with this case? If Southern Valley was somehow involved in Mr. Skinner's death, then his survivors *may* be entitled to damages."

"He doesn't have any survivors," said Cotton.

Goode chose to ignore this. "Now, Mr. Longfellow asks whether my client is an appropriate party to be buying land up here. Fact is, folks, Southern Valley has big plans for your town. Good jobs, bring prosperity back to you all."

He got real close to the jury, their best friend. "The question is, should Southern Valley be allowed to 'enrich' all of your lives as well as Miss Cardinal's? I think the answer to that is obvious."

Goode sat down. And Cotton came at the jury. He moved slowly, his bearing confident but not threatening. His hands were in his pockets, and he rested one of his scuffed shoes on the lower rail of the jury box. When he spoke, his voice leaned more southern than New England, and every single juror except George Davis hunched forward so as not to miss anything the man said. They had watched Cotton Longfellow bloody the nose of what they assumed was one of the finest lawyers from the great city of Richmond. And he had made humble a company that was as close to a monarch as one could get in a country of democracy. Now they undoubtedly wanted to see if the man could finish it.

"Let me give you good folks the legal side of the case first. And it's not complicated at all. In fact it's like a good bird dog, it points straight and true in one direction, and one direction only." He took one hand from his pocket and, like a good hound, pointed right at Hugh Miller as he spoke. "The reckless actions of Southern Valley killed Jimmy Skinner, you folks can have no doubts about that. Southern Valley's not even disputing it. They were illegally on Louisa Mae's property. They posted no warnings that the mine was filled with explosive gas. They allowed innocent people to enter that mine when they knew it was deadly. It could've been any of you. And they did not come forward with the truth because they knew they were in the wrong. And now they seek to use the tragedy of Louisa Mae's stroke as a way to take her land. The law clearly says one cannot profit from one's misdeeds. Well, if what Southern Valley did does not qualify as a misdeed, then nothing on this earth ever would." His voice up to this point had been slow and steady. Now it rose one delicate notch, but he kept his finger pointed at Hugh Miller. "One day God will hold them accountable for killing an innocent young man. But it's your job to see that they are punished today."

Cotton looked at each and every juror, stopping on George Davis; he spoke directly to him. "Now, let's get to the *nonlegal* part of this business, for I think that's where the struggle you folks are going through lies. Southern Valley has come in here swinging bags full of money in front of you, telling you that it's the savior of the whole town. But that's what the lumber folks told you. They're going to be here forever. Remember? So why were all the lumber camps on rails? How much more *temporary* can you get? And where are they now? Last time I checked, Kentucky was not part of the Commonwealth of Virginia."

He looked over at Miller. "And the coal companies told you the same thing. And what did they do? They came and took everything they wanted and left you with nothing except hollowed-out mountains, family with the black lung and dreams replaced with nightmares. And now Southern Valley's singing that same old tune with gas. It's just one more needle in the mountain's hide. Just one more thing to suck out, leaving nothing!" Cotton turned and addressed the entire courtroom.

"But this isn't really about Southern Valley, or coal or gas. It's ultimately about all of you. Now, they can cut the top of that mountain easy enough, pull out that gas, run their fine seamless steel pipeline, and it might keep going for ten, fifteen, even twenty years. But then it'll all be gone. You see, that pipeline is taking the gas to other places, just like the trains did the coal, and the river did the trees. Now, why is that, do you think?" He took his time looking around the room. "I'll tell you why. Because that's where the real prosperity is, folks. At least in the way Southern Valley defines it. And all of you know that. These mountains just got what they need to keep that prosperity going and their pockets filled. And so they come here and they take it.

"Dickens, Virginia, will never be a New York City, and let me tell you there's not a damn thing wrong with that. In fact, I believe we have us enough big cities, and a dwindling number of places like right here. Y'all will never become rich working at the foot of these mountains. Those who will claim great wealth are the Southern Valleys of the world, who take from the land and give nothing back to it. You want a *real* savior? Look at yourselves. Rely on each other. Just like Louisa Mae's been doing her whole life up on that mountain. Farmers live on the whim of the weather and the ground. Some years they lose, other years are fine. But for them, the resources of the mountain are *never* extinguished, because they do not tear its soul away. And their reward for that is being able to live a decent, honest life for as

ong as they so desire, without the fear that folks intent
n nothing more than making a pile of gold by raping
nountains will come with grand promises, and then leave
when there is nothing to be gained by staying, and de-
troy innocent lives in the process."

He pointed to Lou where she sat in the courtroom.
"Now, that girl's daddy wrote many wonderful stories
bout this area, and those very issues of land, and the
eople who live on it. In words, Jack Cardinal has en-
bled this place to survive forever. Just like the moun-
ains. He had an exemplary teacher, for Louisa Mae
Cardinal has lived her life the way all of us should.
She's helped many of you at some point in your lives
nd asked for nothing in return." Cotton looked at Bu-
ord Rose and some of the other farmers staring at him.
"And you've helped her when she needed it. You know
he'd never sell her land, because that ground is as
nuch a part of her family as her great-grandchildren
vaiting to see what's going to happen to them. You
an't let Southern Valley steal the woman's family. All
olks have up on that mountain is each other and their
and. That's all. It may not seem like much to those
vho don't live there, or for people who seek nothing
ut to destroy the rock and trees. But rest assured, it
neans everything to the people who call the mountains
ome."

Cotton stood tall in front of the jury box, and though
is voice remained level and calm, the large room seemed
nadequate to contain his words.

"You folks don't have to be an expert in the law to
each the right decision in this case. All you got to have
s a heart. Let Louisa Mae Cardinal keep her land."

CHAPTER FORTY

LOU STARED OUT THE WINDOW OF HER BEDROOM AT the grand sweep of land as it bolted right up to the foothills and then on to the mountains, where the leaves on all but the evergreens were gone. The naked trees were still quite something to behold, though now they appeared to Lou to be poor grave markers for thousands of dead, their mourners left with not much.

"You should have come back, Dad," she said to the mountains he had immortalized with words and then shunned the rest of his life.

She had returned to the farm with Eugene after the jury had gone into deliberation. She had no desire to be there when the verdict came in. Cotton had said he would come tell them the decision. He said he did not expect it to take long. Cotton did not say whether he thought that was good or bad, but he did not look hopeful. Now all Lou could do was wait. And it was hard, for everything around her could be gone tomorrow, depending on what a group of strangers decided. Well, one of them wasn't a stranger; he was more like a mortal enemy.

Lou traced her father's initials with her finger on the

lesk. She had sacrificed her mother's letters for a miracle that had never bothered to come, and it pained her
so. She went downstairs and stopped at Louisa's room.
Through the open door she saw the old bed, the small
dresser, a bowl and pitcher on top of it. The room was
small, its contents spare, just like the woman's life. Lou
covered her face. It just wasn't right. She stumbled into
the kitchen to start the meal.

As she was pulling out a pot, Lou heard a noise behind her and turned. It was Oz. She wiped at her eyes,
for she still wanted to be strong for him. Yet as she focused on his expression, Lou realized she had no need
to worry about her brother. Something had seized him;
she didn't know what. But her brother had never looked
this way before. Without a word, he took her hand and
drew his sister back down the hallway.

❧

The jury filed into the courtroom, a dozen men from
the mountain and the town, at least eleven of whom Cotton could hope would do the right thing. The jury had
been out for many hours, longer than Cotton had thought
probable. He did not know if that was good or bad. The
real card against him, he knew, was that of desperation.
It was a strong opponent, because it could so easily prey
upon those who worked so hard every day simply to survive, or upon those who saw no future in a place where
everything was being carved out and taken away. Cotton would loathe the jurors if they went against him, yet

he knew they easily could. Well, at least it would soon be over.

Atkins asked, "Has the jury reached a verdict?"

The foreman rose. He was a man from the town, a humble shopkeeper, his body swollen from too much beer and potato, and from too little effort with arms and shoulders. "Yes, Your Honor," he said quietly.

Hardly a single person had left the courtroom since the jury had been given its charge from the judge and sent out. The whole population of the room leaned forward, as though they all had just been struck deaf.

"What say you?"

"We find . . . for Southern Valley." The foreman looked down, as though he had just delivered a death sentence to one of his own.

The courtroom erupted into shouts—some cheers, some not. The balcony seemed to sway with the collective weight of the decision of a dozen men. Hugh Miller and George Davis exchanged slight nods, lips easing into victorious smiles.

Cotton sat back. The legal process had had its day; the only thing absent was justice.

Miller and Goode shook hands. Miller tried to congratulate Wheeler, but the big man walked off in obvious disgust.

"Order, order in this court or I'll clear it." Atkins slammed his gavel several times, and things did quiet down.

"The jury is dismissed. Thank you for your service," he said and not very kindly. A man entered the courtroom, spotted Cotton, and whispered something in his ear. Cotton's despair noticeably deepened.

Goode said, "Your Honor, it now remains solely to appoint someone to represent Miss Cardinal's interests and assume guardianship of the children."

"Judge, I've just received some news that the court needs to hear." Cotton slowly stood, his head down, one hand pressed to his side. "Louisa Mae Cardinal has passed away."

The courtroom erupted once more, and this time Atkins made no move to contain it. Davis's smile broadened. He went over to Cotton. "Damn," he said, "this day get better and better."

Cotton's mind went blank for a moment, as though someone had smote him with an anvil. He grabbed Davis and had it in his mind to deliver him into the next county with his right fist, but then he stopped and simply heaved the man out of his way, as one would shovel a large pile of manure off a road.

"Your Honor," said Goode, "I know we're all very sorry to hear about Miss Cardinal. Now, I have a list of very reputable people who can represent these fine children in the sale of the property that has just now passed to them."

"And I hope you rot in hell for it," cried out Cotton. He raced to the bench, Goode on his heels.

Cotton pounded his fist so hard on the mighty bench of justice that Fred the bailiff took a nervous step toward them.

"George Davis tainted that whole jury," roared Cotton. "I know he's got Southern Valley dollars burning a hole in his pocket."

"Give it up, Longfellow, you lost," said Goode.

Neither man noticed the courtroom doors opening.

"Never, Goode. Never!" Cotton shouted at him.

"He agreed to be bound by the decision of the jury."

"I'm afraid he's got a point there," said Atkins.

A triumphant Goode turned to look at Miller and his eyes nearly crossed at what he was seeing.

"But Henry," pleaded Cotton, "please, the children . . . Let me be their guardian. I—"

Atkins was not paying attention to Cotton. He too was now staring at the courtroom, his mouth wide open.

Cotton slowly turned to see what Atkins was looking at, and felt himself feeling faint, as though he'd just seen God walk through that door.

Lou and Oz stood there before them all.

And between them, held up almost solely by her children, was Amanda Cardinal.

Lou had not taken her gaze from her mother from the moment Oz had led her down the hallway and into the bedroom, where her mother was lying in bed, her eyes wide open, tears running from them, her shaky arms finally reaching out to her children, her trembling lips forming a joyous smile.

Neither could Cotton take his gaze from the woman. Still, he had unfinished business before the court.

In a cracking, halting voice he said, "Your Honor, would like to present to you Amanda Cardinal. The rightful and true guardian of her children."

The sea of now-silent people parted and allowed Cotton to walk slowly over to mother and her children, his legs stumbling along, as though they had forgotten the proper motions. His face was smirched with tears.

"Mrs. Cardinal," he began, "my name is—"

Amanda reached out a hand and touched him on the

shoulder. Her body was very weak, yet her head was held high, and when she spoke her words were soft but clear. "I know who you are, Mr. Longfellow. I've listened to you often."

TODY

THE TALL WOMAN WALKS ALONG A FIELD OF BLUE-
grass slowly curving in the wind. The line of mountains sweeps across in the background. Her hair is
silver and hangs to her waist. She holds a pen and a paper
tablet and sits on the ground and begins to write.

*Maybe the wishing well did work. Or perhaps it was
the unwavering faith of a little boy. Or maybe it was
as simple as a little girl telling her mother she loved
her. The important thing was our mother came back
to us. Even as our beloved Louisa Mae left us. We had
Louisa but a minute, yet we came close to having her
not at all.*

The woman rises, walks along, and then stops at two
granite tombstones with the names Cotton Longfellow and
Amanda Cardinal Longfellow engraved upon them. She
sits and continues writing.

*My mother and Cotton were married a year later.
Cotton adopted Oz and me, and I showed equal love*

and affection to him and my mother. They spent over four wonderful decades together on this mountain and died within a week of one another. I will never forget Cotton's great kindness. And I will go to my own grave knowing that my mother and I made the most of our second chance.

My little brother did grow into those big feet, and developed an even bigger arm. And on a glorious autumn day, Oz Cardinal pitched and won a World Series for the New York Yankees. He's now a schoolteacher there, with a well-deserved reputation for helping timid children thrive. And his grandson has inherited that immortal bear. Some days I want nothing more than to be holding that little boy again, running my fingers through his hair, comforting him. My cowardly lion. But children grow up. And my little brother became a fine man. And his sister is truly proud of him.

Eugene went on to have his own farm and family and still lives nearby. He remains to this day one of my best friends in the world. And after his performance in that courtroom so long ago, I never heard anyone ever again refer to him as Hell No.

And me? Like my father, I left the mountain. But unlike Jack Cardinal, I came back. I married and raised a family here in a home I built on the land Louisa Mae left us. Now my own grandchildren come and visit every summer. I tell them of my life growing up here. About Louisa Mae, Cotton, and my dear friend Diamond Skinner. And also about others who touched our lives. I do so because I believe it important for them to know such things about their family.

Over the years I had read so many books, I started to write one of my own. I loved it so much, I wrote fourteen more. I told stories of happiness and wonder. Of pain and fear. Of survival and triumph. Of the land and its people. As my father had. And while I never won the sorts of awards he did, my books tended to sell a little better.

As my father wrote, one's courage, hope, and spirit can be severely tried by the happenstance of life. But as I learned on this Virginia mountain, so long as one never loses faith, it is impossible to ever truly be alone.

This is where I belong. It is a true comfort to know that I will die here on this high rock. And I fear my passing not at all. My enthusiasm is perfectly understandable, you see, for the view from here is so very fine.

ACKNOWLEDGMENTS

I would be remiss in not thanking various people who helped with this project. First, all the fine folks at Warner Books, and especially my dear friend Maureen Egen, who was wonderfully supportive of my trying something different, and who performed a marvelous editing job on the novel. And thanks also to Aaron Priest and Lisa Vance for all their help and encouragement. They both make my life far less complicated. And to Molly Friedrich, for taking the time from her extraordinarily busy schedule to read an early draft of the novel and provide many insightful comments. And to Frances Jalet-Miller, who brought her usual superb editing skills and heartfelt enthusiasm to the story. And to my cousin Steve for reading all the words as usual. And to Jennifer Steinberg for her help.

To Michelle for all she does. It is a well-known fact that I would be utterly lost without her.

And to Spencer and Collin, for being my Lou and Oz.

And to my dear friend Karen Spiegel for all her help and encouragement with this work. You really helped make it better, and maybe one day we'll see it on the big screen.

And to all the fine people at the Library of Virginia in Richmond for allowing me use of its archives, providing a quiet place to work and think, and for pointing me in the direction of numerous treasure troves: remembrances penned by mountain folks; oral histories documented by diligent WPA staff in the 1930s; pictorial histories of rural counties in Virginia; and the first state publication on midwifery.

A very special thanks to Deborah Hocutt, the Executive Director of the Virginia Center for the Book at the Library of Virginia, for all her assistance with this project, and also with the many other endeavors I'm involved with in the Commonwealth.

To access the Special Reading Group Guide, visit our Web site at www.twbookmark.com.

JOIN THE ADVENTURE!

Get involved with All America Reads, an exciting new nationwide literacy project. All America Reads is a national collaborative reading program centered in the nation's middle and high schools to encourage students to read and to provide them with the tools to do so.

All America Reads is proud to announce the program's inaugural book, WISH YOU WELL by David Baldacci (Warner Books, 0-446-52716-5, 0-446-61010-0).

For more information about All America Reads please call 1-804-779-2054 or visit www.allamericareads.org.